Praise for Susie M

The Thirteen

"An eerie blend of *The Stepford Wives*, *The Witches of Eastwick*, and *Desperate Housewives* . . . features a cast of bewitching characters and a creepy story that will stick with the reader long afterward."

—Library Journal

"A deliciously wicked piece of work . . . Moloney continues to stretch the genre."

—The Winnipeg Free Press

"Moloney has been called Canada's Stephen King . . . *The Thirteen* is a creepy-fun read, with characters ready-made for a Hollywood casting call."

—Maclean's

". . . a compellingly uncanny narrative, binding the tropes of small town paranoia and cliquishness with the chokehold of family obligations and religious fervour, and the very real claustrophobia of poverty and desperation. . . . [L]ike a gonzo, mirror-universe, occult version of *The Stepford Wives*, with a dash of Stephen King thrown in."

—The Globe and Mail

The Dwelling

"A refreshingly original take on the traditional ghost story. I sat up all night to finish it—and not just because I was afraid to turn out the lights."

—Kelley Armstrong, #1 New York Times bestselling author of Omens and Wild Justice

". . . downright terrifying."

—Chatelaine

"Moloney is skilled at blending the expected with the original. *The Dwelling* shows a fine understanding of human nature."

—The Globe and Mail

"Moloney manipulates the tension artfully, giving the reader glimpses of the house's history and leading to a suitably grotesque ending."

—Quill & Quire

"The author, while creating a living, pulsing and macabre structure, also treats her human cast of characters with great care. . . . This is a great psychological thriller written in good taste with a suitably imaginative conclusion."

—*Books in Canada*

"If the best measure of a horror story is how scary it is, Susie Moloney's new novel is a success. This book will scare the bejesus out of you . . . not via an excess of blood or violence, but by conveying a pervasive atmosphere of the macabre. *The Dwelling*, like most good horror stories, contains a large dollop of mystery . . . [and] stellar characters."

—*The Winnipeg Free Press*

A Dry Spell

"A rare piece of work. . . . Reminiscent of early Stephen King. . . . A story that is heartfelt and contains a touch of myth."

—*Chicago Tribune*

"A fast-paced . . . blend of ghosts, curses, bad weather, oddball characters and romance. Moloney is a gifted storyteller, drawing her likeable, credible characters with bold strokes and subtle touches."

—*The Globe and Mail*

"A fine read. . . . Like joyriding rural teenagers aching to get airborne, we're soon swept away by the breathless pace of Susie Moloney's novel."

—*The Toronto Star*

"Absorbing. . . . Moloney intertwines powerful psychological, supernatural, and sexual undercurrents."

—*Entertainment Weekly*

Bastion Falls

"The setting and the characters alone make this worthwhile reading. . . . Take this thick white book home to read on a long winter's night."

—*Geist*

THINGS WITHERED

STORIES

SUSIE MOLONEY

WITH AN INTRODUCTION BY KAARON WARREN

ChiZine Publications

FIRST EDITION

Things Withered © 2013 by Susie Moloney
Cover artwork © 2013 by Erik Mohr
Cover design © 2013 by Samantha Beiko
Interior design © 2013 by Kerrie McCreadie and Dan Seljak

Distributed in Canada by
HarperCollins Canada Ltd.
1995 Markham Road
Scarborough, ON M1B 5M8
Toll Free: 1-800-387-0117
e-mail: hcorder@harpercollins.com

Distributed in the U.S. by
Diamond Book Distributors
1966 Greenspring Drive
Timonium, MD 21093
Phone: 1-410-560-7100 x826
e-mail: books@diamondbookdistributors.com

Library and Archives Canada Cataloguing in Publication

Moloney, Susie, author
Things withered / Susie Moloney.

Short stories.
Issued in print and electronic formats.
ISBN 978-1-77148-161-8 (pbk.)
ISBN 978-1-77148-162-5 (pdf)

I. Title.

PS8576.O4516T54 2013   C813'.54   C2013-905160-0
          C2013-905161-9

CHIZINE PUBLICATIONS
Toronto, Canada
www.chizinepub.com
info@chizinepub.com

Edited and copyedited by Sandra Kasturi
Proofread by Michael Matheson

Canada Council   Conseil des arts
for the Arts   du Canada

We acknowledge the support of the Canada Council for the Arts which last year invested $20.1 million in writing and publishing throughout Canada.

ONTARIO ARTS COUNCIL
CONSEIL DES ARTS DE L'ONTARIO
50 YEARS OF ONTARIO GOVERNMENT SUPPORT OF THE ARTS
50 ANS DE SOUTIEN DU GOUVERNEMENT DE L'ONTARIO AUX ARTS

Published with the generous assistance of the Ontario Arts Council.

Printed in Canada

For Gary & Dale,
who have given me a sense of home

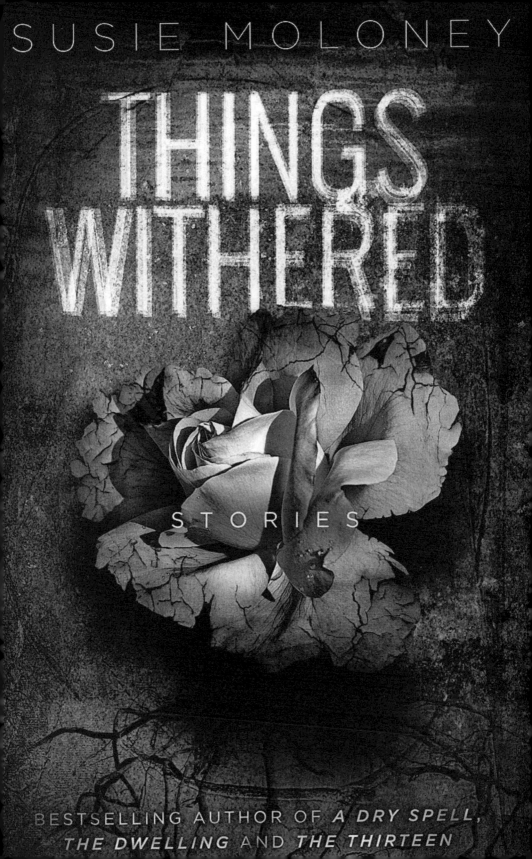

SUSIE MOLONEY

THINGS WITHERED

STORIES

BESTSELLING AUTHOR OF *A DRY SPELL*, *THE DWELLING* AND *THE THIRTEEN*

CONTENTS

Introduction

Susie Moloney is a revelation.

I love these stories because they're about people who have lived, so that they bring all their experiences, all their past, to the story and this evokes a deeper response from the reader. It means that at the end of each story, I'm left momentarily stunned by what I've read, and somehow bereft that it's over.

There are no clichés of storytelling here. Middle-aged, overweight women have as much right to a story as anybody else, and Moloney tells us so in no uncertain terms.

It's gorgeous lines like this one in "Night Beach," one of my favourites in the collection, that wreak the magic: . . . *a great hairy man who reminded Laura of an uncle she used to like*. Moloney won't give us the story of that uncle, but there is so much history in the line, so much hint of damage, that already the character has more meaning.

Some stories are like a slow burn and leave the same scars as burns do. In "Reclamation on the Forest Floor," another favourite, the clumsy romance between Shara and Donald is almost painful to read, and Moloney's description of Shara's physicalities is truly horrifying.

Moloney captures the essence of what it is to be ordinary, to be trapped in a life expected. She takes the moments many will understand and she twists them, undermines them, until they fall to pieces. She writes in "The Neighbourhood," *When I look back on my life now, I think of all those times when I was rubbing invisible dirt off something when I could have been reading a book, sewing; phoning my husband and hearing his precious voice a minute more*, and if that isn't a truth for all of us, I don't know what is. "The Neighbourhood" is the longest story in the collection, and Moloney uses every word to lead us inexorably to the powerful ending.

At times, in stories such as "The Last Living Summer," it almost feels as if Moloney is chronicling a time in the future, when the world is tired and things have changed. This is a sad, melancholic, devastating story where, again, she gives us people with a whole life behind them, bringing this to bear in how we react to the characters and how things play out.

Things Withered is a brilliant collection, showcasing the work of a writer everybody should be reading.

— Kaaron Warren
Canberra, Australia
October 2013

The Windemere

"You must be Stephanie."

"Yes."

The two of us stood just outside the wide awning over the front entrance. The sky looked about to break open.

"Shall we take a look?" I said. My doorman let us in with a remark about the weather. We took the elevator to seven.

She looked like a nice girl, legitimate, and I could feel my relief counter going up, checking out her Louboutins and her Prada bag. Too often I start out with great expectations only to find my client has brought three giggling girlfriends all decked out in their Macy's best to look at a luxury apartment that none of them could afford. I allow myself this small relief because lately, I have to take it where I can find it.

"Nothing lower than six and at least one bedroom, is that right?" The girl smiled politely.

"That's right," Stephanie said, as the doors opened on seven.

The Windemere was nearly the oldest building in the neighbourhood, bested only by the Paramount, on the same block. The Paramount had been built by the family of the current Mayor, and had been in the news lately, mostly for code violations that were routine with a building more than seventy years old, but which were a fun read when your Mayor's mother was quoted as saying, "Well, I'm certain we have people on that, don't we?" in response to the collapse of a wall in an upper floor hallway. A real *cause célèbre*.

It was like being in the shadow of a more glamorous older sister. In fact, there were other differences that made The Windemere's more low-key presence a bonus. Overwhelmingly the tenants of The Windemere were from very old families, some on leaner budgets than in their glory days, but more importantly, when their own scandal hit, it got far less ink than it would have, had it been The Paramount.

I would know. I live in the Windemere, 2C. A modest apartment, part of a larger apartment that had been split in the '50s. Lovely nonetheless and I was a big booster of the building. I felt responsible for its projection in the community.

I opened 7A with as much flair as I could manage at my height and general unremarkable sparkle. The apartment, thank the gods, spoke for itself. I swung the door open and mentally offered a *ta-da*.

The view from the threshold was spectacular. It opened across from a bank of four floor-to-ceiling windows that from the 7th floor, overlooked a dozen mature, budding Gingko trees. Through them you could see the street, pretty and refined, quiet. Even the parked vehicles were genteel: Mercedes, BMW, Lexus.

Stephanie gasped, clapped her hands together, and went right to the windows. She hiked one open and leaned out. She giggled like a child.

I was very pleased.

She spun around and smiled happily at me, spinning back in a mini-pirouette and walked the length of the apartment, her bag swinging beside her.

An apartment like this one could be a tough sell. It was broad and wide, previous tenants at some time in the last forty years had torn out walls where they could, stuck in retaining posts, created the look of a studio loft in the place of what had once been a Victorian-style apartment, with a warren of smaller rooms. While it greatly improved the look and air of the apartment, with just one bedroom it was a hard sell for families. And at the price, it was tough to find single renters.

Ms. Prada bag and Louboutin shoes was just the kind of girl I was looking for.

"You have a friend in the building, is that right?"

"I do," she said. "Tracy Killens and I went to college together. She's in—"

"9A, yes, I know Tracy." Stephanie flashed a smile full of very white, very straight teeth.

The mention of Tracy Killens relaxed me even more. She had been in the building a long time—maybe as long as ten years. Which seemed crazy, because Stephanie didn't look out of her mid-twenties. With these people, though, it was all genetics.

Then it came.

"This is the apartment where the woman died, is that right?"

"A lot of our tenants are elderly. It's to be expected." The girl turned and looked me right in the face. She was still smiling, but there was an element of smugness to it this time.

And I thought: therein lies the difference between us and them, new girls and old ones. When they catch us in something, they like to point it out.

"The *other* woman," she said.

"That's right," I said, caught.

"She jumped out the window."

"Or she fell. I don't think they really know. Would you like to look at the kitchen?" I turned to the east wall and did my game show sweep of the area. It was very modern, with a stainless steel fridge and stove. The dishwasher was hidden behind a cupboard panel. The counter was L-shaped, and jutted out into the open space like a cudgel.

She didn't take her eyes off me; even as I smiled and pointed out appliances, I could feel her looking at me. I finished extolling the virtues of minimalist cooking and turned back to her, expecting of course, the inevitable request for the gruesome details, followed by a polite request to think about it, followed up with an email before the end of the day, bowing out.

Instead, she said, "I'm not squeamish." She took a last spin, a near-pirouette like she'd done when we'd come in. "I'll take it. When is possession?"

"Beginning of the month, May 1." It was April 13.

Stephanie frowned. "Oh no. I need it sooner. Can you do something?" She looked disappointed. There was still the odd smudge of fingerprint powder on the window ledge. There were plans to paint. And the police had to sign off on it. It was probably just paperwork.

"I'll see what I can do," I told her. She beamed.

"Thank you. I won't forget it." She clapped happily and waved her arms around in the air, a strange little dance-like move again.

"I can sign today!"

And I thought *thank god*.

I was ten minutes late for the weekly brokers' meeting, or the Confederacy of Assholes, as my husband Kevin called it. He was a big fan of John

Kennedy Toole, and a great paraphraser. On the way to the meeting I called Kevin and told him I'd made the commission and he was thrilled, always my biggest fan and supporter. Sometimes the things he said could bring tears to my eyes, especially if the day was otherwise a bad one. The weekly Assholes meeting was usually a bad day.

My weeks hadn't been great in the last few months and I could feel the pressure. But this week, I had something to announce and I was very pleased. The Windemere was an unusual success, with tenants locked into leases for years, just sitting in their great rooms, getting older and older. It was essentially a deathwatch, that building.

Kevin joked on the phone thanking Alzheimer's and gin. I chided him for the tastelessness, but chuckled anyway. Poor Clara.

Clara Burns had been eighty years old when she did the high diving act. It was a mystery to me, and continues to be to most, I suspect. She'd been spry and not at all soft in the egg, so how or why she'd flown out that window was suspect. Even the police theories were silly at best, that something might have fallen from the sill and she'd overreached to catch it; that she was leaning out to get some fresh air. That she might have waved to someone on the street.

Nothing was found by her body, not so much as a potted plant; what could she have been reaching for? It was a chilly day, even for spring. If she'd waved to someone on the street, would they not have seen her fall?

But there was also no evidence of anyone else in the apartment, no foul play, as they say. No note if it was a suicide. A mystery. But Kevin was right, it was a boon for me, and would bump up my figures for April.

I was late for the meeting and when I walked in everyone turned to look, expectantly. When they saw it was me, their eyes all shifted back to the droning at hand, disappointed.

My announcement of the purchase was met with the usual mandatory applause, if somewhat unenthusiastic and truncated, ruining it a little for me. Maybe I read too much into these little slights at the office, as Kevin would say. I wanted to believe that, but I didn't, not really.

In the old days—and I was one of the few who would remember them—there was more inter-office support. The '80s had been a kind of Golden Age. Everyone was making money and real estate was a glamorous occupation. Everyone was a tycoon. I was young then, and passably pleasant to look at, but the years had not been kind.

I am five feet, two inches tall, and weight had seemed to arrive out of nowhere and stick to me like scandal. I had lately developed a wattle that horrified me. My pants had long ago reached sizes that I previously hadn't known were available without a prescription, and I was perpetually cheating on some diet or other. These days it was the soup diet. I was eating only soup, and peeing like an infant. Poor Kevin had taken to eating his big meal at his office, and I tried not to feel bitter when he came home smelling of Bolognese or BBQ. He was gracious over dinners of chicken soup, vegetable soup, onion soup (no cheese or croutons, just onions, sadly).

Over the last two years, as the weight gathered, I had taken to the fat lady's diversion of overdone nails and over-processed hair. Recently I'd dyed my hair a luscious red, suitable, the stylist assured me, to my fair complexion, which was a nice way of saying "doughy." The hair might have been a tragic error on my part. It was *very* red and in my worst late-night moments, I felt sure it was clownish.

But you can't overthink these things. I am fifty-six years old and I've spent a lifetime trying to compete with prettier girls, slimmer girls, girls who sparkled. It wasn't happening.

"Sparkle," was our team leader's favourite expression and he could work it into any circumstance. Apartments and buildings had to have "sparkle." So did ads, addresses, sell-sheets, and most importantly, realtors. His favourite usage was, *you might want to try some sparkle.* The first time he said it, I had misheard it as "spackle." Funny now.

Richard Maynard. Oh, how I hated him.

At the end of the meeting, Himself asked me to stay behind, like grade school.

"Anita," he said, "Can I have a word?"

I had a feeling the word would not be *sparkle.* So while everyone else filed out, without even the decency to shoot me a sympathetic side-eye, I stayed plunked in my seat at the far end of the boardroom from Richard.

"Of course," I said. I pasted a smile on my face, even though my gut was turning. It was never good, this kind of staying behind.

It started bad, and got worse. "One sale does not a career sparkle, Anita," he said.

That would be me.

I had been having trouble sleeping lately. It seemed that I would drop into bed, dead on my feet, and crash into something deep and settling, only to wake up three hours later to stare at the ceiling for what seemed like hours before I fell asleep again. That was where I was at when I got the phone call.

Kevin was beside me, lightly snoring, probably dreaming of pork roast and gravy, because by then I was on Weight Watchers and actually doing quite well. I had lost about four pounds over two months, and that was the best I'd done in years. It wasn't my weight that was keeping me up at all, but rather a desire to *sparkle* and bring up my numbers before the end of the quarter. I'd been warned by Richard and while it wasn't yet at the dire point, I was likely within spitting distance.

The phone rang. I was awake, but I couldn't help but feel dread. I looked immediately at the clock. It was after 3 A.M.

Kevin rolled over, eyes opened. He looked at me without speaking. When you get to a certain age, phone calls in the middle of the night never mean anything good. He took my hand.

"Hello?" I said. First there was nothing and then a little static. "Hello?"

I realized it wasn't static at all, but crying.

"Anita? It's Myrna Crane. I'm sorry to call but—" her voice broke with another deep sob.

"What is it?" Kevin sat up beside me, alarmed. I shook my head at him and covered the mouthpiece. I tried mouthing "Myrna Crane," but eventually, I just shook him off with a wave. *Nothing.*

"It's Barney Kloss, on eight—he's dead!"

"Barney?! Oh Myrna . . . what happened?" With that, Kevin groaned and fell back to the bed with a grand sigh. He shook his head and turned over onto his side.

"He fell down the back stairs today—he's been trying to get *fit* for crying out loud, I told him he was just going to hurt himself—and he did! He fell down those damn stairs and had a heart attack. The ambulance took him. But the hospital just called. He's gone—"

"I'm so sorry, Myrna." Barney and Myrna were both building old-timers and rumour had it that they'd been doing it since Lincoln was a baby. Whether or not that was true, or whether they were just two people who'd become like family, I didn't know and I guessed it didn't matter now. "Is there anything I can do?"

"Will you come and sit with me? Just for a moment? That new girl is here, but—" Myrna's voice dropped to a whisper, "—*I hardly know her.*"

"New girl?"

"From 7A. She called 911. Stacy."

Stephanie.

"Oh. How nice." I looked at Kevin. His chest was rising and falling with ease. He was asleep. It was now 3:15. I was unlikely to get back to sleep whether I went up to comfort Myrna or not. I said I would just get dressed and be up.

Myrna was tearily grateful. "That would be so nice of you, Anita. Thank you."

I threw on yoga pants and a hooded sweatshirt. I didn't look my best, but it wasn't even dawn. I avoided looking at myself in the elevator mirror. The new diet had really kicked in, but I could feel the brie cheese cobbler I'd had for lunch a couple of days earlier.

The elevator doors opened on the 8th floor and Stephanie was standing there. We had a surreal moment of surprise, the tiny tick of misplaced excitement that you can sometimes get when you're up and about when no one else is.

"Anita. How nice to see you." Unlike me, Stephanie looked well put together considering the hour. Her hair was pulled back into a pony tail that looked chic and sporty, in a way that only very young, very pretty girls can pull off. I felt fatter.

"Yes. I guess I'm taking over. How is she?"

Stephanie shrugged prettily. "Poor thing," she leaned in a little closer, like a girlfriend. "I think her and Barney were involved."

"That's the rumour. It *is* sad." I opened my palm and showed her the tiny pill I had there. "I've brought her something to help her sleep."

"How clever of you." We awkwardly changed places, I held the elevator doors open for her to get in and stepped out.

"I'm sure she'll be fine," I said by way of closing.

"Of course she will," Stephanie said. She held the door open a moment. I smiled and turned to head over to Myrna's.

"Anita—" I looked back.

"I have a friend, Lily. She's wonderful. I've known her since I was a girl. I don't know when Mr. Kloss's apartment will be ready to rent . . . but, I hope you'll consider her. I hope this isn't too forward."

"Oh. Well," was all I could say. I raised a hand in a half-wave and went to poor Myrna.

I managed to make two commissions through May, one impressively large, the best I'd pulled in for more than six months, sadly. I was copying some paperwork when I ran into Richard on his way back to his office.

"You barely scraped through this last quarter," he said by way of greeting. *But I did.* I didn't say it, but rather just looked at him expectantly, wishing he would go away. He didn't.

"Can you stop by my office when you're through here?" he asked. He offered no explanation as to why. I said I would. He turned to go and just as I was breathing, he turned back and said, "Way to sparkle on the

Cavalier Street haul. That's a good sale."

"Thanks." I took my time.

His door was partially open but I tapped lightly anyway. He called out for me to come in.

"Anita, I'd like you to meet Lacey Johnson, the newest member of our team."

Standing next to his desk was a young woman, about thirty, in a well-cut suit which I noticed right off, since wearing such a thing was so far in my past I might have winced with longing if I'd been alone.

"Hello," I said, attempting a smile. Her smile was electric and so white, like all the young people have now, those wonderful teeth, bought and paid for with pre-child disposable income.

Lacey? Really? *Lacey*?

"Very nice to meet you, Mrs. Lockwood."

Richard leaned back on his chair, arms up over his head. He was in shirtsleeves, very relaxed for the middle of the day. As for herself, Lacey leaned against the edge of his desk. It was all very cozy. I wondered if I should slip off my shoes and sit cross-legged on the sofa.

"I want you to take Lacey around with you, show her how we do things," Richard said.

"Oh," I said. "I'm not sure I understand."

Richard sat forward again. "Just take her on some showings with you. I need a senior to train her. She's going to be a broker." He smiled baldly at her, and I read into it. How could I not, it was written in neon.

"Of course," I said.

"Thank you, Mrs. Lockwood."

Richard said, "You can start tomorrow. Does that work for you? You're showing something tomorrow, I trust?"

I was. I had a 10:30 with a couple from Germany. I didn't have a great deal of faith in the first two apartments I would show them. The apartments were well-placed, but expensive and the couple would only be in the U.S. temporarily while the husband worked through a contract. The wife was along for the ride as far as I could tell.

"Of course," I said, and managed to sound a little indignant.

"Great then, it's all set."

When I left the office, I walked the long hallway back to my desk, in "the pit" at the front of the building, same desk I'd had for twelve years. I had a window, and in fact could remember my argument with my previous boss, Don Marko, to get my desk moved to a window spot. My argument—unimpeachable—was that I'd earned it.

Between Richard's office and the pit, there were five offices on either side of the hall. Most of the doors were open, and I could see people at their desks, heads bent over tidy Mac Books, plants on windowsills.

All new faces.

I realized that, back then, I should have argued for an office.

The Bramleys on ten went to the Caribbean at the end of May, and I dragged Ms. Lacey around by the nose for two weeks. The only showing I cut her out of was in my building, The Windemere, and it was as much out of spite as it was out of fear. I showed Stephanie's friend, Lily, poor Barney Kloss's apartment, vacant and not on the market officially, since paperwork was such a bitch in these sorts of circumstances. It was not premature, not really, although morally it might have been a jab to poor Myrna, but it wasn't like I ran up to her apartment and started bragging about my big commission. It was all handled delicately and in the best of taste. And it put my numbers up for May.

I didn't take Ms. Lacey on the showing with me because it was likely to be a done deal, a token showing. What I knew from Stephanie was that Lily was very keen to move into the building, and not at all squeamish about living in an apartment someone had died in. Those, of course, were Lily's own words, from a telephone call. She said, "I'm not squeamish."

I also didn't take Lacey because she was young and looked much more like Lily and Stephanie and that sort, and I was secretly afraid that they'd hit it off. In my paranoid state, I had envisioned all sorts of betrayals—a refusal to use me as broker in favour of Lacey, was one of them—but also an exchange of business cards and secret handshakes and promises of lots of business from Lily's friends.

It seemed prudent just to leave her out of it.

Lily moved in as soon as the paperwork cleared, which was thankfully quick. Someone out there at least, was on my side.

Blessedly before the month was even up, Richard decided that Ms. Lacey was ready to take on clients of her own and she was off my hands. I celebrated that day with a pulled pork sandwich, dripping with BBQ sauce, not my finest hour, although as glorious as a June day. I received no special thanks, but still considered it enough that it was over, my pro bono completed for the year.

Of course no good deed goes unpunished. Richard rezoned some territories and shifted a number of people about, explaining at meetings that a shake-up was always good, kept the blood flowing. I expected to hear a lot of bitching about it. For instance I was shifted so that part of my best grouping was split, and my new territory was a more down-market area. It potentially could cut my—occasionally soft—commissions by a significant amount in a bad year. I expected a lot of brokers would be feeling bitter. Hot young woman comes into the office, the gravy gets spooned a little thinner, so when no one said anything, I wondered if we had begun operating in an atmosphere of fear.

I brought it up with one of the brokers I knew a little bit.

"How about the new zoning, huh?" I said, running into Cathy at the copier. It was a little close to Richard's office, but I'd lost about five pounds recently and was feeling the bravado.

To my surprise, she said, "I know. I've almost doubled my numbers this month. Brilliant."

I think my jaw dropped, but I said, "Yes. Brilliant."

The office distracted me. I went dutifully up to ten to water the Bramleys' plants through the two weeks they were gone. I collected mail and it piled up on the island in the kitchen. Sometimes I lingered; the empty apartment was twice as large as mine and the cavernous silence gave me a kind of peace. The view was spectacular, of course. If I opened the kitchen window and leaned out, I could see clear down to the river, the quaint old-fashioned water towers surrounded by pretty park-like roofs with chaise-and-teak lounging stations on each one. It was nice.

I continued to struggle with sleep. I had my little helpers, but I tried not to overuse them. I knew too many stories of women my age getting dependent on chemical help for everything. When I went through menopause, I was the only one of my friends who did not succumb to the seductive powers of hormone replacement. My fear of aging was surpassed only by my fear of cancer and somehow when offered the choice between a young-looking corpse and dying alone in an assisted-living room, I decided the latter wasn't so bad. You could always watch television. And if it got too lonely or undignified, I could take all the rest of my little helpers and end it all on a date of my choice.

I preferred a natural hell to a foggy complacency.

But sleep was often elusive.

I was having a cup of tea in the kitchen, the light over the stove the only illumination, since I didn't want to disturb Kevin. I drank my camomile tea—a guaranteed cure for insomnia according to television—

and flipped through the new *Vanity Fair*, staring at celebrity faces I didn't recognize and political scandals I no longer cared about.

And I heard singing.

The window was open to the front street and I thought of course that it must be coming from there. I went over and peered out, but couldn't see anyone outside. I checked the clock and it was well after three. Still, listening, it wasn't the drunken frat-singing that you do occasionally hear on lovely summer nights when the college kids band together and walk over to the park to watch the sun come up. There was nothing mirthful or disjointed about it. It was more like *chanting*. Churchy.

I opened the screen and stuck my head out. It served no better to prove anything, except that it was coming from above. I twisted my head up as though that would vet something, and it didn't.

The music faded in and out with the breeze and I decided someone's radio was tuned to NPR.

I ran into Gig Morton a few afternoons later, at the front desk. I was about to collect the Bramleys' mail and take it up, when she stopped me.

"Anita, have you heard?"

"Heard what? I'm just getting the mail, come with me." We walked to the mailboxes and she kept talking in that breathless way of hers. With Gig everything is an exciting event or a horrible tragedy that had to be shared in great hunks of breath.

"It's the Bramleys! Their cruise ship! Some horrible virus or food poisoning or something. Everyone is sick! It was on the news—oh are you getting their mail?"

I pulled their mail out. Bills and invitations to half-off sales. The Bramleys were America's greatly appreciated tax bracket, the upper middle class and their disposable income was snatched at as often as possible, one half at a time.

"Are they ill? Have you heard from them? They're due back day after tomorrow."

"But they might be quarantined! It's on the *news*."

I begged off a longer chat and didn't think about it again until Kevin got home and put on the news. I wasn't listening at all. I was distracted. Things at work seemed to be getting worse, or I was getting paranoid. I was feeling isolated, between Lacey, the new territories, *sparkling*. Too many new faces at the office. I had never really thought about how often I had been passed over for promotion. Sometimes now, I felt almost a sense of embarrassment, like a cougar at the club. As if I was overstaying my welcome. Or at least that I should be in one of those offices, *dammit*.

I was obsessing over that when Kevin said something.

"I'm sorry darling, what?"

"I said—isn't that the ship that Marg and Teddy are on?" I looked up and the video was of a cruise ship at a safe distance. The caption under the video was "Death Ship."

"Oh my god, that's a little dramatic, I hope?"

"Apparently twelve people have died." He looked at me, concerned. "Maybe we should call someone."

Later that night I couldn't help but remember the thing the Queen of England had said the year after Diana and Charles had broken off their marriage, when affairs had been exposed, when her favourite castle had burned up, favourite paintings included, when her daughter-in-law was caught on tape discussing the family, when her son was caught on tape discussing feminine protection. She had said it was her "annus horribilis."

So it was for The Windemere.

The Bramleys were dead. It took seven phone calls, but we reached Marg's sister in Florida. They'd gotten news that afternoon. Marg had died the day before, and Ted that morning.

Their son-in-law would be picking up the keys from us in the next couple of weeks.

The Bramleys. Barney. Poor old Clara.

Horribilis. I hoped not *annus*.

There were, unfortunately, several more bad nights after the news of the Bramleys. My poor sleeping habits became worse. The Bramleys had four children and six grandchildren. They had just begun a happy retirement. It was just a terrible thing that served to make me think too much and too often of my own mortality. And Kevin's. What would I do without Kevin, should anything happen to him? Poor Kevin woke up more than once to find me staring at his chest, making sure he was breathing. He joked, was I waiting for him to die, or making sure he didn't?

It distracted me at least as much as my other thoughts.

I had decided that it was time to speak up about a promotion. I had been much like a kid when these things were announced, trying very hard to be happy for the winning person, so to speak, and not too bitter over my own disappointments, especially since the disappointment belonged to me and me alone. I rarely if ever put myself forward for much at all, beyond tossing my name into the ring. I didn't politic for these things, expecting instead to be rewarded on a system of, if not merit, then surely seniority. This had turned out not to be so.

Along with this morbid turn of thoughts and newfound gumption, I found myself more than once at the mercy of a terrible anger. It would rise in me unexpectedly and be a devil to put down again. I raged internally at my infernal co-workers, my pitiful desk by the window, the denial of new territory when a colleague left to join another firm.

My face would get nearly red with it, and there was always the same, easy—which was not to say, undeserved—target: Richard Maynard. The devil in my eyes.

I still had a friend in the upper ranks, Oscar Barns. Unlike me, he'd benefited from time and merit and occupied the position under Richard. Of course it had been many years since we were in the pit together, but at least he remembered me as a young thing, attractive and ambitious, and hopefully, more than a few nights of boozy flirting from the days before Kevin and I were married.

I waited until the end of the week and tapped on his door near the end of the day.

"Well look who's stopping by," he said, with what seemed like genuine affection. "Haven't seen much of you these days, how are you? How's Kevin?"

"Well, you know, I'm still in the pit. I suppose our paths rarely cross."

He had the decency to colour at that point, but his smile never wavered. "Come on in, Anita. Let's catch up."

By the end of our meeting, I was so grateful that had it been even three years earlier, I might have cried. Which was strange to me, because the result of the meeting was not entirely positive. Not entirely. But I felt heard, I felt stronger for it, as though forcing the issue without wavering was a bit of magic. But throughout my tenure in that chair, what I felt was that tingle of anger. My hands closed into fists just before I closed the door behind me and stayed that way for a very long time.

I was clear in my words: I wanted to move up. It was time. I resisted using the word "fair," since that smacked of girlhood fights on the playground and I wanted to stick with merit and seniority as long as possible before I played such a card. To my benefit, he agreed with me. We went over my numbers and when he raised an eyebrow over the last few months, I bristled and told him my side of things.

Without getting too detailed, I told him how time and again new territories were split up among all the brokers, how in that system I was no more valued than the newest broker. I tried heartily to keep the bitterness from my voice when I told him about Richard's heavy-handed demand that I train the newest girl, and his insinuation, real or imagined, that she could be my replacement.

All the while, my hands were rolled into fists, my fancy, silly, fake fingernails digging into my palms in a way that felt oddly, painfully good. When my voice rose or wavered, my blood pressure climbed and I felt as though my face were getting red and puffed with buried resentments and anger, I would take a deep breath and smile and repeat in my head, *Oscar is not the enemy.*

It worked. To a point.

The unfortunate ending to our visit was Oscar telling me, "If I could do something more, I would Anita. The best I can do, is to put your name forward when the time comes again."

"With emphasis," I pressed.

"As much as I can," he said. "Richard is not a . . . malleable man." I understood this to be true. I was grateful and I said so. There was a long enough pause at the end of the conversation that I knew it was over.

It dragged me home. The best I could do had been done, and I had been grateful for Oscar's *as much as I can.* I disgusted myself as much as I was terribly thrilled with the feeling of that anger. Once home that afternoon, I ate the rest of Kevin's takeout of roast beef from several nights earlier. Ate the whole thing, standing at the fridge.

Delicious.

I went to the memorial service for the Bramleys, held a few weeks after the tragedy. The memorial was for their New York friends, since their children lived all over the country.

Kevin and I arrived almost late; I had been showing an apartment on the upper East side that I felt quite good about. The block was mid-range for the area, and my commission wouldn't be very high, but I'd hit it off with the couple I'd shown it to, and they were young and in their thirties, just the perfect age for moving up on the real estate ladder. I was expecting that they would recommend me to their friends when the time came. I planned to leave several business cards with them when we completed the paperwork.

We walked into the memorial hall and up to the front of the pews. We slid in to sit next to the Turgots, who lived in the apartment directly below ours. We said our hellos and caught up a little bit on whispered gossip about the cruise ship disaster and the Bramleys in general, when I glanced back and happened to catch a row of beauties in a back pew.

It was Tracy, Stephanie and Lily, the full trio of new girls from the building. The three of them sat with a fourth girl, whom I didn't recognize.

They spotted me the same time I spotted them and as I raised my hand in a discreet, but rather pleased wave, the three of them smiled back at me, in unison. It threw me a little.

White. Toothy.

Identical. My hand dropped and I turned back to the front. The memorial was starting.

Requiem eternam dona eis, Domine.

It was a lovely service, with lots of tears, which is all one can hope for at the end of one's life. Afterwards Kevin and I were going to dinner with some friends. I waited outside the hall while he got the car.

He was only gone a moment when the girls stopped to say hello. We exchanged a few pleasantries and then Lily introduced the fourth girl.

"Anita, I'd like you to meet Gwendolyn." I smiled and shook her hand, soft as flower petals, but strong.

"How do you do?" I said, watching for Kevin out of the corner of my eye. She was very nice.

"We're old friends—" Lily started.

I interrupted with what I hoped was a light tone, "From college?" The girls all laughed.

"I think you've found us out!" she said. And then nearly in the same breath, "I'm sure this is very bad time to bring this up—" her tone apologetic and at the same time, firm.

"What's that?" I said. The other girls stood very close, Mona-Lisa-smiling with their lips together.

"I know it's soon, but of course the Bramleys' apartment will be coming up for purchase soon, and we wanted you to know we think Gwendolyn would be a *perfect* addition to the building. She wants very much to see it. Don't you, Winnie?"

"Very much. It's a lovely building."

I had nothing to say. I was quite shocked. My mouth opened but nothing came out. I tried to say *pretty name* but it . . . wouldn't come out.

"We know it's soon," Stephanie said.

"We just want to get in line, really," Lily said. Gwendolyn—Winnie—held her smile, confident and poised.

"You're lovely to consider her," Tracy said. She touched my hand and bent a little in my direction, mindful of her heels. "We'll be in touch soon." She turned and looked at the crowd, still congregating around the doors of the hall. "Wasn't that just the nicest service?"

It had been.

Kevin pulled up and I excused myself. They all waved.

I had forgotten all about the Bramleys' memorial a few days later, when one of the Roberts announced he was leaving the firm. There were two Roberts, they had been so shortly at the office, that I had never learned to tell them apart. They had become the Two Roberts in my mind and that was how they stayed. When I got the intra-office email stating his resignation, my first thought was to scroll down to the bottom and see his title.

Junior Partner, Senior Broker.

My second thought was that I would now be able to tell them apart.

I didn't reply to the email, but I did quickly jot one off to Oscar, saying how *nice* it had been to catch up recently, and wasn't that just so sad about Robert.

I felt pretty big in my shoes; it felt like a bold move and the right one.

Leaving Robert's last day was the following Friday and there was a little send-off, a glass of champagne in the pit, as though he'd suddenly realized those of us on the bottom rung would miss a mentor and benefactor. As far as I could tell, the most popular part of the reception was not Leaving Robert at all, but the champagne, which people seem to over-consume. I limited myself to a single glass and sipped daintily. Not that anyone noticed. I remained invisible.

So better to see things.

Bunches and cliques are common in any office, and I happened to note them, perhaps for the first time. Except for Leaving Robert and two of the other office-dwellers, there were no senior staff on the scene until ten minutes to quitting time. They came into the pit en masse and got drinks and ate a bit of the leftover cheese and crackers that had been laid out for the send-off.

Oscar was among them, as was Richard. I thought about wandering over to their group, knowing the names only of those in my division, my colleagues, some of years, some of months, such as The Lacey Thing, my shadow that long month now well past.

I just couldn't. I attempted simple eye contact with Oscar, a smile and a nod, and went home. Enough.

It was strictly due to nerves, when I couldn't sleep that night. I was overwrought with the idea that I wouldn't be getting that office. That, after all this time, I wouldn't be moving up. That I would be retiring in ten years at the same desk I was at now.

To calm myself I was cleaning. It was after midnight and I had yet to go to bed. I was in my good robe because I had recently begun a campaign to try and look my best. The diet had topped out at about six pounds and it was beginning to feel like I was wasting my time, that there would forever be six pounds out there with my name on it, and no matter where I dropped it, it would find its way home to my arse.

Instead, I was using makeup, hair and clothing tips to camouflage my problem areas. It was a great deal more work and rather than the scale, it required much more mirror gazing than I was used to.

Worse, I wasn't sure it helped.

I began cleaning a junk drawer that had plagued us for years. It was amazing how many odd things accumulated. For instance in that drawer were no less than three packages of birthday candles and for the life of me I couldn't remember the last time a birthday had been celebrated with cake in this apartment, let alone candles. They went into the garbage.

It just so happened that I ran across a spare key in the drawer too, with a rubber Marge Simpson on the fob.

Aw. The Bramleys' old key. I held it a moment, remembering how very long ago Marg had given it to me, back when her children were younger, and I kept plants, and the occasional time conflict that required one or the other of us to unlock doors for school-aged children, or water something.

Oh the days.

I took the key up to the Bramleys' apartment. I would put it inside for her older son to find. The fob at least, was a nice reminder of his mother, who could be quite a funny woman when she wanted to be.

I slid the key into the lock and it worked smoothly in spite of gunk clinging to the grooves on the key from years in a junk drawer (likely source: birthday candle wax). I stepped inside and stepped onto something. The floor was gritty.

I looked down. Along the edge of threshold, there was white something. It took only a moment to figure out what it was.

Salt. It ran in a line across the doorway, except for where I had stepped and disturbed it. I frowned, stepped more carefully with my other foot, not to disturb it.

Curious. And oddly familiar.

There was more I saw. There was salt on each window sill and what might have been more in the bottom of the light fixture in the dining room.

I put the key on the counter in plain view and went out the way I came in, careful not to disturb it any more than I had.

Oddly familiar.

Just after Clara had died, I had gone into her apartment to take a few measurements, to look the place over, since I would be brokering the place. Of course out of curiosity, I went to the window where she'd done the high dive and leaned out as far as I could to see the trajectory. I put my hand on the far corner of the sill to do it, holding on lest there be some kind of wild, unknown wind tunnel that yanked women out apartment windows to their death. And when I did, I put my hand into a kind of . . . grit.

Which turned out to be salt. More or less undisturbed in the corners of the window by police and investigators (which makes you wonder, somewhat).

Curious then, too.

It was only after midnight. I took a chance and went up the elevator to seven. The building was old, the walls thick, but if you had very good hearing, you could hear the murmurs of folks going about their business behind the closed doors.

7A was no exception. Behind that particular closed door I could hear a kind of singing, a *kind* of singing. I tapped on the door, very lightly, uncertain and yet completely convinced. In just a moment, Stephanie answered the door.

Even in the middle of the night, she was lovely, fresh as morning. Wasn't that nice. Perfect, really, except for her confused look.

"I'm sorry to disturb you so late," I said.

She didn't answer, and I sensed, or maybe heard something, from the back of the apartment, in spite of the hour. I had a horrible moment when I thought maybe I had interrupted a moment with a boyfriend and felt my cheeks getting red, my resolve fading when she said, "Not at all. Would you like to come in?"

I did. She led me to the living room of the apartment, which looked so different from when Clara lived in it, for a minute I was rubbernecking, almost forgetting why I had come. Then in the living room, I saw it was true, Stephanie had not been alone at all. There were the two girls, her friends, Lily and Tracy, and Gwendolyn. Winnie.

"Nice to see you all again," I said.

They smiled.

I frowned, "It's nice that you're all here. I have some possible bad news. I'm sorry to say that I'm obliged to show the Bramley apartment to someone else. He had dibs on it, if you will." Their faces were very serious.

I shrugged helplessly. "I'm sorry, girls. There's not much I can do. Of course, if something comes up and he can't take the apartment, I'll happily show it to your friend," and I nodded, smiling, at Gwendolyn.

I looked at my watch, "Oh my," I said, "I can't believe it's this late. I'm sorry again to have disturbed you. I heard singing."

Tracy said. "We have a sort of a club."

"A glee club?" I said and we all laughed.

"Something like that," Lily said. Tracy giggled behind a perfectly manicured hand.

I was about to leave when Gwendolyn said, "These other people, who are looking at the apartment?" I nodded. "Who are they?"

"Well you see, he's my boss, Richard Maynard. It puts me in an awkward position. If not for him—" I let it hang.

"Richard Maynard?" Tracy said. "And he works in your building?"

"That's right." The four of them looked at me, unblinking. I could almost hear their thoughts. "Richard Maynard," I said again. Stephanie and I locked eyes for a moment.

"I'll leave you to your club," I said. They smiled broadly at that, and Gwendolyn let out a throaty laugh that we might have called smoky, back in the day when people smoked.

I waved to the girls sitting and let Stephanie walk me to the door. She opened it. Smells from the hallway were warm and clean.

"Well, goodnight," I told her. She smiled, but it was small and tight. I held the door a moment longer and looked her right in the eye.

"I hope I have good news soon. About the apartment, I mean."

"Yes," said Stephanie.

I shrugged helplessly. "If something changes—"

She smiled. "Let's hope for the best."

"Let's," I said and I waited as she shut the door.

Two major events happened in the next two weeks. I lost ten whole pounds, enough that I rewarded myself with a decadent lunch of a double cheeseburger with gravy on my fries. And poor Richard died, an accident on the freeway.

Terrible thing.

My commissions for June were very good. I had a sudden increase in clients, as is what happens when friends refer friends. There used to be a TV ad like that *and I told two friends and they told two friends* until the television screen was full of faces. It was like that. Lucky me.

I think Richard would have liked his funeral.

It really *sparkled*.

TRUCKDRIVER

That September, none of them knew what they were going to do after college, least of all Corey. Until he saw the truck. It was that kind of truck, it made you dream.

He'd first seen it in a flash, driving past him when he pulled up beside the store. They called it the corner store, but it wasn't really on a corner, it was situated in the middle of a vacant lot. People parked on one side of it, but then on the other side there was room for anything. They used to have baseball games in the lot, football games. In the winter they played street hockey in the lot. No one ever had to quit those games to yell "Car!" Not in their neighbourhood, because they had the lot. Which was where he'd first seen the truck. He was coming back from Bernie Able's, where they'd been smoking a fattie and shooting the shit, wondering if the Bombers were going to do shit this year or what.

Almost laughable, it was really, the truck. At first blush. Some twit had painted it lime green and that was all you saw until you checked out the bumper-less back end, the snub-nose front with the pattern-grill, the huge headlights, rounded old school, like maybe inside there were tiny little candles burning that some guy in galoshes and a cap had to relight every night. It was vintage something and too bad some idiot painted it, probably painting over the vibrant red script of some dairy farm, (*Meadoway Farms, Milk for Growing*), rendering it impotent and worse, maybe ridiculous.

Then it was gone. A flash.

The second time he saw it, it was parked halfway between his mom's place and Rocky Penner's. He'd been walking down to see what Rocky was doing, to shoot the shit, maybe smoke a fattie, see if Rocky found a job yet. Then he saw the truck again.

Except, it wasn't exactly like that.

Really: It was more like he'd been walking head down, head practically between his knees whining in his interior dialogue, as his sister called it, thinking maybe his life was the shits, since the best he'd been able to do since finishing school was to work part time at Target, shifting boxes from one end of the warehouse to the other. He could have been shifting boxes from one end of his old man's Grand Prix to the other, and no one would have noticed.

Truth was, he'd thought it would be different, getting out of school. He thought it would be something better. He'd applied to Barstow-Fedler Industries, taking great care with his application and query letter. For the first time he'd really put himself into the picture—like Goodman, the career counsellor always told him to. For the first time he'd done some real positive affirmation and visualization shit. In fact, he got kind of caught up in the fantasy of it all—working in the office at BFI, wearing a tie, punching shit into a computer, maybe moving out of his parents' house, getting an apartment with a dishwasher and a big TV. What he would do at BFI was less specific, he imagined only as far as the desk, the computer and the tie. The fantasy was sweet. He found himself entirely wrapped up in it, *expecting* it—he went, for instance, and bought a tie, dark blue with small dots that were either gold or beige—just waiting for his start date. Then last Monday they sent a letter. A form letter. *Nothing at this time keep you on* (circular) *file—*

Whatever.

So he'd had his head down and he was pretty deeply lost in thought. He didn't know what had made him put his head up in time to see the truck. He could have easily just walked past it. This he took as a sign.

There it was, like a revelation. Parked in a driveway, like any other vehicle might be, except it was nose out, and it was sweet as hell, even if it was lime green. The green stuck out like nothing else, the only bright spot of colour on the street. Even the houses were mostly brick-fronted with the wide, silent lawns that kids stayed off of. The street was quiet, except for the screaming of the lime green truck.

Over the flat front window was a sign, held fast by an impossibly long wiper, it said "For Sale by Owner."

Corey became giddy and excited. "Owner," he presumed, meant

whoever lived behind the set of bamboo blinds closed over the window in number 362. All he had to do was walk over and knock—

And it could be his.

As long as he could remember, he'd liked old things. When he was a kid, he and his old man would go to equipment meets, his dad on a constant quest to get Corey to play more sports. His old man would be bitching somebody down for the newest of the old stuff at the meet and Corey would be talking to the old timer selling the leather pads and crotch cradles, the scuffed, lace-up skates with no plastic forms over the ankle. But not just hockey stuff, he liked anything old. He'd once spent twenty bucks of his own money to buy this thing called a Tru-Vu 3-D stereoscopic viewer, first manufactured around the '30s and '40s. He got a set of filmstrips with the viewer, tourist destinations with inflated, exotic names, like The Grand Canyon, and Yellowstone National Park. Most of the reels had scenes with people and old cars, little houses in them, and it was these that Corey liked to look at most. Everything seemed smaller, quieter (he didn't want to say easier because he was sure it wasn't; he never got drafted or had to go to war, shooting Krauts or anything else); it just seemed *calmer* in the old stuff. He'd just always liked it. Like maybe the folks in those days cared less about cash and titles. Simpler.

He'd be looking at those old folks in those old pictures and he'd be thinking, *They're all dead.*

"Yeah?" said the guy who answered the door at 362. The guy was younger than Corey expected. He half expected a grizzled old guy, the kind of guy who maybe knew someone who'd driven a milk truck like the one in the yard, maybe he'd rescued it from a junkyard, but had to pass it on. Someone Corey could sit and shoot some old shit with. Not this guy.

He was grizzled, but he wasn't old. His hair was long, but not cool-long, just uncombed. The beard was a mix of grey and black.

"I was looking at your truck."

The guy leaned in the doorframe. "You want to buy it?"

Corey shrugged. *I do*, he thought.

"How old is it?"

The man grinned, baring teeth stained pink. It was startling. "Old as the hills, kid. That truck's been around a long time."

"Oh yeah," he said, and he couldn't help it, he looked back over his shoulder at the truck.

It practically glowed green, and it was beautiful, the narrow snakes of paint where it had dribbled down the sides after the indifferent spray job looked like ribbons of tickertape; the flat front from his angle was chiselled like the jawbone of an old-timey actor, the taillights and their slight, jocular hoods winked. It tugged at him.

The guy went on, his voice a pleasant drone, background music. "It's got a celebrated history, this truck. It's journeyed up and down this great country, a lot of accomplished men got their start in life behind the wheel of this big fella."

Corey's eyes were at half-mast like the hoods on the taillights, his voice quiet. He wasn't exactly sure he spoke it out loud. "Fella?" he said. "I thought vehicles were always women."

"Not this one," the man chuckled. "This one's all man. That's a 37-horsepower engine, four-poster, gravel-eating, old-school V8. Himmler drove a truck with that very engine. German engineering, built to conquer."

"Yeah," Corey whispered. The lines of the body rose straight and tall on the six-foot box and cantered to the flat front without a single deviated rivet, not a single dent or even chip in the paint. The drivers' side door was flush with the side of the truck, appearing seamless. "You've taken great care of it," he said.

"Not just me. Every man who's owned Him has treated Him with respect. Oiled Him, cleaned Him, painted Him when He needed it. Nobody really owns this truck—it's only borrowed from history. You want take it for a ride? You put it in first gear and you can feel the shift of the earth under your ass—"

"I'll take it," he said. He pulled his eyes away to look at the man. "How much?"

For just a second the guy hesitated and Corey thought he saw something falter in his eyes. "How old are you?"

"Twenty-one."

He nodded. "Good age for starting out. Gimme $400 and we're square, deal?"

Corey put his hand out, his face almost splitting with a ridiculously happy grin—he had $600 squirreled away in a shoe box under his bed at home. *Four hundred dollars!* He would be able to buy insurance, fill the tank—

Delivery truck.

"I'm starting a business with it—a delivery business," he blurted. After he had, it felt right.

The guy leaned forward to shake Corey's hand and for the first time

Corey smelled his breath which was bad as if the guy had been sick, and he saw the red veins in his eyes, the dark circles of long nights underneath. It pushed him back a little.

"Hey," he said, "it's not stolen or anything, is it? It's not been used in some kind of crime?"

The guy laughed, slapped Corey on the shoulder as if he'd just told the funniest joke in the world. It was contagious. Corey laughed with him. They were still laughing when he reached into his pocket and pulled out the keys.

He told him to come back with the money, dangling the keys in front of Corey.

He hesitated. "Ah," he said. "Aren't you worried I'll just take off with it? Skip town?" he joked.

The guy chuckled. "Not a bit. I'd find you—and then I'd kill you and eat your heart." He thumped Corey in the chest hard, but playfully and then he threw his head back and laughed. Corey tried to join him.

"Right."

Corey took the keys, closing his fingers over the fob, a leather strip embossed with *Ambrosia Candy Com*, the last bit bleeding so close to the key ring, it was impossible to read. Corey rightly assumed *p a n y*.

Corey drove the truck home without registration. He was feeling pretty good.

His sister and her roommate Madeleine were there, talking to his mom in the kitchen. Madeleine—Maddy—had long black hair and a pixie face, like the kind of fairy you'd see in a children's book (if pixies in children's books had nice honkers). But as usual, when Corey walked into the kitchen and saw her, his face went red and hot and he couldn't speak.

The two of them had an apartment downtown, a television kind of place with a huge open area, the rooms not rooms so much as places behind screens and curtains and makeshift walls. His sister was an administrative assistant at RCA and Madeleine was getting her stockbroker's license. He thought that meant she was still in school but the way they talked about it, it sounded like she was out of school and working somewhere. He couldn't keep up. Half the time they were talking it was all big shit and he couldn't concentrate with Maddy's awesome honkers jiggling.

It was all unbelievably exotic to Corey, who had struggled to finish a BA and had struggled since then to find and keep a job. He'd done the shit job route, fast food, stockrooms, waving flags on the highway, but nothing a man could call work.

Until now, of course. Oh gawd yes, until now.

The truck was parked out front and with his face red as a grape he told them about it. His mom smiled encouragingly—if somewhat indulgently—his sister ignored him except for a quick roll of her eyes, but Madeleine looked him straight in the face and raised an eyebrow, her soft pouty lips turning up at one corner.

"That's wonderful, honey," his mom said. Then she asked Madeleine how often she had to get her hair cut for it to stay so fashionable.

"I go every six weeks," she said.

Amy said, "Sometimes you have to go more often, you know, different seasons."

"Really?" his mother said.

"It's outside now," Corey said. "Come and check it out."

Then Amy gave him her full attention. She sighed and her eyes half-closed in long-suffering fury. It was like when they were younger and Corey had the audacity to interrupt her, or take the last piece of cake.

"You *bought* a truck," she said, "as in paid money, wrote a cheque, that kind of thing?"

"Yup," he said, beaming in spite of Maddy's honkers and his mother's sudden tensing up as she did whenever the sibs were together.

He didn't like the way Amy said it, but he decided to let it go—a sudden and oddly welcome fantasy of diving across the table at her, his hand closing around her slender, smooth throat, and squeezing, *squeezing* while her eyes bulged and her teeth bit down on her fat, bitchy tongue, the blood pooling in her mouth and running out the crook of her lips—

It was enough. Just thinking about it.

Amy sniffed, her smile insidious.

And suddenly in that second—the second where Madeleine should have stood up and run to the window and *ooohed* over the retro cool of the baby parked in the drive and should have asked for a ride, which he would indulgently give—he felt himself flinch, remembering how quick to the mark Amy could be and how powerless he usually was in the stream of her words.

Then he remembered *squeezing* again.

Squeezing.

But his brain was sluggish with images of Madeleine in the truck, standing in the open space where a passenger seat would be, gripping the safety bar, a terrified *squeal* and the brush of her thigh against his bicep when he took a corner just a little too fast. This was mixed in with what was the ongoing, fantasy image of his hands on Madeleine's breasts, pawing, *squeezing*, stroking.

And his sister's voice, so high, so sharp, like knives and axes and the spikes on the branches of the hedge—

"—so you have no job but you spent your savings on that stupid truck? Where exactly do you need to be, that you need a truck at all?" She finished. Her eyelids fluttered and blinked in dismay and astonishment, in *personal affront*.

How *dare* he.

"It's a delivery truck," he said calmly, even though his palms suddenly felt itchy and the only thing that made his voice possible was the image of Madeleine's long thigh pressing up against his arm as he manoeuvred the truck around the block, her clinging to him, the side, the door sliding open wide rounding the corner, loosening her grip on the bar, her body tumbling—

"I'm starting a delivery business; it's all planned out," he said. He was sorry as soon as he said it.

Corey felt tired then, had the most overwhelming feeling of wanting to just drag his feet down the hall and fall onto his bed and sleep. It was 7:30.

Amy gave a pretty little laugh. "Delivering what, exactly? Bullshit?"

"Amy!" his mother said. "That's enough. You two get along!"

His sister stood, as if in resignation, but even his mother must have heard it, the undercurrent in the kitchen, the subtle smile in her voice when she said it. If he could see her face, meet her eyes, he would see them twinkling. She stomped to the kitchen window.

Corey imagined himself in a cartoon lunge—*Noooooooo!*—tackling her before she got to the window, like when Homer goes for the last donut.

Doh.

"*That's it!?*" she snarled. She didn't even laugh. She just turned to him and shook her head in disgust. "Great. If it runs you can deliver big boxes of dork."

This of course caused a casual stampede to the window. His mother stood up and walked over to the fridge to get the milk and on her way she glanced out the window. It was small, but he saw her face fall just a little, her cheeks slacken with a familiar disappointment, only to bounce back up with forced and customary maternal encouragement.

"Good for you, Corey. You're taking some initiative!" she forced out. "Amy, you're too hard on your brother."

Madeleine, in the meantime, picked up her coffee cup and gracefully, casually, carried it over to the sink. She glanced out the window at the truck.

Corey wanted her to turn and see him looking at her. He wanted to tell her that it was a classic machine, that her grandmother had probably had milk delivered in just such a vehicle. He wanted to tell her that during the Depression when money was tight and gas was expensive, they used to drop the motors out of those trucks and get a couple of horses to pull them. He wanted her to enjoy such information.

She never even looked at him. Her even, lovely features never changed from when she lowered her mug into the sink, to when she saw his treasure. Not once.

Madeleine of Steel, studying at the School of AmyBitch.

"It's probably not drivable," Amy snorted.

"Amy, that's enough!"

Corey noticed a real edge in his mother's voice and it surprised him. Amy was the darling. To her credit, she was an actual darling: acing school, not getting knocked up, not smoking or bringing home goth-boys who smelled of despair and glue. Corey had been a disappointment even as a fuck-up. There were no drugs (except pot and they didn't know about that, not even Amy). No girlfriends, no boyfriends, no arrests, no weird obsessions, nothing that he could even be pitied for; there was just *nothing*—

That they knew of.

He was perfectly normal. He was normal, and quiet. Pleasant. The sort of *fella* the neighbours all liked.

"I'm going to take it down to Rocky's to show the guys—"

"Oh good. Your buddies—*Mad*, do you remember that guy we saw on the way here—with the mullet?" Madeleine looked confused and vague and beautiful. She shrugged, half-smiling, bored.

Corey didn't wait to hear what the answer would be but from the foyer he heard them laughing and as he was flinging the door shut behind him he heard Amy exclaim happily, "*That* was Rocky!"

On the front stoop he stood a moment, catching his breath. He dropped his hands down to his sides. He dropped his hand discreetly to the front of his pants and brushed it against himself. He had a boner. Well, a half one.

But not for Madeleine, in spite of that creamy skin, in spite of the endless hair, everywhere; it was not for her.

It was for *Him*.

He'd gotten the boner the minute he'd got in the truck, the second he'd grasped the tall stick shift rising up through the middle of the floor and cranked it into reverse. She—no, *He*—was unyielding and balky, and when Corey finally made contact, it sounded like the bottom of the truck was going to pop rivets and drop out, but he'd made it move. The whole thing was all phallic and gay on the surface but that only popped in and out of his mind, like a notion. Because that wasn't it. The truck made him hard because grabbing the stick was like grabbing himself and the truck moving around when he did it was like a woman, a warm, pliant, cooperative woman.

When he turned the corner at the end of the block there was a trace echo of a feminine squeal of fear mixed with pleasure.

He didn't go to Rocky's.

Instead he drove the truck around the neighbourhood and wished that someone would see him. He drove until it was dark.

Around ten-thirty he parked in the lot by the store, with the engine running, the whole machine thrumming under his feet on the textured steel floor. It was like singing, soft singing. One of those oldies stations on the radio that were hard to get during the day, but sometimes drifted in at night.

The interior was as interesting as the outside of the truck.

The cab was built for a driver only—there was no passenger seating, but there was a safety bar that went from the middle of the top of the cab to where the sliding door opened. There were also four hanging straps in the back. The right side of the truck was almost all door, the panel split in half, the door sliding open with a satisfying rumble, smoothly slipping into a fastener so you could ride with the side wide open if that was the kind of day it was.

Or you could keep it closed, snap the lock, squeeze silicon into the workings so it couldn't be opened from the inside. If it was that kind of day.

It was nice in the truck, with the lights out and engine running. Gusts of warm air leaked up through the floor from the engine, smelling faintly of gas. Corey parked outside of the ring of lights that still protected the store. If the cops drove by they would take particular interest in a delivery truck parked outside a store that had been closed for nearly ten years. The front was boarded up, the plywood planks long since covered with graffiti of the lowest order: tags and *fucks* and *Dani's a slut!*

Even the padlock had been spray-painted over in black. He wondered if the paint had gobbed up inside of the lock, but supposed it didn't matter.

(When he went to pay the guy for the truck, guy stood there on the stoop, eyes glued to the stack of bills as Corey counted them out with forehead-scrunching math, ones and fives and tens and twenties; guy held the money in his palm with his thumb like it was covered in fleas and he said, "Delivery business, huh? Make sure you hose it out real good." It had the same effect on his dick as getting in the cab seat—*you bet your ass I will* he'd thought but hadn't said, not sure why he'd thought it.)

They used to buy caramels and Oh Henry!s and Good & Plentys and in the summer they'd have Creamsicles and grape Popsicles. Larry Beems wore braces and he couldn't have anything sticky, no taffy, no Kraft caramels, so he always had Dairy Milk.

(There were perennial rumours of a grow-op being in the basement of the store, but Corey had never seen any evidence of that and he'd spent a lot of time in the lot. If the cops came around snooping, he guessed they'd think he was a part of that.)

He kept the side door wide open. Air passed through and it smelled like the first day of school, especially when he had his eyes closed. Now and then, as if to spoil it all for him even when she wasn't around, his sister's hateful voice broke through the silence in his head. *You can deliver huge loads of dork!*

"She's awful," Corey said. The radio played something soft and sad, with lots of horn.

Corey'd had the truck two weeks the next time he saw his sister. And something was up with her. He thought she might be bumming cash off their mom.

When he walked in on them their heads were together, his mom's purse on the counter. Amy looked up at him when he said *hey* coming in and she smiled instead of sneering or cracking wise and then he knew *something* had to be up, right?

Hey, he'd said. And she smiled at him. That was why he knew.

Whether or not he'd ever seen that expression on his own face was up for debate, nobody runs to the bathroom and checks their mug after bumming twenty off the old lady, but surely he'd felt the way Amy looked. Her eyes widened first and then looked away and narrowed. But her cheeks got red and if she'd had skin like Corey's, he knew you would have been able to see the red creeping up from his neck, bleeding into his hairline. He knew how it went.

I'm just a little short this month, Ma. I'll make it up next cheque.
Oh don't worry. That's what a mother's for.
I'll pay it back.
Be a good girl. That'll pay me back.

But at the time, he'd just caught them both unawares, feeling like he'd walked in on a conversation about maxi-pads or something. He went to his room and got his jacket—it was colder, the end of September, especially if he drove around with the side door open—and it wasn't until he caught his face in the mirror that he realized what was familiar about Amy and his mom, in the kitchen. It didn't cheer him. Not like it should have.

In fact, what the hell: the day before he'd bummed a ten off his mom for gas.

I'm driving around trying to find delivery work, eh Ma? I'll pay you back.
Be a good boy. That'll pay me back.

He couldn't help but wonder why Miss Perfect needed to supplement though. Maybe she lost her job. Maybe things were getting real for Miss Bitch.

Rocky said he should put a sign in the window. Rocky sucked back a whole reefer, telling him this. They stood in the driveway by the truck, hanging out.

"You should make a real good . . . sign," he sucked. He held the smoke, eyelids drooping. "Something cool. 'I'll Take Your Shit.'" He laughed. "Or 'Devilivery.' Oh yeah," he said, nodding.

"You have to call it that, no matter what you put in front of it: you have to call it: *Devilivery.*" Rocky repeated it a few times and Corey had to admit that it rolled off your tongue pleasantly.

By then he had spray-painted the truck black. It had come to him one day while he was driving around. Little kids kept pointing at the truck. It gave him a weird feeling, so he went over to the hardware store and put the last of his cash down for rental of one of those sprayers and did it in an afternoon. Turned out not bad. No worse than the green job, there were still dried ribbons of paint in rivulets from the top. He'd thought about painting them red.

"Awesome," Rocky said. They sat on the steps to Rocky's mom's house. "Or like 'Hell's Devilivery,'" he added, nodding.

"Hell's *Angels*," Rocky whispered, without purpose.

Corey didn't make a sign. He drove around the neighbourhood with his side door open, even after it got so cold that he had to wear a scarf around his neck. He found an old one of Amy's, an orange, yellow and brown thing from the Gap. He wrapped it around his neck and let it hang around his crotch. When he caught a glimpse of himself in his bedroom mirror, coming or going, he looked good.

He looked good in his rearview mirror.

It got to be a habit, stopping in the lot at night, sitting there while his mom's money exhaled out the tailpipe. He imagined loading and unloading the truck, figuring out the best combinations of layouts, like a game of Tetris. He'd been good at Tetris. He'd played a lot of it while he was supposed to be writing papers in school. It came with the computer.

He didn't like computers much.

Whatever.

Corey's dad had worked for the railroad from the time he left school until the time he left them all, moving in with this woman named Wanda, who had two other kids, about the same ages as Amy and Corey. It was weird, like a JJ Abrams movie or something, going over there to see their "other selves" in their dad's life. Wanda's kids were a boy and a girl, the only difference being that they were reversed, with the boy being older and the girl younger.

The girl had an old-school View-Master collection, and Corey and her hung out in her room, checking out the View-Master whenever they had to go over there, which wasn't that much. She had *The Jetsons*, *Thundercats*, *The Ninja Turtles* and the Transformer series, including the one where Optimus Prime is killed. She was Vonna.

You and Vonna were making out, Amy would tease when their mom would come and get them. The best Corey could do was to protest. But Amy would *you were so* and then their mom would tell them to shut up. He didn't even know if Amy played with the boy, Cliff, or if they all sat around in the kitchen or watched TV or what. They four of them weren't around each other often enough to fight.

His dad got run over by a train when he was moving loads from one car to another in the yard. He was crossing to have a smoke with a buddy when one of the cars thought his dad was signalling for him to go and pulled forward. His dad didn't even scream.

He took it like a man, one of the guys from work said to them all, they were standing around in the living room, not in the kitchen that night. *Didn't scream. Not once.*

I woulda screamed, he added, when none of them said anything.

By then his dad hadn't been living with them for at least four years, and if he thought about it, he would have said that his dad had been living with Wanda for at least two years and he had a vague memory of an apartment complex with a pool with yellow, sad-looking water from the months just after his dad left.

His mom cried. At the funeral the other family sat in the front row opposite his dad's urn full of his ashes.

Wanda sobbed loudly with Vonna on one side and Cliff on the other, kind of holding her up. Corey and Amy had cried too, but from closer to the back of the funeral parlour. Their mom didn't cry *that* much. She cried just enough for the back of the funeral parlour. Their Auntie Meg got up and talked—their dad's sister—apparently their dad had taken up *golf*; Corey had enough trouble with that, that he didn't even spend any time thinking about it, just once in a while he would think, *golf?*—and that was it.

His mom held up okay. And apparently that was the plan, because later he heard his mother on the phone talking about how she hadn't made a scene and no one was going to feel sorry for her.

She didn't scream either.

Most of the time, he tried to think of how to start his delivery business. He wrote lots of notes, filled notebooks in fact, with details of how he would pick things up, how long it would take him to get from (various) points A to (various) points B; he even had time schedules mapped out. He did this while parked in the lot. He wrote things at the top of the notebook like, *It Can Be Done!*

This Will Work!

Monday!

He could make, like, fifteen bucks an hour, if he played it right.

Sometimes the truck attracted the curious eyes of strangers.

His parking every night in the lot made it somewhat of a feature and once in a while the kids hanging around smoking would wander over and look at the truck. There were a couple of young kids, about grade seven or eight, who hung around after the other ones had got bored and wanted to see the engine and stuff—even though there wasn't much to look at. It was located in a curious position, though, and was inordinately large and so he made a deal out of popping the odd, nearly vertical hood and poking around at the tubes and wires there. He knew enough basic shit to mouth off to the kids. He liked the look of their nods, and for a minute it would seem like they were a syncopated team of know-nothings, Corey mouthing off, the short dark kid giving him an *oh*, and the other one with the thing on his chin, giving out an *ah* and passing it back on to Corey. But he didn't like to think about that; he liked talking about his truck, whether he knew anything for real about it, or not. Didn't really matter.

So what do you use it for?

It's a delivery truck.

Girls came around, too.

It was just like that when these two girls came through the lot, looking for boys, other boys, not Corey who was too old for them. They were maybe, they were sixteen, seventeen. Probably. Not.

Corey was twenty-one by the time he'd bought the truck and was staring at twenty-two in the not too distant future. He felt himself, at times, a man of substance, when he drove down the nearly deserted streets of his neighbourhood, checking out Mr. Bergen walking Teepee out for her late night piss; when he saw someone from the street putting their garbage out late, muttering and stepping around carefully over the damp, cool lawns in slippers. He felt sometimes that he was *taking care of business*. Like when he had a book full of notes, schedules of how long to here, how long to there, the price of gas and the weight of materials, the *ladings*.

BOL: bill of lading. It was about transportation.

Making sure things were to rights in the neighbourhood; making sure there were no strange cars around; checking out whose sensor lights were working, checking out that Brenna Lassiter pulled the shades down on her bedroom window. And Hannah Twill. And Gina whatever, who had the kind of dark hair that he liked.

Sometimes there was an empty, hollow feel to the box behind the driver's seat, almost an echo—a cry for help from the bottom of a canyon. It sometimes handled funny, too, when the streets were slick with rain. He looked it up on the internet and they all said he needed weight back there, something to counter-balance the weight of the engine in the front.

They suggested sandbags. 125 pounds.

This one time he picked up four discarded tires from the back of the vacant lot and loaded them on his truck. He grunted as he did this, in the dark of the night, feeling both somehow hard done by and noble. He tossed them in, then climbed in the back to stack them neatly. They toppled over on the first serious turn but he drove them all the way out to the dump, through the city.

Another time he hauled a sofa that someone had left out on the street.

And a lawnmower that someone left too close to the edge of their property. And a long rug, rolled up and tied with jute, a circular stain of unknowable origin spread from the outer edge and disappearing inside the roll. It was heavier than it looked.

He took that stuff places. Not always the dump, which charged fees. It always felt good when there was weight in the back. It handled better. It counterbalanced.

Those times, that time, he felt like a man, not a shit-kid who borrowed gas money from his ma, but a man with a *delivery service*, who worked late at night and drove home tired. He *was* tired when he got home.

He found out that the girls who hung out at the store were there to watch the boys playing scrub or smoking dope or whatever. The blonde one was going out with the kid with the thing on his chin, so Corey's estimation of them being sixteen was probably wrong.

Didn't matter to him, they were no one to him. They were just two girls, too young, one light and one dark. They stopped to stare at the truck, with the curious eyes of strangers. They seemed older. They seemed sly and interested.

He didn't know them, although one of them was vaguely familiar in the features, like maybe she had an older brother or sister he might have known. He'd say that: *Hey do you have a brother?* Sometimes they did, and he would pretend to know the guy. The girls relaxed then. There was a bunch of them, heading into November when it was cold as a witch's tit and looking like snow most days. They were all blonde or mousey brown. Except for the dark-haired girl, they all looked like they had dye jobs. So fucking young to be doing that shit to themselves. He didn't say.

Hey the blonde one said one time. *What's that truck for?* the blonde said.

Delivery truck, he answered shortly. He'd opened the hood and Corey noticed that the cap for the oil thing was gross and cruddy. He'd grabbed a paper towel to wipe it off. He'd stood there, enjoying himself in front of the truck, rubbing old oil off the threads in the cap. He'd noticed a deer carcass the night before, when he was driving around the outskirts of town. There was a bar out around there. Sometimes he drove out that way and parked at the far end of the parking lot and watched the drunks come out and get in their cars. Lots of times they'd have a drunk girl with them, and the two of them would do it in the back seat. There was now a pair of binocs in the glove box. Corey found them around the house.

Probably they had been his old man's.

He was thinking he might go get the deer carcass, get it off the road. Take it somewhere. Get rid of it. Maybe take it out to Berk's field and burn it.

He'd spotted the girls through the break in the hood. He stood there, rubbing, watching them, waiting to see what they would do.

What do you deliver? she said. He thought it sounded provocative, he thought she'd made it deliberately so.

Corey shrugged as though they were asking a complicated, tiring question. *Go away little bug.*

They stayed.

They were Coral and Diane, they told him. He told the blonde one she looked familiar and it turned out she had a brother. Brett some-such-shit. Corey nodded as if he knew him, and that put everyone at ease. They talked about what Brett was doing (he was working for their dad at the glass shop, cutting glass to order and slicing his hands up real bad) and they talked about the neighbourhood. They didn't remember when the store was open, but they remembered playing in the lot.

Coral was a year older than Diane and remembered something about when the store had been open. They all agreed it was a long time ago, but only Corey had any memories of it.

Pop rocks.

Pixie sticks.

Twinkies. Of course, they were still around.

Coral's hair was black like licorice jelly beans. They all remembered licorice jelly beans, too.

Diane wanted to go for a ride. She widened her blue eyes and bitched about the guy with the thing on his chin—all he cared about was goofing and smoking pot with his loser friends. She dropped her head back in disgust and shook out her long blonde hair, grabbing it with her hand and pulling it forward over one shoulder. Coral looked away when she did that.

"Some other time," he told her. "I got to go pick something up."

The two of them walked away, sharing a smoke.

He drove out after that, to the place where he'd seen the deer carcass. It took him a long time to find it again, and by the time he did, it was dark. He drove around town after that, passing the houses he usually watched, feeling the thrum of the engine under his feet, that vibrated up through the shocks under his seats, letting his cock get hard and waiting while the stiffness faded away. It always did, if you waited.

The weight of the deer in the back was good, the truck handled nicely. But it smelled. He did his thing, taking it out to the field. By the time he got home he reeked of smoke and gasoline. He took a shower and dropped dead into bed.

While he lay there, just before sleep, he remembered that Madeleine had moved out of his sister's apartment. He asked her out, after that. He thought he did. He spent the moments before sleep grabbed him trying to remember if he did—if he really asked her out or if it was just something he thought about while he drove around.

His brain was getting fuzzy. He had to start writing that shit down. Take pictures of himself doing shit. Like he took pictures of the loads he carried in the back of the truck. He'd taken about six of the dead deer in the back of the truck, different angles. It must have been hit by a car because its neck was broken and twisted to the side surreally. There was little blood, most of it was on the muzzle, the rest was on its skinny front legs, where it had fallen maybe when it got hit. He dragged it up into the box by grabbing all four of its legs, and when he dropped there and jumped out, they were still in a little elegant bundle all together. He took a picture of that. And of its neck, up close and far away. A spot where the thing's fur and flesh had been stripped away.

In all, he figured he had six pics of the dead deer.

There was a picture of Madeleine on the phone, too. He saw it when he was scrolling through. He couldn't remember when he took it.

The dark-haired one, Coral, lived on Washington in a crappy little house. He saw her sometimes at night when she was walking home from whatever basement she spent her time in. Sometimes he drove past her in the truck. But he never looked out at her. Once she waved, but he didn't wave back.

Ignore to score. Amy always said that, whenever a boy phoned the house for her when they'd been in school. *Ignore to score.* Now that she was back living at home, no one called.

He started parking the truck behind the house. He could see it from his bedroom window, when the streetlight caught a corner of the window, it would gleam. He took to looking at it in the dark at all times of the night, sometimes checking to make sure it was there, sometimes to see what it was doing.

Every time, it would just be sitting there, light glinting off the edge of the window. He couldn't see inside the windows, not from where he was, not at night, not with the light bouncing off the glass, and he was always glad. He didn't want to look inside.

Some mornings he got up and would sit around with coffee thinking, *I'm going to see a movie today*, or *I think Ma said Benedicts was hiring in the stockroom*. It was on the surface though, what he was really thinking was *not getting back in the truck*. But every morning he did. Sometimes it would smell bad, like odd things burning, or the way it smelled in an old cottage that had been boarded up. Like something had crawled in there and died.

He googled the serial number #31081.

At one time

(*old as the hills, kid this fella's old as the hills*)

it had actually been a milk delivery truck. That didn't surprise him. He found a couple of old handwritten sales slips—like the one he had, now kept in his underwear drawer under a couple of old *Playboy*s from the '60s—one was a bill of sale for *One 1911 flat truck ceriel nummer 31081 <u>AS IS</u> sold to C. R. Starkweather this day Agust 14, 1954 Lincoln, Neb.*

He thought it was funny what could come up on the internet. There was a receipt for three tires from Theo & Sons Auto in Kansas City, Kansas, made out to a Richard Hickcock, K. C., dated Nov 1958. There were other things, too. Some strange. A colour photo, undated, uncredited, with no caption, of his truck (he was sure of it) in the middle of the desert. Scrawled across the side was D E A T H T O P I G S, written in what was probably paint.

It was probably paint.

He was having really bad dreams. He was thinking of selling it.

He was thinking no such thing.

It turned out that he had asked Madeleine out. Or maybe he had. In any case, she called him one night. Maybe bored. Maybe it was a joke. He drove around to pick her up.

"You're not serious," she said when she saw him pull up. "There's no seat."

He explained about the safety bar.

She said, "Uh uh, no way," and she started yanking at the sliding door which he'd gallantly opened and closed for her, before getting back in on the driver's side.

"Uh uh. Open this thing—"

And then because for a brief second it had seemed like things were looking up, only to come crashing down, hard *hard*, he started to cry, feeling horribly sorry for himself. She wasn't sympathetic. She was just

all *uh uh no way nope get me out of here open this door OPEN THIS DOOR.*
    Another disaster.

Later, feeling sorry for himself and lonely, he was turning off of Washington and he saw the girl, the blonde one, Diane. It was dark on the street, too late for a kid to be out—
    He rolled up to her and said, "Hey," scaring the shit out of her.
    She spun and saw him, alarmed for just a second. Then she laughed, "You scared me" and grabbed her chest. "I almost had a heart attack."
    They shot the shit for a minute; she lit a smoke and dragged on it. It was cold out and the smoke blurred her face and he could hardly see her. She offered him one. He didn't smoke. Just pot. You gotta stick to the safe shit.
    "Hey," she said. "Can you give me a ride home? I'm just a couple of blocks over."
    She tugged up her hood and tucked her hair into it on both sides. She looked her age suddenly.
    He thought about it. He was busy. The seat was vibrating in idle, the vibrations shaking his lower half. Felt good. Gave him a chubby.
    "I can't," he said, finally.
    "Come on, Corey. It's fucking cold."
    She was so small. No more than a hundred pounds he figured, and she was begging him with her eyes. He was sorry for himself and lonely. Things were not great. He wasn't sleeping well.
    "Please?"
    He didn't want to. *He didn't want to.* The engine purred, the beauty of German engineering reached inside him, soothing away edges, calming him.
    "Okay," he said. "But you have to get in on my side—the door's jammed." Out of the corner of his eye he could see a tiny hard curl of silicone gel sticking up out of the lock. He got out his side to let her in.
    "There's something in the back," he said, his voice smooth, even.
    She hopped in.
    That's what he remembered. He took the corner to hit the highway, heading out to Berk's field. The load in the back shifted and rolled. His fingers were sticky, sticking to the steering wheel. The front of his jacket was a little sticky too.
    But there was weight in the back of the truck, and she handled beautifully.

WIFE

It was noon by the time Karen got around to the dishes. Ted would want lunch any minute, and there she was up to her elbows in soap suds and dirty plates. *A real woman would have timed this better*, she thought. At least the water was in the sink, and she could add the lunch dishes in after Ted had eaten.

She had a specific order that she did the dishes in, learned six billion years ago in a home economics class when they still taught things like how to vacuum in a house with wall-to-wall carpeting, how to sew an invisible hem, what constituted a well-balanced breakfast, and what order to wash your dishes in: glasses, porcelain, plastic, flatware/silverware, with pots and pans pulling up the end. If the dishes were done when Ted ate, then she could start over again, with his glass, plate, etc. If he finished before she was done, then the order would be skewered—maybe the plate mixed in with the flatware, or the fork being stuck with the pots—it would never do.

(Would it?)

For a moment the conundrum seized her, and she thought once and for all she would be discovered to be the fraud she was. The household police would come into the house—wipe your feet—and point their guns at her.

"SHE'S A WHORE!" they would scream, and she would have to go with them.

Karen decided that she would feed Ted *after* she did the dishes, and start all over again, with his.

Sometimes she had a great deal of trouble being organized. Other times, like today, she would whiz through the house, having the dishes done, the carpet vacuumed, and a load of laundry in the dryer before noon. Those were the days that she kept a list, a written reminder of what she had to do: a note to herself to keep on trucking, don't let the bastards get you down; *act normal*.

Once, she remembered, this guy and her were walking down the street, she was drunk, she couldn't remember if she'd even known at the time if the guy was drunk or not, but they were walking down the street at about four in the morning, and he saw someone he knew, and he said to her, "Shh, act normal." She tried.

It was one-thirty and she was doing Ted's dishes and he said to her, "Didn't you just do the dishes?" and the conundrum seized her again, and she wondered if she wasn't supposed to do dishes more than once a day, if it was suspicious, if she would be caught, found out, taken.

(act normal)

She looked at him and he was smiling, amused at her. Oh, this was one of the things he considered her *idiosyncrasies*; she relaxed, let out a breath. She giggled, "Well, you know," she said. He kissed her on her forehead and said he was going out to the garage. He gave her upper arm a little squeeze on his way past her and she felt so much better, and it was, it was, okay. She was happy. Yes.

The bell on the dryer went and that was her second load of laundry that day. She was a successful housewife, getting her work done. She let herself feel it for a moment, imagined the self-sacrificing satisfaction of children running in and out, and her thinking about making something special for supper because they were celebrating a small occasion in a normal life, a goal scored in hockey (a hockey mom), someone getting their ears pierced, an A in Science. She should cut her hair short. So far she just hadn't gotten around to it, besides, Ted liked it long. These days she wore it up in a ponytail, or sometimes she curled it so that the sides framed her face and made her look—slightly, and from an angle—like Audrey Hepburn in *Roman Holiday*. On those days she always had a list, and always got the work done, and usually felt exactly as she should by the time night fell and she and Ted were in bed, lying close but not touching and she was going over the day in her mind, giving herself good and bad marks.

(A in House Science, A in Drama.)

At night, she let herself be.

The funny thing was, she had expected the guilt. She had prepared herself long before the ring was on her finger, but the plan was in her pocket, that she would feel bad from time to time, as though she was feeding Ted a line, betraying him. That long ago she had still had a certain opinion of men, and it had been easier to warn him silently, "caveat emptor, caveat emptor," or to imagine his mother should have brought him up smarter, some mothers do raise fools, etc. He had, after all, been lumped in with the others: as a member of the sex that she had to put up with, work with, be with, but she didn't have to like it. It was like faking an orgasm, something she was adept at. Could she fake it for the rest of her life? That had been the only concern she'd had then. Not getting caught.

She had been prepared for the guilt. The guilt was something she had simply learned to live with, now, and she barely felt it. It was like having bunions and faking orgasms. How long could she do it? Forever.

She had not been prepared for the mind-numbing boredom that seemed to accompany the safety; she had also not been prepared for Ted to become a person to her, to lose his status as man and become lover, friend.

(victim)

At night she listened to him sleep, and if she was feeling okay, if she'd had a good day, maybe she'd changed the sheets that morning and she could smell the faintly present fabric softener—the liquid kind, not dryer sheets—and could feel the cool softness, the clean feeling, then she let herself smile while listening. His breath would go in and after a long time, it would come out. Sometimes he was disturbed in his sleep and his breathing became erratic, or he would mumble and rustle, and she would wonder if he was dreaming of her.

Karen rarely fell asleep before two. She had a lot of thinking to do before she fell asleep, like that poem, "Miles to go before I sleep; miles to go before I sleep." Except the poem made it sound clean and goodhearted, the way a day of hard work felt after the fact. The problem was, her miles to go were fraught with snakes and awfuls and bads and secrets; before she could sleep she had to convince herself that no one had read those things on her during the day, during an unprotected moment, say when she was dusting a window ledge and the motion reminded her of something bad. Did it show on her face?

Like this one time she was in the back seat with her friend's date. They were smoking a joint and it was about ten at night and they were waiting for her friend who had gone into this building to score some beans and she and this guy smoked the dope and she gave him a handjob. The motion was just like dusting a window ledge.

On Tuesdays Karen helped at the old folks' home. Jane Meyers, who had a four-year-old, asked her to help out at the co-op daycare in the neighbourhood. Karen had told her she just didn't feel comfortable around small children just yet. It was one of the many convincing lies she could have told, and had actually thought of:

"Well, you know Jane, Ted and I are still trying, and sometimes it's hard to be around the little ones." Sympathetic pats on the arm.

"It's just that I'm not used to children, Jane, and I don't seem to have the patience just yet. Maybe when I have some of my own." Understanding and slight envy.

"Fact is, there were no children in my life for so long, what with working and all, I just don't know how to deal with them." Obvious envy, followed by self-serving contempt for childless-by-choice women.

What she had ended up saying was that she just wasn't comfortable with small children, but she said it in a self-deprecating way so that Jane would assume something kinder than a lack of patience or affection for children.

(It was very dangerous to mention past careers since past careers might be remembered and asked about, or worse, just remembered by her.)

Tuesdays were good, long and good. Karen did the dishes in the morning, after Ted had left for work. Sometimes she cried if she did the dishes in the morning. Ted liked to make love best in the morning and somehow the cleanliness and simplicity of making love to her husband and doing the dishes made her weep with self-loathing. But it was better once she was in the shower and thinking about one day when she would be old and the past would really be the past and someone would be preparing to forgive her, or she would die and her secrets would die with her.

There was an old woman in the home named Mrs. Taylor. Karen called her Margaret when they were alone, but when they were in the lounge or the lunch room, Karen was supposed to call her Mrs. Taylor because all the nurses did. Mrs. Taylor was ninety. Karen liked her best because she could almost read the death on Margaret's face, see the peace about to be there, the relief in sight, from holding in your breath, keeping all those secrets inside; Margaret would soon die, and let out her breath. Karen sometimes imagined that she was Margaret and peace was in sight. But to Margaret, Karen was just another worker who had some funny stories.

The mind-numbing boredom was never more than an inch under the surface of her skin.

"Ted?"

He was reading the newspaper. He didn't look up, but just tilted his head so that she would know he was paying attention, without really having to; it was cute. It was what Karen imagined husbands doing. At ten o'clock he would turn the news on. On Wednesdays he watched *Star Trek*, and she liked *Roseanne* on Tuesdays.

He said, "Hmmm?"

"I think I'm going to go for a walk." Was that right? Did people really, "get some air," in real life or was that just for TV? How was the grammar. She didn't say *gowin*; she said *going*.

"Sure honey," he answered. As though it were nothing.

(act normal)

Karen and Ted lived in a small semi-suburb, where the people who wanted to live in the suburbs lived, the people who couldn't quite afford the suburbs, but still had decent lives and jobs and some kids that needed a decent school where they didn't teach swearing and safe sex, and where a kid could still get through grade six without smoking.

Once, she stole a pack of cigarettes off a table at a party, and lied when confronted. "Fuck you," she said to the guy. She said they were hers. They had just been opened. She smoked the whole pack.

Karen stood outside the store. It was open twenty-four hours because they weren't exactly in the suburbs. It was the sort of place you'd imagine getting robbed, or a woman being abducted from. If some guy mistook her for some fragile little housewifey he would be in for a big surprise. She didn't have a knife on her but she wasn't afraid to gouge some guy's eyes out. She would love it. As she approached the pool of light thrown out in a wide arc from the store window, and from the outside lights in the parking lot, and the sign, she realized that if she gouged his eyes out she didn't think she would be able to stop there. All the secrets would come out and turn into madness and she would rip his skin off with her bare hands and tear his insides out and punch and punch and punch.

"Marlborough Golds," she said to the man behind the counter. She picked up a package of matches from the counter. She didn't know this man, she rarely came to the store at night. He wouldn't know her. She suddenly realized that if Jane or Louise or Dana came into the store they would see her buying cigarettes and they knew she didn't smoke.

(What else are you lying about?)

"Wait a sec," she said to the man. She went to the sliding door fridge at the back of the store and bought a small container of half-and-half cream for the coffee in the morning.

(If they saw her she could say, "Oh, I've just had this *craving* for cream in my coffee," and they would smile and wonder if she was expecting, or maybe even say it. "Maybe you're *pregnant*!" Then they would laugh.)

The man put the cigarettes and cream into a paper bag. She smiled and said thank you, not forgetting her manners. That pleased her, but it didn't make up for the cigarettes.

Outside the air was cooler and less stifling than in the store. Outside the air belonged to everybody, not just people who belonged in the store, late at night, in the suburbs.

There was no real place she could go to smoke a cigarette. She only wanted to have one, and then she would throw the pack away. She just needed to have one. She wasn't addicted anymore. She just needed to have a cigarette. She hadn't smoked in eight months, and had no intention of blowing everything for one cigarette.

She took the road that ran behind the store, the darker place where a car full of men would be parked, ready to abduct her and they would get a healthy surprise. There was no one there. The road went all the way to the highway, past the houses almost, into the industrial park, where the huge, mountainous buildings would be dark, and quiet and frightening—even at night when empty—with their power.

When she was past the last house before the industrial park, she was past any house that had anyone she knew in it. She stuck the cream and bag into her jacket, stuffing it hard into the pocket, forcing it in a way that quality-conscious housewives, with an eye for longevity and getting their money's worth, would never do to a jacket. She was too far away from the houses to remember that.

She unravelled the cellophane from the cigarette pack, crumpling it up and stuffing it into the other pocket. She did remember that it could be found there, if Ted went looking for something or other in her pockets, after all they were married and they had no secrets from each other

(except some)

and he could surely look in her pockets for the car keys or some change for the parking meter, couldn't he? She tossed the cellophane into the wind. It was so quiet, she could hear it rustling on the concrete of the sidewalk as the wind took it away.

The cigarette was smooth and white in the glow of the street lamps; it was cool in the air. It was perfect.

What she would like to do would be to sit on the ground, leaning against a building, and smoke that cigarette, listening to the sounds of people talking, deals being made, business, while she inhaled and exhaled and thought about getting stoned.

There was this building downtown where you could get a beer and dope any time and there was this asshole that hung out there named Reeses like the pieces and he was always grabbing her tits and anyone else's. One time she and her friend Cindy? Samantha? gave him a joint that had a load in it and watched him smoke it until it popped in his face and he was all stoned and everything and pissed his pants. It was the funniest thing they'd ever seen and he never felt her tits again.

Karen turned the cigarette over and over in her fingers. If she smoked it, he would smell it on her breath, surely taste it at least, when they went to bed. He always kissed her goodnight. Sometimes he even kissed her hand, or her fingers, because he frequently held her hand.

Tears stung her eyes. Ropes tightened around her chest. She brought the cigarette up under her nose and closed her eyes and sniffed, deeply. She lit the end of it with a match, without touching it to her lips. She lifted it, lit end down, to help it burn. She inhaled the air around the cigarette.

(could say the man at the store was having a cigarette)

Smelled like sitting around having a beer. Having a few laughs. Smelled good.

She put it to her lips and inhaled. The smoke, foreign-tasting, not at all what she remembered and yet still good, hurt her throat and her lungs and felt good. She let it out. She closed her eyes, and did it again. Smelled like

(whore)

being drunk, getting fucked, stealing, puking.

Karen smoked and cried.

"Should we make a baby?" Ted whispered in her ear. He always said that before he made love to her, slowly and thoughtfully, as though he needed or wanted permission at each step. She answered him by pressing her body against him, in the same slow thoughtful way.

In the beginning this ritual amused her, and she almost found it contemptuous. Later she began to look forward to the routine of it; the safety in the knowing. Now when she pressed her body against his, she could sometimes blank her mind out in such a way that her body wanted his in an innocent way, the way a wife wants a husband, the way a woman might want a baby.

Her body would never accept a baby. Ted didn't know and she would never tell him, but her womb and ovaries and vagina (up past the place where his penis reached) and her eggs and her uterus and all of it was full of worms and fungus and dark red blood that was poisonous. He could never know that, and she would never tell him.

Sometimes when she had already pressed her body against his in answer to him, when he had his hand on her breast and was stroking it, and when he would kiss her very gently on the mouth she stopped thinking and for one second, until she felt it and stopped, she would feel white and clean and warm and pure and ready for him and his babies. As soon as that happened the snakes came back and they reminded her of secrets. That happened less now, and once or twice, it hadn't happened at all, until the first thrust of his penis into her blackness. Then she remembered.

She would cry for him if she thought it would mean anything; the accidental murder, the socially acceptable, fatal disease. The apologetic sin; the damage done.

(I'm sorry, I am a sorrow.)

She went for a walk sometimes. If Ted was busy in the garage, fixing things, making new things that would break later and he could fix, sitting, sipping his beer. She would poke her head through the doorway and say she was popping out to the store. That was exactly how it happened; she poked her head in, and popped out; she was at her finest when she was lying. It was honesty that made her seem like she was lying. When she really lied, she was infallible.

Karen walked farther now, passed the store, passed the industrial park, passed the highway, up to where the lights got brighter, and there was some traffic. For a long time she just stood on the corner where the highway divided the suburb from the rest of the world and she would stare at the flashing lights.

She had hidden the pack of cigarettes under an industrial garbage can, on top of a rock, and they had stayed mostly dry. She would have one cigarette when she went on her walks. She didn't feel like she was getting addicted again, but at various, random times of the day she would check herself: *Do I want a smoke?* The answer, whether true or not, was always no.

She stood on the corner of suburbie and the rest of the world, and watched the sign flash.

"Eddies," it flashed off and on. There was no apostrophe to show the possessive, Karen at least knew that much, even with her limited education, and so she wondered if it was perhaps some inside joke, as though three or four Eddies owned the bar, and they all had their names on the sign. She eventually convinced herself that was true, and laughed at their little joke herself. Underneath the sign was another that read, "dancers." She just looked, and then moved on, home.

She was always careful now to bring along gum and a Rolaid, which seemed to effectively hide the smell of the cigarette. She washed her hands carefully when she got home, and put off kissing him as long as possible to give the mouthwash/gum/Rolaid a chance to do its work. She stopped at the store and bought some little doodad so that Ted would know where she had been.

"Did you enjoy your walk?"

"Yes, I did," she said. "Would you like some toast?" She was so smooth.

Jane Meyer invited her to a wedding shower. "Bring something," she told her. She hadn't been able to bring herself to ask what exactly she was supposed to bring, or what she was supposed to wear. She didn't feel right asking Ted. Her mother was of course dead and she had never met her father, although she told Ted for convenience's sake that he too, was dead. Who could she ask?

She brought home six magazines. There was *Modern Bride, Today's Bride, Ladies' Home Journal, Country Living, Glamour,* and *Today's Woman.* They all featured a beautiful, delicate-looking woman on the front, and the bride's magazine's featured lovely, clean, pure, brides.

It was Laurie Perkins who was getting married. It was a second marriage, and Karen had no idea if that made any difference or not, but Jane had said—in such a way that it sounded both as though it might, and Karen must know how—"It's a *second* marriage, you understand."

(no)

The magazines told her nothing. The clothes were beautiful, and there was a good article in one of them about how child actors had their lives ruined by fame and money. Karen could just imagine. They knew nothing, but she bet they had their share of secrets. She felt gleeful after reading that article, but forgot to put fabric softener in two loads of laundry and the socks clung to the shirts. It was six of one, half dozen of the other, as Ted would have said.

By the end of that day she hadn't figured out what to wear, but had decided that she would bring flowers. Flowers were associated with weddings in all of the magazines, and they were so beautiful, perhaps no one would see through her.

The shower had gone over without a hitch.

Ted had smiled at her when she left the house. "You're looking so pretty, I don't know if I want you to go anywhere," he told her, looking her over in a way that he rarely did. She was so familiar with that look that she snapped back from the robot-dressing, flower-carrying, supper-dishes-done, there's-a-cold-roast-in–the-fridge-if-you-get-hungry, and felt her eyes narrow and turn hard. Did he see? She stopped in time.

The flowers were in a clear plastic box, provided by the flower shop. Karen had tied a ribbon around the middle of the box, slightly hiding the flowers inside, but allowing them to peek seductively through; that was on the advice of the magazine. It was supposed to be for centerpieces being stored in the refrigerator, but Karen had adapted the idea, and was quite satisfied with it.

She had decided upon a red blouse with a black skirt, not too short, not so long that her legs didn't show. Her legs were smooth and long, and like the flowers, might be something she could hide behind. She wore nail polish, a light pink that clashed with the blouse, but no one wore red anymore.

(act normal)

The flowers were a big hit. Laurie called them chic.

"Oh! So *chic*," she squealed when she saw them, in a brittle, half-hysterical way that made Karen do a double take. She'd heard herself talking that way in the very beginning. She watched Laurie carefully after that, but never heard it again. She did see Jane looking at her skirt, and later saying something to someone in a surreptitious way. The others were wearing fat dresses and pants.

(sorry or fuck you)

She was dressed wrong, and she suspected the flowers weren't chic at all, but were wrong. She wished for a cigarette but never got one that night.

It wasn't long before she crossed the street to look at Eddies. She would carry her cigarette over there and smoke outside the building. She could hear the voices inside, laughing, the music, the clinking glasses.

She imagined herself saying it. "Just stopped in for a drink, hon. I got so thirsty! Want some toast?" She would just have a Coke, smoke a cigarette. While she imagined the Coke some men drove by in a car and shouted out the window at her, and laughed. It was that kind of place.

The first night she crossed, she didn't go in.

"Want to make a baby?" They were sitting at the breakfast table.

Karen's eyes were carefully hooded, as she had to be careful in the morning, when she was tired and more of her real self was awake than her home self. She looked at him tiredly, wondering what he meant, assuming that he was just making a little husband-wife joke, since his sperm was still in her, running out, soaking into her underpants and robe. She would wash clothes again today.

She smiled.

"I mean it," he said, seriously.

He looked deep into her eyes, and she knew that he couldn't see anything unseemly there. She became very aware of the feel of his sperm running out of her. It felt warm on her cool skin. Because it had been in her body? Because truth hurts?

He reached over and took her hand. He lifted her fingers to his mouth and put one in his mouth. "I mean it, sweetheart. Darling. Let's go again, this time, we'll make a baby," his voice got husky and deep with desire.

She stared blankly at him, but let herself be led away.

One time this guy in a bar who looked like a nice guy, way back when she was still to learn that there was no such thing, before she met Ted and found out there were, there was this guy who seemed really decent, and offered to give her a ride home on his motorcycle. She was a little drunk and feeling like she should be nice because he was nice and maybe he would like her if she was nice and then the motorcycle ride would be something they did together. He took her for a ride and stopped in this park and fucked her without taking his pants off, even, just pulled them down. He took all of her clothes off, though. She refused to feel bad about it. She stole his pot.

It was Tuesday and Karen was at the old folk's home. She was reading to Margaret. When they got to something that Karen couldn't read, she just pretended. Margaret was very hard of hearing and Karen suspected she only really liked the attention. Karen loved to read for her.

While Karen read to Margaret, she noticed that the old woman would sometimes zone out, as though her mind had simply ceased to function. Her eyes would go blank, the muscles in her face would go slack. Where did she go? At those times Karen would wonder if Margaret was dying. She looked so peaceful. That was what peace would look like: like not thinking at all.

"Margaret?" Karen would whisper. So far, she always answered. It wouldn't be long though, and Karen looked forward to Margaret's peace.

Karen lay on her back and her husband moved up and down above her. She couldn't let go, her muscles, every muscle in her body, was tensed and panicked.

(what if? what if?)

She went in. She walked in as though it was something she did every single day. As though she wasn't Mrs. Karen Stevens, but was Karen. Or "Kren," she used to be.

Insides of those bars all looked the same. The same people sat at the same tables, their backs against the wall as though they were actually important enough for someone bad to be looking for.

"Gimme a Club," she told the bartender.

It was early, ten-thirty. She could smell the urine coming from the men's washroom, where last night or today someone must have pissed on the way in. They (she) used to laugh when someone did that. Underneath the beer and piss and cigarettes you could smell the more sinister smells, puke, pot, blood.

The music for a dancer came on. Kren kept her back to the stage. The bartender put the beer in front of her. She was only going to have a Coke, but it was as if the place had overwhelmed her, as though the last three years had stripped the first thirty from her and here she was, back at ya.

"Déjà vu," she whispered. The bartender looked disgusted at her.

She wished she had a cigarette, but that would be going too far.

"Got a smoke?" she asked the bartender.

"I ain't a fuckin' store. Go buy a pack," he said. He gestured to the machine in the corner, a dark corner, of the bar. There was a man sitting at the table right next to the machine. He was drunk, or at least, he looked pretty drunk.

Kren knew the people in this bar, especially the men. A lot of them would be married. None of them would be like Ted. These ones were the bored ones, the ones that expected something different out of life but were too stupid to go get it themselves, but too smart to live without it. She was suddenly so lonely for Ted, for home.

"Gimme some change then," she said, and handed the bartender a twenty. While he got her change, in quarters, she took a gulp of her beer, delicately wiping her mouth with her fingers.

The quarters slipped in with a familiar ching, dropping into slots in an organized, determined (deadly) way. Kren looked up at the stage where the woman was taking her clothes off in a bored, off-key way. Only one man watched, and his eyes never left her.

She reached out to push the select button.

(what the fuck??)

The taste of the beer was in her mouth. Not the taste of beer that was there during—say—the back yard barbecue they'd had with the Meyers this summer where Garry Meyers had cooked hot dogs for their two kids and Karen had helped Jane make her "famous warm potato salad" and Ted had put his arm around her waist and given her a tickle every chance he got just to hear her say (he told her after), "*Ted!*" How had that beer tasted? That whole day had had a taste to it, and now, in retrospect, she thought it tasted like that sour topping they used in place of sour cream in cheap restaurants. It tasted exactly real, just like real sour cream when you first put it in your mouth, wrapped up in your baked potato, or your warm potato salad and then when you weren't thinking about it, it turned to wax in your mouth and you couldn't taste anything else.

Wax beer. Bees wax.

(fuck you and the horse you)

Kren pushed Marlborough. Already, she could smell them.

At eleven-thirty Ted wondered about his wife. He supposed that she had run into someone and was just visiting over a cup of tea or something. He smiled when he imagined that. A cup of tea. Tea wasn't exactly her cup of tea, as it were; but she had developed a taste for simpler things since they'd been together. You never know, he thought, smiling.

He checked the clock on his way into the bedroom: midnight.

She was drunk. She couldn't have articulated it in her state, but in the deepest, darkest part of her mind, where the snakes and awfuls and bads were, it was as though something had shifted and the world was once more in balance. She was where she belonged and Ted was where he belonged. Suburbia was smoke-free, it knew when to say when; it knew safe from sex.

She was dancing with the man who couldn't take his eyes off the dancer. He was holding her too close.

(bees wax)

Her mind had slipped to the place where Margaret's went when Karen saw her zone out. She was at peace. The anger she remembered wanting to feel was dissipated; if the imagined car with a stranger in it ready to abduct her were to appear, the anger would by then have turned to fear.

(don't kick me)

(fuck you and the horse)

They didn't really talk, although sometimes the man breathed in her ear, words she couldn't hear or wasn't listening to. Words she'd heard before, the intent clearer than language. There was the same rhythm always.

"Let's get out of here."

That's how it was when the man led her away, to his car opened the back seat instead of the front. She got in, a fluid, remembered motion, coming more easily to her than spinning the dryer dial to forty minutes, than snapping clean sheets over the naked bed.

"You're a sly one, aren't cha? You don't say much. You do your talking with your body, don't cha? Hey?" His hands were the hundreds of hands from forever and always. A part of her slackened, settled in for the duration, her mind shut off. It didn't last.

Karen. Stevens. *She should have brought a cake to the shower. Food.*

There should have been someone to tell her, some way to find out. There never was. Never. There was never any way to know what she was supposed to do.

She realized too late that it wasn't Ted. They weren't making a baby. Her hands curled into fists and she hit him, as hard as she could.

(so sorry)

He shouted and it sounded good.

She beat against him, pulling his hair, trying to smash him with her knee, while he squirmed above her, grunting, and screaming, "Hey!" and pausing long enough to look at her.

His eyes.

Karen plunged her thumbs into his eyes so he would never ever see her and she dug in. He screamed. Blood ran over her hands, down her arms, into the sleeves of her blouse. Secrets flew out in all directions.

Poor David, or,
The Possibility of Coincidence in Situations of Multiple Occurrences

It was David who found her. Later, at the bar, he was all, "smell my *fingers!*" laughing and shoving his hands under people's noses, but he wasn't like that when he found Aunt Bedelia's dead body. Not when Myra got there. When Myra showed up at, David had been crying like a little kid. Myra, of course, handled it all.

David and Myra had been a twosome as far back as anyone remembered. They grew up practically in the same house and someone said one time that they first did it when they were eleven, which could be true because the family that Myra came from was always a little nasty. Whenever they started, they must have kept doing it, because by the time Myra was in the tenth grade, she had a bun in her oven and no one ever wondered whose bun.

That first bun was a dud. Myra dropped it into the toilet after gym, only about eight weeks into the whole thing. She screamed because it hurt and she wasn't entirely sure what was going on. The gym teacher came running, ready to read the riot act and found Myra screaming behind a locked bathroom stall, with twenty girls crowded around the outside.

After the gym teacher coaxed Myra out and got an ambulance to take her away, no one flushed the toilet.

Marsha, Myra's very best friend at the time, said, "What do we do about—" and looked around for support, but no one finished the sentence. You could smell it, a kind of coppery, period smell. They stood around, arms crossed over breasts still covered in identical "Breakout Mustangs!" t-shirts. There was much shifting from leg to leg as they decided.

"Should we, like, say something?" No one knew. What did you say to a blob that would have had high school parents? *Way to luck out.*

Eventually Sandy Degas said she needed a ciggy and left, with two of the other girls in tow. The four girls left behind avoided looking into the toilet for a few more minutes and then they left too. Marsha told Myra after she got out of the hospital that they were very respectful. They might have been, for the time. They didn't say any words over it, but they didn't flush, either.

When it was all over and done, David acted like she got her period unexpectedly. "Oh," he said, when Myra told him it was gone. "Oh. Okay." And then he wondered about whether or not he should tell his buddies, or if he should just forget about it.

"Did you tell them I was pregnant?"

"I dunno," he said. "I guess so." When Myra told her mom this, she told her that boys weren't like girls. Not at all. And if she knew what was good for her, she would never expect them to be.

All of that had been years before David found Myra's Aunt Beddy after she died, her body on the floor having fallen while carrying lunch to eat in front of the TV. Spread around her body were a half-dozen crackers and a large puddle of tomato soup.

It was almost too much to mention that there was a large, hardcover copy of the King James Sacred Name Bible at an angle just about under the couch on the other side of the room, as if it had been stepped on and slid across the floor. Beddy was a Jehovah's Witness and the rumour went around about how God was getting her back into the fold, but the truth of it was that her heart had given out somewhere between the kitchen and the chair and that was all.

By the time David had walked in on Beddy's dead body, he and Myra had been living together in their own little apartment, and were settling into something like the lives they'd lived as children, but by then, of course, they were the adults. By the time David found Beddy's dead body, he and Myra were exactly as they were always going to be.

David had dropped by Aunt Beddy's to pick up Myra's mother's deep dish pie plate because Myra was making some kind of pie for a thing at some place.

He'd been to Beddy's a half-dozen times in the years he'd been with Myra, always in some kind of formal setting, usually the Big Four: Easter,

Thanksgiving, Birthday and Christmas. He almost didn't recognize the house, since Myra's birthday and her mom's were both in the winter, and so was Christmas, so he'd mostly seen the house with snow in the yard.

The day he found Beddy's body, he knocked on the door and waited. The only thing really on his mind was what the hell conversation he could possibly make with Myra's aunt while she was looking for the pie thing. Small talk made him nervous enough to sweat. He told Myra that he could smell his sweat even when he was just knocking. He had decided to talk about their apartment. The super was replacing all the old pipes with new ones and everybody's bathroom was going to be ripped up for a month or so. It seemed a good topic.

—*yeah they're ripping up the bathroom and such. Copper's a better bet. Water's been running out brown for last year. Smells bad when you first get the shower going then it's not too bad but yeah the PVC's gonna make a huge difference—*

Beddy wasn't too bad for an old lady. She lived alone; her husband had been dead for as long as David had been with Myra, and she didn't just go to bingo and bitch about the price of prime rib, she did regular stuff. She went to movies and used to golf and ran with a bowling league. She wasn't as bad as some.

But he was still sweating about talking to her.

When no one came to the door, David just opened it a crack and called in.

"Hello! Aunt Beddy, it's David—I've come to—" By then he was stepping inside the door, still knocking, and then in the next instant he saw the old woman's feet sticking out past the TV and of course he thought the tomato soup was blood.

And then he screamed. He slammed the door by instinct and then, stupidly, called her again.

"Beddy?" he called, already a tremor in his voice. "Beddy! Are you all right?" But he knew she wasn't all right—no one who was all right just lay on the floor with their feet stuck out like the witch in *The Wizard of Oz*. What would be the point? He knew she was all wrong. Just like he knew he had to go in there, to make sure of that. And he had to call someone, the police or the hospital or someone and he wasn't exactly sure which. All of this was running through his head—even as he knew he would call none of those people at all; he would call Myra at work.

He managed to push the door open a crack and peeked in, the sweat pouring down the soft insides of his chest, soaking into the tops of his Y-fronts. He gaped at her stuck-out feet. They didn't move. Not a twitch or a roll. Nothing, and that was when he started figuring she was really, truly dead. And that probably that reddish stuff on the floor was blood.

Blood that smelled like Campbell's Tomato Soup.

It was splashed around by her feet, and it took him a minute to recognize the pieces scattered around it, each piece smeared with the same substance. He noted the regular blue stripe at each of the edges of the bits of white and nodded approval and support to himself with the recognition: *It's a plate.* He must have seen those plates a million time. He and Myra still had her meat platter, with the same blue stripe around the edge. Broken bowl.

Killed by a goddamn broken bowl. For some reason, that relaxed him.

"Aunt Beddy?" he called again.

He pushed the door with his foot and it swung open in a wide arc, exposing the rest of the front room and the stairs that led to the second floor. The smells of the house hit him in the face, the usual, vaguely unpleasant smells of a house that spends too much time with closed windows and the same person. And soup.

He leaned in until he could see as much of Beddy as he was going to see. There she was: Beddy from the bosoms down, on her back, one arm straight at her side. The other arm he couldn't see, so he figured it was up over her head.

Oh god.

David's family did not hunt. They fished, but fish were fish and hardly worthy of a second glance until they were on the plate. He could remember gutting and cleaning one when he was about ten, but he did it with his older brother, and there were so many jokes and experiments with the insides that he could scarcely remember it as a living thing. Outside of roadkill poked at with sticks in the summer, he'd never seen someone he knew, dead. Never once. He'd not lost anyone and had attended no funerals.

But he was sure she was dead, and that he had to either go in there and check, or call someone who would.

It was the door that stopped him. The door was open, but he had remained on the step, the very idea of sticking his foot over the threshold just seemed too much to bear.

So he sat on the step and called Myra. He waited for her there.

Once she arrived, the machines of the business of death took over. A silent ambulance arrived, the lights turning without siren. A police car. Finally Myra's crappy little car. Once they arrived and whatever invisible salt had been laid over the threshold had been spoiled, he went inside the house, following behind the uniformed cop, and Myra's straight back.

He'd looked only once. Beddy's mouth hung slackly open. A great dark maw.

Myra put her arm around him and asked if he was all right. He lied about having gone inside. With Myra there, he felt brave and was all, "She looks like she went okay, not hard," and "I knew you'd want to see her," and "Guess it was just her time, baby."

When the paramedics took her away and Myra was cleaning up the bits of bowl and soup between making phone calls to family, David burst into tears and sat on the sofa for ages like that, bawling.

Even though once the hours had passed and they were out for a drink at Macon's, even though he was all *smell my fingers*, it was still a hard thing.

Beddy was the first one, but it was a bad year.

David's mother and Myra got along pretty well, for the most part. The only time there was tension was during the holidays, like Christmas, when there had to be choices made about who went where for the big dinner. Lorna, his mother, always wanted David to spend Christmas Eve at "their house," even though he hadn't lived at home in four years. She wanted him to sleep in his old bed and get up with her Christmas morning to open the presents. The first couple of years, he went on his own and Myra went back and slept over at her parents' place, for mixed reasons. For one thing, Myra's two sisters, Grace and Peggy, were still living at home then, and it was kind of nice to spend Christmas in that familiar way. But the third year they lived together, she and David had a big fight about it, ending with both of them going over and sleeping at his Mom's Christmas Eve. She put up with it then, she told him, but it had to stop. They were adults, they had their own home.

"It's just an *apartment,* David, not a real home," his mother had said when he'd tried to explain it.

Lorna was well thought of in the neighbourhood, since she'd raised David all on her own, never once having a boyfriend, let alone a second husband. David's father had left when David was five and had never come back. There were rumours that he didn't live very far away and that he had, over the years, made contact with Lorna and she flat-out refused to let him have anything to do with their child. David claimed to never think about his father. Myra, especially around the holidays, got curious about him and wondered what kind of a man had started up with Lorna in the first place. By the time January rolled around, it was business as usual.

Lorna was a nurse, a good occupation for a single mother, since she could work her schedule around taking care of David. Myra's mother had been a clerk in a grocery store the whole time she'd been growing up, working bizarre hours. It had made her close to her sisters and her dad, who in spite of having to take care of them on his own two or three days a week, never lost the ineptitude that dads sometimes have. So Myra had cooked, since she was eight or nine years old. It meant Myra was a pretty decent cook.

Lorna was a tall woman, thin like they usually are, with a nose that got hawkish around her fiftieth birthday. Myra thought maybe she was a lesbian and that was why she never remarried, and that was fine, but she spent far too much of her time doting on and protecting David. He didn't resent it, exactly, and it had turned him into a polite man, which is a bonus no matter who you are, but he didn't put a stop to it, either.

Ah, Ma, was as far as it got when she launched into her fussiness. Myra suspected, in the beginning, that he liked it, but also respected the fact that he never expected it of her.

Never expected it.

And as Myra would have said, if anyone asked her, she and Lorna got along just fine (when it wasn't the holidays), but she did find, after the first year together, that she maybe competed a little bit—just a little bit—with Lorna, if not for David's attention, then certainly for his comfort.

Myra would remind him to wear a scarf in the winter. She always asked him if he wanted seconds. If he had a cold, she went out in the snow and got him vitamins and aspirin. She made the soup he liked. It wasn't that she mothered him, not that exactly, but she did give him the same comforts he had had at home.

Not that he ever asked for them.

The first year in their apartment had been more or less idyllic. Without discussing it, they settled into traditional roles, where Myra came home and made supper, set the table, and cleared and cleaned. David took out the garbage and fixed things that broke, mostly without success and that wasn't an issue anyway, since the building had a super. But he would make a vague effort, leaving a plugged toilet with the plunger still sticking out, for Myra to find, tidy up and call the super. He accidentally nailed a drawer shut in an attempt to repair the loose front without removing it from the slot. But he tried.

Money had been a whole other issue.

Both Myra and David worked. Myra was putting in time, punching a clock at the meatpackers, a horrible, smelly, lower-back-destroying job that nonetheless paid a sweet $18 an hour. David worked at a warehouse across the city, shuffling crates for an amount they never discussed. She'd tried to talk him into applying at the meat plant, but he just wouldn't. He did later, after the thing that happened, but he never did get on.

Myra's dad did all the yelling about money when she was growing up. He paid bills, once a month, at their kitchen table in the middle of the action.

He'd open a bill and hold it up, staring at it intently as though getting unheard messages from it.

If it was the electric bill, they were going to get the electric cut off and no one would ever dry their hair again. Then what would they do?

If it was the gas bill, they were all going to freeze.

If it was Myra's mother's Sears card bill, and she wasn't home, then the girls were going to start sharing clothes and buying secondhand. They were growing him out of house and home.

Then what would they do?

His was the only voice on those nights, which were—in spite of how it would seem to an outsider—no more tense than any other night. It was as though that was his night to voice opinions, every other night belonging to the girls and their mother. He didn't rant and rave like some fathers, he just talked. It was all talk. He was the man, the head of the house, and he paid the bills, and goddamn it if he wasn't going to have a thing or two to say about it his one night of the month. The rest of the time he was his normal, mostly incompetent, self.

When Myra and David set up house together, Myra came home every other Friday and handed over her cheque to David, who deposited it in the bank. When the bills came in they went on the table in the hallway, in a neat pile. The cheque book was in the little drawer in the table. Myra had to nudge him at first, but then, once a month, he paid the bills.

Their phone had been cut off twice, incurring a huge reconnection fee. The electric bill came so often on pink paper that Myra thought they were printed on pink paper.

Eventually she was joking that they were the only people she knew who had a utility bill from Last Notice.

By the time they were together their second year in the little apartment, Myra was sitting at the kitchen table once a month, paying the bills. After that there were no more cheques paid to Last Notice.

And whenever she saw Lorna, she felt a little smug.

I'm taking care of business here, Lorna.

David's boss at Manitoba Shipping was a big guy, Raymond. He had a tattoo of a daisy on his right bicep and just after David started there, he called him "Daisy," like a joke. It wasn't funny.

Raymond got up close to him and in his face. "What'd you say my name was?" he nearly whispered it. David felt his breath on the top of his head. The guy *loomed* over him.

"Hey," he said, his mouth going dry. "Just a joke, right?" He held his hands up—no offence—and shrugged. "I mean, you got a daisy on your arm."

"Not funny." His breath was eggs and cigarettes.

"*Okay.*"

"What's my name?"

David swallowed before answering. "Raymond."

Raymond shook his head, his hair plastered to his scalp with some kind of shiny cream. "No. Not to you. I'm *Mr.* Shotski until further notice. Right?"

"Right."

"Right, *who*?" Another guy—Barry or Garry, David couldn't remember, but he met him on the dock first thing—had come up behind Raymond. He stood there quietly, waiting, pretending not to listen, but listening just the same. He was smirking.

David expelled breath and muttered a small *fuck* under his breath. "Mr. Shotski," David muttered.

Raymond smiled, friendly, nodded. "Alright then. Don't be an asswipe. We're clearing out the back section for some TVs coming in. It's all gotta be cleared by lunch. Barry'll tell you what to do. You'll be *lifting*. You think you can handle some *lifting*, Davey?"

David sighed. Nice first day. First *hour*. "Yeah. I'm an ace at lifting," he said, with a touch of smartass. Raymond smacked him hard on the back.

"Good. Get back there." And he turned around laughing to face (oh) Barry.

Asswipe, David muttered, under his breath, as he walked to the back of the warehouse.

About eight months after Myra started getting on his ass about applying at the meat plant, David was starting to think his work at the warehouse had shown enough promise and fortitude that it was time he got an evaluated raise. Of course he'd had to go through Daisy—as Raymond had remained inside the dark places of David's mind—in order to talk to Mr. Harris, the big boss, but the months had mellowed the big man and the incident of the first day (first *hour*) had never been brought up or repeated. He'd called him Mr. Shotski for about a week when Raymond got disgusted.

"*Raymond*, Dave," he snarled, as though it were an act of rebellion on David's part. He didn't like Dave, or Davey, but preferred the more respectable David, but hadn't said anything to any of them. The guys in the warehouse seemed to take their lead from Daisy, and so David was Dave, or spitefully Davey, when he dropped something or ran the forklift into the wall. *Nice driving, Davey.*

So that morning he went in early, hoping to catch Daisy before he hit the dock.

He hadn't said anything to Myra about it, but she was still on her kick to get him to apply at the meat plant and make a little more money. Money was one of those things that sat between them like a big, grey elephant they never talked about, and what he'd come up with was: he really just didn't want to work with Myra. He would not have been able—even to himself—to articulate the reasons why, but knew instinctively that if he worked with her, even within entire rooms of her, somehow his level of esteem would drop for one of them. It wasn't that he wasn't a good worker, in fact he worked hard when he had to, and didn't bitch or whine about it either, and also in fact, enjoyed his work. He did what he was told and was, after an acclimatization period, able to identify additional, unassigned aspects of the job, and perform those tasks with an equal degree of competence (this was from his three-month evaluation report; the one he did not get a raise from).

That wasn't it. It was something indefinable that had to do with her basic femaleness that he equally did not apply to his upbringing in the hands of a super-mom, but usually when he thought about working with Myra, there was an unbidden but definitive image of her breasts in the mix that made him feel small, horny and unable.

So he hadn't mentioned his plan to ask the big boss for a raise. He sure as shit didn't want to go home, where she would be paying bills at the kitchen table while making supper and doing laundry—all at the same time—and tell her he didn't get it.

Daisy was at the big desk set near the double doors at the back of the warehouse, where everything came in and was recorded. It was sort of Daisy's nest. Scattered around the floor at his feet were dozens of little wrappers. He bought bite-sized Hershey and Dairy Milk bars by the box. Lately he had been into Riesens and their little gold wrappers sometimes caught the big overhead lights and sparkled.

"Hey Raymond," David said, and realized that he was going to first have to make his case to Daisy. The thought made his mouth dry.

Daisy said, "What the hell are doing here so early? Catch a ride with the milkman?" This made him laugh and so David laughed too.

"Heh heh, yeah," he said. "I actually wanted to talk to you." Daisy looked up, and looked him over, probably frisking for the reason, thinking of the things he might call—*asswipe*—him if he was quitting.

"So what is it?"

David's face reddened, "Well," he began. "I've been here eight months now. I got a good eval from Mr. Harris. I'm on full-shift days now, and I'm thinking I might like to talk to him about a raise." His face burned. Daisy kept a beady eye on him through the short speech.

He grunted and looked back down and marked something on a sheet, looking up briefly as though the answer was written on the pile of stereos in their boxes just inside the loading dock.

"So?" he finally said.

"So, do I just go knock on his door, or what?"

Daisy dropped his pen in an authoritative manner and leaned back in his chair. "First of all," he said, holding out a finger and pointing to it with his other hand, "things aren't that great around here. Bob's—Mr. Harris to you, right?—got the tax bastards so far up his ass that he's sneezing toupees. Second of all—" and here he put out another finger and pointed to it. Visual aids. "—you haven't even been here a year. Raises come at the end of the first year."

His face nearly bleeding humiliation, David said, "I didn't get my three-month eval raise."

Daisy raised his eyebrows and grunted again. "Oh yeah?" He licked his lips. "Time's have been rough around here." But he sounded unsure. "No eval raise?"

David shook his head.

"You been here six months?"

"Eight months," David said.

Daisy shrugged, "I dunno," he said. He pointed to the front of the warehouse. "Mr. Harris is in his office. Go now," he said. David nodded, utterly servile in his gratitude and terrified it showed. Right then he felt like he loved Daisy. Even enough to call him Daisy, like in an affectionate way.

"Great, thanks," he said. And started to walk back there. Daisy called him back. Pointed the pen tip at him.

"Look," he said, seriously, all eyebrows and beard. "You be *respectful*, you got it? Things have been rough around here." He jabbed the pen at him.

David bobbed his head like a dog in the back of a station wagon.

"All right. Good luck, *Davey*," he snickered.

David had only been inside the warehouse office twice, once when he was hired, and then again for his three-month evaluation. The office was really no more than a small separate room with a bathroom beside it. He'd been to the bathroom, but had tried to avoid mostly. Since only men worked in the warehouse, cleaning the bathroom was an afterthought at best, and you could smell it. They kept the door closed. David used it on an emergency basis, usually holding it until lunch when they all trooped across the road to the doughnut place.

The office door had a textured glass window, with ancient lettering on it saying simply "office," although most of the gold on the tops of the "f's" was scratched off.

He stood outside the door and got a sudden attack of the sweats. What the hell was he going to say?

Mr. Harris, I'm David Hoffman, from the back? Mind if I talk to you for a minute?

Or *Mr. Harris, I'm David Hoffman and I wanted to talk to you about my three-month evaluation raise. . . .*

The first time he ever applied for a job, his mother had given him a pep talk the night before. She said the key was confidence. *Be confident in your ability to do good work for your employer, and be confident that they will benefit from your presence.*

What would *Lorna* say?

He smiled a little. *Mr. Harris, my son—a very good man and a hard worker—has not yet received his three-month evaluation raise. Don't you think it's high time—* He could hardly walk in and start demanding high times.

Mr. Harris, I'm David Hoffman (shake hands). *I'd like to talk to you about my three-month evaluation, sir. I haven't yet received—*no—*my paycheque hasn't yet shown—*no—*I would like to talk to you, sir, about my performance. I feel I've—*that was it. When he got a positive response, or any response, he would bring up the raise.

He was pretty sure that's what *Myra* would do. The skin under his arms was damp and cool. He was sweating. David looked around him and when he saw no one, he gave himself a surreptitious sniff. It wasn't bad. Anyway, it was probably good to smell a little bad, like he'd already shifted a load to the back.

David took a breath and knocked on the glass window. It shuddered in the frame. There was an answering squeak from inside, like a rolling chair on the floor, and he put his hand on the knob and turned, pushing the door open not much more than a crack. He stuck his head inside. (*Mr. Harris, I'm David Hoffman and I would like to talk to you, sir, about my performance here at—*)

"Mr. Harris? I'm—"

He stared at an empty chair. The squeak sounded again, coming from above and he looked up naturally, to the source of the sound and saw a pair of shoeless feet swinging in a short arc, above the floor. Each swing in either direction produced a *skreek*.

He beheld Mr. Harris hanging; above the back of his head, a thick yellow nylon rope extended to the ceiling. His face was grotesquely swollen, his eyes open and bulging out. His face was purple, lips pursed.

Mr. Harris?

David screamed and slammed the door shut. He screamed a second time, losing it completely. He yelled, "Daisy! *Daisy!* Mr. Harris is—" and then he couldn't finish. Mr. Harris's face stuck in his mind's eye and he leaned over on the spot and barfed. Lucky for him, he'd eaten no breakfast.

When Daisy showed up, he pulled David's hand off the knob, finger by finger.

Myra came and picked him up about an hour after the paramedics had come and gone, taking Mr. Harris with them. Daisy—who had yet to say anything to David about being called the D word—was pale and grim through the whole episode.

"Holy fuck," was what Daisy said about the whole thing.

Myra took over right away, just as she had when Beddy died. She said, "We can pick up the truck later, or tomorrow if you want. We'll just get you home. You feeling any better?"

David's stomach was tight and the inside of his mouth tasted like shoes. He felt shaky, but not bad. If he could get the picture of Harris's head out of his mind, he would be much better. But there it was, every time he looked, Harris's head, Harris's head, Harris's head, and it was kind of like having a sore tooth or a stick in his hand, where he had to keep poking at the thing, getting some kind of morbid pleasure in horrifying himself.

"Did he leave a note?" Myra asked as they drove across town to their apartment. He didn't ask her about the meat plant, if they were pissed off that she left, or if they would dock her pay. "Did Daisy say anything?" Myra thought Raymond's name was Daisy, because that was the only thing David called him when he spoke of work at home. He couldn't remember if she'd even spoken to Daisy. All he remembered was seeing her standing, silhouetted in the doorway, the light from outside wrapping itself around her body and glowing at the edges, like an angel.

"His name's really Raymond," David said.

The warehouse went into a temporary shutdown, but most of the guys saw the writing on the wall. Everybody went back to work the next day, but little was accomplished. They mostly did things half-heartedly, and it wasn't just because the boss was dead, because even Daisy seemed drag-ass and uncertain. They mostly stood around in a clutch talking about the possible reasons the old guy did himself in. That's what they said, *did himself in.* Not once did they say, *committed suicide*, for instance, or *killed himself.* It was mafia movie talk. Harris's widow, Justine, had come around a couple of days after the funeral—which most of the guys attended, since no one got docked for funerals. She said that there were a number of *issues* that had to be *dealt with* and that they were shutting down for a few days so they could get an accountant in to take a look at the company's *viability.*

"With pay, of course. At least for the first week," she said. Her face was red, but not with tears or grief, they all agreed, but embarrassment. No one expected either full pay or their job at the end of the *viability* thing.

"Guess he went broke," Barry said. They stood around Daisy's desk after Mrs. Harris left. Only Daisy sat, looking defeated. David realized Daisy would lose his job, too. His was a cushy job. Ever since Harris had done himself in, Daisy had wandered around in a kind of haze, mouthing the same trash he'd always said, but without conviction.

"Tough break, you finding him like that," Osprey, who worked in Receiving, said. He grinned. "Screamed like a little girl, didn't ya?"

Only David and Daisy had seen the body. The other guys didn't have a snapshot of Harris to carry around inside their heads, tucked into a file folder inside their heads, with their girlfriend's Aunt Beddy in a pool of tomato soup. Harris had been much worse, of course. His face all purple like a face shouldn't be. He knew it ran through Daisy's mind, too, because Daisy glared at Osprey.

"Shut your mouth, asswipe," he said. Osprey did. Daisy was still foreman, at least until the end of the day.

There were handshakes all around at quitting time.

David wanted to find work at another warehouse after they closed down Manitoba Shipping, but Myra thought he should set his sights a little higher. "Apply at the meat plant," she said. "But not in shipping. Shipping is where they put the imbeciles, and you're no imbecile, David. You've got to start thinking bigger."

He'd told her, of course, his reason for going into Mr. Harris's office in the first place that day, and she was thrilled with his gumption. She'd wanted to hear what he was going to say. When he gave her his little speech (without the handshake) she nodded with approval.

"You probably would have got it," she said. There had been a final cheque from Man Shipping but missing forever was the 3% evaluation raise. There were no letters of reference, although there was a contact number they could use for "enquiries." He figured at his next job interview, he would just explain what happened when they asked him, *why did you leave your last position?*

My employer did himself in. Just kidding.

He would never say it like that.

David went drinking with some of the guys he worked with at the warehouse on the Friday night after the big to-do, and got very drunk.

"You know," he slurred to Shamus, who worked mostly at the dock, "Life is very fragile. One minute you're there, and *poof!*" he snapped his fingers and leaned indelicately close. "And the next minute you're lying in front of the TV, in a bowl of soup."

"Hey, did he shit his pants?"

"Huh?" David slurped beer from the bottle. The table was littered with empties, the waitresses busy on Friday nights.

"Harris. He shit his pants? I heard you shit your pants when you die. Especially when you kill yourself."

"I dunno."

"That would be an awful thing to happen. So private, you know?"

David nodded sagely. "Dying should be private." Then indignantly, "People should die on their *own* time."

Lorna had called seven times between Tuesday, when David found Mr. Harris hanging from the beam in his dirty office, and Thursday when he went back to work. Myra had counted. The first time she called Myra told her that David was napping in front of the TV. After a few calls, Lorna finally got through to David and Myra had to listen to only one side of the conversation. It consisted of a series of, "Ya, Ma's" followed once in awhile with an "Aw, *Ma.*" The other two calls had been for Myra, exclusively.

"Is he there?" Lorna asked covertly.

"Yeah," Myra said, "I'll get him."

"No! I want to talk to you."

Myra rolled her eyes, but no one was looking. David had been on the couch—his usual spot—watching *Jeopardy!*. Myra listened to Lorna at the same time she listened to David answering Alex Trebeck. He never answered in the form of a question; he always just said, "Connecticut," or "leatherback turtle." It drove Myra mildly crazy. Between the two of them, she could have *spit* crazy.

"Is he all right, Myra? In your opinion, is he all right?"

"Of course he's all right. *He* didn't die."

"I realize that," she sniffed. "It's just that this sort of thing can have an effect on people. David is delicate."

"No he's not."

There was a long pause, during which Myra rolled her eyes a couple more times. Then Lorna said, "Where is he now? Is he lying down?"

"He's watching *Jeopardy!*."

"Should I come by, do you think?"

"Everything's fine, Lorna. He's going back to work. The problem now will be whether or not he still has a job."

"They can't fire him for this!"

Myra held back a sigh. "Well they wouldn't fire him for *that*. The owner of the company is dead. That might cause some problems. David said they weren't doing very well or something. Maybe that's why he did it."

"Mmmm," Lorna said, thoughtfully. "Myself, I would suspect marital problems. No one kills themselves over business."

"What about the stock market crash in '29? Didn't people jump out of buildings and stuff?" She grinned evilly, but did not add, *You must remember that.*

"Mm," Lorna said again. There was another pause while the two women tried to think of something more to say. "Well, I suppose I should iron my uniform for tomorrow."

"Yes, probably," Myra said.

There was a breath and what sounded like the beginning of a word on the other end. "Did you say something?" Myra said.

"Well," she said, "since you asked, there is something I wanted to bring up, but I don't want you to take it the wrong way, Myra."

"Shoot."

"I don't think right now is a good time to go and get yourself pregnant again," she said in a single rush.

Get myself pregnant?

"What are you talking about?"

"I just think that this is a bad time—with David's job up the air, you never know what the fallout from this sort of thing will be—"

Myra took a quick peek into the living room. David was staring at the TV, looking just fine. "First, I did not get *myself* pregnant. What am I, a plant? And second of all, I don't know why you're bringing this up now. We have no plans to get pregnant."

"Please don't be offended, Myra. That was not my intention—" she said, with the same huff. "It's just that with what happened with your aunt, now this situation, I don't—"

"Lorna, I have to go. Nice talking to you. Everything is fine. We'll see you Sunday." And she hung up. Myra counted to twenty. Then to thirty. Eventually she was able to call into the other room, "Hey, David, you want dinner?"

Life was too short. As David lay on the couch, watching *Jeopardy!* and thinking about how fragile life was, listening to the comforting drone of Myra's voice on the phone in the other room, he made a decision.

What would happen to him if something happened to Myra? What would he do without her?

He would have to marry her, he decided. Before it was too late.

On Friday night, David, red-faced and as earnest as he'd ever been in his life, asked Myra to marry him, asking her as she walked in through the door after her shift at the plant.

"This is so sudden," she said, without a trace of irony.

"Well," he said, "are you going to?"

She laughed a little. "Yeah, of course," she said. "Of course I am. We were always going to, weren't we?"

"I guess so, yeah," he said. They grinned and decided to go out. Before they did, Myra called her mother and her sisters. "Hey," she said, "David and I are getting married." They went out for dinner, and except for that one little thing, everything was the same as it had always been, just a little more solid.

On Sunday they told Lorna when they showed up for supper at five o'clock. Without a word to David, she turned to Myra and said, "I thought we agreed you weren't going to get pregnant."

"*Ma!*"

"I'm not pregnant, Lorna," Myra said.

Lorna looked down at Myra's belly as though there might be a flashing sign. "Then why are you getting married?" she demanded.

"*Ma!*"

"No reason," Myra said, and pushed past Lorna, into the living room where she turned on the TV and made small talk for the rest of the evening, bringing up the pending wedding about forty-six times. Her jaw was tight; David could see the muscles working there when she spoke. Lorna, for her part, seemed quiet.

Myra held back with the guys at the meat plant, not saying anything for a week, about David asking her to marry him. There was an intimacy working the line that you had to experience to understand. On the surface it usually looked just like bantering and kibitzing; whatever jokes were making the rounds usually got heard on the line. Everybody had a nickname, and the nickname never left the plant.

Joe Alexander was "Rocky," because he sparred at a place downtown. He was a most unlikely looking boxer, skinny from head to foot, with a chest that seemed to have been deflated, like a beach ball that had lost some of its air. Plus he was a real gentle guy.

Tami Clammoti was called Tammy Faye after the long-dead Tammy Faye Bakker, some evangelist's wife mostly famous for wearing too much makeup and having a jailbird husband. She didn't wear too much makeup, though, and she wasn't married to a preacher, but she was already named Tami, and that was her misfortune. The line was rife with middle-aged tabloid readers.

Bradley was Badly. That came from an accident with the slicer.

Sue Ellen Morgan was Vegas cause that's all she ever talked about from Christmas until the end of February when she and her husband went off on one of those under-$300, round trip weekends to gamble. She talked about gambling for months and planned strategy, and wondered out loud about ways to beat the club, but as far as Myra knew, never won anything substantial.

Arlen Tibbs was Dube and since he was there before Myra, she didn't know how he got his nickname, and considering, it wasn't something she was going to ask about.

Everybody had a nickname.

Myra was Baby Girl, because when she started, she was the youngest person on the line. She still was.

But, after David found the second dead guy, the guys on the line— Badly particularly—had taken to calling her Crypt Keeper, like the bony dead thing from the comics. She was good-natured about it, and thought it wouldn't last, that they would—even if just out of habit—go back to calling her Baby Girl eventually.

Things on the line, though, moved slowly and every day, every minute, really, was much like the last. After your first few days your hands flew, and your mind wandered, searching constantly for things to amuse it. Something, anything, different was welcomed, embraced. Even Vegas's constant rattling on about gambling was welcomed by the time it came around; she always had a new scheme and everyone put their two cents in, having seen such and such on TV the night before, having read this and that in a magazine at the doctor's office (where they were probably having stitches removed from an accident with the slicer).

As such, in the constant search for novelty, stories about one's life outside the line came naturally. There was an intimacy, a familiarity, about everyone's life that didn't exist in friendships outside the line. The others literally knew everything about you. It came up as naturally as the weather, and was discussed as deeply as the bomb and the end of the world and the possibility that the current president (whoever he might be) was the Antichrist.

When Tammy Faye lost her baby and was off the line for a few weeks, Myra told everyone about her and David and their pregnancy in high school. When Rocky's girlfriend went in to have a mole removed, everyone heard about everyone else's surgeries. They knew who was fixed and who wasn't. They knew about every close call ever experienced in and out of marriage. They knew that Dube's brother was gay. They knew Badly had once been part owner of a thriving computer business and that his partner had absconded with all the assets leaving Badly with all the debts and nowhere to go but down with the ship. They knew his wife left him over it, packing up the kids and moving to Kitchener, and that he only got to see them a couple of times a year at best. They knew that he considered it his own damn fault because he had left all the accounting to his partner, never once even looking at the books, which had not just been cooked, but fried. They knew he was up late into the night sometimes thinking about the what-ifs and making himself crazy and getting an ulcer.

They all knew Trace had gotten herpes from her ex-husband and that she hadn't had sex since 1999 because she left him over it and couldn't face telling someone about it. They were all sorry for her, and after the first couple of weeks of knowing, got over not wanting to touch her, stand near her, or certainly, eat anything she touched. No one ever offered to fix her up, though. They all knew that Tammy Faye and her husband were trying to have a baby and that she took her temperature every day at lunch and sometimes met him in the parking lot. They speculated as to what they were doing out there, but no one ever—not even in a spirit of fun—went out there to see. They talked about it every time, though, grinning when she snuck out.

So of course, when David found Beddy, they knew. Myra told them everything: about the soup, the Bible, the broken bowl, the paramedics, and even about David sobbing his heart out on the steps. They knew that he called her instead of the police. They knew that Beddy had been the one to tell Myra about the facts of life, a fact that she wasn't sure even David knew. They knew that.

They also knew all about Lorna, because work was the only place that Myra allowed herself to vent about the other woman in David's life.

But they also knew that David, only months later, had found his boss hanging from the rafters in the warehouse office and that David had called Myra to come and get him.

Two bodies was two too much.

"Hey, Crypt Keeper," someone yelled at least once a day, "what're you and Death doing this weekend, digging up a couple of old friends for a night on the town?"

"Hey, Crypt Keeper! If you ever come to my place, don't bring Death. I'm too young to die."

"Hey, Crypt Keeper, where'll you two be tonight? I want to make sure I'm somewheres else."

So she kept the wedding plans to herself until Friday. She had to tell them. It wasn't like they were family, it was something different, something more than that. It was like they were a kind of diary, a human record of the steps she—all of them—took in life. It wasn't about judgement or advice, or even sharing. It was a registry system.

Myra had been unusually quiet for most of the week. She'd been asked twice if she was feeling all right. They even let up on the Crypt Keeper thing, suspecting not that they'd offended her, but that she was sick or something, and so left her out of conversations altogether, leaving her to ail or recharge. By Friday she was almost sweating the information out of her pores and had to speak.

She told Tammy Faye, feeling probably closest to her because they were only a year apart in age, and yet Tammy Faye had already planned out most of her life (marriage, kids, house in the country eventually) and was struggling to make it so, with thus far disastrous results.

So just before biting into her boloney sandwich at lunch, she said casually, "David and I are getting married." Then she chewed and flipped the page of the *People* magazine she was reading. It was from an April three years before.

Tami stopped eating her own sandwich and punched Myra a little too hard in the upper shoulder. "Fuck *off*!" she said, a little too loudly. Dube and Henry (new guy, no nickname yet) were sitting at the next table and Dube leaned back on his chair and looked at them.

"Hey, keep it down girls, unless you want me to get out the oil," he chuckled.

"Like from your hair?" Tammy Faye said. The new guy laughed. She turned back to Myra. "Well?"

Myra shrugged, but found herself smiling. "Well, what?"

"Tell me everything! How did he ask you? *When* did he ask you?"

"A couple of days ago."

Tami-Faye lifted an eyebrow and was silent for a moment. She sipped her coffee and stared forward. She nodded a little.

"Okay. Well, have you set a date or anything?"

"We haven't really—"

"So, is this supposed to be a secret?" she asked in a whisper.

Myra shook her head, but didn't deny it, and kept her voice low when she said, "Just, you know, with the Crypt Keeper thing . . ." Tammy Faye nodded and winked.

She nudged her with her elbow. "Just bring it up low key when the whole thing dies down," she said. Then she laughed. "So to speak," she said.

In the days following David's almost impromptu proposal to Myra, a feeling of chaos began to overtake him. He felt like the triangle ship from that old *Space Invaders* game at the bar, spinning around, shooting wildly, just trying to keep it all together.

He was getting married. He wasn't sure what that would entail from him, but he suspected he was supposed to do something.

He was looking for a job again, and wondering why Myra wasn't pushing him to apply at the meatpacking plant. (It was suspiciously apparent: when they were together he told her where he was applying, what they were paying and where he was interviewing, the whole act, after awhile, designed to get her to say *something* about the meat plant. But she didn't. It made him want to apply there. That would make him think she was practising some kind of stupid reverse psychology on him and he would stop, rethink the whole thing, and his brain would swim because he was: getting married, looking for a job, and—)

He was suddenly afraid of everything. Jumpy.

After the dinner with his mother on the Sunday after he and Myra had told her they were getting married, he figured he'd better meet his mother for lunch or something. Her nose was seriously out of joint and that wasn't something easily discussed with Myra present. Since he wasn't working and was out and about most days anyway, he called Lorna and said they should have lunch. She said they should eat at the hospital.

His mother always wanted to eat at the hospital, just like she always wanted to have dinner at her place, and always wanted to feed them on major holidays.

In the morning before their lunch, David applied for a job at a car dealership, not because he wanted to work at the dealership, but because it was near the hospital and seemed both convenient and responsible. And something to bring up over lunch, because his mother would ask. She *would* ask.

He parked in the paid lot and went through the front entrance. The receptionist waved to him. "Hello, David! Here to see your mom?"

David smiled and waved back. "Yup, having lunch."

"Well, you have a good time," she said and he stood in front of the elevator with an older couple who were waiting to go up. The button was lit up, but David gave it a push anyway, just for something to do. The hour bothered him; it was not quite noon. He wondered if the couple thought he didn't have a job (which he didn't). He gave the button a second push, as though in a hurry to get somewhere (as if he had to get back to work). What did they know anyway, he could have a sick grandma up there. Maybe he was on a mission of mercy. Maybe he worked in the hospital. There were all kinds of reasons why he might be wandering around on a weekday before noon. All kinds.

While they waited, a nurse showed up to stand with them, pushing a wheelchair awkwardly, her other hand pushing an intravenous pole, with a bag filled with suspect-looking yellow liquid. It looked like pee. He also thought that it could be apple juice, the two were nearly indistinguishable. He wondered whether or not to push the button again.

Man in a hurry here. (Which he wasn't.)

The guy in the wheelchair was slumped forward, clearly incapable of pushing his own intravenous pole. The elevator doors opened and they all pushed inside. The nurse and the chair came in last, cramping things up enough that David and the chair stood side by side. There was a brief tangle as the man and the nurse pushed the buttons for their floors at the same time. The nurse pushed six, David's floor.

The man was from the Chronic Care ward. His mother's ward. He wondered what was wrong with him. His age was hard to gauge. He could have been anywhere between fifty and seventy. The grizzle on his chin showed patches of grey and he was as wrinkled as any old poop David had ever seen, but he didn't really have that sucked-out look that the truly old seem to have. But if he was in CC, then—

The realization hit David like a hot flash. Sweat suddenly appeared in his armpits, and the hair on the back of his neck stood at attention.

What if he pops off?

A stray heebie-jeebie crawled up his spine, sending his skin to gooseflesh. His mouth dried up, all his saliva busy making sweat stains on his clean white shirt (put on that morning in anticipation of dropping off his resume at the car dealership near the hospital—they always wore suits and ties in that place).

Oh gawd. What if he pops off in the elevator? Right beside me?

The nurse was a pretty young woman, who smiled professionally at him. No clue there. She *seemed* calm enough. He smiled back a little roughly.

The elevator cranked its way up to three and the doors opened. There was some shuffling about as the older couple worked their way around the nurse and the man in the wheelchair. They mumbled smiling *excuse me's*. The woman, slightly rotund, bumped the wheelchair gently on her way past, sucking in as best she could.

Don't bump the chair!

David's face grew red and sweaty. The nurse looked at him sideways, her nursing skills kicking in; he noted a slight concern cross her face. Then there was a muffled grunt from the chair and she looked down at the guy in the chair just as the doors were shutting.

"Is he all right?" David asked, too quickly.

She bent over him. "Mr. Gumble?" she said loudly. There was another small noise.

"Is he all right?" David asked again, too urgently.

She patted the man's shoulder. "He's fine," she said stiffly. "Just a little breakfast coming back. *Isn't that right Mr. Gumble?*"

The elevator laboured past four. Then five. There were no more sounds from the man in the chair and David's situation was increasingly panicked. What if he was dead? What if that breakfast coming back on him was really a death rattle?

I've killed him.

David leaned over slightly and snuck a look. He stared at his chest. It didn't seem to be rising at all. He stared intently, willing either the doors to open or the man's chest to rise in breath.

"Excuse me?" the nurse said, peevishly.

The man's chest rose, barely perceptibly, but it did. David sighed.

"He's all right," he said, grinning.

"Of course he is," she said. She stared ahead. Her cheeks were pink.

The doors opened on six and David pushed his way out first, in a most ungentlemanly way. Although he did say *excuse me*.

By the time he found his mom he was better, but his hands were shaking, his face was flushed and he'd sweated through his shirt.

"Good lord, David," his mother said, pressing her palm to his forehead. "You look terrible. You must be coming down with something." And then she made him sit through his temperature and pulse being taken. He sat on a chair in the hallway, the thermometer sticking out of his closed mouth, hair stuck up in the back from his mother's hands feeling his head, looking like one of the deranged patients from another floor. Psych Ward.

His pulse was elevated. She snuck him some meds from the cupboard and they went to lunch.

After his experience at the hospital, David began avoiding things without really meaning to. He avoided, for instance, going back to the hospital, which began to seem to him to be filled with people who could, at any moment, die.

He also had problems with people who were sleeping.

Days after Myra told Tammy Faye about her pending marriage, Myra started making plans. She was careful to poll him on any and all decisions, but he had been with her long enough to know that she was really just telling him what she was doing, not looking for input per se. This was fine with him. While he didn't actually say it, all he really needed to make the experience a grand and fulfilling one for him, was a date and a time to show up. Maybe a little help picking out a suit.

It was to be a small wedding, just a little something at the church, followed by a lunch at the Olive Garden downtown, and then a few hours down time before a big party at their friend Hugh's place. He had a big basement, partway finished, with a wet bar.

"It's not like we're inviting the whole world," Myra told Grace, her youngest sister on the phone. Grace was protesting having the reception in someone's basement. Her next youngest sister, Ellen, said it was tacky.

"It's not a reception anyway," Myra said. "It's just a party. Like, to celebrate." All that sounded fine to David, because until Myra started talking about the how-to, he was very worried that something important like a hall or a caterer would be dropped in his lap. He was all for cold cuts and cheese squares in someone's basement.

It should have helped.

The whole event, considering how little planning it was taking, was still more than a month in the future. But to Myra this seemed somewhat of an emergency and just a couple of weeks after he'd proposed, she started looking for a dress. She said she wasn't going to get one of those princessy things, but just an ordinary dress that she might be able to wear again someday. "Maybe at my next wedding," she would joke whenever she told someone about what she wanted for a dress.

Ha ha, David would think.

But she did want the dress to be perfect. Same for the shoes, the jewellery, her nails, hair and skin. All of these things had to be sorted out, appointed to a day in appropriate reference to the wedding time, and it seemed only the shopping was flexible. But not that flexible. She and her sisters started shopping for the dress just a couple of weeks after the decision had been made.

"You have more than a month," he said to Myra and her sisters as they got ready right after dinner to "hit some stores."

Her sister Peggy, the one closest to Myra in age, turned to him, hands on her hips and said, "You know, David," she said, "some women get married just so they can buy and wear one of those big dresses."

"So?"

"So," she said, shaking her head and curling her lip slightly, "*that's* how important the dress is." Myra kissed him and said she wouldn't be more than a couple of hours.

She did that every night for a week, the only variation being who she went with—Peggy, her other sister, Grace, or her mother. Sometimes they went back to the same stores they'd already been to, to get the opinion of the other females, who talked on the phone about the dresses they saw on a daily basis. It seemed exhausting to David and he was very worried that the same attention would have to be applied to his suit.

Without working, and still performing the frequently discouraging task of looking for a job, David's life began to feel very confined and dull. By the time Friday had rolled around, he was about ready to whine if necessary to get Myra to stay home. He came home early from job-hunting and started supper. He made spaghetti. He'd bought a bottle of cheap wine to go with it, hoping that it might inspire in Myra a bit of romance. Between working all day and shopping all night, she hadn't been feeling exactly romantic, and it was heading into a week. David had much more time on his hands and so spent a good part of the day thinking about sex, only to be ignored at bedtime.

When she got home from work that night, she smelled the spaghetti.

"This is great," she said, coming into their little kitchen, where the counters were wiped clean, most of the prep dishes already washed (foreplay starts in the morning), and the sauce was bubbling on the stove.

SUSIE MOLONEY

"Maybe I should keep you at home. Make you my bitch," she said. He took this as encouragement and grabbed her around the waist, kissing her thoroughly on the lips. She kissed back, and that was all he needed to know. His planned, off-handed comment (prepared in the event of another shopping trip) to be expressed casually and hopefully jokingly over dinner, of, "You'd think if we were going to be married, I'd actually get to see you sometime. . . ." would go unsaid. So far she had said nothing about shopping and the phone had not rung.

David poured her a glass of wine—*Oh, wine, too! Can I pick 'em or what?*—and she took it into the bedroom with her. The bathroom was off the bedroom and in a moment he heard the sound of the shower, which caused him to start humming as he put water in the pot to boil the noodles. He hummed some Barry White and then another song that was just stuck in his brain until he realized it was a Justin Bieber song, and he deliberately went back to Barry White. He heard the shower turn off just as the water was ready for the spaghetti. He heard the bathroom door open and suddenly wondered if he should really be starting the spaghetti or just turn everything down. (Or if he should just put the spaghetti in and—but that was a bad idea.)

So he turned the sauce down to minimum and shut the water off completely. He stuck the spaghetti back in the box with limited success. He breathed into his hand, and it seemed all right to him. He took a sip of wine from his glass and put it back on the counter before quietly making his way to the bedroom. The door was slightly ajar, the wonders inside just out of his sight, just tantalizingly close enough. He pushed it open, slowly, drawing out the anticipation.

"Oh baby—" he started and then he saw her.

She was laid out flat, sideways across the bed, where she'd fallen. The towel wrapped around her wet hair had come loose and partly covered her face. Her arms were stretched out sideways from her body, limp.

Dead.

"OH GOD!" he screamed, and dropped to his knees. "Not MYRA! *MYRA!*"

And she jolted up, eyes wild, "What! *What!?*"

David's head went light, the room swam. He fainted, crashing to the floor.

He came to with Myra waving a peeled clove of garlic under his nose. He opened his eyes and she was staring down at him, the towel gone from her head, her hair hanging in wet tendrils down her face.

She bent close to him. "You fainted," she said. "You're not pregnant are you?"

He closed his eyes again and exhaled with relief. Of course she wasn't dead. "I thought you were dead."

Myra lay down beside him, propped on one elbow. "That's kind of nuts, David."

He hadn't told her about what had happened at the hospital. He rolled over on his side, and propped himself up. Myra's robe had slipped open. He could just about see one of her breasts.

"Never mind," he said and, tugged at the robe, giving both breasts a bit of air and Myra let him. He was grateful to have something else to do, and they both worked at taking his mind off things, nicely and slowly. Near the end, he caught Myra staring up into space, as though she had something else on her mind. But it all ended well.

David found a job two weeks before the wedding. He almost had his pick of two jobs. He had applied at another warehouse, this one much closer to home, close enough that he might have been able to walk to work most of the time. He'd also applied at the on-line catalogue branch of a major department store, working in the basement, filling orders for delivery, not very far removed from a warehouse job, but because it involved retail goods, it paid slightly worse. He would have to drive. He ended up taking the catalogue job, because at his final interview for the warehouse, he told them up front that he would require three extra days off the week of his wedding. He and his bride were going on a short trip, he'd said, although that wasn't entirely true. Myra and David had decided that in lieu of a honeymoon (and having lived together for four years already it was almost unseemly to spend their wedding money on a trip somewhere), they would each take a few days off work and do things in the city that they never got to do. They would go to the museum and the racetrack and splurge on a single night in a local hotel with room service. Myra got the time off without question.

(The day she handed out the invitations they'd made on the computer—a comic couple wrapped with ropes, the caption reading, "We're tying the last knot!"—she had lots of input: *I dunno if I can come: I'm too young to die*; and *Is it BYOC? Bring Your Own Coffin?* Someone asked if they could give the eulogy. Hysterical.)

So David had to take the catalogue place. Primarily staffed by women, including the one who interviewed him, they seemed much more sympathetic to the idea of a honeymoon trip.

A few days into the countdown to the wedding, his mother showed up at his new job at lunch time. "David," she said, "we have to talk."

He took her to the diner around the corner from his building where he ordered a BLT and fries and she had coffee and toast.

"If you're still set on getting married," she said, "then it's time to get serious about your life." He stopped in mid-chew. What did she mean? Now?

"Yeah," he said, his mouth full of toast and tomatoes.

She reached across the table and took his hand. She said, "You can't work in a warehouse for the rest of your life. You're young enough now that you can still go back to school."

The word *school* conjured up such a conflicting set of emotions that for a moment, David couldn't swallow. On one hand, school was safety, home after school, chocolate cake and cold milk from the fridge; *Friends* in reruns on TV until five. On the other hand, school was endless amounts of paper and reading, strange calligraphy in meaningless order.

"What are you talking about, Ma?" he finally said.

"If you agreed to go back to school, get some kind of trade, I will pay for it." She leaned back against the cracked red vinyl of the booth, folding her arms across her chest. *My work is done.*

"School?" It sounded drastic to him.

His mother leaned forward, "What are you making at the warehouse?"

"It's on-line shipping," he said.

"It's a warehouse. How much are you making?"

Reluctantly, he told her. She grimaced.

"Do you know what a machinist makes?"

He shook his head and she paused. "Well, neither do I. But it's not an hourly wage, I'd bet. I bet it's an annual salary. An annual salary allows you to plan for expenses and to save a little money.

"How do you expect to open doors for yourself, if you refuse to turn the knob?"

Of course, with that turn of phrase, she lost him. The ends of his fingers tingled with the sensation of turning doorknobs, followed by the hollow-throat feeling of a rising scream.

"What?"

It took all of the lunch hour, but David finally agreed. He would look into going back to school. He had no idea what Myra would say. His mother's expression was victorious. As if it was a final reward for his pliancy, she told him she's made an appointment for him to be fitted for a tuxedo.

"One of my wedding gifts," she winked, implying that the other was the schooling. She had him. Myra might not like the schooling idea, not right away, but she'd lately been in a tizzy over what to dress him in for the wedding.

He went the next day to be fitted, right after work. Mr. Rabbinowitz was the name of the tailor and he was a tiny little guy, with quick movements. You had to keep your wits about you, David found, because if you didn't, you were apt to get stuck with a pin, or find him with his hand up your crotch, measuring something.

It turned out he was pretty close to a standard size. He wasn't sure if that was a compliment or not, but it did mean that his tux would be ready in just a couple of days.

"Pick it up Tuesday," the little man said, very quickly; in fact, "Tuesday" was the only word David actually heard. But the beaming smile from the man indicated that not just anyone could pick up their tux on "Tuesday"; he was bestowing a gift of some sort and David felt compelled to be appropriately gracious. He thanked him profusely and asked him if there was a picture, like in a catalogue or something (he was used to catalogues now), that he could take home to show his girlfriend.

As the man was digging something out from under a long cutting table cluttered with bolts and pieces of fabric he said, "Not girlfriend for so much longer, eh? Wife, next."

"Yeah, that's right," he said, and took the proffered illustration of his tux from the man.

Wife.

Driving home he felt a kind of urgency, for the first time.

He had opened the conversation about school with the tux. He gave Myra the picture and told her that his mother had offered to pay for it. He'd expected—with all her fuss about dressing up—that she would be pleased, and maybe better.

"A tux?" she shrugged. "Buying or renting?"

"Buying," he said.

She shrugged again. "Really? When will you ever wear it again? Her money, I guess." But he could see her calculating in her head what else could be done with that kind of money.

David shrugged too, as though he didn't care. He wondered about bringing up the prospect of school, and thought maybe he would be better off to just feel it out first. He said, "You know, I'm starting to really get into this marriage thing," he said. The plan for the next bit was going to be something about *responsibility to a family*, and maybe the phrase, *getting somewhere in the world*.

But Myra interrupted him: "Why doesn't she pay for the food? Now that would help."

"I dunno," David said. "You know, I've been thinking about the future—"

"Or flowers. Or why doesn't she split that cash and help me pay for my dress? What's a bloody tux *cost*, anyway? It's gotta be nearly a *grand*." She threw her hands up into the air and then covered her face and started to cry.

David floated, paralysed, unsure as to what had happened, but fairly certain he shouldn't bring up school. At least not right away. Maybe after the wedding. Myra was sobbing on the couch. Nerves. With his mother, it was often nerves. He put his arms around her and told her that everything was going to be all right.

It felt good to be on top for a change.

On Tuesday he left work a half hour early to go and get his tux. The women at the catalogue centre were fluttery with excitement for him. *A wedding*, they kept saying, without adding anything else, as though it were a thought all on its own. There were lots of sighs and dreamy looks.

He was glad he was taking off early.

The little bell over the door tinkled when he walked in. He thought he recognized his tux hanging on the rack, covered in plastic. But then, they all looked alike.

The door to the back was closed, voices coming through, muted and insistently cheerful. He wondered if someone was getting fitted and contemplated waiting.

Instead, he knocked on the door.

"Mr. Rabbinowitz? It's David Hoffman," and he pushed open the door. The minute it met with resistance, he knew exactly why; without even looking down, he knew what he would see.

He looked down anyway, and his eyes met what was becoming a familiar sight.

What he saw was the top of Mr. Rabbinowitz's head, his bald spot a grey circle in a patch of dark hair. From inside the room a voice said, *"For lovers only, here's Frank Sinatra's beautiful 'From the Bottom of my Heart.'* . . . *Sing it Frank—"*

"Oh fuck," he said. "OH FUCK!"

It had been a brain aneurysm. "These things aren't always picked up, David," Myra told him. *It's not your fault*, she meant. And of course it wasn't, but who was to say?

David had gone into a kind of shock after finding Mr. Rabbinowitz. Much more so than when he found Mr. Harris or Aunt Beddy. He had closed the door and went to the phone on the counter and dialled 911.

"Mr. Rabbinowitz is dead," he told the operator. "I found him." He gave the address and then, in a repeat of Beddy's terrible last day, he waited on the steps for the ambulance to come. He called Myra and she came and got him, driving him home in her car, even remembering to take his tux with them, her face white and grim. She didn't say much.

He didn't pay for the tux, he told her later. "I just saw it there and pulled it off the rack. Then—you know."

"It's all right," she said, grim and all. "It's all right, David."

David spent his time on the couch. He didn't go back to work. Someone had called them and he tried to explain why, but in the end it was just too complicated. *Well, see, I guess I'm the spectre of death. . . .*

Myra had remained white and grim for a few hours, sometimes suggesting to him that it wasn't his fault, that it was just bad luck, and he should just sleep it away. But then she would switch over to telling him to just snap out of it. Like Cher in *Moonstruck*, when she slaps Nick Cage. Myra didn't slap him, although she looked a couple of times like she might.

He wondered if he and Myra would still get married. Whenever he thought of getting married, he remembered shoes. Myra came home from work on the Friday and saw him using a black felt-tip marker on his running shoes.

"What the hell are you doing?" she asked, impatiently.

"I don't have any shoes for the tux."

"Your mother bought you a pair. She brought them yesterday. *You tried them on.*"

"Did I? Oh," he said. He capped the marker and put it on the coffee table.

Myra crossed her arms over her chest in a remarkable imitation of his mother. "You better snap out of this, David. We're getting married tomorrow. We're going to dinner with everyone in four hours. Get drunk or something, but *get over this.*"

She picked the remote off the table and shut off the TV, leaning in close. "It's okay, David. You didn't *kill* them. They *died*. You *found* them. It happens all the time." She sat down beside him. He could tell by her face that she wasn't sure that was true.

All David heard was *kill, died, found.* He saw them each in his head, like old, dead friends.

"You know you're spending the night at your mother's, right? You remember that?"

He looked at her. Why was he spending the night at Mom's? He nodded.

"Do you want me to pack your shit? You won't need much." She pinched a bit of fabric from his sleeve between her fingers with mild alarm, but sympathetically. "I guess you can wear what you have on to dinner, and then tomorrow, all you'll need is the tux and stuff. Okay?" He nodded again. She snapped her fingers in front of his face.

"Snap out of it, David. You're freaking me out."

He cleared his throat and sat up straighter. "Okay. I'm cool." He looked around the room as if seeing it for the first time in a long time. There were plates on the table from the night before. He should have cleaned those up. He got off the sofa and wandered over there. He stacked the plates up together and put them on the counter.

"I'm going to have a shower," he said.

Myra perked up. "That's a great idea. I'll put some clean clothes out for you. This will be fun! It's our last night together as singles!" She came over to him and grabbed him around the waist. She wrinkled her nose, "Maybe we should go to the pub and pick up other people. Our last chance—"

He tried a laugh and it came out sounding fairly real. "No, I don't think so," he said mechanically. He couldn't think of anything else to say. He felt like big bad luck.

"Get in the shower. I'll lay out your clothes."

"Lay?" he said, getting that one.

"No sex until after the wedding," she grinned. "I know it will be hard to keep your hands off such a lovely bride as me, but just try."

He laughed. He thought he did, anyway.

When David got out of the shower, the room was filled with steam. He swiped his hand across the mirror. It fogged back up quickly. He finished drying himself and tucked the towel into itself around his waist. He felt better. Period. He took a deep breath, but got the sickly, warm, foggy air, tasting vaguely of soap. David ran a comb through his hair and turned to leave.

The door was shut.

He put his hand out, brushed the knob. His heart started to pump hard, he felt like he couldn't get a breath. Droplets of water trickled down the side of his face and gathered uncomfortably around his hairline, making him feel dirty, sweaty and greasy. He tried to take a deep breath. It caught in his throat.

"Myra?"

Beddy? Mr. Harris? Mr. Rabbinowitz?

David put his fingers on the knob, pressed his flesh into the smooth, warm surface of the glass, but couldn't turn. His chest was tight. He thought he was having a heart attack.

There's nothing on the other side.

He started to turn the knob, and then let go of it as if it were burning. He swallowed. Squeezed his eyes shut.

Just turn the bloody knob. There's no one there dead—killed died kill found—on the floor, bed, dangling from the ceiling. Myra is putting clothes out. She's probably waiting to put her make-up on. Just turn the knob.

Grasp and turn.

David swiped his fingers on the towel, his hand damp with either the mist in the room or fear. He put his fingers on the knob again. Swallowed.

He was trapped. Never getting out.

The knob turned within his fingers and Myra's face appeared in the crack. "Are you done? I gotta get in here," she said. Then she saw his face. "What?"

He shook his head. "Nothing." He kissed her forehead. David brushed past her through the open door, hardly noticing that his eyes did a quick once over of the room before stepping completely into it.

"Let's go," he said. "I'm starving." And as soon as she turned her back, he dropped onto the bed and sucked at the air, unable, it seemed, to fill his lungs, not hungry at all.

There were doors everywhere.

His buddy Shamus opened the one at the restaurant. David drank minimally at dinner and did not visit the bathroom after his first attempt, which left him standing, sweating, outside the men's room, unable to even push it open. He spent the night in a semi-cold sweat that if noticed, he hoped would be passed off as wedding jitters. If Myra noticed, she didn't let on, although twice he caught her looking at him, but thought it might just have been a kind of dreamy-eyed disbelief, the conclusion to their single days. She had a few glasses of wine, too.

When they left the restaurant to go back to Myra's sister's for a nightcap, David made sure to pull up the rear. Myra opened the door when they left. There were no problems at the house, someone else did all the opening, it wasn't his house. No one stayed long, thankfully, but David held his water until they left. It seemed an interminable time was spent at the door saying good night and making wedding jokes, and finally Myra's friend Gloria gave Myra and David some space and David knew Myra wanted him to say something romantic, it was right there on the surface of his brain, but unfortunately he seemed to be operating at a much more buried level in there—the best he could do was to mutter *I love you* a few times, hopefully with the right degree of warmth and sincerity. While he muttered, he thought to himself, *I will make this up to you, I have a lifetime to make this up to you—*

When they got to Lorna's—finally—David beelined for the can and left the door opened while he peed.

"David!" his mother shouted. "Close the door!"

Ha ha ha ha ha ha ha—

David slept poorly in his old room, after drinking most of a bottle of rum, going over the evening in his mind, over and over again.

Hey David, check it out: you find dead people, followed by hysterical laughter for most of the night. Even Myra laughed.

He woke up with a headache and a dry mouth, but felt surprisingly refreshed. It was his wedding day. The mother of all days. He popped a couple of aspirins and drank a full pot of coffee before they even started getting ready.

Myra called just after ten to make sure he was up. "You should be there a little early," she reminded him. "At least by 12:30, right?"

His mother plagued him with a constant stream of questions. Did he have everything? How were the shoes? Did he like them? When were his friends coming to get him?

A buddy from the old warehouse called to see if he wanted a car, a fake moustache and enough money to get him out of town. Ha ha.

It was all coming together. It would be okay.

Hey David, check it out: you find dead people. Hilarious.

The atmosphere at the apartment was festive and swirling. Both Myra's sisters and her mother were there, along with Gloria, who'd spent the night. They'd all drunk a bit more when they got back, but not very much, although they'd still both woken bleary-eyed and achy. It might well have been the hour. Myra had found herself awake just after seven—having not gone to sleep until after two—but couldn't fall back to sleep. She was too excited.

Her dress was hanging under plastic in the hall closet where the winter coats were, guaranteeing that it would not be touched before that morning. She'd settled on a delicate off-pink number, cocktail length, with a fitted bodice and an a-line skirt. Worn with the crinoline Janis had talked her into, it was a real princessy thing once she got it all together, but without the crinoline, could be worn just as a dress. The colour set off her skin nicely, making her look like she had a bit of a tan. For jewellery she would wear pearl earrings and leave her neck bare. Her shoes were plain pumps, dyed to match the dress—just slightly off-colour, but not noticeable. Beige stockings. Unused to such fussy dressing, she was surprised to find herself excited about wearing everything put together, which she had only done once, the day she finally picked the dress (she'd had seven on hold at various shops in the city).

The sun was shining by the time she grew bold enough to start the coffee and it looked like the weather was going to be perfect. Gloria came stumbling off the couch once she smelled breakfast and they picked up where they left off.

"You really think he's losing it?"

Myra shrugged. Then she said firmly, "He'll get over it. It'll be fine."

Mostly she worried that her buds from the meat plant, unaware of David's latest brush with death, would hear about it at the wedding and start bugging him. She had decided sometime after 7:30 that she would corner Tammy Faye and Vegas in the church and tell them everything, and tell them to get everyone else to keep their mouths shut.

A pre-emptive strike. It was good enough for some.

David sat around drinking coffee and eating toast and peanut butter until he'd gone through nearly the whole loaf.

He and Lorna played a hand of Hearts, and even had a last drink from the cupboard over the stove—so rarely opened that David's mind was actually taken off the events of the day and the previous few days while he peered curiously inside.

At eleven-thirty, when Hugh called, he started getting dressed. In his old bedroom he put Aerosmith on the stereo and cranked it. When "Amazing" came on, he stopped what he was doing and sang it out, at the top of his lungs.

It was all good. David was getting married and that had nothing to do with anything.

Pumped and cheerful, buzzed by the drink and uncomfortable in his stiff, new clothes, he and his friends and Lorna too, got to the church about quarter to one. The wedding was at one o'clock. Cars were parked up and down the street and it took them a couple of minutes to find a place, but they did, on a block behind the church. They walked, feeling odd and obvious in their suits and ties (especially David who had tied his own bow tie, crooked and lopsided had been the best he could do, but figured he looked pretty natty).

The reality of the whole thing was just beginning to sink in when they got to the side door of the church.

David stopped, one foot on the first step, the other on the ground.

Hughie said, "What's up, man? Cold feet?" he giggled. Then he burped. "Oops, breakfast coming back."

"Wow," David said. "Getting married, the whole deal. I feel like I've hardly thought about it."

Hughie smacked him in the shoulder. "Well, I guess I should say something deep and wise. I will say only, 'You'll find a way to fuck it up, *Grasshopper*.' Now let's go."

He nodded. Hughie held the door and the two of them went inside.

There was a buzz coming from the church. It sounded like hundreds of people, when David knew it could only be a couple of dozen. His throat was closing again. His mouth was dry. And his two beers were coming back on him, through his bladder.

He and Hughie peeked through the door separating the rectory from the pews. The carpet seemed redder, the pews shinier, than they had seemed when the four of them had been in for the brief rehearsal and to talk to the minister on Wednesday.

"Where are the girls?" David said.

Hughie stuck his hand through the crack in the door and pointed to the other side of the church. "I think they're over there. We're supposed to be out there." Someone in the audience saw his arm and waved. He waved back.

David swallowed. He could smell perfume and it was overwhelming. He wondered if it was the flowers or someone sitting out there. Through the crack left between Hughie's head and shoulders, he saw his mother, sitting in the front row with her hands folded in her lap. She was wearing a hat. He didn't remember the hat. He didn't think he'd ever seen her in a hat.

"Oh man," he said.

Hughie looked at him and they started laughing. "I gotta take a piss," David said. "Where's the can do you think?"

The two of them wandered toward the back. There were three doors more or less the same. The last door had glue smears where a sign once must have been. "There, I bet," Hughie said. He opened the door and jumped, shouting, "Aha!" The room was empty, except for a gleaming urinal and a single stall. "There you go. I'll head out there. Meet ya." They locked eyes.

"Good luck, buddy. And when she kicks you out, and you come to my place? Bring beer."

David laughed. It was happening. *His life.*

David checked his watch while he peed, holding himself awkwardly as far away from the urinal and stream as he possibly could, and stay upright. It was five minutes to.

He zipped up and washed his hands. Checked his tie. He pulled one side a little further until it looked more balanced. Fixed his hair.

Ready as I'll ever be—

He stopped.

The door was closed. His breathing came in shallow, weak gasps and he felt the first trickles of moisture down the insides of his arms, ruining his shirt.

From somewhere in the church he heard the music start.

When it stopped, because he knew it would, knew they couldn't bring out the bride without the groom standing up at the front, waiting for her. It was in all the movies. He stands there and watches while she walks up the aisle.

And he wasn't there.

He panicked.

"Myra!" he called, pressing his face close to the heavy wooden door. "Myra!" She was somewhere in the church. She would hear him. He called again, and then waited. His hand itched to go to the knob, itched to turn it, itched to yank the whole thing open, let the bodies fall where they might—

The idea that he might forever be trapped in a tiny room, while weddings and baptisms went on and on forever occurred to him. It occurred to him that there were doors everywhere, all over the world, and usually there were people behind them, and that people expired, got tired and keeled over, that this was going to be something that would ride with him forever and ever and as each of these thoughts ran through his mind, he panicked, he screamed, he shouted—

And Myra came. He heard her voice through the door.

"David? Are you stuck?"

There was such relief in hearing that voice, it was a sound of such home and comfort and pleasure, that without thinking he grabbed and turned the knob. There was only one second when—

Beddy?

—he hesitated, but it passed and the thick perfume of the place and Myra gave him the woozies, but just for the one second. And then he saw her head tilted, a little bit impatient, it showed on her face, but content at the same time. She was beautiful. He pushed the door open.

"You rescued me," he said.

She rolled her eyes. "Save the crazy shit for after the wedding, okay?"

"Absolutely." And he did. And they got married. And he didn't find anyone else dead behind a door for the longest time after that.

Nearly a year. It would be his personal best.

THE LAST LIVING SUMMER

It was Donna who brought up the odd change in the air. I had noticed too, but I hadn't said anything about it. There was something in it, an aftertaste that shouldn't be there after a gulp of it. Metallic, like aluminum would taste if you put it on your tongue. She thought it seemed thinner, too. It might have.

It smelled like fish.

She stopped in when she was done her walk for the day. She beachcombed. Such an old-fashioned name for it, sounding very blue and green and smelling like salt, peaceful and quaint; it was more like a reconnaissance mission or the act of a militant, scouting for signs of the enemy.

I was on the porch and saw her coming long before she called *hello*. My house faced the water, just as hers did, six hundred feet to the east.

Donna got all the way to the post at the end of my "yard," the one with the fake seagull gruesomely nailed through the feet to the wood, before she looked up and saw me through the screen.

"Air tastes funny," she said. She stopped at the foot of the steps and took a big breath. "Like metal."

I nodded. I was sitting with my notebook, playing, not doing much of anything, waiting for a time when I could pour myself a drink. There was still propriety. So I got up and pushed the door open as if I was going to give it a sniff.

"Just come on up."

She looked around up at the sky and down the beach where she'd come from and then did come up. She was tanned, her teeth unnaturally white against her skin. Outside the door the air was still. The only sound was the slapping of the waves against the shore, against each other. No birds. Not for weeks now.

The wood seagull was the only one I'd seen since June.

"Tastes like metal," Donna said. She put her hands on her hips and looked outside. The sky was grey, like the water, and cloudless. It looked like October, and here it was the end of August.

"Want a drink?" I said. "It's five o'clock somewhere." You couldn't tell by the light, but it was just a little after two. She hesitated, shrugged and then grinned *ha*. I took out glasses and poured us one each, from the bottle on the table. I'd brought it out earlier, thinking she might be by.

A glass full of wine is always half full.

"It's almost the last of the white. There's still at least four red. And some pretty brown whiskey for emergencies."

"The air tastes funny," she said. "That could be an emergency."

I nodded seriously. "Could well. Let's drink to that." We did.

"I was down by Augar's Hill this morning," Donna said. "As far as the marina. Only thing I saw was that Marmaduke dog used to belong to Paul Burl, remember? I tried to get him to follow me, but he's skittish."

"Coolidge."

"That's right. Coolidge. If I see him tomorrow I'll call him. See if that works."

I nodded again. It would be nice to see a dog, I guessed, but even thinking that, I could still feel coldness in me. To what end, seeing a dog?

I would almost rather see Ann.

She tended to disappear for short periods and then reappear when whatever collapsing hell she was going through had righted itself, or at least stabilized. She was no longer the person I used to secretly make fun of the way she kept an organizer in the front seat of her car, or how she never just said *oh look at the stars* but rather was compelled to name them, *oh doesn't Orion look fierce tonight?*

Not seeing her was somehow both better and worse. The last time we ran into her had definitely been worse.

Donna and I had been chatting in front of my house *blah blah blah*ing over whether or not it was prudent to read *An Infinite Jest* while in our state of mind. I said it hadn't done very much for Wallace, but the joke fell flat, as those thoughts were starting to. We were thankfully distracted by screaming from the east side of the beach. Our heads swung in that direction, as if on identical pivots.

"Hey! *Hey!*" she screamed. It was Ann. She was a doctor, lived a couple of houses up the beach. We'd seen more of her a couple of weeks earlier and then not at all for a while. She'd played emissary to the folks on the other side of her place, when there'd still been folks on the other side. She used to bring us chocolate, and stay and have a drink. Lately she'd been getting squirrelly. A person could hardly blame her. But that shit was catching, and it was hurting my opinion of her.

She'd started dropping by at odd times and complaining about whatever was handy. We were all of certain age, the three of us. Complaining was a slippery slope. You had to stay off the edge. Particularly now.

"Mr. Kruger's gone," she shrieked. Donna pushed open the door and went down a step, no more. She stood there, holding the door open. Ann ran as best she could, panting and stumbling the last twenty feet. I tried not to judge but I felt a sneer on my lips and was glad I was inside the porch where she couldn't see. Mr. Kruger? What had he ever done for us.

She panted and gasped, stopping on the sand near my seagull. "I saw him get in his car. I waved and flagged him down, but he wouldn't stop. He's gone and left us," she held her chest and heaved. I didn't react. Ann was about two syllables from hysterics, doctor or no doctor and I couldn't take it on.

She wore a skirt, with a pretty turquoise top that I suddenly coveted. I avoided eye contact, even through the screen.

"He wouldn't even look at me." Her eyes bounced from my shadow through the screened porch to Donna, back and again.

"*Ann*—" Donna said. Like I knew she would, Ann Baxter grasped at this like a lifeline. Her bottom lip quivered, and her eyes washed a little with tears.

"He's gone and left us here—" She covered her face.

I stopped it there. I put my hand out onto Donna's shoulder. She stiffened, and shot me a nasty look over her shoulder, but she stopped.

"We'll be fine. What difference does it make?" I said. "Want a snort?"

That shut her cake hole. She straightened up.

"It's barely past lunch."

"It's five o'clock somewhere," I said. Donna snickered. Ann side-eyed me.

"Did you take my schnapps? When I was on the pier yesterday? Did you?"

I narrowed my eyes back at Ann, theatrically. "I rarely leave my house." Her expression shifted rapidly from stricken to suspicious and she smiled.

"That's not an answer."

"Do you want a drink or not?" She scanned the frightful horizon and considered this. It was dreadfully quiet, just the water slapping, which could sound like thunder if you were alone. Ann told us once that she saw a man get shot, at the hospital, a gang thing, and when the bullet left the gun, she really thought it was thunder, as if her brain had to rationalize it.

"Do you have any schnapps?" She looked at me slyly. If she had looked at me slyly with humour I might have got her some, but it was just sly as if the whole thing was just about catching me in some lie. I said I didn't. She would have to make do with wine.

They came into the porch. We sipped and watched the sky darken to an eggplant purple on the horizon, like it had almost every day since May.

It was the last time we would see her.

Donna went somewhere every day, up and down the coast, nose poking into the few remaining boats, knocking on doors. I rarely left the house. I knew there was nothing out there for me and I was too old to prove it to myself. I had everything I needed where I was. I had my books, my papers; I was down to ink and notebook for writing, but that was probably best. It took more concentration, kept my mind off the worst of things. I tended to get morose when I wasn't drunk, and tried not to be drunk until the afternoon.

In the mornings I worked and puttered and waited for Donna to come back from Out There.

I knew she swam in the ocean, sometimes doing laps until her arms shook. She'd come over then, her lips blue, fingers pruned, hair soaked and tangled. I don't know how she did it, but she was the kind of woman who preferred staring into things to looking away. I was not, by nature.

I could look away from the glare of the truth without batting an eye. I could in fact toast a lie, smile in its face and drink to its health even as the truth was in the glass. This was a new skill, since Dick died.

The exception was the night of the fish.

I lost track of the days quite a while ago. I know it's August, and it might be Thursday. It might be Friday. The night of the fish was four nights ago, maybe five. Time has gotten funny.

Donna and I were in our usual positions, parked on my veranda, feet up, drink in hand, staring out at the beach. Storms came nearly every night now, and they could be spectacular. We were storm people any way, Donna and I. Almost how we met. We'd been summer neighbours a long time, her house just up the beach from ours. Sometimes when the sky got black as shit I'd stand out on the sand as long as I could, the wind tangling my skirt around my legs, whipping my hair so hard against my face it stung, I'd stay out right up until the rumbling scared even me and then I'd watch from the veranda. When I had a husband, he'd be in there hollering for me to come in before I got knocked over. I would wait until the last minute.

Often as not, when I was running back inside, getting wet, I would see Donna doing the same thing, the two of us the only living things out in the storm.

When it got the way it finally got out here, she just came over and we'd watch from my veranda. *Fill me up and let's see this*, she'd say. We'd drink a bottle of wine watching it, then maybe another one brooding about it.

It was just like that the night of the fish.

Fill me up.

If I think about it, it had been an odd day, too, maybe the second or third day in a row where the sky never lightened past the dull silver it was nearly all the time now. But the fish had been less than a week ago. It wasn't a case of the sun never breaking the clouds so much as it was the sun having lost its brightness. What remained was weak and grey. Donna had done a little beachcombing that day and had come around with a bag of goodies, including a can of cheese she'd taken from a boat she'd found banging against the Bushnell's dock. She said the inside was done in this hideous pink-and-blue décor as if by a pregnant teenager. There was also a ratchet set, some blue sea glass and a pristine set of four wine glasses, which she presented to me with a *ta da* like a gift. I was delighted. So many of the glasses from my old life had ended up broken, thrown hard against walls and into sinks, the leftover wine in them spreading out at the site like a splatter of blood, eventually swept into corners. Dead soldiers.

We used the new glasses that night, filled with a nice red, with a white on deck for when the red was drained.

The storm started way far out on the horizon, so slow that we could watch it come in at our leisure, like ladies at lunch.

I must say.

Oh yes please do.

They'd all been strange, the storms. One day the sky had stayed a brilliant azure blue even as hailstones the size of golf balls tore through the top of the canvas gazebo Jeb and Heidi Keenley kept in their back yard on the slope. Heidi would have had a chicken if she'd seen it like that, but Heidi had been MIA for at least two months, gone along with the rest of the neighbours and that didn't bear thinking about. And one day the sky had just stayed that near-black all day, one bright beam of sun stabbing through and hitting the beach. Could've burned an egg on the sand right there on that patch of sun. It was crazy, right down to the bloody sky

But I was talking about the night of the fish. So when the clouds grew black on the horizon, there was not much to remark on. In fact, in general, it began as an unremarkable storm, which was sort of nice, calming. For a while.

The clouds moved in, across the water, never rising above the horizon line, not even when they were close enough to make out the asymmetrical blooms like blackened cauliflower that made up the clouds, they still seemed to be resting on the top of the water. The sky hadn't brightened in weeks by then, being colourless rather than grey or silver, really, but the clouds were so sooty and fulsome, the contrast against the sky so complete, there was a kind of eerie beauty to it. The kind of beauty that can, for a moment anyway, make you gasp a little and clutch your chest.

I must say.

Oh yes please do.

The wind came up and turned the water nearly as black as the clouds, so the only way to see the difference between sky and lake was through the angry, foaming whitecaps that swirled and fell into darkness.

Rain came in a burst, torrential, coming down so hard and thick it obscured everything else, a veil of water, a wall. It was like being under the falls at Niagara. Just after the rain started, the sky *exploded.*

We had been in our usual positions, lounging in my pretty wicker chairs that in another lifetime had been a special joy of mine. I used to change the cushions by the season, pretty green-and-white pin stripes with pink-and-green pillows for spring; blue Wedgewood through summer; gold-red-burgundy-brown for fall. Red and white through the winter. Of course this changed every season also, when I got bored or tired of the old look, I shopped for new cushions. Shopping seemed a surreal concept now.

Since everything changed, the cushions had become lost in the fog. Maybe since Dick had died. That seemed unlikely since I could hardly remember when Dick died, and I surely remembered putting out the blue cushions. But a couple of those had torn, or been stabbed with scissors and tossed to the floor of the veranda, fluffy white guts kicked into corners with the shards of broken wine glasses.

Me and Donna were lounging on a mix of the green-and-white, the red ones, and the few blue cushions that had survived my lapses of sanity, and drunken raging against the unseen. Feet up on the ottomans. Wine glasses dangling elegantly from our veiny hands.

The sky burst and flashed and we jumped. Wine sloshed in my glass, but didn't spill and so I said *look ma no spill*—

Just as another flash—

Not a flash. An eruption. A cannonade. A bombing.

Whatever fist had busted through the sky hit the water's surface and flared. What had been black burst into a flash so bright it stunned me, I lost all sense, heard nothing, certainly not the explosive blast that must have followed. Instead, everything just stopped, hovered under the audacity of that blaze.

For a moment the face of the water was absurdly keen, every wave scored, the water such as I had never seen it, still, serene, flat, as if not water at all but a piece of glass laid over it. Then sound.

A low rumble like the expected thunder, it rolled and rolled, a build so long that I looked at Donna, maybe my eyes like dinner plates, like a child, because Christ would know it, I was scared.

Donna said *what the fuck?* And I heard that, and it did *not* help since unlike me, she is not a natural curser, but saves them up for the most appropriate time.

I would have answered but then the sound hit us, a crack that made me shriek, that got lost under it, although I knew I did it, just as I knew I dropped my wine and clapped my hands on my ears. My own shriek or the thunder was the reason we didn't hear the roar of the ocean, heaving up its contents.

That we heard as the thunderclap died away, as they all ultimately do, in spite of how it seemed it was going to last forever. The silence afterward was just as terrible. I spoke for that reason alone.

"What was that?"

Donna didn't answer. She ran her sandal through the wine draining towards the corner of the porch. She held up her glass. It was empty.

I poured us both a couple of doozies. We drank those and had some more. And then again.

At some point, I remember she asked me *what came out of the ocean?*

I meant it to be funny when I said *everything*.

Maybe I should have said *afternoon* of the fish.

I woke up on the wicker sofa and Donna was gone. My head was pounding. When I got my ass moving, slowly, slowly, I made coffee on the woodstove and drank it in the kitchen with my hands shaking. So I didn't see it at first.

I smelled it. Fish.

I've lived at the beach all my life. My mother used to say I had sand in my veins. I've certainly not known a time when I didn't have sand in my hair, under my nails, or on the floor, and the smell of fish in my nose.

Not like this.

This was heavy, oily, also familiar, but in the worst sort of way, the kind you would stumble upon rock-walking, the picked-over corpse, usually just the head and spine, the gulls circling overhead. It got into your clothes, your hair. A smell you carried with you all day.

I changed my clothes after that and cleaned up as best I could in the bathroom. The water was working only intermittently then, but I had filled the bathroom and Dick's room with buckets of water, some of it from our taps when they worked, some of it at the empty houses of neighbours. What did it matter where it came from? I washed up and changed and felt nearly human and went back into the veranda. I would clean it up, I thought, and see if I couldn't find some kind of track to get back on.

The storm had scared me in the same way falling down the stairs can scare a person sober. That, thankfully, had not yet happened. But the storm had freaked me out enough to make me want to sit up and take notice.

To look things in the eye, so to say.

I went out to the veranda, plastic bag in hand to fill with bottles and corks and broken glass and cushion stuffing and bits of life that hadn't worked out the way they were supposed to, written on pieces of paper rolled into balls and tossed into corners and under chairs and sofas. I unfolded the piece I found in the corner of the kitchen, drunken sprawl hard to decipher, although not hard enough.

. . . *always I expected to be happy when I was alone alone alone and yet I* . . . I rolled it back up and stuffed it in the bag.

It was then I guess I looked outside for the first time and saw the shoreline.

At first I thought it was nothing more than sea foam, the saliva of the sea, ocean vomit, as Dick used to call it. Over the last few years, it had been getting worse, or more prevalent and so at first—

At first I thought *holy shit what a lot of ocean vomit*—

Of course it was too much for that. What I was looking at was wide enough from the edge of the water as to be nearly halfway to my fake seagull on the post. *Halfway.* I pushed open the screen door and squinted. The sun was out.

There was Donna, with her plaid treasures bag, coming up the beach. "Hey!" I called. She waved.

"You have to see this," was what she screamed back. And for the first time, I thought maybe I did.

The smell hit me bad as soon as I landed sand level. It was the smell of the sea, of the dark beach at night, of fall at the shore. This was peaking, under the familiar smell was the dead smell, waiting. It would not be long. It was overwhelming.

Fish. Everywhere. Dead. Fish.

Sunlight glinted off the silver scales, sickly white bellies, thin red jelly under the gills, nothing moving.

Thousands of them, all sorts, I could have named maybe six of them, maybe eight, no more. Enormous mounds, in an uneven, meandering ribbon going along the coastline, as far as I could see to the east and as far as I could see to the west.

I had no words. My mouth simply hung there. Donna was crying.

"They're dead," she said. She pointed needlessly up the coast. "I walked the whole length, and it's the same, all the way up as far as I was going to go—"

I put my hand up. "It's okay. This shit happens. I've read about it."

"I saw a shark! *A goddamn sand tiger shark*! There's tuna, and whitefish and swordfish, a ray, a fucking *Finding Nemo*, Rosie, they don't even *live* here—"

"Okay," I said, but I didn't have the stomach for it, to stop her, to comfort her. I wanted to fall over. The smell was horrible. It was getting to me. I wanted to swoon.

How?

Donna dropped to the sand on her butt. She dug her skinny heels and fingers into the sand. She dragged them through, making patterns, deeper and deeper. Then she read my mind.

She got up and brushed the sand from her hands on to her skirt. I watched and she picked up one of the fish. Just before she threw it in, she looked at me. Hurt. Not that I had hurt her, just hurt. She tossed it into the water.

We watched it arc and then it hit the surface. There was a tiny flash— like a glint of sun hitting the chrome on the side of a car as it drove by, nothing more. Might have been the sun hitting the scales, except there really wasn't any sun. The sky was grey, like it had been.

"What the hell is happening? There's no mark on them, no blight or tumors or anything. Nothing bit them. Tide brought them in. They're still coming." I looked out to sea. It was true. With every comforting—

—Dick used to say the tide said *mensch mensch mensch*—

—wave, more fish dropped and were dragged back out, pushed in, pulled out.

"Electrocuted?"

"I think so. Must have been."

Mensch mensch mensch. The water slapped hollowly against the slabs of flesh. It was hard to hear it, but I forced myself to listen. To not hear it as it was supposed to sound, would be to go crazy. I heard it. I listened until I could feel my heart and breath slowing down. Donna dropped back to the beach, curled herself up, tucking her head into her knees.

"What now?" I said.

She stared out to sea. The horizon was disappointing, the sun bright through a single, white cloud.

"You're going to get your skirt dirty. How'll you wash it?" I said, trying to smile.

"Do you think they're all dead?"

I shrugged. *The whole ocean?* No. I couldn't think that.

"Ann's gone," she said.

I had an urge to lie down on the sand and make an angel like I used to do when I was a little girl. I couldn't even remember being a little girl, except for that feeling, suddenly so clear, of damp, cool sand on my back, scratchy and giving. I tried to say that I needed a drink. *Now we can have the schnapps*, but the effort seemed not to be in me. It was all I could do to stand there.

"Do you think the water's safe?" She said it so plaintively that we might both have been children, making angels in the sand.

"I don't know," I lied.

I went back to the house, leaving Donna on the beach. I tried to coax her into coming with me, but she waved me away. "I'm just going to sit here a minute. I'll come later, Rosie," she said. When she said my name, I felt something break inside me, but I left just the same.

Honestly? I had no words in me anyway.

I'd had an ongoing argument with Dick for the forty years we were married about who should die first. We would have this argument after lovemaking, after fighting and making up, over dinner in the city, sometimes in the car on the way home from a night out with friends when you perfectly tag-teamed every quip, every story, and left feeling so good about yourselves that the very best parts of yourself were then on display: every generous notion, every forgiveness, every single *oh no, after you dear*. When things were at their very best, those moments in the marriage when you feel for a little while like it hadn't been a big mistake, I of course always said that I wanted to die first.

I was lying.

Most women, I believe, have a dream of a time *in the future* when it was all over, when they were absolved of all responsibility for others when *go forth and sin no more* would be gloriously whispered in their ear. *In the future*. I don't know that it comes very often for normal women, I don't think children stop needing parents, or spouses stop needing each other, until someone dies. I saw a time when Dick would be gone—statistically before me—as a time when I would get my time. I would read. Write. Eat what I wanted. Let myself go.

Dick got sick at the beginning of all of this, but not like the others. Ann looked him over and said discreetly that she thought it was cancer, but unless she got tests done, she couldn't say for sure. Tests of course, were out of the question. The world in which tests were done had disappeared. It must have been cancer though, because he died. It was mercifully fast.

There'd hardly been time for anything, but he told me a few things. He told me to change the batteries in the smoke detector. He told me there was a box of pornography—mostly nude pictures cut out of *Playboy* magazines in the '70s—under the moving tarps in the garage. He told me that the key for the safe deposit box at the branch in the city was in his sock drawer. All things I already knew. Toward the end he babbled about these things over and over.

A couple of days before he died, he was sick, but lucid. Lucid enough that I accused him of palming his meds, a great sin because by then pain meds were not easy to come by, Ann had given him the last of what she had in her house. That made him smile, but not laugh, which still makes me think that I was right.

A fact extraordinary enough to remark on: he was braver than I would ever have been. No matter how well I would have wanted to go out, dignity, grace, etc., I would have taken the pain meds. The fact he didn't makes me weepier about him than any of the other things he said, or tried to say. The fact he wanted to be present and with me the last few days showed me a courage I guess I'd forgotten to look for. He was a good man and sometimes I forgot that, and dear god I hated remembering it.

But a couple of days before he died, he tried to talk to me about what was going on outside there. A real Donna, he was.

It's going to get worse. I read some awful things—

I shushed him.

Don't go into the city. Stay here. Money's not going to be worth shit. There's the generator if you need it. Collect fresh water. Food for a long time—

I will, I am, I did, I will, I promised him.

Ann came every day. When he died she gave me a valium and said she'd come back in the morning and give me another one. I got up in the night and poured myself most of a bottle of burgundy. It's my drug of choice.

So instead when she came back I made her and Donna help me get Dick into the boat. Ann tried to get Mr. Kruger to come and help us, but he declined. Bastard. I hope cannibals eat him. We were three old women. It took us better than an hour to get Dick up the dock and into the boat. I got him out to sea and rolled him over myself. I didn't watch him sink and I didn't look back. When I got home I didn't tie the boat up. Haven't seen it since.

Ann had been so good. But we all changed.

About an hour later, Donna was at my door.

"I found Ann," she said. And then turned around to walk up the beach. I followed her.

"Should I come?" Donna shook her head.

She gestured towards Ann's house. "She's inside," she shrugged, her voice flat. "I covered her with a blanket."

I nodded. "Good."

"I don't blame her."

I didn't either. But I did. I wondered if it was because Kruger left. Maybe she and him had started something up. It was a crazy thought. We were all over seventy, Ann was probably seventy-four. Then I felt bad for thinking that, thinking of Dick.

And then I thought *apparently she saved some of the meds for herself.*

"You want a drink?"

"No." She gave me a wan smile and held my gaze. "Later."

I fired up the genny. It made a ghastly noise, but lit up every light in the house. I even went outside to look up at it from the beach. It looked like goddamn Christmas. I pulled a chair out onto the sand, sitting about a yard from the wall of stinking fish, and got my bottle and drank. I guess

I was waiting for Donna. Didn't see her.

I thought I would like being alone. I did, in a way. In the first weeks after Dick died, I tried to wrap my head around all of the things I said I wanted to do when he was gone. I stacked books on all the tables. I kept my notebook open. I ate apples while I walked around and cooked absolutely nothing, not even tea. I let myself go. My hair was wild, my makeup smeared, my belly out, my underwear off.

It got good. I missed him more than I thought, but by the time I recognized that, the world was topsy-turvy and people were gone, and missing Dick got tangled in missing the way everything used to be, and it was easier just to have a drink.

When I was good and drunk I got the flashlight and went stumbling along the great wall of fish. I saved that in my head.

I thought *I have to tell Donna that one, Great Wall of Fish, she'll like that.*

I found her about a mile up the beach. Her body was caught in the tide, swooshing up against the Great Wall of Fish and sweeping back out to sea because there was nowhere for her to go, her bathing suit a bright spot in all that grey. She'd gone for a swim.

I watched her for a long time.

Mensch. Mensch. Mensch.

Now I've finished writing this all down. I'm glad I did. I have no one left to tell it all to, and I proved to be a poor talker anyway, unless you like a joke more than a story.

The sky's a little darker today. The fish have really started to smell. I haven't seen or heard a thing other than the regular movement of the ocean, in days.

I have a few things I have to do. I found the shovel Dick bought last year for the deep flower beds I was going to try my hand at and never really did. It's got a red handle. Pretty red. I notice things like that now.

Donna was my friend and I don't think she wants to be left where she is, washed up on the shore. Her hairline and the tips of her fingers were blackened.

The house is tidier than it's ever been. I've closed down the genny and I like the quiet, but actually preferred the smell of gas to the smell of the fish. It's getting bad.

I've changed.

There are no good bottles of wine left, I've saved nothing for a special occasion. The bottle I've brought to the beach with me is pedestrian and impersonal. No notes of humility, no bite of regret, no nose of resignation.

It's just a dry red. Open, of course.

I think about karma. I know somehow that we did all of this. The fish are like chickens, coming home to roost. It's all coming home to roost. The beach is silent. Everything is silent. I'm alone. Alone. Alone.

I put my head back and swallow the long swallow. When I'm done I grind the bottle into the sand so that it stands upright, not spilling. You never know.

I hope I don't see Coolidge. I'd hate to see that dog now. I'm a dog person.

I've changed into my bathing suit. I'm going for a swim.

THE AUDIT

Poor Janet lay in bed listening to the alarm, trying to ignore it and knowing it would never, ever go away. In the first few blinks of waking up she had nudged at Les, curled up on his side beside her. When he slept on his side, he didn't snore as badly. She nudged him and felt his body roll with the force of it, but otherwise, gave no other response. She was about to speak *Les get up time for work* when she remembered that Les wasn't working these days and then the day ahead washed over her and her stomach tightened and any thoughts of sleeping in or not getting up were lost in churning waves of stomach acid and tightened shoulders.

I'm being audited.

The alarm kept up its tinny shriek, a cross between bells and a rattling aluminium door. It sounded just like one of those wind-up alarm clocks of the sort that she remembered in her parent's room from when she was a kid, but it wasn't. It was a plug in. The wind-up clocks wound down eventually, and after a minute of the ringing, you could go back to sleep. If you could stand a minute. In January you could; when the floor was cold and the car had to run a full fifteen minutes before you could drive it without stalling, and if the coffee had to be made and if you forgot to make your lunch for work before going to bed, you could stand it. Probably you could stand two minutes of ringing if it meant not putting your bare feet on to the cold January floor. The plug in alarm didn't run down. It rang until the little button was pushed. It was Les' mom's old alarm clock. She gave it to them when Jan complained about Les not getting up for work. The clock was procured like magic, practically out of a hat. Les's work record embarrassed his mom. They fought about it all the time. When he wasn't working, they avoided his mom's place.

Les-than-a-man. That was what Jan's mom called him.

It was all the way across the room. To shut it off, you had to get out of bed. You couldn't even crawl to the end of the bed and reach out to the dresser and shut it off. He'd done that too many times. They started to put it on the chair in the corner. Something about the chair made it sound louder too. *It's the acoustics,* Les-than-a-man had said, grinning. *Makes the chair vibrate with it.*

Janet didn't know if that was true, but it did seem louder.

"Shut off the fucking alarm," Les mumbled from under the blanket. Jan was already half-way out of bed by then, so she didn't say anything back. The bedroom was freezing. They all but shut the heat off at night *save a little dough*, Les said. Les-than-a-man.

It was 5:30. She had five hours to get her shit together before her meeting with the government accountant. She was being audited.

I'm being audited. Jan thought it to herself as she pushed in the little button on the back of Les's mom's alarm clock in hopes that the words would lose some of their power, the power they had held over her for the last two weeks, but in spite of the two weeks that she had to get used to the idea, it all still made her stomach tight and sore and her head ache.

I'm just a dumb waitress, she thought. *I'm a big nobody. What do they care what I have?* She'd said this and more to everyone who would listen for the last two weeks, until Les-than-a-man told her to can it. She scuffled a foot under the end of the bed fishing for her slippers and found one and put it on. She got down on all fours to find the other one. Les had pulled it off her in a stupid gesture (it was supposed to be romantic or something but it had just been *stoopid*) last night when he wanted to have sex. She told him she wasn't in the mood, but he said *I'll make you in the mood* and then what was she supposed to do? But her slipper had gone flying.

He always did the wrong thing at the wrong time. Like mornings, when he slept instead of going to work.

The house was cold enough that she wrapped her robe around her middle tight and hugged her arms to her middle. She slipped out of the bedroom and closed the door behind her. The first thing she did was turn the heat up. No way was she doing bullshit paper work in a cold house. Then she made coffee. Strong.

It was still dark out when she went down into the basement and started hauling boxes of receipts upstairs. She brought the first two up and even just the sight of them, with their box tops folded in on each other in a pinwheel felt so overwhelming that she decided to start with just the two of them and then work her way up to the other box, still in the basement, and then the assorted bags and folders with the other papers in them.

The boxes were from the liquor store, from when they moved. One was a Captain Morgan's Rum box and the other a Canadian Club. Scratched out with black marker was the notation "kitchen" in her handwriting. Written under that was "tax shit," in Les's handwriting. *Ha ha*, she thought, Les-than-a-man. That's what it was, though. Shit.

The coffee maker gurgled as though there wasn't a care in the world that couldn't be taken care of by Maxwell House in the Morning, but it filled the kitchen with such a warm and homey smell, that Janet thought she might cry. It reminded her—the dark, the coffee smell, the tight stomach—of when she was in school. Her dad would get up and make coffee *come on girls* and then call her and her sister to breakfast. Her mom worked a night shift at a bakery and she slept while the three of them ate and mumbled quietly at the table before school and work. Jan hadn't done well in school, mornings before she went filled her with a familiar, comfortable sort of dread, based more on the tedium of the long day ahead than any real fear. It wasn't she was worried about failing a test, or a grade or getting a bad mark on a paper. She didn't do well, and wasn't expected to by either her parents or teachers. Sometimes it just worked that way. She left after tenth grade, not exactly with her parent's blessings, but with a basic understanding that neither she nor school were doing each other any favours. She went right to work at a diner on Rail Road, making $3.25 an hour. She'd been a waitress ever since. And she was a damn good one. She even liked it. Her parents had her sister to be proud of. Betty had gone all the way through school and then, in a move that was incomprehensible to Jan, went on to more school. She was a medical secretary now, and worked at one of the hospitals in the city. She was married with two kids. Her husband was a mechanic. He made good money too.

But no tips, was their joke together. Not very funny, considering it was the tips that got her into this mess.

I could just kill Terri Pringle.

Janet had been waitressing for ten years. Never once had she claimed any tips. Not once. Ten years, ten tax reports filed, not once had anyone said fuck all about tips. Then she was talking to a new waitress, Terri

Pringle, who said, in passing one day, that you had to claim your tips on your income tax.

"They'll come after you, if you don't," she'd said. Terri worked part-time. She was a student at the community college and she had said the whole thing with such confidence that it shook Janet up.

Tentatively she had said to Terri, "I've never claimed my tips." She'd tried to say it with as much mustered confidence as the younger, student-y Terri, but hadn't managed as well.

"My dad's an accountant," she said. "They'll come after you for that." Then the shift had changed and everybody went home. Terri didn't even work there long.

Jan had asked around after that. She asked the other waitresses and they would sigh and the debate would start, but most of them said they never claimed their tips. One girl said they automatically assume tips on top of your wages. "Ten per cent," she said. "Look over your last year's return. Where it says: undeclared income?' Look there. They'll have added ten per cent."

They hadn't. Her mother and dad said not to worry about it. "You get it done at the H and R Block, don't you?" She did.

"They do it for you there." But her mom had looked a little frowny over the whole thing *you don't want to do anything to get into trouble,* she'd said later, when they were alone.

Don't be such a putz, Les-than-a-man said. "Declaring your tips would be like when we borrow ten bucks from my mom and then declaring it as income." He laughed at the very thought and then watched tv. He reminded her, though, when they were going to the H and R Block to get their taxes done. *Don't be a putz,* he'd said, and he shook his finger at her and raised his eyebrows in a perfect imitation of his mother when she said to him, *You get a job now, you hear? Don't be a bum like your father.*

In the end, she declared her tips. Or at least, a rough estimate of them. The H and R man had raised his eyebrows, too, and Jan had trouble deciding whether that was because she was claiming them, or because the number was so low, or too high. Her face had reddened and she felt like she'd been caught in a lie, but of course she had no real way of knowing if she was lying or not because Terri Pringle—*I could kill Terri Pringle*—hadn't even mentioned declaring tips until nearly October. Jan had guessed based on what she made from around November-mid when she decided inside her head to play it right to the end of the year. She thought she was safe in her guess because people tipped more around the holidays, and she counted them.

She poured coffee into her bunny mug and got down on her hands and knees on the floor in front of the first box. She cracked it open, not knowing even what year she was about to see, let alone whether or not it would be her stuff or his. Les had a business on the side sometimes, fixing bikes. His stuff was mixed in with hers, but he only claimed the money he made working extra for his buddy Tom, who had a bike shop, because Tom declared it.

The box was filled to the top with little pieces of paper. A musty smell came from the box, like old books at a garage sale. A couple of little pieces fluttered up and settled back down, like fall leaves when you swipe by them on your bike on the way to school. Thinking about school set her off again. She wanted a Tums, but she'd eaten the last of them the night before.

Gee-zus.

Her and Les were both savers of paper. Paper had some kind of authoritarian hold over her feral self. Paper made her feel more feral than human, or certainly sub-human in some way. Especially white paper. Around very white paper with lines and numbers or words on it, she felt stained and dusty and smudgy. The lines, even and black or blue, the careful tally of numbers in a row, the dots matching up with each other, they seemed like representatives of some kind of legal authority. She also felt this way about soldiers and policemen, doctors and dentists; pieces of paper felt like they could boss her, regardless of what was written on them. Could as easy be a receipt from the drugstore for tampax as a subpoena, didn't matter. Coloured paper wasn't so bad. She kept the pizza flyers and the two-for-one deals that came from the carpet cleaning people, and ads offering her fifteen per cent off her next oil change, with a sort of grown-up sigh, and filed them in a pile on the table beside the front door. Anything that came in a white envelope (especially a white envelope with a little window on the front) went reverently over to the desk in the corner, where she paid bills. She even kept the newsletters sent by her member of parliament, just in case. You never knew. Someone might ask. Something.

You never knew.

She didn't claim much on her income tax. She claimed panty hose and her uniforms, of course. And shoes, but they were the special (ugly) orthopaedic shoes that she had to wear because of her bunions—an occupational hazard of working on your feet for ten years. In a few years she imagined she would have to have some sort of an operation on varicose veins. Annie had it done last year after she nearly couldn't walk for the pain. The operation fixed her up pretty good, she said, but by the end of the year—*when Terri Pringle left never to return—I could kill Terri Pringle*—new ones were troubling her.

She claimed gas mileage whenever she had to work extra at a catering job that her mother sometimes got her through the bakery. Mostly Bridge Lady teas and things, but once a Sweet Sixteen party. That had been quite a bash. Not only had it been catered, but the whole place had been professionally decorated by one of those balloon joints. They turned the No. 16 Legion Hall into a pink cloud, with a real balloon waterfall in the corner. Not just streamers, either, but yards and yards of pink fabric had been draped over walls and tables and the whole thing had been just beautiful, although a little hard on the eyes after an hour or so. Most of the teenagers took off after the presents were opened, but that was okay because the mothers and aunts and old ladies had stayed for hours, wanting only more tea and the waitresses weren't too taxed on their feet and were paid for the whole day. Her mom and the others had made tiny little cakes—twelve kinds—the sort that were just a bite and sickly sweet after the first couple, but lovely to look at. Just perfect. They were tipped as a group and shared after those events. She wondered if the others had claimed the tips on their income tax.

Janet started going through the receipts, one by one, noticing that while her whole body felt sick and tired, and shaky, it was only her hands where it showed.

Sometime over the next two hours, Les woke up and ambled into the kitchen and poured himself a cup of coffee. Janet, engrossed in 1996 fuel receipts didn't even look up. In fact, didn't realize he was up at all until he kicked and scattered a pile of health-relateds (Les's filling, but paid for by her, ergo *her* health-related receipt, plus two massages and a visit to the chiropractor, all from 1998) receipts when he opened the fridge door to get the milk. They went flying towards the free-standing cabinet where she kept her baking stuff and Tupperware.

"*Don't,*" she shrieked, shocking them both. She bent over double from her position, sitting on the floor surrounded by boxes and pieces of paper (almost of them white), and fished out two receipts that had slipped under the cabinet. "This took me *hours,*" she said.

"*Sor-reee,*" he said, and muttered something about someone being a little cranky under his breath. He settled in on the living room sofa, out of Janet's line of vision, but she heard him open the paper.

She felt mildly guilty for snapping at him when he'd just woken up—

Les was not a morning person—and so called to him in the living room, "How come you're up so early?"

He grunted. She waited for his answer, and realized the grunt was going to be all she got, and so bent back over her receipts, searching for something, anything, over the last six years that would save her ass.

"Dear Mrs. Lancaster," the letter has started. Right away, reading it, before she even opened the envelope in fact, she knew it was bad news. The long, thin, pristine white envelope was addressed to her and her alone, the erroneous "Mrs." making it somehow worse. The corner was stamped with a government of Canada logo and no return address. Under the logo was "Department of Revenue," and her stomach had tightened.

She had come home after her shift smelling like French fries and mud pie and wanting nothing more in the whole wide world (ever again) to take her shoes off and sit on the couch. Les's truck hadn't been in the drive and that had given her a little lift. The house would be empty and quiet. She didn't even wonder where he was, didn't give it a thought (although hoping in the same breath that he was out looking for work and knowing that it was more likely he was playing pool at the legion or else was at his mother's cadging twenty bucks). She grabbed the mail not even looking at it and threw it on the table. The letter from the government skittered out, sliding across the Formica with its weight.

"Dear Mrs. Lancaster," it began. "A review of your 2000 tax remittance noted that you filed $362.96 in income under 'other source.'

"Your explanation of the additional income was for gratuities received through your employment at the Happy Diner where you are listed as 'serving personnel.' A sequential review of tax information filed for the years 1996-1999 indicated that while during those years you were also employed by the Happy Diner as serving personnel, no gratuities were claimed for those years.

"You are therefore required to appear at your nearest tax office on or before February 13, 2001 with records indicating this discrepancy in an independent audit. Please call the number at the bottom of this page to make an appointment with your auditor, no later than ten days after the receipt of this letter."

It was signed by a secretary for a director at Revenue Canada (Auditor's Department!) whose name was Mr. Peter Norris. Peter Norris. She'd never heard of him, never would meet him, but she had a vague feeling from then on that he had her file on his desk ready to

125

be stamped, "Guilty," the implications of which could only be dreamed about, in a nightmare fashion.

She'd left the letter lying around for a couple of days, never once forgetting about it for even a moment. That had been a Friday. Saturday night her and Les had gone out for a couple of beers with their friends Gord and Paula and Janet had drank more than a couple of beers, uncharacteristically, pissing Les off because it meant he had to drive them home and he'd had a warning four years earlier for drinking and driving. "They'll cut my ass off, I get caught," he'd said, petulantly, more than a little in his cups himself. She'd laughed at that. "They won't *cut your ass off*. They'll take away your license," she'd said, matter-of-factly. "Cut your ass off. What does that even mean?" She could get snarky like this only when she was a little drunk.

"Same thing," Les said. She fell asleep in the car and *even then*, didn't stop thinking about the audit.

She finally told Les about it that Sunday, when he was trying to watch football and nursing a hangover with a beer. "Get yourself a lawyer," was what he said.

She told her mom and dad that same day, walking over to their place right around supper time, needing just a little comfort food and maybe a bit of advice. What she thought she really wanted was to hear her dad tell her it was all right and then to tell her to bring her stuff over to him and he would take care of it. Maybe call her Princess, like when she was little.

"Just get your things together and explain to the government that you didn't know you had to declare your tips and that you're very sorry and you won't do it again," her mother told her. She made beef casserole with shell noodles. It tasted like grade five and homework, because of how she felt.

"You never should have declared them in the first place," her dad said, from his chair in the living room, where he was watching the game and switching over to Matlock, between quarters.

On the following Monday, Abby at work said, "You get yourself a good accountant and let them do the work."

She got herself Ramona Jacobson, who *tsk-tsk-ed* and *oh my-ed* everything, called her *Lancaster* and charged by the hour and talked really fast. The woman wore those half-glasses that old people wore, even though she didn't look more than ten years older than Janet, and sometimes she peered at her over them as though Janet were some sort of alien creature worth a second study.

Ramona Jacobson scared her almost as much as the audit, but at least she was on her side.

The phone rang at eight-thirty just about knocking Janet out of her slippers. Her eyes were stinging from being open so long and her fingers were black and coated with ink. It rang twice before she realized Les wasn't going to pick it up and she got up off the floor, very careful not to disturb any of the fifteen piles of varying years and subject matter (unfortunately in no particular order) that were distributed around the floor in the kitchen.

Les was still reading the paper. He shifted without looking at her, his bulk moving slowly over the vinyl seats of the sofa, so that air escaped from one of them making a hissing sound, like a fart.

She grabbed the phone on the fourth ring.

"Hello?" she said, like a question.

"Lancaster, I just wanted to remind you to bring all the co-malgamated T-7s. And while I got you, don't forget the super-annuated close forms. Even the ones for your spouse." Ramona Jacobson spoke *very* fast on the phone, breathing it all into Janet's ear like sitting too close to a speaker for too long.

"Huh?" she said. "Bring the what?"

"That's right. And the T-6s, too. From the legion work. Gotta go. If you need anything, I'm in a meeting for the next hour and then you can get me on my cell. You have that number?"

"I don't know."

"It's—" and then at the speed of light she rattled off what seemed to be an account number at the world's largest bank.

"Um thanks," Janet said.

"You can get me on it until 11. *Shit!* I have your Geswins! Well, that's all right. What time's the appointment?"

"Um—"

"1:30, right. Hmmm. Forgot about that. Anyway, I'll meet you there. If you need me, you can still get me after the hour. Gotta go, I'm late, good luck!" And she hung up.

Janet hung on to the phone, desperation creeping over her face more quickly as she realized that Ramona Jacobson had hung up before she had a chance to ask what co-malgamites were. And the super-annuated thing? Had she said that? malgamites, or something. What was that? Something else too. She hung up before Jan had a chance to ask—

What everything is.

She hung up and stared at the phone as if it was going to ring again. It didn't.

"Who was that?" Les said from the couch.

"The accountant," she said, bewildered.

"Oh yeah, when's that thing?" He turned a page of the newspaper with such slowness, such snapping of newsprint, such rolling of fat that she wanted to turn and scratch him to pieces as though making him bleed and scream would somehow release the rising pulse of terror inside her.

"1:30," she said. The only thing she knew.

"Well, you're in for it. Shouldn't have claimed them in the first place," he said, then he chuckled. And he folded the paper over, smoothing the pages down against the coffee table. Jan went back into the kitchen, glancing up at the clock. It was 8:35. She had three hours left before she had to get in the shower and get dressed and down to the auditor.

There was a fourth box in the kitchen when she re-entered. It was perched on the edge of the vinyl chair that was covered with brown flowers, a cast off from her mom's place. Their old kitchen suite. The kitchen chairs of her youth. If you got close enough they smelled like her sister and mashed potatoes.

On the side of the box was written, "taxes 1997." She thought she had been through all the '97s. Her heart sank, and yet lifted at the same time, as though in this new box might be the answer, the legendary, mythical piece of paper that would lead to the path that kept her out of prison. The Holy Trail.

Ignoring the rest of the receipts in the box she'd last opened ("tax crap '98 or '96"), she went right to the new box and pulled open the flaps. Little pieces of paper fluttered up. She grabbed one closest to the top.

"Windlemiers," it said at the top. She frowned. Windlemiers? She shook her head. There were a series of code numbers at the top. Then a lonely figure. "$267.95." Two more figures followed, the only two she could puzzle out. The itemized taxes: Provincial and federal. *Okay that's good.* Janet nodded encouragingly to herself. *Taxes, right, good; that was what she was looking for, right?* Under the taxes was the total and then another series of codes. A figure that might have been the date seemed absent. She puzzled over the first series of codes, in case that was it, and then the one at the bottom. Nothing seemed remotely date-related. She tried to think of what on earth might cost $267.95 all at once and could come up with nothing but a car repair. They rarely had $267.95 (or even just $267.00) all at once to pay something. Not after pay day, anyway.

She nodded to herself. Car repair. That would be good. She could say it was car repair to get to a Legion job. There was no date. Her heart pumped a little harder with the lie. (Not that it was *necessarily* a lie, it could be true, how did she know? *How on earth* was she supposed to *know?*)

She dropped it with haphazard abandon in the vicinity of the pile supposedly of "car repair." The year no longer seemed to matter. She could hear the clock ticking in her belly.

The phone rang again about twenty minutes later and it was for Les. Jan had just cut her finger, a paper cut, and it stung. She stuck it in her mouth and sucked, the pain exquisite and small. Through that, she heard him mumbling into the phone, listening with only half an ear (he wasn't currently cheating as far as she knew, and he wasn't actively seeking employment and so it would only be some bum friend or other and therefore was not very interesting). Then he called from the living room.

"Hey Lancaster!" he called (he had taken to calling her that when she told him about the accountant calling her that; he thought it was funny). "Call-waiting for you." She stumbled into the living room, her eyes unable to see great distances after all their small work.

She looked at him questioningly. He shrugged.

"But get off, 'cause I have Beaner on the other line." A bum friend.

She took the phone and the man on the other end was talking before it even got to her ear.

"—confirming your 1:30 P.M. appointment. You understand that you're expected." Her mind snapped awkwardly on the moment and gave her all her reference material out of panic.

"Yes, I understand. I will be there. I am meeting my accountant," she said, hoping the last bit came out with some authority.

"Good, good," he said, and then paused with horrible time-stealing importance and affability. "So many people just try to avoid the inevitable by not showing up, you understand. It's not that I believe you won't be here—I'm not saying anything at all about you personally, it's just that many people try to avoid the inevitable," he said. It seemed to Jan that he had just spoken in a loop, saying every word with such deliberation that the time it took excluded the others and so he repeated them, endlessly.

"Yes," she said, because she couldn't think of anything else.

"And you'll be sure to bring your liabostities?" he asked.

"Yes?" she said firmly, having no idea what he was talking about. *The accountant will take care of it*, she heard her father's voice in her head. And Abby's. And her mother's. Even Les might have said something like that right after sex. Maybe.

"Good, good," he said again, his voice on a loop. She nodded into the phone, eyes glazed over, looking towards the sunburst clock over the dresser they kept in the livingroom to keep their CDs in. There were sweaters in the bottom drawers. "Yes," she repeated, because he seemed to need something more.

"Good, good, then," he said. It was almost 9:30. "At 1:30 A.M., then," he finally finished, as though it were an affair or something pleasant. His voice was *affable*, something she'd only read about and that filled her with suspicion. He hung up and she handed the phone back to Les.

"Thanks for taking so long," he said, sarcastically. She went back into the kitchen.

Three more boxes were in the kitchen when she came in.

One was beside the stove, and written in big, bold black letters, all capitals was, "Existentials, 1999." The other two were half-hidden under the table, but she saw them, even as they tried to wiggle closer under. The box she had been working on was only just started, but she tore into the new one with a fierce sort of will. The kitchen was littered with paper, her comings and goings had scattered some of the neat stacks until they were literally piles. *You get piles from sitting on cold cement in your pyjamas,* she thought wildly; her mother used to threaten that.

Ripping open the new box she stared blankly at a receipt that appeared to have no dollar figure. The date was '99, though, as the box had promised. For this, she was eternally grateful. *June 16, 1999. Thank you, Jesus, I am absolved of sin in the blood of the receipt. Thank Jesus.*

Jesu anumi ablo.

What would Jesus do?

"Jesus wouldn't have claimed them in the first place," Les said from the door. "I'm picking up Beaner and we're getting that starter for the pickup," he said vaguely. "I might stop over at mom's after," he said. She didn't look up. He picked his way around the piles of paper and said nothing about them.

Good bye. Maybe she only thought it.

Ramona Jacobson called back at ten. "Don't forget the willimusteers and the mono-magnisiums. Also the Pat-Rilancers; they're with the S-2 forms. *Okay?* Gotta run. You know you didn't bring them to the last meeting and that was your choice, Lancaster. Oh! For god's sake, jiggle things around and make sure there's at least a thousand bucks in your mainstream, eh? Get me on the cell, 873dog95-24eat at sam's30" And she hung up.

Janet cut her finger, a paper cut, on the pad of note paper by the phone. She sucked at it.

There were six more boxes, all unopened when she walked back into the kitchen. She stared at them with a baleful, exhausted sort of defiance. They were marked only randomly, some had the routine, black felt marker scrawled across, others didn't. They were marked, "Hornets, 98." "Case Histories, 1996." And worse, "Receipts and Recipes for Disaster, 1998."

In one she found a bird's nest.

Her grade ten orienteering report.

A bill of sale for a car she'd never owned.

A copy of the *Desiderata* on pink paper, decorated with filigrees on the edges.

A receipt for fourteen pairs of panty hose (taupe) in size 7.

"*Go placidly among the noise and haste—*" she recited, remembered from a vague and unmemorable adolescence.

Sometime after four that day, Les and Beaner walked into the house and heard the phone ringing. They'd picked up the starter for the truck and then dropped by Les's mom's place. She'd given him twenty bucks after a hard ride. *You get a job, Lester. Get a haircut, Lester. You're living in sin, Lester.*

He and Beaner had laughed at this at the Kegger on Main, Les a little less hardier than Beaner, whose mother was dead and in her grave fifteen years.

"You gotta tape that, Mom, put it on a loop so I can play it back later, like a motivational thing, you know," Les had said to his mom. They'd repeated this bon mot up until their fourth beer when they got into sports with more of a vengeance.

"Janet," Les screamed when he walked in. The phone rang. "Let the machine get it," he said to Beaner. "Old lady's not home. Must be working," he said to Beaner.

"Wanna beer?"

"Does the Pope shit in the woods?" Beaner answered. This struck Les as hilarious.

In the livingroom the machine picked up the phone. A woman's voice screamed fast, into it. "Lancaster! Lancaster! Lancaster!" The boys ignored it.

Beaner followed Les into the kitchen. The fridge was blocked by an enormous pile of paper, literally blocked. Everywhere in the room was paper. It reached as high as the counter.

"What the *hell?*" Beaner gasped.

Les tried to get the fridge door open and couldn't. He looked around at the mess, a mess he sure-as-shit wasn't cleaning up.

"She had some tax thing. Guess she didn't get it cleaned up. She'll do it later," he said, but his mouth was dry. It was more paper than he'd ever seen, ever. He brought a hand up to shield his eyes, the sunlight, filtering in the west window was shining off the endless white, nearly blinding him. "Fuck," he said, equally vaguely, utterly unsure as to what to do. The paper presented a problem.

"Holy *shit!*" Beaner said. "What the hell is that?"

Les looked at his buddy and then followed his gaze to a spot on the floor where the mountain dipped nearly to linoleum. Pinky-brown flesh showed against the blinding white. A slender wrist and hand.

Without a word, Les stepped one giant step around the mound nearest the fridge and crouched, piles of paper reaching right to his crotch, a necessary lunge that pulled his groin muscle.

He picked up the hand, gingerly, like he might a mouse. "Cold," he said, but not without feeling. "Better call someone," he added, his voice cracking. Beaner didn't move.

There were tiny scratches all over the arm, little nicks in otherwise, white, smooth flesh.

"What are those marks?" Beaner said.

"Looks like paper cuts," Les said, nodding. One summer Les had worked at a heating and ventilating company in the city. Mostly he had stuffed pink insulation into walls and then covered them up. He stuck his hand through the mounds of paper, along the route of the arm that he'd just felt, curious.

The body itself was warm.

"Body's warm," he said. He looked over his shoulder at Beaner's pale, sick face.

"Paper's a good insulator," he said.

PETTY ZOO

The woman with the naturally occurring pigment hemp bag—Trudy knew it was hemp because the word HEMP was (probably) vegetable dyed in large-cap sans serif Helvetica across the off-centre of the bag—was staring at them. The woman's daughter followed her mother's gaze and as soon as she looked at Trudy and Timmy, the mother tapped the girl on the shoulder, forcing her to look away. *Don't stare, it's not polite.* Parenting practices learned on *Bewitched* and *The Partridge Family. Nothing to see here folks, just another Saturday. Mother gripping toddler's arm too tightly during quality time.*

East Fairfax Mall and the petting zoo. Or as Timmy had so appropriately mispronounced it to his father, the petty zoo. *Wild Kingdom Mobile Safari* was at least an hour late opening the gates set up in the centre court. The area was sectioned off from regular Saturday shoppers with clanging portable fencing. Inside the fence was festive papier-mâché jungle trees and plants (Trudy assumed) and life-size papier-mâché treatments of the animals offered beyond the cubicle walls and metal gate. Jungle sounds came over the PA system, screeches and hoots that could have just as easily been mimicked by the hundred or so children left to run Wild Kingdom-style out of boredom. Parents had stopped controlling their children about twenty minutes earlier; in another ten minutes or so, Trudy sensed there would be a huge parental uprising, in an effort to make *someone* pay for the delay in the opening of the gate, and the kids would all be called back to hold places in line while parents ran to the mobile Starbucks or the mobile

Moxie's in the corner of the food court for a little infusion.

She was gripping Timmy's arm too tightly, it was true. Her face was screwed up in that harried way he no doubt recognized. She was tired, her feet were sore—why did she wear goddamn heels, for chrissake?—and she was bored out of her skull. Her *fucking* skull; she would have liked to shout it. *Pitter patter assholes.* My baby wants his picture taken with an alligator.

"Mom?" Timmy wiggled in an effort to break some of the hold on his arm and she yanked discreetly, about to lean over and snarl *enough*, but he said, "Mom, you're hurting my *arm*," and he said it with such deliberation, such equanimity, she immediately broke hold. She shot a look at the hemp-bag woman. She was still looking. Equally discreetly. Trudy noted with amusement that the woman and her daughter wore the same shoes. Daughter's attempt to look older, or woman's attempt to be hip. Did they still call it *hip*, or was it *with it*, now; or something else; *happening* maybe. They used them all when Trudy was the daughter's age; she wished they would get their own words.

"Sorry," she mumbled to Timmy. Quality time. The petty zoo. She and Sam got stoned the night before and came up with variations on the petty zoo. Her favourite was *A Visit to the Petty Mall at the Zoo*. The neon lights were giving her a headache. There was little action behind the gates—which were padlocked (like someone couldn't just move them two feet to the left and walk right in—just the odd green-jacketed *Wild Kingdom*er strutting by, careful to keep his eyes ahead in case he caught the beady, angry eyes of a consumer about to go a little *Wild Kingdom* on his petty zoo ass for making her stand an hour in line with a four-year-old.

Timmy wanted to run in the fake jungle like the other kids. The other kids were unparented. She already had a *Bewitched* mom staring at her. What would Samantha do? It wasn't that easy, of course, because Tabitha was a preternaturally well-behaved sitcom accessory. While sitcom kids regularly did typical four-year-old acts like shove purple crayons up both nostrils, there was never a moment of preternatural sitcom horror when the sitcom mom couldn't get them out when the sitcom kid couldn't breathe. The kids usually sneezed on cue. Therefore, not applicable.

In front of them was a woman who had presumably brought a child with her, since she had a Hello Kitty knapsack in her free hand, but no child present. Behind them was a man who had brought two children, a little girl who had stood quietly at daddy's side throughout the whole ordeal, and whose son was raising hell amongst the papier-mâché rainforest. He came back at intervals for quarters implying a video game somewhere in the jungle.

Pitter patter, let's get at 'er, pitter patter—bastards at these things didn't give a shit that parents had exactly forty-eight hours worth of love to shower on their offspring, none of which should be spent in a mall—yet somehow always was. It wasn't like they were shopping. When she was a kid, her mother dragged her to the mall for school clothes and to buy her dad and brother a Christmas present. Now kids wanted to go.

"What's the damn holdup?" the man said. She admired his free use of the curse word. Men had balls, even when they were with the kids.

Trudy turned, shrugging. "I can't tell—" She had to look up to meet his eyes. They were blue. Of course they were.

"This is crazy, waiting this long—" he ran a hand across his jaw. His blue eyes were watery, red-rimmed like he'd been up all night reading, or playing Xbox. He was wearing a long coat, unbuttoned, with a jacket underneath and a black t-shirt. Black was probably in an effort to look slimming: the white Nike swoosh strained at the waistline.

"They should at least come out and say something—" From behind the jungle-cubicles came an animal screech, a real animal, not through the PA, loud and sudden. The crowd in line and around the papier-mâché jungle turned en masse toward the sound. Trudy jumped a little, startled by the suddenness and clutched her chest, grinning. She turned back to the dad behind her—*I don't think the alligator wants his picture taken*—when a flutter of something terribly bright and garish even in the neon-lit mall flew wildly up from behind the cubicles, screeching in a repetitive trumpet that made all the people lean back and crouch at the same time.

It was a parrot. Once identified (as not the alligator or leopard or tiger) people laughed and enjoyed the show. The bird flew as high as it could—not very—then dived back down, obviously confused. From the floor there were a series of *oohs* and *ahhs* like at an air show. The bird swooped low over the jungle and a little child screamed. A mother dashed out of line, crouching as though the parrot were a bat, looking up over her shoulder, and made her way to the screaming child (a girl it turned out) and Trudy said, "Oh no, it's *The Birds*." She said it to the man, who didn't get the reference.

The mother crooned to the child, but did not come out of her crouch, instead squatted beside the crying child, who had thrown her hands over her head. Lines of green ink ran from the child's fingers on her left hand to beneath the cuff of her sweater. Green wasn't bad, it wore off; Crayola orange marker stained the flesh for a very long time, the mark of the beast. The mother crooned mostly that it was all right.

It was apparently not.

The bird swooped next over the line of people waiting. There was a group shriek then, and some people in line broke ranks, diving low themselves, hands over their hair. They were not all women. Once the mothers or fathers screamed, the children lost all sense and began bellowing for their parents, running randomly from the centre of the fake jungle to the outskirts as though for the safety of corporate culture Gap Second Cup Suzy Shier Disney. There was still some laughter among the crying, parents feeling foolish after their initial panic, and the new panic of having lost their place in line. The bird flew up to the rafters and perched. Someone said something about *heads up* and *umbrellas* and while they were laughing, they prudently moved up in line, closing the spaces left by the timid. The bird continued to trumpet at intervals. People looked up sympathetically, now concerned for the poor, cageless bird.

People from behind the gate came out in official-looking green bomber jackets with *Wild Kingdom Mobile Safari* embroidered over their pockets. All looking up, not at the crowd at all. A young man stood tentatively half behind and half inside the gate. His left hand was wrapped in a bandage. He looked back over his shoulder a couple of times.

That's when Trudy realized that not all of the howls and animal screeches were coming from the PA system. There was a sudden roar from behind the kid at the gate and he ducked instinctively. The PA cut out suddenly, and all that could be heard was the crying of kids and generic crowd noises, helpfully pointing out the parrot.

Metallic clicks and white noise replaced the piped-in jungle for a moment and then a voice came on, "Good afternoon Shoppers, welcome to the East Fairfax Mall Wild Kingdom Mobile Safari. There will be a slight delay as crews from the Safari prepare for your visit. Please be patient." There was an overall cry of indignation from the crowd. A slight delay? Trudy and Timmy had been waiting an hour.

"Oh, Timmy, it's going to be later still. Why don't we skip this and we'll come next time? Hey? We can go to McDonald's—" She was all for just dragging him out of the line and through the endless mall hallway to (C? D?) where she had parked the Range Rover, but then desperation could be smelled coming off her four-year-old only child (*do you know how much it costs to put a child through school?!*) in waves, heady like fear-sweat.

Timmy yanked on her arm this time, repeatedly, desperately. "Nooooo, please stay? Please stay? *Pleeeee-ssssse?* I wanna stay. I wanna wait. Pullleees?" The commercial had run all week, savvy marketers playing the commercial fifty times between four P.M. and six. Prime kid time. That easy-to-reach after-school crowd: captive, reliant, and with tired, guilty, working parents trying to make supper. They laid it on thick with the wild animals: a fast-cut montage of creatures, constant reminders that you could have your picture taken with an *alligator*! They might as well have told the kids to go get mommy's purse.

Trudy made a feeble attempt at a deep-breathing calming thing that had been the focus of a lunch-hour workshop in natural stress reduction four weeks earlier when someone screamed from behind the cubicles. Something soft but *HUGE* fell to the floor behind them, with an upsetting and primally familiar *ooomph!* Trudy reached down in a smooth motion and picked Timmy up; the two of them stared ahead. A bizarre stillness seemed to settle on the crowd for just a second, like holding a breath. Trudy craned her neck around the people who still stood in line. There was nothing to see, really, but there was this pregnant kind of feeling, of something major happening just beyond view.

Something *roared*.

Then there was screaming. People scattered like ball bearings in all directions. Little kids fell in the wave of bigger bodies scrambling. Shoes clattered on the hard mall floor. For a moment it was impossible to see what had happened, but Trudy backed up, towards the west corner of the centre court, to the Disney/Gap/Tommy Hilfiger triad. She backed into the man who had been standing behind her in the lineup for the Safari. She spun around.

He stared wide-eyed ahead, still as a statue. His little girl had her face pressed into his overcoat and Trudy could see her body shaking in absolute silence.

"What is it—" she began. The man backed up a step, stepping on, nearly over, his little girl and she squealed, but didn't take her face away from his coat, instead buried herself deeper in its folds.

The man sucked breath up, as though he were going to speak, but air just sucked in and out in gasps like a fish. More shrieks and howls joined the wailing of kids, hundreds of people, until it was impossible to tell which was which. The animals behind the cubicles called. There was a clatter of metal behind the jungle walls. Timmy clung tightly to her neck, cutting off the circulation in her arm—he'd gotten much much heavier and Trudy wondered inanely, *When was the last time I carried him?* They spun around to the sound of the clatter, just as the little girl whose Hello Kitty knapsack had been her calling card, screamed from her mother's side.

"TIGGER!" Was what she screamed.

A human cry of pain and terror followed an inhuman cry of rage and power and the glimpse of a green-coated thing sliding? across the floor. Trudy followed its path thinking, *What? Tigger? Disney? Pooh Bear? Can't be Tigger did she say TIGGER?*

Tiger.

The man in the faux cammo coat screamed in agony as the monster, not catlike at all but hugely out of proportion to cats or anything else she'd ever seen—massively out of proportion, monstrous, enormous, a mutant festively coloured and not real—leaped upon the cammo-man and the screams of the crowd mingled with the screams of the man and people ran and ducked and fell and some just lay, playing dead like they taught you to do in the event of a shooting in a public building.

Trudy ran blindly, squeezing Timmy to her, into her. Behind them the cat roared and she heard the squawk of the parrot—or maybe something else, something larger. She ran smashing into children, women, men, a teenager who pushed past her hard saying *excuse me.*

Out of the corner of her eye she caught a glimpse of the hemp-bag lady. She was screaming too, and something the size of a dog was buried in her arm. Her pretty blouse, cropped pants, both were coloured red, the red splashing huge drops as she shook her arm, up and down and still the thing clung.

"*Get off get off get off,*" she shrieked, backing away from it, as if she could.

Trudy pushed past a man who was kicking a raccoon, even as another leaped from the middle of the crowd and landed on him. He did not scream but each movement of his body was punctuated with an *oof!*

People fled into stores, behind displays. Merchandise scattered dangerously around the edges of the centre court. Trudy stepped on something that squeaked. She couldn't see where she was going for the press of bodies until she hit a glass wall. She dragged the two of them along it pressing against bodies that grunted and sobbed and shouted names—*Gloria! over here!* Someone screamed that he dropped his phone. Trudy hit something soft, synthetic. It fell into something solid and the two of them went with it. Her face pushed into the soft plush of a toy, smelling like plastic and gas. When she was able to move her head, she saw the painted face of a doll. Nearly life-size, the sort of toy weekend fathers buy their daughters, garish, bright—

Ariel. *The Little Mermaid.* A big one.

They were in the Disney store. Trudy and Timmy had landed in a pile of stuffed toys. The corner display. There was Woody, Pooh, Ariel.

Trudy laughed. Hysteria, panic, adrenalin all fought over the place in the toy pile.

Disney.

From somewhere beyond her scope of sight there were terrible sounds, clearer somehow than the cacophony of voices: guttural, growling, sometimes worse. She pawed away at the pink softies, the blues, the greens, the lurid reds of the toys they were buried under, they scattered over her head, and pressed into the window. She kept doing it until she could see through the glass.

What she saw: just past the blond fluff that was the top of Timmy's head she saw a single papier-mâché palm tree, still standing. Someone ran past the window, hands raised over his or her head, their mouth open in a shriek, almost cartoon-like. The person hit a patch of something slippery

(blood don't say it, don't think it, blood)

and went down. The chasing-thing rose on hind legs and then dropped out of view.

A bear. Trudy thought it might have been a bear. She turned away.

This isn't happening. This is the petty zoo. Saturday. Forty-eight hours of uncompromised quality time. Timmy had not let go of her neck. Trudy was almost on top of him.

"Timmy, let go," she grunted. Her voice was muffled by the toys. Under the screaming and weeping, Elton John sang over the store PA. "Hakuna Matata," from *The Lion King*. They had it at home.

"Tims, we're in a store now. We're safe—look—it's the Disney Store."

Timmy wouldn't take his head out of her neck. He had been silent. His hand clutched her wrist, digging her watchband into the soft flesh. She realized that she had lost a shoe, her bare foot resting on one of the plush toys. Her mind stumbled over thoughts fast, like: the wristband and the fluorescent lights and the bump and press of other bodies as they tumbled into the pile of soft toys and rolled off or jumped away.

Trudy tried to slow her breathing, tried to calm herself to calm him.

Hakuna Matata

She dug her hand out from under a huge stuffed Lightning McQueen, one shiny headlamp eye staring cheerily up at her, the other buried somewhere under her neck. She brought her hand up to her baby's neck and stroked. Around them were the shouts and cries of chaos, the crash and clatter of things that fell and the grotesque wild call of animals.

"It's going to be okay . . . we're in a store. We're in Disney," she said. She laugh-sobbed, "Nothing bad can happen in Disney—"

A flash of orange and an ungodly sound and then
Tigger?
was upon them.

Night Beach

The beach had been deserted the four or five times she'd been down there. When she mentioned this to the lady at the store, she said, "Oh, you really have to go at night. It's a night beach."

A dirty patch on her breast was embroidered with *Sylvia*, but there was a look of the second hand to the smock. Her husband, a great hairy man who reminded Laura of an uncle she used to like, shot *Sylvia* a look, a quick one. Not too nice, maybe. The woman stared him down.

"What?" the lady finally said. He shook his head and disappeared into the back of the store, saying nothing.

Laura bought the city paper, a carton of milk for her coffee and a package of hot dogs. She added a candy bar while she watched the woman punch in her purchases on an old-fashioned, manual cash register. The store was utterly deserted, as it had been each time Laura had been there.

The woman gave her the total. While Laura dug in her purse for the money the woman leaned on the counter and said, "Yup, lots of people on that beach at night. Gets real lit up if there's a moon," she said. She watched Laura steadily as she spoke.

"Oh," she said, because it seemed to need something.

"Are you enjoying our little town?"

Laura stared into her purse, not quite sure what to say to such a thing. She wasn't enjoying anything these days, and the town, she decided, was a little creepy. It was empty all the time. It was the beginning of July, beach season, and the town was less than a mile from one of the country's "The Ten Most Beautiful Beaches." The main road ran along the rugged shoreline of the rest of the lake, with tiny little coves dotted here and there. In spite of this, the place was dead.

Laura's cabin was about a city block from one of the little coves and she'd been down there a handful of times. It was always empty. One day she shared the beach for a full afternoon with a big black dog that ran in and out of the water, barking. He'd run about ten feet in—to where the water would just be touching the underside of his belly—bark madly for about thirty seconds, and then run back out, looping the cove for a few minutes, and then back in. No owner had shown up to take him away, no one had called for him. It had been surreal. Her only company.

"It's very quiet," Laura said, because to say otherwise would be impolite. And she wasn't sure if it was the town, or her own circumstances. She wasn't sure she would enjoy anything for a while. Not even St. Kitts.

(He'd taken her to St. Kitts one year, on a conference. She'd had to spend the whole time in the hotel, going out only when it was dark so that no one saw them.)

The man returned from the back. He loaded some things onto shelves behind the counter, eyeing his wife. She ignored him. To Laura he said, "You have to be careful swimming. There's an undertow."

This annoyed the woman and she snapped. "There's no undertow. For chrissakes Bernie, don't scare the girl from the water." He looked chastened. He allowed himself one glance at Laura and then went back to stacking.

"We need bodies on the beach," she said to Laura, more kindly. "Don't listen to him. You go swimming. Try that West Beach. It's a good beach. It's a night beach."

The woman put Laura's few things in a plastic bag with the logo from a famous toy store on the side and handed it across to her. The store was shabby, with a fine and invisible layer of failure over everything. The meat counter was empty and used to store things still in boxes, with anonymous names stamped on the outside. Handwritten across the side of one box was *Mephist* and the rest was hidden behind its neighbour, on another she could clearly read (*362 Belisle Street No COD!*). The printing angled off until the final D was only about a half inch high. A file folder blew open and closed with the rotation of a small fan. The papers inside fluttered like the gills of a fish, as if it was breathing.

The place smelled funny. Like an old auntie's bedroom.

"It's better at night," the woman added as Laura nodded her goodbye.

"Excuse me?"

"The West Beach. It's better at night. Go tomorrow," she turned her head, looking out the big, grimy window at the side of the store. "There's a moon."

It was just after ten A.M.

The store was at the other end of town from where Laura was staying. It was nestled in a short strip of businesses, most of which were boarded up, as though waiting for clientele to decide on opening day. The hot dog stand was open and as Laura passed by, a tall man ducked his head in a nod and watched her walk. She waved and smiled a greeting. He didn't wave back.

The main drag—such as it was—was barren. Farther down, heat waved up off the concrete in front of the mini-arcade, and distantly she could hear the ping and click of the games as they played themselves. A single car was parked outside the arcade, coated in dust from the gravel road into town.

The place should be packed. But it wasn't, the whole thing was downright creepy, and completely deserted.

Laura hadn't come to the beach for a party, regardless of what the woman at the store thought, she was not looking for a busy beach. The main beach was close enough to walk if you had nothing else to do with your day—and she didn't—and had she wanted loud company, that would have been the place to go. It was unofficially, strictly regulated: the body beautiful, the young and tanned, occupied the middle section of the beach. The east side beach was for the campers and families and the guy at the beach stand that sold drinks and dogs (that was the name of it, in fact: *Drinks 'n' Dogs*) said the water was warmer on that side from the kids peeing in it. The west side was where Laura had sat the day she'd gone. It was mostly old people who didn't want to walk far from the boardwalk and didn't mind sitting near the rocks.

She belonged in the middle group, but had her fill of sexual heat and innuendo. Maybe forever.

The week before her holidays Tom had walked past her desk and given her the signal, a casual tap on the cubicle wall as he passed. Ten minutes later she met him in the coffee room and as they poured coffee he leaned close to her ear—reaching for the sugar—and told her that he couldn't see her anymore. It was because of his wife, he told her. She was suspicious.

"But you know, maybe we can meet up once in a while at the hotel. See ya, kiddo," and then he did the worst thing, the very *worst* thing he could have done, ever. He slapped her on the back. *Good knowing ya. Don't take any wooden nickels. Catch you on the flip side. Sayonara. Toodle-oo.*

See ya, Kiddo.

For two years her life had been about secrets and sex and love. (On her part; bravely, boldly she had told him on a trip to Bemidji that he didn't have to love her! She had enough love for them both! Darling!)

When she got back to her desk she looked up beach rentals on the net and called this one sight unseen. After all, she could cry anywhere.

It was the worst thing that he'd done, in a list of worst things that could go all the way back to the fact that he was cheating on a wife whom he had three small boys with, a woman whom he had also taken to St. Kitts, she found out later.

Kiddo. Really? *Kiddo*?

It was the worst thing he'd done. But not the worst thing *she'd* done.

That would be the packet and photos.

The cottage was about seventy years old. There was electricity, but it was without plumbing. She hauled water from the city and it wasn't as bad as she had thought it might be and was just preoccupied enough for the extra, unfamiliar chore, to be a distraction. There was an old back house at the end of the yard, abutting onto an overgrown, unlit pathway and that was the bad part.

At night she used a flashlight. There was a powerful yard light over the back door and she kept it on all night long. But when she had to use the outhouse, rather than make the trip easier, it simply deepened the shadows in the yard. The flashlight was used to dispel those. While she wished she hadn't been quite so impulsive, it was not that bad. Laura read during the day, a lot of light stuff, suitable for the beach, the sort of thing that occupied only enough of her mind to keep her from crying all day. It was a lot of John Grisham and Sue Kellerman. She would read a paragraph or two and then stare into space until she was crying hopelessly; then she would blow her nose, dry her eyes and go back to the book. That cycle took about a half an hour, and so were her days filled.

She'd taken a lot of walks.

The road in front of the cottage ran alongside the shoreline that was the fat cousin of the *Ten-Best* beach. The shore was at the bottom of a steep drop-off, carefully secured by an eyesore, a clumsy metal guardrail, but there was a nice view from the road. And you could always hear the water. Wild waves smashed against enormous rocks the colour of slate when they were wet and even during low tide when the water lapped instead of pummelled, it sounded violent and discouraging like tight knots of teenagers at the 7-Eleven. The sound was always there, low and growling or as loud as highway sounds, but always there, under everything else.

Laura would walk the full length of the road, a good long walk that took the better part of an hour, and if she was hot and sweaty, or not quite ready to go back and face the routine tears of Mr. Grisham and the incredible lightness of reading, then she would slip down the steep incline and wander along the rocks up to the far end, where the rocks ended briefly and there was a small patch of blond sand. The west beach.

It was always empty.

She would wear her bathing suit and carry a towel, but never went in past her knees. She'd sit an hour or so on the coarse sand, staring out as far as the water went—and you couldn't see where the water ended on the other side; it was all grey water and blue sky, forever.

It was as if she *thought* she went in. Like trying to remember if something happened on a Tuesday or a Wednesday, the final outcome not really important.

Then she would head back and try to do something.

In the mornings she went for supplies, if she needed something, or if she wanted something. A candy bar, a newspaper. The store sold no magazines, the woman said it wasn't worth the effort to bring them in, because folks brought them from the city. But both papers were there every day and the first two days Laura was at the beach, she bought both papers and did the crossword puzzles in both, and the Jumble.

The days were long, and sometimes, if she had to, she went for two-three-four walks. The second night in the little cottage she decided around ten P.M. to take a walk through the town.

It had been disturbing.

The town itself was completely motionless. The night had been breezeless, the moon reflecting off the water in little white lashes, like the flick of a cat's tail, there, then gone. The water lapped against the rocks in little gasping breaths. But for the length of her walk, she saw no people outside, no lawn chairs parked to face the lake, no cars on the road.

Sound carried, however, and she could hear people laughing and the low jumbled hum of voices or radios, maybe coming from the campground, maybe from across the lake, where at night you could see a single light burning, no bigger than a star in the sky. (She liked to think it was a lighthouse, but knew it wasn't; she asked the woman at the store the next morning and she told her it was the yard light from a John Deere dealership.)

Laura hadn't walked long that night. Instead she'd gone back to her little cottage, glad to see its light through the front curtains, circa 1949. She poured herself a glass of wine and let it warm her to sleep.

The day had been a restless one. She'd walked down to the beach again, and it was deserted, although as she was leaving a tired-looking woman with a small boy showed up, him scrambling down the sandy hill with a towel around his neck, her pulling up the rear with less enthusiasm. They'd shared a wan smile each before the woman suddenly shouted, "*Johnny!* Take your *damn* sandals off!" startling Laura so badly, she actually jumped.

She'd gone home and finished the Grisham, starting on a Laurel K. Hamilton, but put it down when the words started swimming in front of her eyes. She ate one of the hot dogs she'd bought at the store, raw, and then out of guilt made herself a small salad with the limp works she'd brought from the city. She dressed it up with the last glass of wine in the bottle and it seemed like she might be feeling (starting to feel) a little bit better. At some point through dinner she realized she hadn't thought about Tom—

or that horrible other thing

—all day. She convinced herself that she really was feeling better.

After the wine, she fell asleep on the sofa. She slept for hours. In self-defence.

Laura woke hours later, fighting some demon she could no longer remember. The room was dark and she realized she'd slept through the sunset and that it had to be close to ten, for the room to be so dark. Beside her on the coffee table were the remains of supper, a few pieces of lazy lettuce drowning in Italian dressing, fork-knife-napkin a crumpled package and her empty glass. It was disorienting. Her first thought was panicked—she'd slept too long! She would never be able to get through the night! She could *not deal* with another sleepless night!

The curtains were drawn against the sun, an attempt to keep the cottage cool, in vain. She was sweaty and hot, unsure of the time. Laura pulled herself to sitting and peered through the tiny crack in the curtains, seeing only the night.

Tomorrow his wife will get the package, was what she thought once fully awake. The thought made her stomach tighten and her face hot. If she'd been an excitable girl, she would have felt her heart pounding like in a bad novel. She thought about that scene in *Psycho*, when Janet Leigh looks at the money in the envelope.

It was like that, except that there was no money in the envelope, just some photographs that would damn Tom to hell forever.

But her, too.

And his wife.

Oh god, his poor wife.

Laura had only ever seen her in the flesh twice, both times viewed through hair hung over her face as though the woman would take one look and somehow know. *You! You there!* The wife (Betty, her name was Betty) was lovely, in an older woman sort of way, with blonde hair carefully dyed and a figure kept trim. At the time Laura hadn't spent her time thinking those things, although she'd viewed her critically and judged her fairly on her shape, comportment and fashion sense, none of which had she come up short on. She was a good-looking woman for all her fifty years, and could have passed for less.

What she really remembered was her laugh.

The wife (Betty? *Betty*) had dropped by to pick up Tom for lunch. He hadn't warned Laura at all, so perhaps it had been a surprise. (That was what she had told herself and she'd never had the heart to ask, didn't want to hear that it wasn't a surprise, didn't want to hear about little domestic intimacies such as dropping by to take your husband for lunch.) Betty was, of course, well known in the office, Tom being a senior vice. As she made her way through the office she paused to chat with other senior people, and at each desk had laughed or made someone else laugh, as though she hadn't a care in the world, as though—and at the time this was a fact, Laura would have staked her life on it, really truly—her husband wasn't about to turn her in for a younger model (specifically, Laura). She'd moved swiftly past Laura's cubicle, without knowledge, and had stopped in the broad hallway not fifty paces from Laura's chair and talked to Mr. Devereaux, another senior vice. Her perfume lingered.

Anaïs.

Or Chanel. Something like that. Soft. Probably expensive.

Her laugh had been the laugh of a bright and funny woman, empowered and pleased with her place in the universe. Someone's wife.

(Except she was more than that and Laura didn't like to think about it, but she was the director of marketing at some upscale pharmaceutical downtown. And the mother to Tom's sons.)

The second time she saw her was by accident, coming out of the building at the end of the day, walking with Janine and them, happy the day was over, and she saw the wife (Betty, her name is Betty) in the car. Tom's car. A car she'd had sex in, with a pearl rosary that danced from the rear view mirror with every thrust. The woman was sitting in the driver's side, her head resting lightly on the headrest, blonde hair slightly mussed, otherwise perfect in a little beige suit. Laura had been wearing a too-short skirt with a blouse that had a Peter Pan collar—in the morning she'd felt it whimsical and smart, and suddenly it seemed an embarrassing, poor choice, a failure. The wife's (Betty's) eyes had been half-closed, waiting for her husband to leave so they could drive home together, have dinner with their sons, probably watch a little television while the boys did their homework. Later, maybe they'd make love

(Laura knew the underside of the driver's seat most intimately. She could pick the steering wheel out of a line-up, if she had to. Knew the markings and odd stains on the floor mat on that side. She'd viewed it all a lot of times, her head in Tom's lap.)

The wife hadn't seen her. And if she had, would it have made a difference? An office girl among four others.

It would make a difference after tomorrow.

Laura had done one other thing after spontaneously booking her two weeks at the beach, renting a cottage sight unseen. She had sat down at her computer and very carefully, using her daybook when she had to, compiled a list of dates.

Trysts, rendezvous, assignations. When she could, she supplied snaps for visual backup. *Do you remember the conference the company had in Miami, Mrs. Freeman?* The photo was a selfie of the two of them on the balcony of the hotel, *snap*; the two of them cuddled close and grinning lovers' grins. *Snap.* Because that photo could have been a friendly shot of two people during an office conference on business, she also supplied another—a shot of Tom coming out of the shower, laughing, a towel dangling just in front, conspicuously casually. *Snap.*

Mrs. Freeman, the trip to Saratoga Springs wasn't "no wives." A snap of the two of them taken by a waiter in another hotel, the second night of the conference. (She'd spent the day cooped up in the hotel and refused to have sex with him until he took her out; she didn't put that in the letter.)

I went with him on the Merchant junket.

Here we are at Niagara Falls.

Check his credit card statement for August of last year. He brought me a pair of earrings from Arizona. Real jade.

But the worst one, the very worst one, was the picture of Tom making a kissy face to her. A day trip to Rochester. In their car, the rosary swinging with the motion of the car, just slightly out of focus.

Oh god.

She hadn't intended to do anything with the list, not really, hadn't thought beyond the statement of it, made to herself a sort of reckoning of their time together. But still, she printed it off her computer and folded it neatly into three parts, carefully placing the snaps—her snaps—of the two of them, or just of him, into the middle of the folds. She'd addressed the envelope.

Betty Freeman.

Personal and Confidential.

And like Janet Leigh, had simply stuck the list in the envelope and walked away.

Thing was, after writing it all out like that—it had taken most of the afternoon, what with doing her regular work at the same time and switching screens whenever someone of note moved past her cubicle— she had been spent. There had been no *after*. The after had been much like the after from sex, when you no longer feel the need. Few things are as over as sex, that way.

Except maybe writing an incriminating letter to your ex-lover's wife and adding a few snaps to make it all real.

She'd put the envelope somewhere on her desk and gathered her things up to leave for the day. Her heart at the time was pounding and she ached in every joint, like an old woman. Her stomach hurt. Mary Ellen had asked her about her plans for the evening and she'd said something about Lean Cuisine. The two of them had walked to the elevator. Susie showed up and said it was raining. The three of them left the building with their sweaters over their hair, handbags lofted in the air like flags.

The letter on her desk.

Mail room picked it up around seven. Of course.

There was no way she could stay in the cottage and brood about the facts any longer. It was very late by then, but there would be no sleep. There would be nothing but great black holes of guilt and the horrible twisting of her stomach, her body getting hot and obvious every time she allowed herself to think.

She would be fired, of course. And while she didn't sign the letter, her face was in most of the pictures. She didn't think for a minute that the wife (Betty) would remember her from office visits or from the street, or even from the annual end-of-year, lame company get-togethers. But she would make it her business to find out who she was.

And she would be fired.

It wasn't even car payments, rent, VISA; it was two years building some kind of job equity. A reference. Getting another job.

(also car payments VISA rent)

There were times when she could hardly breathe.

The night was utterly silent. The few cottages that were occupied had lights on inside, but she swore she didn't see anyone in chairs, no blue glow from portable televisions, no one casually strolling to the kitchen. The cottages that were unoccupied had looked lonely and sad in the daytime, but in the night without the sun shining over them, they seemed more sinister, more desperate for human company. Or company of any sort.

He, of course, *he* would be punished for nothing. The company would never know. It was unlikely she (Betty, her name is Betty) would leave him—they had small children, a life together. Instead, it would just eat away at their marriage until everything she said to him had an ugly edge to it, until eventually that would just be the way they communicated and their little boys would grow up hearing that loveless, pained and angry tone and in some kind of cosmic circle, probably cheat on their wives because of it. That's how it had worked in her family.

Laura kept her eyes forward and followed the road. Even if there turned out to be no one on the beach, the beach was familiar enough. The walk was twenty minutes of her time.

She remembered what the woman at the store had told her—that west beach was a night beach. A night beach. It was a strange idea that didn't matter anyway, but it did mean that there might be other voices there, that could drown out the horrible in her head.

Even focusing on the road, watching the light play between streetlamps and the way the moon looked on the water, the way it shimmered there, jumping from swell to swell, she still couldn't quite shake the feeling that she was somehow obvious. There was a book in high school, by some dead author that she hadn't liked much—*Silas Marner? The one with Heathcliff?*—where the woman was marked for her adultery with a big A on her chest. She felt like that: as though you could tell by looking at her, not only that she had sinned, but that she had *told*.

Maybe they would get a divorce. It wasn't like someone like her (Betty) needed the rent money.

It took a moment for Laura to recognize voices, as she got closer to the beach. She was used to hearing sound coming over the lake, and at first she thought it was that. As she got closer to the west beach, she realized the voices were closer. She pulled her cover-up a little tighter around her—feeling suddenly shy—and shifted her bag to her other arm. Other than the people at the store, she hadn't spoken to a single soul since she'd arrived.

(Once, they'd walked with a bag and picnic lunch. Out of town, of course. She'd brought what she thought was a lovely surprise.

Laura, what's this?

It's a bottle of wine. For later.

We're at Martha's Vineyard, for chrissakes.

Oh.

He'd rolled his eyes, but said it was cute. She suspected he was lying.

Probably tomorrow she wouldn't seem quite so young-dumb-silly and that was maybe the only good thing but at too large a cost. *See ya, Kiddo.*)

She rounded the corner and fumbled only briefly in the dark for the path. Down below there was definitely the low rumble of voices.

It didn't seem at all like the beach she had visited during the day. In the dark, the beach seemed to glow, the full moon on the fair sand, the lights on the water. Light seemed to come from everywhere, and she realized that the lone streetlamp at the top of the path filtered down to where there were a dozen or more people on the normally deserted sand.

At the bottom of the path, the black dog from days earlier bounded up to her. He barked loudly, startling her, his tail wagging. He leaned low and jumped up on his paws before rounding in his loop, heading back towards the water. She laughed nervously.

A young man saw her and smiled. "Hey," he said. He held out his hand to help her over the few large rocks that cluttered the last couple of feet to the beach. She took it, laughing self-consciously.

"Is that your dog?" she said.

He shook his head. "His name is Rider." He pointed to the water where the dog had run. There were people in the water, most of them having waded in only up to their knees or so.

"The water's pretty cold," he said.

He wore a half wetsuit, the sort that people wore when they surfed or dived. He was young, about her age. Handsome in a beach sort of way, with sandy hair and a tan, even in the dark.

"Are you surfing?" she said.

He shook his head. "Lost my board. Just a boogie board. Might look for it later." He shrugged. He nodded at her, almost formally. "Welcome," he said. And then he turned and jogged back to the water's edge.

Rider barked, and no one paid much attention.

It was almost like a party.

People milled about and spoke in low tones, as seemed fitting for the hour. It had an elegance to it, and a kind of beauty. But it was an odd assortment of people. There seemed to be no fixed groups, everyone mingled together. Laura wondered who was with who, but didn't ask.

She chatted with a girl from the city who wasn't dressed for the beach, in fancy capri pants and a top with shimmery threads through it, like the water. Another girl, Jessie, was dressed similarly. She had been at a party, she told Laura. A set of car keys dangled from one pretty, manicured hand. Her words were a little bit slurred and Laura wondered if she had been drinking. Now and then the girl jangled the keys. Laura asked her if they were staying in town, and the girl looked confused.

"I don't think so," she said. For a brief second her expression was very confused, her forehead bunched. It didn't last and she brightened up and said, "I *love* this song! Don't you love this song? I'm going to crank it!" She jumped happily and ran down to the water.

Except there was no song, no music played and Laura decided that the girl was drunk.

It was chillier by the water than on the cliff road. The wind came up across the water and you could feel it. She shivered under her cover-up.

The water's edge was definitely where the action was. Standing around in the shore was an old guy, about fifty, with an enormous gut, smoking a cigar; a lady with a little kid, who kept pulling off her water wings, protesting when her mother kept tugging them back on; the guy who lost his boogie board; an extremely attractive couple wearing nothing but their bathing suits in spite of the chill, walked hand in hand up and down the beach. Laura caught a little of what they were saying as they passed.

"—up to sixty—" he said.

"—it's too fast—" she said.

"Are you going in?" a woman who said her name was Ramona asked. Ramona was in her thirties somewhere. She was in shorts and a t-shirt. The picture on the t-shirt was of a psychedelic swirl with "Sock It to Me!" in bubble letters.

"Cool shirt," Laura offered. "Is it vintage?"

"Vintage?" Ramona said. She ignored the question. "Are you going in?" She repeated. "I don't think I'll go in again," she added.

On closer inspection, Laura saw that her hair was wet and tangled. A bit of sea plant had worked its way through the tangles. Laura reached up to take it out, but the girl pulled away. "Don't. It's okay. I'll float."

She was talking to a guy named Kevin about charcoal vs. gas. He was quite handsome, explaining that the only way to cook was with charcoal.

"You get a good hot coal going and the steak is smoky. I'm all about coal. Briquettes. Laura, we've all done things we regret."

"Excuse me?"

"Want to go in the water? Just to the edge. Come on, let's go," he said. He reached out as if to put his hand on her arm, but he didn't. His hand hung in the air.

"What did you say about regrets?"

He smiled, and she noticed that his lips were blue with cold. "Come on, let's get in there! The water's beautiful in the dark!" He walked away from her, backwards, to the water, waving his hands playfully, *come on, come on*—

She shook her head. The water didn't look beautiful. It looked vast and dark, the surface as black as the night surrounding them, the moon reflecting a million tiny skeins of light that looked alive, a million tiny snakes slipping under the surf, reappearing somewhere else.

She wandered away when Kevin slipped into the water.

The girl in the sparkly top was beside her then. "I'm going in," she said. For the first time Laura wondered if she was dreaming. She looked the girl over—she wasn't wearing anything that seemed water-friendly.

"In that?" Laura giggled. And she noticed the girl was wearing high-heeled shoes. They were really cute.

"Come on—" she said and dashed for the water. "We're all going in!" Laura watched her run to the edge and then into the water, slipping in up to her knees, almost silently.

Laura moved closer to the water. A lot of people were in there now, more than were left on the beach. She joined a heavy-set woman close to the edge. The water slid gently up on the sand, like a tongue coming out for a lick and then pulling back.

"Hi," she said. The woman looked up blankly. "There seems to be a lot of kids on the beach tonight," she said.

The woman answered slowly. "Are there?" Laura looked around in illustration. A pair played in a few inches of lake not four feet away. Deeper in, a little boy was up to his shoulders.

"Seems kind of late."

"Never too late for a swim," the woman said. "I'm going now. You should come."

She walked to the water, and didn't stop, up to her knees, then the bottom of her black suit, then up to her belly, then her chest. Laura watched her do this, watched until the woman turned back and stared at Laura intently.

Laura was alone on the beach. Everyone was in the water. They all had turned to look at her.

(*seems kinda late for kids*)

"It's good water," said the man with the big belly and the cigar. He was still smoking it.

The dog—Rider—jumped in the water near them. Barking. He swam around the attractive couple who were holding hands, knee deep. She could see their mouths moving, but they were just out of hearing distance. If she was a lip reader, she bet she would read *too fast!* on the woman's lips. There were a few people farther out, bobbing. It all looked so inviting.

From out in the surf a man she didn't recognize waved. "Laura!" he shouted. "Come on in! Get yourself wet!" He waved again when he caught her eye.

They were all looking at her.

Laura. Laura.

They knew. She looked in their faces and thought they knew all about her, every moment of her life, from how she cried the first day of school to what she wore to prom to the moment she sealed the envelope with the damning photos, to be sent to a woman she did not even know to destroy a family not because she cared but because she was angry.

Kiddo.

"Come on in, Laura—" It was the woman with the black bathing suit. Rider was at her left shoulder, floating in the water, tongue lolling out.

She had to. She could feel the cool sand under her feet, the occasional pebble that hurt. She wasn't dreaming.

The water was cold and her skin puckered with it immediately, but not in an unpleasant way. Kevin waded in, closer to her. His hair was wet. His arms were wrapped around his middle.

"Deeper," he said. It seemed, almost, like a dare.

She waded in to her knees and then, the water lapping up over her thighs, she dived. It was smooth and clean-feeling and she wondered how it would feel on her naked breasts. It was good to finally be in the water. She kept her head under for a few strokes of her arms, letting the water rush over her, under her. It was good, clean. Cleansing.

She swam, for want of a better purpose, out to the man who had waved, then stopped, felt around for the bottom and stood. The water was just over her breasts. Her skin had goose-bumped, but the water was warm by then. Nice.

"Hi," she said to the man. He was a full foot higher in the water than she was.

The man grinned at her.

"Welcome to the water." he said, and she had just enough time to look confused. They stared. Mouths moved without sound.

Stay.

Her hair clung uncomfortably to her head and neck in great wet clumps. She dipped her head backwards into the water, submerging for the first time, the world around her going silent. Water slipped into her ears, around the soft curves of her face, it slid over her breasts and thighs with the tide and with the motion of her hands. As her eyes closed she could almost remember the way his hands felt on her, the way he would squeeze her thigh and then stick his hand up under her skirt, as if that were foreplay.

It hadn't even been worth it for that.

Laura opened her eyes to look up at the sky. The night was clear and there were so many stars it looked fake. The moon was so bright, you could see it in every ripple in the water.

It was cold. Her teeth started to chatter.

"I'm so cold—" she said, and turned to her right. The man was gone. She swung her head the other way, and there was no one there. "Hey—" Laura spun herself awkwardly around in the water, treading with her hands, kicking with her feet. Panic rose with confusion. Had she drifted out past the others? All around her was black water, the moon glinting off small waves like winking eyes.

"HEY!" she called. There was no one. She could see the streetlight beyond the path. The beach was deserted. Laura tipped herself forward and began a jerky front crawl in that direction, her arms already tired from treading water. She made little progress, fighting the tide, and rising panic. When she gained a few feet she stopped, and caught her breath.

"Hey!" she tried again. Her own voice echoed back to her from all sides.

The water was so black. Laura leaned into the water again, and tried to swim. Her feet splashed with every kick, the big muscle in her thigh cramping. She barely kept pace with the tide. Her arms weakened, exhausted. Her lungs ached.

Then one kicking foot hit sand. She groaned with relief and stopped, standing on tip toes, her feet digging into the floor of the lake, her head tilted, sucking air into her lungs in great grasping breaths. It was going to be all right.

She pushed herself forward, half-floating, half-walking, ignoring the cold, the ache in her thighs, the sharp sting on her feet from the rocks buried in the sand. When the water was at waist level, she stopped again, to rest.

Laura looked out at the beach, toward the streetlamp for reassurance.

At first, she saw just shadows, backlit by the tall, orangey light. The shadows moved down the path. Light from the moon reached their faces.

Laura waved, and lunged forward through the sandy bottom of the lake. "Hey! Where did—"

They were not the people from the beach. They were old. They struggled on the rock and stared out at the water.

She recognized some of them. The guy from the hot dog stand, Drinks 'n' Dogs. The old couple on the rocky main beach. The woman from the store, who told her to try the west beach. What had she said.

It's more of a night beach.

"What's going on?" she said, close enough to see their expressions. They looked at her oddly. Expectantly.

"It's okay," the man from the hot dog place said. "Just close your eyes. It'll be over fast."

Laura started to ask *what will be over*—

"Gotta do it, sorry to do it. Gotta do it for the town," the woman said. *Sylvia*, that had been on her smock.

"I don't understand," Laura said, but even as she did, even as the panic rose inside her, the line of them, a wall of stone-faced old townies made her stop. *What?*

"There's an undertow," Sylvia's husband said. The water under Laura's feet swelled and retreated, forcing her forward slightly and then pulling her back. First at her ankles, then higher. Calves. She dug her feet in, tried to walk. The water tugged at her thighs, and she stumbled, caught her balance. Her eyes were huge bright circles on her face, lips blue, her mouth a black O open in a scream that echoed back to her over and over.

The water swelled up once more and pulled her under. The last thing she heard was a cascade of voices.

Stay.

The brown-haired girl waited impatiently in line and was beginning to think twice about the two Cokes and big bag of ketchup chips she was holding, but she had the munchies and then her boyfriend came up behind her and ran his hand over her ass. That made it better. The line moved very slowly to the front of the store.

As they got closer, the young couple looked over the meat case. The roast beef looked good, mouth-wateringly so, and so did the corn beef. He whispered in her ear *get a half-pound of corn beef and I'll go get some rye bread* and she watched as the big hairy man dragged out a long roll of bologna for someone and started slicing it on the machine.

By the time she got to the counter there were another half-dozen people behind her in line. She told the hairy guy about the corn beef, first ordering roast beef, and then correcting herself with a giggle. The woman behind the till rolled her eyes.

Act straight! she told herself. She was twenty-one and on her first camping trip without her parents (who would flip if they knew who she was really with).

In an effort to appear older (straight) she said to the woman as she rang up her purchases, "Man! It's so busy in here! Is it like this all summer?"

The woman tucked the girl's corn beef and rye into a second bag so the Cokes didn't crush the bread and said, "Sometimes the summer's slow in starting. But once the first young person comes, it gets much better. That'll be $12.50."

The boyfriend appeared chivalrously from behind and gave the woman a twenty.

"Looks like you could use some help," he said.

"We had some," the woman said and gave him the bags. "Watch while you're swimming. There's an undertow."

THE HUMAN SOCIETY

There were two dogs, and without a drink Dass had trouble remembering their names. His mind was jumpy when he hadn't had a drink. He'd no sooner be trying to remember the name of the black-one-with-the-white-tip (on his tail), than he'd be figuring out a way to get some money. Then he'd be thinking of who he owed money to, and how unlikely it was he would ever pay it back, and then he'd be thinking about all of the places he'd have to avoid going, in order to avoid running into those people, and because some of those places were BARS he'd be thinking about how to get a drink.

But the dogs were important today. He had to take them away. Marnie was going to dry out. She wouldn't go unless someone took care of the dogs (Beachie? Bitchie? Barbie?). He told her he'd take care of it. Just as soon as he could.

She was going off in a cab, but she wanted to see him go with the dogs first.

She had cab money. And him with no drinking money.

"You're not taking them to kill them, are you?" Marnie looked bad. Drink bad. Her hands were shaking so hard she had to take three tries at the lipstick.

"No no no," he said, thinking about the cab money (in her purse, maybe). He wanted so badly to ask her for a couple of bucks for the dogs, you know, but she'd see right through that, and she'd know it would be drunk up by noon. (Sooner, but then without the cab money she would have to take the bus, or get on the horn and start calling around their bum friends for a ride and that might be bad news, bad bad news cause you can't control the car unless you're driving and there were people who'd just as soon drive her right down to Andy's Bar, down the street aways and Marnie was shaking bad enough to say okay; so it would be noon at the soonest.)

The dogs were barking at someone going by. They were always barking. It was a busy street, lots of people home during the day. Dass had fixed the gate up a few weeks earlier (and was damn proud of that work, four nails and a piece of board from the alley, but damn proud just the same—most days just finding the hammer would have been cause for celebration). Course, he'd been drinking that day. Pay day. That was why they had the front door open and the dogs running all over the street. People kept coming over and taking off, leaving the door open. Dogs kept getting out. Barking, scaring the little kid across the street. Kid was bit by a dog when he was barely walking. Scared since, the kid's mom told Dass, all the while angling for a beer.

Dogs liked being outside. Dass left Marnie in the bathroom and he opened the door. They barrelled out past him, the big one (yellow dog) knocking him into the front door. It bounced against the wall and popped him back.

He would've liked a drink.

Sun was out. No snow yet, but coming. Winter was such a stupid, evil bitch, dangerous like acid when a man had to remember his coat and boots and gloves when often he couldn't remember the names of his wife's dogs.

"What the hell's the big one's name," Dass called into the bathroom. "Digger?"

Digger. How the fuckin' hell was he supposed to remember Digger? Especially since he was already Yellow Dog in his mind.

Marnie came out of the bathroom tucking her shirt into her jeans. Her lipstick was more or less straight and she'd combed her hair and pulled it back in a tail. She looked not bad except for the scary look in her eye and he nodded as much to her.

"You're not going to party while I'm gone, are you Dass?'

He groaned and looked away from her, watching the dogs bark and run along the fence at someone walking by. "No," he said into the window. "With what? My good looks?"

You go get straight at a hospital and I'll just get straight here on my own.

Nice fuckin' world.

"And you're going to take the dogs somewhere nice?" He grunted again. She knew fuck all. "You know you can't take care of those dogs on your own."

Then like a cat or something she was right up behind him, her shaky hands on his back. He shook her off. "I'm feeling awful low, Dass. Scared and low."

"Maybe you should take an ambulance," he said. Deferred cost.

"I got my cab money. Is it out there? Did you call it?"

"You get anything else from His Almighty?" She tapped him lightly on the back. He had a feeling that she might have liked to give him a good sock with her fist, but she wasn't feeling up to that.

"You know I don't. You know I'd give you," she said. "I'm sorry. You got any cigarettes?"

"No. You think the bastard would spring for a nice breakfast for you."

Behind him, Marnie restlessly went through things, looking. Looking for cigarettes, looking for money, looking for booze, just looking. There was nowhere new to look. They both did it, all the time. It was their way of pacing.

"No fucking cigarettes," she said. "Nice goodbye." Then she started crying.

The cab came late, reluctant. The driver sat in the car and honked for her. She took her little shopping bag with a change of clothes and her cab money (or maybe it was tucked in her shoe; to his credit, it wasn't like Dass had really, really looked) and waved from the cab. She looked scared and sick. He waved her off and realized he forgot to ask the other dog's name.

By noon Dass was shaking pretty bad. He ran a hand over his wobbling chin a few times, ignoring the beard that was now growing there, no longer just stubble, and did his pacing. He peeked in vases, in drawers, under the rug, pulled the cushions off the sofa, checked inside the zippered sides of the cushions, under the back, under the sofa, under the rug again. The looking itself became a huge distraction, an activity so filled with futile hope that it completely, happily occupied him. He poked in emptied ashtrays, went through Marnie's underwear drawer, in the chocolate box she kept her jewellery in, looked in the medicine chest, in the cutlery drawer, on top of the fridge, gave all the empty beer bottles a shake looking for a sip of something.

He did every room probably twice.

The dogs barked, more lazily by noon. They ate the dried crumbs in their bowls and slurped water from the toilet, and did their own version of the pace. They nosed under the usual places for bits of forgotten food, not realizing or not having to, that they'd been all those places already.

Maybe he could get money for them.

If he had to take care of them anyway he might as well see.

Marnie was damn attached to her dogs.

Shaking bad and feeling sick by one, Dass found a length of rope in the back shed and tied it to the collar of Yellow Dog. He did no better than clothesline for the other one, the black-one-with-the-white-tip (on his tail) and tied it with a half-knot to the collar. It slipped off a couple of times anyway, and he finally just tied the line around the animal's neck and hoped for the best.

The Humane Society was a good twenty blocks from their place.

Marnie'd be eating some kind of lunch by then, he thought. Drying out for two weeks. Shots of stuff, probably to take away the worst of it. Food, bed, heat, people to talk to (about not drinking). Nothing to drink. It was a real toss-up.

Nothing to drink was harsh thinking.

Marnie was attached to those dogs. It was unnatural. They were there before him, even. He could remember (slightly) Yellow Dog sniffing around him. He poured a little beer into a dish for the dog as a way to impress Marnie. They'd laughed like hell when he slurped it up. He wished he had that now. That was the thing about drinks you gave away, you never got them back, and the glow of the generosity faded fast.

"Get some chow, hey boys?" Dass told the dogs periodically. It was cold out, and he tugged the zipper on his jacket all the way to the top. His nose was freezing. He held both leads in one hand and kept the other tucked in his pocket. Without thinking about it, he would do a search once in a while for loose change, through all the pockets. It was comforting, and unconscious.

The dogs pulled him along. Get some chow.

All the months they'd been together, some real bad ones (which was why her brother was sending her off to dry out, nothing to drink, ha ha Marnie, who's your daddy now?) she always fed those animals. She'd scrape up the cash and buy goddamn dog food. Dass had almost hit her once over it, when they were first together, but he never did, of course. He'd never hit a woman. But (in recent memory) that was the closest he'd come.

Sweating with the bad sick, the need-a-goddamn-drink sick, trembling, eyes watering against the cold, smelling in clothes unwashed and unchanged for a while, he pulled the dogs across the street and ignored the people ignoring him from the bus stop with wary eyes.

It was unnatural, the way she was attached to the dogs.

Besides, they could get them back. Wasn't that what the Humane Society did? Wasn't it like a pawn shop, but for dogs. And cats.

The christly things slept with them, for bloody sake. Leaving their dog hairs everywhere. They'd get inside your clothes and itch like the dickens. Get in the food. Eat you out of house and home.

They could get them back in a couple of weeks. Who the hell would want to buy a couple of mangy mutts that barked at every living thing? He'd get some money for them and then have them back lickety-split, before Marnie even knew they'd been gone.

"Get some chow," he muttered, halfway to the dogs.

Dass took the two dogs into the low-bricked building with the small painted sign that didn't exactly scream money, but looked just sleazy enough to remind him of a pawn shop. The door pulled cold air in with him and for a minute all he could smell was dog. It wiped out completely the smell of his own sick-sweat. It was comforting. Homey, even.

Grey hair stuck out over both ears over a fat, florid neck, with the zipper of his brown windbreaker jammed up into it. There was a fresh scab over a long, terrible looking scratch on the top of his bald head and a sore that hadn't quite been healing on his cheek. The two ladies behind the counter looked up when he came in, first at the two barking dogs, and then at him.

That is what they saw.

He saw them see, and he tugged up his pants, self-consciously. He smiled at them, brown teeth poking through grey lips.

"Hi," he said, and was suddenly uncertain as to how to go about it.

The dogs barked.

"Shuddup," he snapped at them.

"Can I help you?" one of the women said.

She stood back from counter, hardly glancing at the dogs and asked the man what he wanted them to do with them.

Dass tried to explain in a roundabout way about Marnie and her "trip," saying she was going out of town (out of this world, off the planet) for a while and couldn't take care of the dogs. He explained for a good five minutes, wrapping words around lies and forgetting which he'd told, truth or lies. He thought at one point he might have said something (thinking he was needing something extra there and not quite being able to put his finger on compassion but remembering something dimly like it, and remarking that Marnie loved those dogs and then calling her poor Marnie and maybe—he hoped not for reasons he also couldn't quite reach—saying something about her giving up the bottle).

"You want us to kennel these dogs?" the woman said. She said dogs like she meant shoes.

Dass was confused. He didn't think that was what he wanted. (What he wanted was a drink). He thought he'd explained it. Apparently he hadn't, and he launched in self-defence into another explanation of Marnie and her love for the dogs and his own inability to care for them. And hit upon what he thought might be the right thing to say.

"Gotta work, you know."

The woman tired and reached under the counter pulling out a long sheet of paper with endless official questions.

"You're surrendering the dogs to the Humane Society, is that right?" she asked without waiting for his answer. She spun the form around so its right side faced Dass. She put a Bic pen on top of the paper.

"Fill out as much of the form as possible—" she said, and turned to the other woman, who throughout the exchange had simply leaned on the counter and watched. She said something to her that Dass didn't quite catch. He stared at the form.

Name, address, the usual shit. He picked up the pen. His hand was shaking very badly by then and he was thinking he was doing a very bad (bad dog thing) thing and no one had yet mentioned money.

His throat was dry. He needed a drink. Couldn't think without a drink. Couldn't fill out the form without a drink. He wished suddenly that he was just home, throwing up into the can, getting on the horn, finding someone with some money. Taking beer bottles in. Looking for beer bottles in the parking lot behind the hotel. Anything. He wished he'd said he'd found the dogs. (Wished he hadn't mentioned Marnie, wished she didn't trust him with the goddamn dogs whose names he couldn't even—)

"This one's Ginger," he said, suddenly. Shook his head. "Digger. Name's Digger. He's a good dog," he added, and petted the head. The other woman was coming around the counter to take them.

Tucker.

"The little one's Tucker," he said. Thought. Tucker. That was it; they called him Fucker when they were happy and drinking.

Marnie. Poor Marnie.

The form sat unfilled on the counter and the woman was holding her hand out for the leads. Dass hesitated.

"Um," he managed.

The two women waited.

"What about some money?" he said, and licked his lips feeling bad about that, but unable to help himself, the need and the dryness and the looking women making him do it.

"It's ten dollars a dog," the woman behind the counter said. Dass relaxed visibly, his heart rising in his throat. (Twenty dollars! twenty dollars! lunch too!)

"It's an administration fee," she said efficiently. The other woman took the clothesline and the yellow nylon rope from Dass's hand even as the words started to work inside his head, even before he became utterly crestfallen even before he had a chance to discard it immediately they don't mean that.

"We'll need cash or cheque—with proper identification, of course— we don't have debit or credit card." the woman said.

The dogs were being led away. They went happily enough, without so much as a goodbye to Dass, the smell of food that he couldn't smell likely heavy in their nostrils like the smell of warm beer in a cardboard carton in from the cold.

Marnie.

I don't have any money. He wasn't sure he said it. So he repeated it. "I don't have any money."

The woman sighed heavily.

"You can take the dogs back with you, sir," she said, but made no move to call the other woman back with them. "Are you able to care for them?"

"I thought—"

From behind a door, dogs yelped and squealed and hollered for release. He thought he recognized Yellow Dog's bark among them. But they all probably sounded the same.

"I thought—"

"We will care for the dogs if you cannot pay the fee. We don't like to—we are a charitable organization, sir. We rely on the donations and administration fees of the people who use our services in order to stay alive," she said, the words heavy with meaning and disapproval, but it was rote, and not necessarily personal. Not any longer. She turned away from him and began shuffling papers, putting a bright orange sticker on each sheet. Letters. The sticker had a picture of a smiling cartoon cat.

"If you could fill out the form, in any case. Any history you know about the dogs, their names and ages—if you don't mind," she said, her back to him.

He picked up the pen, his hand shaking.

Surrender. You want to surrender the dogs to us, is that right?

Was that right? Dass couldn't seem to think. Couldn't remember if that was right at all. Surrender didn't sound right. Not at all.

He wrote Yellow Dog and Butcher for their names. He guessed wildly at ages. He wrote his address and put his and Marnie's name as owners, using her last name, leaving the phone number blank.

"We can get the dogs back?" he said. He looked for a place to put the pen, and there was no place. He thought about sticking it through the narrow coin space in the Humane Society donations can beside the cash register, but it was too small. He poked the pen through the slot a little to test it anyway and the can rattled and shifted sluggishly, fat and heavy with coins and maybe dollar bills. The pen fell off. It rolled off the counter and on to the floor. He ducked to pick it up and just held it.

The can had an orange sticker like the one on the forms, but bigger. There were two dogs on the sticker, a big one and a smaller one, then a cat, tucked nicely between them. Didn't cats and dogs fight? The slot on the top was just the size and shape to fit a folded up dollar bill through. (Or maybe bigger, maybe tens and fives, rich people liked dogs too, didn't they?) He dragged his eyes off the can when the woman started talking again.

"This is not a kennel, sir. You cannot bring animals in and then retrieve them later. If you want them back, there will be fees for their care and feeding, any veterinary bills they might incur, including a standard de-fleaing and bath. Do they have their shots?"

"Yes," he lied. He nodded for emphasis.

"It usually runs to about $80 a dog," she said, and then she looked at him briefly, showing her disapproval. There that'll get ya.

$160. For the two of them.

He nodded, white-faced. Backtracked. "Maybe I should just take them back with me now—" he said. His mouth was so dry, his insides so uncertain that the words came out garbled. But she understood.

"Can you take care of them?" She accused.

The door where the dogs were kept was ice-coloured glass with mesh screen. A heavy door. It sounded like there were thirty-forty dogs back there, all barking, freaking out with the new pair.

"I better take them," he said fast.

"I don't think you're in a position to care for them. Do you have dog food at home?" she fired questions quickly. "You said yourself the primary caregiver of the dogs was going to be away and couldn't help take care of them. Didn't you? You are the dogs' proper owner, aren't you?"

"Yeah. Yup. I better take them," he said.

"Maybe you'd better think about it. If you can't properly care for your animals, they could be seized."

Seized.

"I don't have no $160."

The woman leaned forward and said gently, "We can find proper homes for the dogs, you know. Good homes. They're in good hands here. Maybe you want to think about that."

"Marnie loves those dogs. They sleep with us." She nodded.

"Excuse me," she said, not unkindly. And she disappeared into an office, leaving him standing there.

All his thinking rushed forward on him at once. She didn't seem to be getting the dogs. The dogs were in the back. He thought maybe she was calling the cops. Why why? Why would she do that? There was no reason, but sometimes there wasn't. Maybe security. Would a place like this have security? Maybe big mean dogs they couldn't unload.

Good homes.

Maybe she wasn't even coming back out. Maybe he was dismissed. No she said think about it. Maybe she was leaving him alone with his thoughts.

$160!

And no drink. No smokes even, for a moment like this. He ran dirty hands through his sticky hair and over his stubbly chin and under his neck, scratching his finger on his zipper. No drink no drink no drink no

And no dogs.

Of course he took the bright orange can with the coin (maybe more!) donations from tired fathers and mothers talked into being good homes by little kids. When he had drink in him he'd think better. He'd figure something out.

Truth was, they stole those dogs. Right from under him.

Tucker and Digger. Marnie's boys.

The can rattled all the way to the back of the hotel. He broke it open with a rock, all the time singing in his head Tucker and Digger Tucker and Digger.

Dass's head was full of shadows and fog by then, so rattled with the need for a drink that the actual getting of one was a near-letdown, except for the having it. He drank a full glass right there at the bar and ordered another one—shitty watered-down draft and it tasted like some kind of nectar like they always said. Nectar of the dogs.

Bartender didn't ask him why he was crying at all, just gave him his beer glass, full, golden, icy cold like his fingers and told him to take it to a table.

Their names were Tucker and Digger. Nectar of the dogs.

RECLAMATION ON THE FOREST FLOOR

Shara wondered if the Mac was ruined. The corner was dented as if it had been dropped from a height, like the top of a dining room table. There was blood on the corner that spread across the lid in a delicate spray that reminded her of the Magic Spin Art kit she'd had when she was little. It looked like batik. Groovy.

The Mac was brand new.

Hilary, on the other hand, looked used up and spent. She lay on her left side, arms out in front. She lay on a pile of leaves and forest detritus, where Shara had dragged her. Her eyes were open, staring up at the sky through trees.

There was a dent in her, too. The top right side of her skull was mashed in. Blood made her blonde hair red.

Shara slumped to the ground beside the body, still holding the Mac. She was still shaking. She felt exactly as she did after masturbating, relieved and shameful. In fact, the whole thing was much like that: the exhilaration of arcing her arm over her head and bringing it down, full force, the meeting of force and flesh, and the knee-weakening result.

Leaves and earth clung to Hilary's bare midriff, where the ground had tugged her top up. A single gold leaf and several shapely red ones.

Morus Rubra. Red Mulberry leaves. Kind of rare in Ontario. Some people thought they looked like oak leaves. The *untrained* eye thought that. Shara's eye was quite trained. Wasn't that why they were here in the first place?

She didn't know what to do about the Mac. It was blood-covered. She wondered if it would still even work.

It was shady where she'd dragged Hilary's body, but rays of sunlight cracked the treeline somewhere behind her. It was getting late.

Shara opened the lid and turned on the laptop. It sang awake, popping up a photo of what Shara knew was Hil's favourite flower. *Myosotis.* Forget-me-nots.

"Now your favourite flower should be a lily," she said to the corpse. "See that's a joke, Hil. I do *so* have a sense of humour."

The Mac still worked. She rubbed the blood off as best she could with Hil's skirt hem—a Stella McCartney. Hilary and her mom had made a trip to London that summer to buy school clothes. It was ruined now. But it left a lot of her flesh exposed.

The temperature was cool on the forest floor, Hil's body hidden by overgrown fern and ground cover. Shara heard rustling in the shadows to her right.

She left her like that, in the woods.

Shara had been driving in Hil's car. They'd been sharing the driving, bickering off and on, like sisters, like girls who'd known each other too long to be objective.

I have to pee Hilary had said, right on the heels of *I work just as hard as you do. Why shouldn't I get it?*

She'd said it with that open-mouthed *duh, bitch* that she'd lately picked up using, after summer at tennis camp. Hilary had come back no better at tennis, but with a small tattoo that her mother didn't know about and a snotty attitude.

Shara had spent the summer at study camp, tutoring freaks in science, her first ever paid job.

Her student advisor at the U set it up. Shara had put off the inevitable in a persistent fog of denial for most of the previous year. Tuition had only been half-paid and she was wait-listed for a dorm room. Of course, Hil had invited her to stay with her at the apartment her dad rented for her off-campus. In return she could do Hil's laundry.

(*It's the least I can do* she'd simpered and Shara, remembering all the homework answers and French essays and class notes and assignments she'd given/done for Hil *aw c'mon please Shar-shar-shar you know I'd do it for you*—had thought that it WAS the least she could do for her)

It had all been settled.

I have to pee.

Shara, who was driving, had pulled over; maybe without thinking her eyes scanning the horizon for just this copse of trees. She'd written a paper on the area: *Anomalies in Flora in the Canadian Shield*. She couldn't see what she was looking for from the road, but she stopped very nearly exactly at the spot. And they were talking about The Canadian Shield Award, for Botany. They were both up for it.

I work just as hard as you do, why shouldn't I get it? Anyway, my paper was better.

There were so many answers to that. The thing is, it was about balance. A level playing field. Shara knew that, it was an unspoken agreement. Balance.

Hilary was the pretty one.

Shara had gotten out of the car with Hil and leaned against the passenger side. Hilary had been sorting photos on her Mac. The computer was on her seat.

Hilary had walked about twenty feet into the forest and squatted, her skirt held around her waist.

And then she said—

(with her mouth twisted up into that *duh bitch*—)

—*you're not the only smart one*—

Hilary's paper was not better. Not.

There's a plant genus *Artemisia*—wormwood—that has all sorts of applications and uses in real life, but which is bitter and sometimes even poisonous. Their first year Botany prof had made them put a little on their tongues. Butterflies eat them, jamming their proboscis into the veins of the plant and sucking out the marrow. To the human tongue, however, the taste is repellant regardless of preparation or benefit.

Like poison.

That was what it was like when Hilary said:

You can stay with me in the apartment off-campus

I work as hard as you

My paper was better

Duh

You're not the only smart one—

It all tasted like wormwood.

There had been nothing to say then. There had been no breeze and no traffic—it had been quiet enough that Shara heard Hilary's urine splash on to the Bishop's Weed and ivy.

THINGS WITHERED

What had she even been thinking?

Hil's Mac was brand new with a 17" screen and aluminium casing. Shara reached in through the car window and picked it up. It was surprisingly heavy. Peripherally she saw Hil drop a tissue to the ground, bright white on the brown-green covered earth.

There had a been a snap of panty elastic.

I'm not in love with this skirt I don't even know why I bought it—

Shara saw her life like a single thought in that moment. Not so much a picture as an ugly knowledge, the feel of cancer growing inside you. Nothing good was ever going to happen to her. She was going to be trapped in an ordinary life: no schooling, no money, no future, no boys.

Shara *had* to kill her.

When Hil got close enough Shara brought the Mac down on her head with a godawfulsatisfying *thunk*! And Hil dropped elegantly to the forest floor.

She'd had to do it. It was about balance. One pretty, one smart; one live, one dead.

Shara had dragged her body through the trees, leaves clinging, being pushed aside even as they dropped on both of them from above. Her heels dug shallow furrows into the damp ground. Her head bobbed with every step Shara took. Like the Mac, Hilary was heavier than she looked.

Shara dropped her and she hit the ground, her head lolled to the side a little, like when they posed for photos fooling around at keggers in first year, chin down, eyes wide, head tilted; that was before all of this shit started, before Shara was a thing to be carried, before her father lost everything, before her life was shit and poverty.

They'd vamp for the camera. *Smile! Say . . . Khloe Kardashian!*

The rustling to her right sounded closer; a curious something coming closer to see. It would start with animals, more drawn to Hil as her body putrefied, if it lasted long enough to putrefy. The forest was unforgiving. Fauna, flora, all of it starving.

Most people don't think about it, but an ecosystem is like the human body, with every part having function, every function requiring fuel to operate. The forest floor was a series of systems, intricately involved, consuming whatever fell prey to it, to feed its parts to function, every function requiring fuel.

She left her there like that, for the forest to eat.

Shara parked Hilary's car on the street outside the apartment building. She sat a moment, gathering herself. The building and the street were popular with student renters. The front of the building was lit with a set of spots on either side of the front lobby. *Heathrow*. Everyone called it Deathrow. Funny, that.

Now it was.

They'd always had a system, in case one of them needed the car. Shara put the keys on the top of the tire under the wheel well on the passenger side and left them there.

A girl crossed the street a few yards away, lugging a book bag. She didn't even glance in Shara's direction. Nonetheless, Shara's knees were shaking when she walked across the lot. She made three trips, each time, watching for watchers, dragging up both their luggage, her own laptop as well and the bloody Mac.

On the last trip up, her eyes darted back and forth across the lot, but it was practically deserted. There was a couple standing at the trunk of a car, unloading; two girls dragged wheeled suitcases somewhere. Farther away yet she could see the front of the school. There was a canopy set up, lit with tiny white fairy lights. She could hear faint music. First Days had started, first year students were picking up Welcome packages, and in the quad there would be a mixer. There would be a half dozen activities going on, no one close enough to see her, what she was doing.

Hilary would have been rushing to get there. Wanting to change, to borrow something. She would have coaxed Shara into going. Shara would have gone. Would have spent the evening watching Hil tart around.

No more.

In the hall another girl passed. She looked at Shara a moment, a pause before saying *hello* and passing her on the stairs.

Hello Shara said back, and wondered how it sounded.

When Hil lost her virginity in first year she came to Shara's dorm. *Do I look different? Can you tell?*

That was how she felt as the girl passed her by. She couldn't help it, she looked back at the girl as she swept out the doors, the night air breezing in through the building. It smelled like cut grass and faintly of wood smoke from the quad.

Sweat trailed down her spine and under her arms. Absently she swiped at it, as if an itch.

She'd studied Hil the morning she'd come in to ask *Do I look different?*, studied her for signs of sex and there had been none. *Can't tell at all* she'd said. It would be the same now.

No one would be able to tell.

Her body itched, between her shoulder blades, under her hairline, even between her legs. She was probably covered in bits of leaf and dirt. Hilary didn't exactly drag herself into the woods.

Shara scratched under her hair and headed for her dorm.

Do I look different?

Of course she didn't.

Shara didn't go to the quad, skipped out on the First Days festivities all together. She put Hilary's bags in and around the other bed in the room, as they might be if someone had run in and ran out again without unpacking.

That's what she would say.

"Oh, yeah. She dropped her stuff off and ran out again. I guess she went to First Days," Shara practised it in the mirror. Twice. And then she fell into an exhausted sleep.

She slept heavily, for an hour, waking only once. She woke in the sweaty heat of the room, thinking she'd heard a rustling, and felt a tug, on her foot.

Dream.

"Hey, I know you," said a boy. Shara turned. "You used to study in the library, every night. Last term, right? I'm Donald Keele. I work in the library. I stock shelves." The boy stood beside the registration line, his packet tucked under his arm. Shara stared without recognition.

"It's okay," he said. His cheeks got red. "You hardly looked up from the books. And it paid off. You won that award, didn't you? The big money?"

"It's not been announced yet," she said automatically. She'd been saying it for months. What did Hil say? *They haven't contacted me yet.* As if she was just waiting to hear.

She blinked. Her eyes were dry as sandpaper. A shower and a nap had not refreshed her the way she'd hoped. She'd missed a meeting with her advisor already, but she'd had a terrible time getting out of bed.

She was feeling off; just *off*.

"I bet you will. Me, I'm strictly a C student. I wouldn't know much about prizes," he laughed.

The girl at the table asked her for her student card. Shara gave it to her.

"Oh," Shara said. The boy, Donald, wore his hair longer than Shara normally thought was attractive. His shirt was thin from washing and the collar was fraying. Whether this was student affectation or genuine poverty she couldn't know, but it was disconcerting, distracting. He was a bit hipster for her.

She could smell herself. She had woken to a smell. At first she'd thought it was coming from outside the window, something in the street, dropped and left to spoil. But she could still smell it. She tried, discreetly, to smell herself. The boy was waiting for her to say something else.

"Do you still work at the library?" she asked politely.

"Yup. And the cafeteria in the morning, and I'm a TA for Professor Lange. Philosophy. I'm a Philosophy major." He blushed, as if this were an embarrassing thing. She nodded. She had no electives and so did not take Philosophy.

"Here you are," the girl said.

"A couple of us are going to the Cub for tacos, you should join us," Donald said. The girl at the desk gave Shara a fat envelope and handed her student card back. A space in the small of Shara's back was sore. She rubbed it, closing her eyes. There was a note clipped to her envelope. *See me, P. Duggan.* Her advisor.

"I don't think so," she said. "I have something I have to do."

"Are you okay?"

Do I look different? Can you tell?

She nodded. "Yes, just a little . . ." it trailed off. She was exhausted again. No matter how she slept, she was still dead on her feet. She finished with the registration and went back to the apartment to fall into bed. She didn't call Duggan. Or answer the phone when it rang.

Scrapbook moment: whenever Hilary's mother noted something significant in their lives, she would say, *oh my a scrapbook moment, girls!* The summer previous, when Shara's home had been tense and nervous and filled with sweaty fear, Shara had spent most of her days at Hil's, beside the pool, drinking cosmos and sometimes secretly sneaking a cigarette out of Adonia's stash in the kitchen under the recycling. The first time Adonia caught them, Hil gave her a side-eye and said *bitch please you're not supposed to smoke here* and Adonia just went back into the kitchen. Later they agreed that having something on the housekeeper was a good thing, especially when Hil started sleeping with the guy who came to clean the pool. In Hil's defence, it was practically the only guy they saw all summer.

Boredom and monotony had made them childish and they spent a lot of time looking for the old croquet set, their *NSYNC playing cards for 21, the Spin Magic. They found hardly any of the things they looked for, but they delighted in talking about them, spent whole days doing it. They'd been floating in the pool on their childhood blow-up rafts, Hil's shaped like a shark, Shara on the turtle. Hil's mom had come out of the house and said—

Scrapbook moment! And snapped a photo.

Scrapbook moment: Playing Miss California when they were about ten, California being the apex of glamour to them at ten, and deciding that Shara came in second and Hil first because it was a beauty contest, after all. *You're the smart one,* Hilary had said. Shara agreed. Hilary could be the pretty one if she wanted. At ten, being the smart one was better.

Scrapbook moment: Kevin Murdock kissing Shara at riding, behind the tack shed, and Hilary finding them *he's supposed to be mine* she said, her delicate features twisted into a transparent expression of anger and surprise, at the injustice of it. *I liked him! Cheater cheater—*

More than before, Shara understood that look now, the wide-eyed shock, the fish pout speechlessness, the *unfairness* of trounced expectations.

The Canadian Shield Award for instance, in Botany.

Shara was the smart one.

Scrapbook moment: in the arc between overhead and Hil's skull, when the Mac was on its trajectory, too late to stop, Hil had looked dubiously at Shara and said what sounded like *seriously?*

The memories flickered through Shara's memory like a slide show, the Mac, the pool, *NSYNC 21, Uno, the flare of blood, Hilary's eyes wide open staring up into the canopy of Red Mulberry, leaves stuck to her pale skin—

The pictures flickered and flipped over, fading while Shara fell asleep, now and then scratching absently at a place on her body, her lower back, the soft inside of her thighs, under her arms.

She fell asleep, woke up and fell back to sleep, fitful, noise filtering up into the bedroom from other rooms, the street, feet crunching on leaves, something rustling low in the brush. Sounds.

In the night Shara dreamed she opened her eyes and over her head was purple morning light dappled unevenly and the room smelled very bad, like something dropped and left to spoil, until a breeze blew gently over her and carried the smell away. Hilary's eyes, wide open, stared down at her.

"Something's wrong with my arm," she told the big nurse. There were two nurses, a big one and a little one. The big one wore a name tag. It said University Medical Staff. But the place where her name would be was blank.

"A sprain? Is there swelling?" She reached out and took Shara's left arm gingerly in her hands. She was surprisingly gentle for a large woman, and the surprise of that made Shara feel like crying.

"It's like a rash, I guess," Shara said. She raised her arm up over her head to expose her tricep to the woman. "Here." She ran her hand over the place on her arm where it was so itchy—*one* of the places where it itched, the itch driving her mad—and where it was discoloured.

The nurse squinted and leaned over the counter. She tried to get close and lost patience.

"Come around this side of the counter, please," she said. Shara did. She ran the back of her hand over the flesh that was itchy. The skin felt clammy, maybe even soft, with a scent that reminded her of something.

(pleasant *scrapbook memory* of hikes and camping and the underside of the dock at Providence Bay)

"Don't scratch," came the auto-response from the nurse.

The big nurse looked at her arm. Peered, stared, stroked, prodded, examined and finally stood back and shook her head. She reached into a cupboard and took out a container of wet wipes, yanking one out.

"Lemme see this—" again she was very gentle and looked to Shara once for confirmation that it didn't hurt as she lightly stroked the afflicted underside of her arm with the wipe. It was cool and soothing.

The nurse held it out to show Shara.

"It's green," she said. They looked at it. It was. Green.

"It itches," Shara said. The nurse shrugged and Shara had to go into the little room to wait for the doctor.

Hilary's dad called on the third day. Shara had forgotten that this might happen, her mind on other things

The flies, for instance. The apartment was full of flies.

She stared at the call display number, their name coming up not as J. Peale, her dad, or even E & J. Peale, but the jaunty "The Peales." Of course they were jaunty. Why wouldn't they be? They were also jovial, cheerful and self-satisfied, any number of kindly, happy adjectives.

Why wouldn't they be?

Scrapbook memory: Shara went home from Hilary's house every few days, but only because she had to. On one of those days, she went home and found her mother crying in the kitchen, standing at the new island, the reno so new the range top had yet to be used. Her mother only cooked a couple of times a week. They'd all gotten used to eating out.

What's going on? she asked her mother. She had to say something, even if they weren't really a talky-touchy family like the Peales, always all over each other. The woman was right there, though, crying. She had to say something.

Her mother didn't look at her, but she took her hands off her face. Her face was tearstained. She turned away. Gave her head a little shake.

Shara, Daddy can't pay tuition for next year. You'll have to get a job or transfer to another school, okay? All the words were strung together like a lyric.

And then she went outside through the living room. The patio door squealed open and then shut again. Just like that.

She didn't answer the call from The Peales, but stood there and listened to the message, staring at Hilary's luggage, still piled in front of the bed, as if waiting for her to come and unpack. This would be what she said, if someone asked her.

"Hi Hilsy-Punkin, it's Daddy. Just checking in, we haven't heard from you and your cell is off. I know you're busy sweetheart but just give Mommy and me—"

And so on.

The rash spread along her left side. Shara turned slightly to her right and tried to see it all in the small bathroom mirror, foggy from her shower.

The doctor had gently and carefully talked to her about hygiene before sending her back to the apartment with a sample-sized bottle of hand sanitizer. He told her not to let herself get so preoccupied with school that she forgot to shower and scooted her off with a firm expression and a wave of his hand.

It was moss. Ordinary moss. Garden-variety moss—pardon the pun—*bryophyta.*

That had been a few days earlier. She'd showered and used the sanitizer. Like he'd said.

The moss ran from the soft underside of her arm, down her left side, slightly less in the slope of her waistline, but spreading in a jagged circle over her hip on to the rise of her buttock. It continued down the length of her leg, although she couldn't see it in the mirror, she could see it by looking down. She did not look down just then.

It still had a greenish tinge to it, but if she took a rag and wiped at it, the green came off on the rag and underneath the skin was mottled and discoloured. If she ran her hand over it, it felt soft, spongy.

A fly buzzed around her head, landing and flying off when she swatted at it disinterestedly.

The apartment was full of them. It was the smell.

Donald waved her down in the hall. At very last second Shara thought she would run away, pretend she hadn't seen him, but she was too slow. He grinned, an armload of books leading the way through the scores of students on their way to classes.

"Hey!" he called, waving, but he knew she'd seen him.

She smiled wanly.

Today he wore a suit jacket, something from the secondhand store, she thought, because the lapels were wider than was fashionable. His shirt underneath was crispy-looking, purely white against his pink skin. He was very fair.

"Hi," he said, out of breath. "I thought I might see you in this wing."

She smiled and swallowed. Her mouth and throat seemed full of fluid. "Oh," she said. Again she was at a loss. "Donald," she added.

"Yeah. You remember. I wanted to ask you if you felt like going to the First Days Fair tonight. I want to hear Gibby Chuck play—he used to play for Dizzy Gillespie, back in the day. You like jazz?" He looked at her. Her hair was uncombed and she was wearing dirty jeans and a sweater that had been on the floor for . . . how long? She might have slept in it. She couldn't seem to keep track of things. Her mother used to say such episodes were because her head was "full of flowers," like that scene from Bambi with the skunk. It wasn't far off, this time.

She kept thinking about the woods.

"I don't know," she said. She'd just had a terrible dream.

"I think you would. You wanna go?" She didn't answer.

He said, "The band is new. This is their first tour—"

Hilary had been in her dream.

They had been in the woods. It must have been just at dawn because she remembered the birds were loud, braying, swooping around her head. Hilary would speak, her voice oddly coming from all angles, above, across the big rock, from far away; but Shara wouldn't look at her.

Hilary only said one thing in the whole dream.

Look at me, Shar. Look at me.

"You look like you could use a night out—" Donald said. He stood close and she could feel his body heat. He seemed to vibrate with vitality. She would have liked to lean in and melt against him, extract some of his chlorophyll.

"I have to see my advisor," Shara said. The last message had been for her. *Miss Troit, I expect to see you at 2 pm, and this time your absence indicates—*

"Okay . . . but you'll go?"

Look at me, Shar.

"All right."

"Good." The two of them stood in the hall while the numbers dwindled around them. He stood over her, taller by a foot and a half, his dark hair dangled in his eyes when he looked down at her. His eyes were blue. He was so pleased. She tried to imagine how that would feel. To be pleased.

Shara ached to scratch, all over, but worst between her legs, around her eyes, in the deepest part of her ears, where the itching rash had become something unbearable, something practically living. This morning she had stuck a Q-tip deep in her ear and rubbed it around furiously, hard. It had come out green. It was not Donald's presence that kept her from scratching, but rather an agreement with herself that she was not going to give in to it again.

Green. It had come out green and she recognized the smell.

His mouth was his best feature. His lips were plump and bow-shaped like a baby's.

She'd seen a program on television the other night—a back to school thing with all kinds of experts—and they said student stress was at epidemic levels and caused all kinds of illness, from headaches and rashes to cancer and yeast infections.

It was the stress.

Maybe it was a yeast infection. She imagined tiny grains of yeast multiplying, into so many millions of grains that it was a moving, shifting mass.

"Are you okay?"

"I have a headache." She almost said yeast infection.

"You look a little tired."

"I'm under stress," she said. Her stomach rolled uncomfortably. She put her hand over her mouth, ducking her head forward. Her hair spilled over her face.

He reached out and gently-so-gently, pushed it back. She looked up at him and he was smiling softly at her, with affection and interest.

"Maybe you should crash for an hour, like before I pick you up. I'll pick you up at seven, good?"

She gave him the address, conflicted. Confused by his attention. She had a sudden new feeling in the pit of stomach, heated raw feeling of panic. Like she'd misunderstood the whole lesson and now there was the exam. Where had he been last semester? *I'm not the pretty one.*

Now I'm the pretty one and *the smart one.*

She started to go to Duggan's meeting, but gave up about halfway to the office.

Shara was tired all the time, but didn't sleep. The phone rang so much now, and it wasn't just the Peales. There were other calls, mysterious calls from Out Of Area and Private Number. She didn't answer those. Hil had family everywhere. Everyone was calling Hil.

Her own mom called one night. *Shara it's your mother. Pick up the phone. Shar? Fine. Diana hasn't heard from Hilary either. You two are up to something. Someone give someone a call.*

She fretted about that for a long time.

(Scrapbook moment: her mother screaming at her that it wasn't just about her, they were all suffering over daddy's economic turn-around— *not Hilary she wasn't*)

No matter what she did, the apartment smelled. It was gassy. She was gassy, her stomach stretching over bloated organs. She took Tums but nothing helped for long. Flies had laid eggs somewhere, she suspected, because no matter how many she killed, or shooed out the window, there were always more. They buzzed, so close to her, so close to her ears. The sound of madness she was sure.

Her mind would wander to terrible places. It was the exhaustion. She would think of the forest floor, of the life cycles of bacteria and bugs that reclaimed what fell, for its own. The relentlessness of nature's mood. Of Hilary, slowly dissolving into the woods. The forest was uncompromising.

She tried to clean.

The vacuum was sitting in the middle of the bedroom. It was still plugged in, although Shara had given up trying to keep up with the dirt that seemed to come out of nowhere: soil and twigs and bits of wood rot and leaves. Everywhere. Dragged in, she supposed. But from where? It was always just there.

She would just get it vacuumed and there would be more.

She was losing it.

Look at me, Shara, Hilary had said.

Scrapbook moment: her mother called them into the living room for a family meeting. She said the words as though "family meeting" had been something they'd done always, since their early days of red-checkered-family-picnic-Frisbee-throwing-sing-a-longs. Proof that there'd never been anything like that was in the way the three children sat three abreast on the Montauk while their parents roamed or sat, alternately, the blocking like an Agatha Christie play at the summer theatre.

Things have taken a turn their mother said and she continued in a convoluted, complex series of non-sequiturs, talking one minute about Shara's car insurance and the next about the kitchen cabinets being loose and then to their father's recent bad luck.

Your father's had some bad luck.

Her younger sister Cherie, beside Shara on the sofa, whispered *did you PVR Apprentice?* just as her father spoke for the first time, smoking nervously beside their mother's chair.

I've lost my job he said. Her mother cried.

Shara leaned into her sister and said *No. I forgot.*

Things are going to have to change around here her father said. And they sat like that for a few minutes more, the three kids on the sofa, their dad standing, their mother crying.

Scrapbook moment, as Mrs. Peale would say.

Who wouldn't be stressed after that? The rest of the story came out in dribs and drabs as her grandmother used to say, before giving them $500 for their birthday *you're getting your inheritance in dribs and drabs* ha ha ha.

Three of the six cars were sold, the kids were to share one. Their housekeeper disappeared. The pool went uncleaned. The paper stopped.

There was no money for school. When she finally got the nerve to ask about school her mother threw up her hands and screeched *school? School? I knew you would come at me with school I'm not dealing with this right now can't you see I'm upset—*

It might all have been all right if not for Hilary throwing it all in her face. *You can stay with me at the apartment.*

She was not a charity case. She was the smart one.

Shara belched and wiped spittle off her lips with a tissue. She peeked at it. Yellow-grey matter, with substance and weight. She balled the tissue up and tossed it towards the waste basket by the desk. It missed and landed on the floor.

She sucked up the fluid that seemed to continually pool under her tongue. It was foul, tasting as it smelled, like the shore of Lake Winnipeg in August when everyone was going home.

Doctors Google, Wiki and Yahoo mentioned stress frequently. But also everything else.

The Mac was open on the desk, with numerous opened tabs featuring her symptoms.

With all the mucus

(what she decided was mucus, in spite of its odd colour and texture)

—smell—

because of that, it could be a flu or cold. She did not cough, but her throat and mouth stung with the taste of it. It could be gastrointestinal bugs like a flu or a tapeworm or her period, especially with the bloating.

It could be cancer, of the esophagus, pancreas, lungs, or stomach.

Excessive belching was caused by so very many things.

Clammy, cold hands and feet also had a variety of causes.

(moss no one mentioned moss)

The patches of bubbling flesh that seemed to have sprung up in the last few hours, was a mystery. When she touched them, the flesh was warm, where everywhere else she was cold; and there was something like a pulse beat under there, but not steady. Writhing. Living.

She pulled a sweat shirt on over her jeans to cover up as much of her skin as possible. She was pale. Very pale. She looked *unwell*. Very very *unwell*.

Just before leaving the apartment to meet Donald, she did two things. She closed the lid on the Mac (a tiny bit of blood could still be seen in the seam, if you were looking).

And she brushed red leaves off the bed. They were everywhere. Like the flies.

Dancing in her head over and over, on a loop: *Look at me, Shar.*

Donald slipped an elasticized yellow band around her wrist and shouted over the music into her ear *we missed the first set* but he was grinning when he took her hand and they ploughed through the crowd, all of them eyes forward, heads bouncing, some of them fingers snapping like jazz daddies. The noise was overwhelming/distracting/a blessing, even when a bad thought or two popped up in her head, like thinking how much the bass line sounded like the noise of the Mac making contact with Hil's skull—

—it was fleeting though and Donald's enthusiasm made her both tired and happy. He leaned into her and said something loudly into her ear, but the music covered it up. He laughed, his face close to hers. In the lull between the chorus and verse she heard him shout *the drummer used to go to McGill* his face solemn just briefly at this bit of abutment, then he smiled down at her as he started mouthing the words to the song along with most everyone in the crowd. Shara didn't know the words, but tried the chorus

(throat feeling in pieces with every vibrato)

and felt herself grinning like a madman.

He'd picked her up outside the apartment, getting out to open the door for her and as he came around the car she was embarrassed for her thick jeans and heavy sweatshirt *RTSD Science Camp Counselor 2008*. He wore his other jacket, with the unfashionable narrow lapels and looked handsome.

He seemed shy opening her door and waiting until she got inside.

In the parking lot of A Building where the First Days concert was— jazz, he said it would be like Dizzy Gillespie, except Dizzy was dead like so many people lately—he didn't get out right away but instead touched her hair *I had a crush on you last year. You don't remember. You hardly looked at me, but we talked about plants.*

I remember she said, surprised that she did.

I asked you about belladonna—he laughed. *I was trying to be flip and cool but you said belladonna is an example of god's hand in nature—poison, but that its taste gave you fair warning. I liked that.*

(why didn't you say something last year)

I bet you get the Canadian Shield Award.

Then the car went quiet. He thought she was embarrassed and he tried to make a joke—

But in fact that feeling was back, the unrealized point, a missed message, some kind of impending trip to the Dean. But he touched her hair then and said *what happened to your head*—

The room pulsed like the itching-moving-writhing that seemed to be her body now, inside, in her organs, under her flesh, under her hair. It was distracting and she couldn't get on top of the

Look at me, Shar—

bad memory of the dream. Seemed so real. Hilary's eyes, boring into her *look at me* and she wouldn't couldn't didn't.

Did she? It was hard, now, to remember. She struggled to do that and then Donald was beside her. He took her hand and held it. His hand was warm and hers was so cold. He squeezed it with affection and—

There was a brief moment of clarity when she turned and looked up into his face and thought *big deal about money I can do this*

But seconds later his grin faded. He let go of her. Backed away, surprised.

She stared too *what?*

And the music thumped around them and he raised his hand between them—turned it palm out to show, to see.

He shrieked into the pounding, musical air—and jerked his hand, shaking it, shaking something off—his face twisting into disgust, mouth a grimace, as bits of something scattered around him.

A piece of whatever it was hit the back of a girl in front of them, her blonde hair pulled into a neat tail. The thing stuck there. Lights flashed as people walked back and forth through the stage lights shining from the back of the club and Shara leaned in to peer at what Donald had shaken off his hand.

He shouted something but she couldn't hear it.

The thing on the back of the girl's sweater was a sphinx, a non-sequitur, enigma, puzzlement, poser, entirely illogical.

It was a finger.

She looked down at her hand, in the dark where bodies blocked most of the murky light from the ceiling anyway and turned it over and over and it seemed that maybe—

Some of her hand . . . invisible in the dark. Or gone.

Look at me, Shara.

No one would have heard her scream, not over the music, they were too close to the speakers, but Donald saw her face, the expression and he reached out to her, grabbing her around the arms and just squeezing like you would if you were wanting to help to

—see god's hand in nature—

And through the jersey of her grey sweatshirt, through his fingers, seeped some kind of fluid and she felt a kind of collapse inside herself, inside her arms, to the bone inside her chest. And Donald screamed.

And then the *smell.*

And no one heard him over the music, but around them people twisted toward her, their bodies swivelling in mid-writhe, pretty young faces usually smooth, tortured into grimaces, jerking away from the swollen, sweet-hot, molten stench and over the music there was a collected sound of surprise and repulsion.

When Donald turned away from her in revulsion, Shara pushed her way through the crowd, each and every one of whom turned to look—not at her, but at whatever that horrible—

—smell—

was.

Shara plodded through the parking lot from Building A, screaming, each step a kind of splatting sound, the soft squelch of snails pummelled with rocks, of stepping on Basidiomycota, passing First Days celebrants, most of them already drunk, most of them hardly seeing her, not caring. No one noticed her wake.

The keys were just where she'd left them.

The dream had been so vivid. The scents of the last of the periwinkle, of all the summer dying on the stem, on the vine, shrinking, dying, seeping, melting into rich soil. It was pernicious, that smell.

It filled Hil's car.

Slowly as the student buildings and campus gave way to town, gave way to blank fields and car repair shops and wooden estates, hidden, marked only by reflective numbers on posts, gave way to vast fields of scrub and empty, neatly tilled fall-hardened earth gave way to a twisting gravel road.

And if it was light even on the horizon, she would be able to see a geographical anomaly, a copse of *morus rubra*.

Hilary hadn't even known that.

Shara, now so much closer to the earth, felt that she could smell them. Red Mulberry. They were poisonous.

I work just as hard as you do.

Her pretty, pretty face, always so pretty, grinned and she thought it was funny—she was teasing even if Shara wasn't in the mood for teasing and she said

Maybe I'm the smart one, too.

The moon made everything grey but the leaves of the mulberry were distinctive. She parked and got out of the car. Hilary's car.

And from the road, she peered into the woods, at the figure that stood through a break, and in a clearing, about a hundred metres away. Her skin was pale and soft, a slight tan from tennis camp. There would a perfectly shaped, dark mole in the direct centre between her shoulders. Her hair swept over it most of the time; her eyes were blue.

And she was still the pretty one.

Shara walked towards her, every step wet and near collapse.

Halfway, she could sense Hilary's vitality. Her life.

The two girls stood together under the trees.

"Look at me, Shara," Hilary said.

Shara did. And *saw*.

Shara's reflection lay dead on the soft damp forest floor, and must have for the whole week that had passed. Her flesh was mottled and grey, still bloated slightly through the middle, but internally collapsing into the ground, soft with fallen leaves and twigs and green moss and damp with body fluid.

Hilary stood over her.

"It's about balance," she said. "Now you're dead and I'm alive."

The two girls met eyes. Brains and cranial fluid seeped from Shara's head onto the leaves, her body torpid, flesh pallid and as cool as the ground cover. Just faintly she could smell the moss under her rotting, ending self.

When Hilary got to the apartment, she did two things: she opened the window and shooed out some curious flies. Then she called her dad. She didn't know *what* could have become of Shara. She was such a smart girl.

While the phone rang, she flipped through mail she picked up on the way in.

The Canadian Shield Award for Botany was announced and Hilary did not win. The award was announced and then poor Shara's body was found, in the forest, making it all the more poignant.

Shara's paper won. Reclamation on the Forest Floor in the Canadian Shield.

Hilary was the pretty one.

She erased the history from the Mac. It was nothing she would ever need:

Google

"symptoms" + "rotting flesh"

Domestic Happiness

(with apologies to Stephen King)

Maria is silent as she wipes down the walls in my kitchen. I don't actually watch her do this, I just know that it's her job for the morning: the walls in the kitchen. When I pass through my gleaming hallway, through the living room that smells gently of lemon oil and flowers and into the kitchen— the dishes hiding behind cupboard doors, or in the dishwasher—I smile. She thinks it is at her, and I suppose sometimes it is. But honestly, when I pour my coffee from the gleaming pot, into a brilliant white cup, atop my uncluttered countertop, I know exactly what it's for.

Order.

Good clean order.

When I smile and she sees me, she smiles back. Her eyes are confused, though, even when she smiles, there is always that hesitation, that furrowing of brow. She speaks no English; I think she is afraid I will speak to her and she will have to try to understand.

I don't, even though she gives me *this*. This order. For me, that exchange is profound enough to warrant the silence. There should be silence in the face of, a reverence for, this order that she gives—like the Madonna. Maria. It all makes perfect sense.

Without it, I am at sea. Eyes that should be trained on the page roam rooms for loose pens, unopened mail, threads from clothes I don't remember wearing, curling on carpets like minute snakes. I look for

Sometimes when she smiles at me, she can't help it, her eyes drop down to my left hand, and the missing fingers there. Two: the baby finger and my ring finger. I joke—with those who speak English—that I will never have to marry, because I have no ring finger. In certain rooms it will get a laugh. Maria is Spanish, which probably means she's Catholic. I think she would pity me.

Señora pobre.

She has no idea, of course, how she came to be here, in my home.

I walk through the house on my way back to my office; it smells of lemon and flowers, not dust and chaos. For that I am truly grateful.

Thank you Father (for they have sinned).

Cortario mis dedos para esto. My Spanish is weak. I may be wrong.

I keep my own office. As a result, there is a differing order in there. Books are stacked sometimes on the floor, but neatly, bohemian style, with the titles facing the person who might sit in the soft fat chair in the corner. It's a good chair for reading and there is a lamp above the right side. I tend to lean right when I read, and I read often. I spend nearly all of my time in my office, venturing out into the rest of the house to eat, check the messages that come infrequently on the machine, get the mail that Maria leaves on the table by the door.

The office smells, too, of old body and books, coffee and gum.

Before Maria it was Concepçión and before that, I forget. *La señora es extraña.* They quit.

My friend John says I should marry Maria. He says that not because he believes I am lonely or want a mate, but because he knows what I truly value. He was a great friend of my ex-husband's. He knows how the marriage disintegrated and why; he knows how baffled Raymond still is, even now. Years after the divorce, he sees my contentment and wonders. He wonders if I am a lesbian, but only in self-defence.

I am not anything, actually. I am a sensualist of a sort, but not sapphic or libidinous. I crave and lust for order. All around me I need things to stand to reason. Dishes in cupboards, pillows stacked neatly in a fan, magazines spine side out, toilet lids down, bowls white, blouses hung, t-shirt sleeves folded into the back on the seam, CDs in their cases, jazz, rock, blues separated by gender and then date, food behind doors, lids on pots, handles out, teakettle gleaming, teapot stashed, teabags hidden, television hidden, sofa table one inch from the soft back of the cotton sofa, vacuumed daily, vacuum cord wrapped counterclockwise, nose parallel to the back of the closet, broom not touching.

This is why when I found the ad in the back of Epicurean that said, "Anything You Want," I didn't hesitate. By then Raymond had screamed himself hoarse and left, but the damage had been done; it would have taken me months to sort through his detritus. It made my heart stop. I couldn't swallow. This was infinitely easier.

But it was very expensive. *Anything You Want.*

The ad said, "Anything you want, fees to be negotiated. Some trade negotiable."

So three men came one day, one of them was a doctor, and he cut off two of the fingers on my left hand, with my blessing. Maria showed up the next day, the first Maria, and put things to rights. She comes every day in some form and keeps it all right. Order. So I can think.

What do I care? I am not married. I write for a living, I type with four fingers, only, and my thumb presses the space bar.

I hear the vacuum roar in the living room and I smile. Peace floods over me, bleeding into my scalp, pulling my hair tight. Phantom fingers tap the desk while I wait for words.

I write so much better now.

I ♥ Dogs

Terry ran her hand down Andy's back. His hair was smooth and soft until she got to his tailbone, where it became coarse. Even through the thick hair on his barrelled chest, she could feel the rumbling of his stomach. She repeated the action on his underside and then again, carefully over each of his limbs. The dog stood passively for her as she did this. Other than the rumbling, wet noise in his abdomen, there seemed to be nothing wrong with the dog.

But obviously, something *was* wrong. The room smelled of vomit. For the third morning in a row she had woken to a retching dog and a mess. His stools were loose. His stomach was rumbling.

Her own bedroom was off the dog run. It would smell too, probably. She didn't mind so much lately, probably wouldn't even notice it by the time she went to bed. Elton used to comment if the dogs had made a mess, but Elton hadn't been around in months. Not since Auntie Julie had come to stay. It seemed hard to remember. Three months? He had a good attitude, Elton. When Terry got caught up sometimes, he would tease her. *Life is just moments, til you die, Ter. Just moments.*

Terry sat back on her haunches, at a loss. There'd been no change in diet (although that would be the next step), and while there had been two new dogs in the kennel, they were kept apart from her two. None of them were suffering anyway. She shrugged despairingly and put her hand on the dog's back.

They were normally so healthy and vigorous; she didn't know what to think. So far her Amos showed no signs of tummy trouble. She would wait and see. Terry ran her hands over Andy again, with affection. Playfully he nudged his face under her hand when it got close, in spite of it all.

They were beautiful dogs, her babies, perfect examples of their breed with shining black hair and the barrel chests common to Rottweilers. She didn't like "Rottweiler"; it was too austere and Germanic to describe her dogs. She preferred the more affectionate "Rotties" for her two; it went better with their personalities.

Amos was her little girl, and she looked just like the Rottie *Carl* from the children's books. You could—Terry could—see her smile when she was happy. That happiness was somewhat unpredictable. Andy was the baby, just under two and still puppy-like, although of them both, he had the better temperament. Amos was harder to please.

The two of them scuttled around her on the tile floor in the back room where she'd been keeping them since Julie moved in. Julie was afraid of the dogs.

When Terry stood up to leave, Amos jumped up, her front paws pressed against Terry's shoulders.

"No, no," she said. "Down, Amos!" The dog whined in her throat but dropped to the floor, nails clicking on the tile. She paced around in the circle. Terry mumbled a *good girl* and picked up the bucket that held the stinking water she'd used to mop up the vomit.

Andy panted and sat down in the corner on his bed. In the kitchen they each had a mat. If she needed space or if they got out of hand she said *mat!* and they went. It worked the same with *bed* in their room. But she hadn't said *bed*.

"Big fella? Sore tummy?" Andy panted and grinned and his big brown eyes never left her face. As if he wanted to understand. Amos flopped down beside him.

"I'll take care of it, okay? I'll take care of you. It's okay. S'okay."

Terry latched the small hook and eye closure that separated the dogs from the rest of the house.

"I want coffee," Julie said as soon as she saw Terry.

Terry dumped the contents of the bucket into the bathtub in the trailer and rinsed it out with clean water. She put it away in the cupboard by the back door and put the mop out on the back porch, head up, to air dry.

"I want *coffee*," Julie repeated when Terry came back into view.

"You can't have coffee, Julie. Doctor said."

"Just coffee for me, for Auntie Julie," Julie said.

Terry ran water into the small sink in the kitchen. A few dishes were piled up from the night before, and there were Julie's breakfast dishes: an egg cup, a saucer from an old tea set that she had taken a liking to.

"I can make you a pretty tea. But no coffee," she offered. *Pretty tea* was what they called the raspberry tea Terry kept in the cupboard since Julie had come to live with her. It was red when brewed. Pretty.

"Please? Just coffee for me. For *Julie*."

Terry shook her head. She squeezed soap into the running water. It lathered immediately, clouds of white bubbles. Outside she could hear the neighbour kids playing.

"Julie, coffee upsets your system, remember? Remember what Doctor said?"

The old woman quieted down for a moment, perhaps thinking about what Doctor might have said.

Terry washed the few things there, the saucer, their mugs from the morning, their teacups from the night before. The dog dishes from breakfast.

Across the street the older boy—Damon—was throwing a basketball against the metal pole of their basketball hoop. Each connection made a loud, tinny clang. One—clang—two—clang—three—clang—four—the littlest one, Tristan, yelled at his brother. Something *wasn't fair*. Damon ignored him. He just threw the ball. *Clang.* Until her head ached.

Terry remembered something she wished she hadn't. A silly thing. Nothing. Three months earlier the woman across the street, Damon's mother, Marguerite, had a baby. Terry had wrapped up a small blanket (with a repetitive pattern of two Rotties snuggling, adorable as hell) and a little outfit bought at Sears for $10.95 and dropped it off for them. In a nice bag, on the door. Not to bother them. She'd so far received no thank you card. It was a little thing, a silly thing and it didn't matter. Just once in a while it popped into her head. Marguerite. Margarita. Like the drink. Did her parents name her after the drink?

"I'm older, you have to mind me," Julie said, firmly.

"I'll make you tea." Terry turned away from the sink and wiped her hands on the towel beside the stove. She plugged in the kettle.

"You're mean to me!"

"That's not fair!" Tristan screamed across the lane. "Not fair not fair not fair—"

"Boys!" Terry called through the window all the way across. "How about quit with the banging? Would ya?" At that distance, her voice strained, sounded pressured, hard, unpleasant. She smiled broadly, benignly, in case they could see through the window, and they would see she meant no harm. But they weren't looking. Had they heard her? The ball hit the pole once more and bounced on the driveway.

Damon yelled, "Sorry, Mrs. Bondi."

They'd heard her. She didn't call out a correction. *Miss. It's Miss Bondi.*

There were six dogs currently in the kennel. Terry kept all sorts. She wasn't fond of Retrievers—they struck her as slave-like and diminished when humans were present—but she had a big golden one that she kept regularly; he was here. The Retriever's owner travelled frequently to the city and the dog had always been kept at Terry's, boarding sometimes a near equal split of fifty-fifty with the owner. Difference was, of course, Terry was paid. She didn't like the breed, but she had become accustomed to this one's ways and they were familiar with each other now. No problem.

There was a Newfoundland—a gorgeous animal, but this one was standoffish; there was a smallish Bulldog and a Terrier, Max. She wasn't fond of Terriers either, but Max was a confident, courageous dog and she respected that. And the two Rottweilers, new dogs that she was keeping for the first time. Nice enough so far. Huckley and Ryan. They hadn't answered to their names.

That was all she had right now. She had room for sixteen dogs. It took about eight regular to keep the kennel going. It was slow now, but would pick up once summer was in full bloom and folks started going away again.

In the afternoon while Julie had her nap, Terry cleaned out the stalls and let the dogs mingle. She tried to keep her mind on her work, but it wandered. It did, lately.

Across the street Marguerite had brought the baby out to play in the yard. They were all out: the two older ones, Damon and the girl—April—the little one, Tristan and the infant. The infant's name was on the tip of Terry's tongue, but hung there stubbornly.

They were playing a game, mom too. Whatever it was, it involved a chant of sorts: periodically one of them screamed *Ollie Ollie all-in-free!*

They all played until the baby cried. Then it was just the children.

Marguerite saw Terry and waved a hearty hello.

Terry waved back.

The other Rotties, she kept them apart from the rest of the dogs because on their first day, while they were still in the intake run, the larger of the two—Huckley, she told them apart by size—bent low at the neck when he saw the Newfie. He bent low and growled long, aggressively. Rotties were absolutely a universally misunderstood dog, few people were more certain of that than Terry, but there had been true menace in his growl.

Terry kept the new ones in the intake.

After two, before Julie was due to wake up from her nap, Terry let Andy and Amos out. She opened the door and lifted the latch to their room. She coaxed them out the big door, which led to the kennel yard. They went out reluctantly, sticking together. She followed them.

Amos fussed around Andy, sniffing behind him as he walked, running up alongside him, sniffing his front. Mothering him. Poor Amos, she was nervous and frantic.

Niecing him. Terry smiled. Niecing sounded like something you did surgically. *Auntie Julie, turn over, I've to niece you now. Won't hurt a bit.*

Terry smiled and absently rubbed her hand over Amos's snout. In her throat she made the noises that were just between her and her dogs. Calming things.

Rum-umm-um-ummmm.

Julie had come about four months earlier. She was Terry's aunt, her mother's sister, her mother long dead. Everyone who had cared for Julie at one time or another, was long dead.

Poor Julie, she had been when Terry was growing up. *Oh, Poor Julie.* Poor Julie's particular disability was invisible. Deprived of oxygen at birth, her brain had begun life with the full expectation of a normal course of things, but this was not meant to be. But, to the average outsider, she appeared just plain and simple, helpless; some people just were helpless. It was more complicated than that, more medical, more clinical. And as she had aged, she required more care. This care had fallen to Terry.

She was happy to do it, of course. Julie had known Terry all her life and was comfortable with her.

The children screamed. A new game. No more Ollie Ollie. Now it was some sort of tag that was *hysterically* funny. Terry kept an eye on Amos and Andy even as she cleaned things up around the yard and the kennel. She shovelled shit and moved pails about, filling them, emptying them, filling them again.

When one or other of the children shouted, poor Andy tensed beside her. He was still looking ill and his eyes were striped with red veins, like a road map of the city.

Eventually he threw up in the yard, before Terry had even finished filling the water trough in the back of the kennel. She heard him retch over the squeal in the pipes. She looked up and out through the kennel window saw Marguerite scolding Tristan for something. The girl, April, tossed a ball against the side of the house.

She heard: "If you don't behave, we'll go in. I *mean* it."

But they didn't go in.

Andy retched his breakfast.

Sometimes Julie had seizures. They'd called them "episodes." When Terry was growing up she was made to sit quietly when Julie had one of her episodes. She had to sit on the sofa and wait with everyone until it was over. Her grandmother in particular was adamant that no one move.

Sit still, her grandmother would say, if she squirmed. *Sit or I'll go crazy*.

They were clannish, even now. Except it was only she and Julie now.

Marguerite caught Terry on her way back into the house, Terry still in her knee-high boots, covered in dog shit and smelling of same. Her t-shirt was thin in front from the endless paws and heavy bodies of dogs held there in restraint or compassion or friendship. She had not put on a bra that morning. Everything about her hung, embarrassed or wet or dirty.

The baby was perched on Marguerite's left hip, and the woman listed to the right as a result. She walked with a kind of lurch, likely common to mothers with infants of a certain age. The child clung with sticky fingers in the front of Marguerite's own braless t-shirt. Terry stopped to greet her. She put down the pail of water she was carrying back to dump behind the house and put a hand up over her eyes, to shield them from the sun.

"Hullo there Terry, howerya?" Marguerite said. Behind her, across the street, the children watched, quiet for the first time that day. The older one, Damon, absently dribbled the basketball on the concrete drive.

Conk-ca. Conk-ca. Conk-ca. Conk-ca.

"Hi," Terry said.

"I'm so glad I caught you before you went in! I haven't seen you in a dog's age," she said, her voice unnaturally high. "I just *had* to talk to you."

Marguerite spoke without pause, a stream of words. Terry listened to what she was saying, nodding when she should, again and again. She noted the girl's eyes and how they drooped at the corners, and how they were underscored with heavy bags and how her skin looked a little dull. How dull her hair was. It was distracting. When the conversation seemed to be at an end, Terry nodded more vigorously. *Yes. Yes. Absolutely.*

"Is that okay?" Marguerite asked at the end. "I mean it's scaring the kids, you know? I want to be compassionate and all, but maybe close your windows or something when she gets on it. You know?"

Terry leaned in close to Marguerite and looked into her eyes, around the rims and into her iris. Marguerite said, "You're not mad?"

Terry shook her head. "Marguerite," she said seriously. "You need to get some iron."

"Iron?"

"You look deficient." Marguerite stared. Terry added helpfully, "You can get it in tablets. People take it too. Not just dogs."

By then Julie was up. They both heard her call, their two heads turning in tandem to look at the trailer.

Just before she turned to leave, Terry thought she heard Marguerite groan.

The kids weren't so bad later. Probably the two younger ones were having their own naps. But then around five, the Mister came home. The truck pulled into the driveway, the children started. The older boy revved his mini bike and roared up the street.

The dogs barked. Terry heard the Mister curse them.

Don't those goddamn dogs ever shut up—or words like it. It was hard to tell exactly what he said, with the wind, and the other noise.

At six they barbecued across the road. Marguerite's husband could be seen through Terry's kitchen window, flipping things, fussing at the barbecue in the way only men did.

The slow tender charring of ribs and ground beef wafted across the street, setting Julie off.

"I want steak today," she said when she finished her milk.

Terry ate her cornbread, chewing silently. Julie wouldn't eat. She wanted something else. Something *nice*. She was *older*, Terry had to *mind*. She wanted steak.

"There's no steak," Terry told her.

It was a perfectly nice supper. The cornbread was fresh, made by hand, by Terry after Julie had woken from her nap. Elton used to love her cornbread, it was light and golden. She had a knack. Terry said as much, patiently. *It's good Julie, eat some.* Smiling at Julie without making eye contact.

Look, Julie, there are peas from the garden, along with Terry's tomatoes and she'd cooked up some egg noodles with butter. It was perfectly nice.

When she was done Terry pushed back her chair to rest. They could have tea if she wanted. It was a quarter of seven. Normally, or before everything changed, Elton would be coming around and they might watch *Law & Order* or just walk through Terry's garden and putter about. But not since.

What's this? She's your sister? Your aunt. No. I can't see this. Nope. Nope. Good Christ, Ter, put her in a home.

There were hours yet before bed, although Terry was exhausted. Hours before bed.

Julie's moaning during her seizures was frightening Marguerite's children. The sound carried on the wind across to their house, in through their windows. She said she had to turn up the TV when it got bad.

The middle one, Tristan wanted to know first if Julie was dying. Then if she was some kind of monster.

It had to stop. Marguerite had not wanted Terry to be mad, she'd said. It was just that the sound carried all the way across the street and into their windows. *It was the kids you know, they got scared*, she'd said.

She understood. The sound did carry, very clearly sometimes. Just the other night Marguerite and her husband had guests and they were all sitting around in the yard. And Terry heard everything they said.

She's crazy, the Mister told his guests. *First there was just one of them, now there's two. Two old crazy ladies, screaming and moaning. And about a thousand dogs.*

Just four of her own. Just four I think, Marguerite said.

The other's out of hand though, Marguerite said. *She scares the kids.*

But she hearts dogs, an unfamiliar voice said. *Like the t-shirts, get it?*

And then they all laughed.

Around 11:30 P.M. Julie woke up and shrieked, one sharp, unpleasant sound. Terry was lying in her own bed, the door to her room open so she could hear Andy, should he need her. She imagined lights going on in the house across the street.

She imagined them snarling. *What the hell was that? Goddamn—*

From the side room she heard the dogs shifting, could hear the scratch of claws on tile. The wet snuffle of Amos's troubled sinuses.

Terry had tried to read. Beside the bed was a worn *Fodor's Travel Europe*. It was spine down on the bedside table, open to Spain. At one time she had wanted to go to Spain. Elton had been there in 1988. The book, in fact, was Elton's. They'd teased, somewhat, about going. In the front on the flyleaf, he had written his name in careful, almost feminine script. He had lovely handwriting. Terry felt it was a sign that a man was a gentleman. She'd read somewhere that if you could read a person's signature, it meant they had nothing to hide.

You could easily read his. Elton D. Balfour. The D was for Dennis. An uncle on his father's side. She knew that. That was hers to keep.

The light was out. She'd crawled into bed tired, she'd read four or five pages tired, she'd turned out the light tired, almost too tired to set the alarm. And yet when she turned out the light and laid her head on her pillow, she had been utterly unable to sleep. Her eyes had felt so dry while she tried to read her book, and yet when she closed them they had no relief, and in fact, she opened them within minutes to the dark. Then they'd adjusted to the minimal light in the room, to the fair glow of the single streetlight that she shared with the family across the street, the last two houses on the block.

Her ears adjusted to the silence and she could hear Amos and Andy shuffle and curl up over each other. She heard poor Andy's tummy rumbling, again. Heard him pass gas. There was no cause for it, still, that she could see. Except a nervous stomach. For the morning she would put drops into his water, the ones Dr. Bertrand had given her for Daisy, an old Border Collie that stayed at the kennel months before. Daisy had a nervous stomach.

If that failed, she would take him to the vet, but the vet was a last resort. She'd just had them all in for their shots and she hadn't even had a season yet. There just wasn't the money. Julie had her meds and the kennel licenses were due.

The click and tap of nails on tile came into her room. She turned on her side and peered into the dark. She could tell by the head that it was Amos. The dog came right to the bed and poked her snout into Terry's shoulder. She reached out a hand and scratched the top of Amos's head.

In the dark Terry whispered, "Who's my girl?" And the dog flopped down on the small, thin mat beside the bed, dropping her head with a snort and a sigh. Terry rolled over on to her stomach so she could put her hand on Amos's head. At intervals, without knowledge, she stroked the soft, sleek fur of Amos's forehead.

The two girls slept.

They woke like that, the two of them waking with the alarm, Terry a half second before it sounded, Amos on the first buzz. She reached over and slapped it off.

"Up, up, Amy," Terry said; she sat up in bed, resigned to the dark. She reached over and petted the girl on the head. Made her noises: *rumm-rumm-rummm*. Amos shuffled up, her bulky chest causing her to roll a couple of times before she made it up onto clicking toes. She snorted and hacked in her snout, sounding as much like an old man as a still-baby Rottie. Terry grinned into the room, still dark. She was thinking—*Try those drops on Andy*.

And she was thinking that when she turned the corner between her room and the dog run. By then Amos was already ahead of her, already in the dog run. When Terry turned the corner Amos looked up at her, her ears back, and she whined deep in the back of her throat.

I told you.

Andy was lying so still on his oversized foam bed.

There was a medicinal smell in the room, or something she associated with medicine; under that was a fainter smell of dog shit. From her boots.

Amos dropped her head and dug her nose into Andy's side.

"Amy, Amy," Terry said quietly, holding her breath. Amos whined.

Across the street a car door slammed and an engine gunned. They both jumped. Then Marguerite screamed from a window or maybe the stoop, "Damon stop that right goddamn now," and then she called out to Mister, "Good bye," and "Don't forget—"

Something. The sound was drowned out by Amos's wail, sudden and loud, into the dark room, the still-dark morning. Amos dropped to the floor on her front legs and howled.

No god—please—

Terry buried her face in her hands for a silent second or two before she fell to her knees and crawled over to Andy, her own wail trapped inside her body too hard and solid to come out, her face twisting up, tears running down her cheeks even as she couldn't make a sound. Not until she reached his cooling body and leaned her head against his still chest. She pressed her face into his fur and then she howled. A gulping choked sound that lasted just a second; Amos too, one last wail. The two of them like that, Amos licking and nudging at Andy's body, Terry just stroking then weeping, but quietly, trying not to wake Julie, who wouldn't understand.

It was warmer earlier in the morning and part of Terry marvelled at how warm it was, even though when she carried Andy's limp and dead-weighted body out into the yard, it was still only after six.

Somewhere behind her she could hear Julie, disturbed by either Amos or Terry's crying or maybe just awakened by the free-floating trauma in the small trailer. Either way, behind her as she stumbled and lurched to the kennel with Andy heavy in her arms, his big black head bouncing against her arm, she could hear Julie, screaming. She was crying, Terry thought, because she thought maybe Terry wasn't in the house.

She would be afraid, Terry guessed. She was prone to fears, most particularly the fear of being left behind, alone. *Leaving Julie!* She would question every time Terry left the house.

The old woman called her name, like a child might, in two syllables: *"Terrrrr-rreeeee!"* The name catching in her throat halfway as her angry tears became more acute.

At the gate while Terry fumbled trying to unlatch it, Amos at her heels, running around the back of her legs and then around again in confusion and heartbreak, she heard the neighbours' door open across the street. The screen door slammed on its spring right after that.

She didn't have to look to know that Marguerite would be standing there, her arms holding her robe closed around her body, looking. Behind her on the step would maybe be Damon. Maybe the little girl and Tristan the boy, would be on the step with her, the little one's arms wrapped around his mother's legs.

"Terrrrrr-rreeeeee!"

She didn't have to look. Beside her, Amos stopped and stiffened.

"Terry?" Marguerite called into the morning. Into the mourning.

Terry got the latch lifted and was struggling to keep it up while pushing the gate open. Perspiration dripped on her upper lip from the strain of carrying the dog. Andy had been healthy; he'd weighed an even, consistent 160. She pushed at the gate.

"Terry!? I don't know what's going on but I thought that yesterday we came to an—" Marguerite shouted from across the street even as she walked over, crossing the gravel lane, fast. Terry barely glanced over her shoulder as she manoeuvred Andy's sad bulk through the gate.

I'm so sorry my baby, my love, good dog.

By then the other dogs were awake and there was a cacophony of barking. Terry was still crying. She hadn't noticed, except that she couldn't breathe through her nose, and was instead breathing through her mouth, a catch in her breath that matched the intermittent wail from inside the house. *"Terrrrr-reeee!"*

No. Hers was different.

Marguerite stopped just inside the edge of the property. Terry couldn't turn to look at her, didn't want her to see her crying, didn't want her ugly neighbour eyes on her poor Andy. Instead, she shoved her way and Andy's bulk through the gate suddenly and it caught on holding wire against the inside fence. By accident. It happened by accident. The gate was open wide, but her arms were full of her Andy and for a moment she hovered between two choices, at six in the morning, forgetting one for the other.

Gate. Gate. It was always imperative, of course, that you close the gate, locking up the sometimes angry and unpredictable animals, and her hand wriggled out from under Andy and she slapped at the gate, stuck to the fence. It loosed and swung shut. She heard the latch close her in, with the other dogs and (poor) Andy.

"Terry, do we have to talk about this again—I thought I'd made it clear—"

The rest she didn't hear.

It was only a moment before she realized that the gate had locked—*click click*—before she had called Amos in—

Come

Her mind had been elsewhere on Julie crying and neighbours and the single streetlight joining them and the drops and the vet and Elton, Elton and—

And only a moment more before she turned her head, Andy's heavy body already stiffening *oh god please* and saw Marguerite's mouth open without speech. Only a moment more before she wished it all back even as Amos, her body elegant and slender, elongated, in flight, landed on Marguerite's chest.

Under her breath, hardly meaning to, she might have said *git her* honestly meaning *come here*.

Julie's screams were drowned out by Marguerite's even though it was only a moment more before Terry was able to put Andy down and get to the gate, locking it behind her, before the other dogs got out.

Only a moment when she thought a nasty, cruel thought.

I heart dogs.

Everything was just moments, right up until you died. Just moments.

THE NEIGHBOURHOOD,
OR, TO THE DEVIL WITH YOU

I don't remember when it was I started hating Hazel Kummel, but I do remember the moment I realized that I did. It had been a beautiful, sunny day, the sort of day that always reminded me of being a little girl, the way the sun would shine through wherever you were, through windows, through tents, through screen doors and wind breakers. I was sitting on the bench that my son, Kerry, had parked in the sun beside my rock garden, just to prove I did sometimes. If he'd had his way, it would have gone in the back, in the shade, where I would never see the street. *You'll never use it in front, Ma.* So now I did. At what point did children decide they were the boss of you?

I was enjoying the stark sun, when I heard Hazel raising her voice across the road where she's lived for fifty years, right across from my house, where I have lived for forty. All of us, me, my boys Todd and Kerry, and my now-dead husband, loved Burlington Avenue, the whole neighbourhood, very much. We had wonderful neighbours. Oddly, most of the neighbours who had kept me on Burlington for so long were now dead or had moved away. Except for Hazel, whom at the moment I realized I truly hated, and who was standing in the middle of her lawn with a shovel raised about waist level, shaking it at Josie Tubman's granddaughter, the one with the unusual name.

Keeheisha?

She was shrieking something at the child that I couldn't hear. The poor girl was riveted to the spot, her tiny feet bare and brown against the brilliant green of Hazel's lawn. She always kept a nice lawn.

I hurried across the street, and as I got closer, I heard Hazel:

"—no respect for other people. You keep your goddamn ass out of my yard, off this lawn—"

I shouted at her, "Hazel! For goodness sakes, *language!*" Twenty years earlier I would have been shocked; it would have been cause for conversation all over the block, but times had changed and even my mailman had mentioned the *goddamn potheads.*

"Lower that spade, Hazel Kummel. *Really.*"

I crouched down beside Keeheisha and took her hand. I asked her if she was okay. Hazel interrupted with her side of the story, even as Keeheisha was telling me hers. The child wasn't hurt and that was the main thing.

"For crying out loud, Hazel," I said. "You can't scare a little girl like that! What were you planning to do? Hit her over the head with the shovel? The child is seven years old—"

"The devil will take the child!"

In retrospect, I was surprised by my reaction, which was to get angry.

"I don't want children in my yard," Hazel said, more quietly. "It's not safe." She stuck her chin out.

Once, years before she and I had had an argument about my husband's truck. She said it blocked her view. What it had blocked was her view of what was going on in *my* house. She'd known she was wrong to bring it up, but still she'd stood there in the front street with her chin sticking out, just like that. Wrong and she knew it. Doing it anyway.

"The devil will take them," she added one more time.

That's when I decided I hated Hazel Kummel.

Instead of feeding the anger, the realization seemed to deflate me, to dim my lights so to speak, and I found I didn't have the energy to keep talking to her about it.

"Don't scare the kids, Hazel," I said. "They've got parents who will come over and *give you* the devil, if you don't watch it." I said it all very patiently and calmly, managing to keep contempt and—somehow—pity out of my voice. Maybe I'm a good woman. My Dan always used to say so.

But that day I crossed the street back to my own house and I could feel small doors in my head smashing shut, and a couple—salaciously—staying open: the door to judgement, self-satisfaction, smugness. Sorry to say, but as the years had passed, those doors had been hung, and by the time I got to be the age I am now—a healthy, happy, active sixty-seven—those doors had been in use more often than I would like to admit. I struggled with the changing world around me. When Dan and I first moved to Burlington Street, we didn't know anyone, but nearly everyone on the block looked just like us: young, poor, ambitious, and the colour of an unfinished pine cupboard. Now the neighbourhood looks more like the rest of the world. I have Indira, up at the end of the block, Lanelle on the other side of the next door neighbour, Jack Gillam, who back in the day we might have called "glamorous" as a euphemism. There was Fia and her family, behind me. They were Portuguese. And Josie Tubman, Keeheisha's grandma. Josie's been living on the other side of Hazel for eight years.

One thing never changed: Hazel was a recognizable commodity. There was one on every block. We would have had all sorts of idioms for it— witch, hag, cow, biddy, crank—back in the day, but what we meant was, Hazel was just an old bitch. Never liked anybody, always suspicious.

The neighbourhood had changed slowly. People, friends my kids had gone to school with, grew up and moved out. Their parents started to follow when we were all hitting fifty.

When I turned fifty, Dan and I went down to Mexico for two weeks, my first real holiday ever. We had growing boys for a lot of our lives together, and trips were family affairs involving the outdoors. We went camping, paddling in canoes with Todd and Kerry for miles, sitting around the fire at night, at first talking about animals and how we fit in with the beasts, then school and friends and how complicated it was to be a kid, then things got quiet for a couple of years. After that there was maybe one more year before they scattered off to school, girls, their own lives. In the winter we skied. They came skiing every year. Would still go, frankly, if they thought I'd pay for it.

But we went off to Mexico the year I turned fifty, a kind of birthday present to us both. We had a grand time. We made more love on that trip, I think, than we had trying to make Kerry—a most reluctant human being. We got to talk, sleep late, read on the beach until the sun was dropping low enough that we couldn't read. We did crossword puzzles while we drank coffee for hours in the little cantina in the mercado and I picked up just enough Spanish to embarrass myself.

Thing was, we felt like kids on that trip, not having brought any of our own to compare ourselves to, we got to feeling pretty darn good about ourselves. We had managed, in those two weeks, to put all thoughts of mortality behind us. It was a beautiful trip.

And when we came home, Dan up and died. Just like that.

His heart popped. We'd been home from Mexico for just over a month. It killed him, that trip.

Fifty changes you. Just like fifteen.

I still hate thinking about that.

To look at it now, you would never know that Burlington Street used to be the busiest street in the neighbourhood. There was a little family store at the end of the block—not there anymore. Cars, however, were rare in the daytime unless someone's husband was working shifts or you were having guests from out of town. When my two were little the neighbourhood was deserted from nine-to-five, except for women and children. There were lots of those.

Next door to us on one side were the Carraways, Bob and Wanda, kids Lindsey and Janet; on the other side was the Johnsons, with four girls, Betty, Janie, Carolyn, and Angela the youngest—all a year or so apart. Can you believe that, four girls right next door and not one of them married to any of the boys on the block? Not a looker among them, either. Smart as pigs, but those were the days when a boy wanted looks first and brains second, if at all. I like to think things have changed.

Across from us, was Hazel with her boy Cuthbert. Cuth. They called him Cootie when parents were out of earshot, even my two and it wasn't because there was anything wrong with him, just because his name nearly sounded like cootie. Hazel tried to ruin that boy but never managed it. Sports saved him from a miserable existence. He's on the coast now.

One over from Hazel's on the east side were the Arlingtons and like us, they had two boys around the same ages, and their claim to fame is that their oldest is a doctor. Big whoop. My oldest is an engineer, but talking to Linda Arlington you'd have thought I said my Todd was washing dishes at the Y. *Oh that's so nice for you dear, did I tell you what Sean has been doing? He's been teaching at the—*

Big whoop. Didn't see Sean down on the weekend, but I made sure to stand and talk to Todd while he sat in the car getting impatient, for a good fifteen minutes. Todd could've killed me, and I know he was thinking that I was getting old and senile, but he would've been more upset if he knew I had been using him to get Linda Arlington's goat. Ha ha.

But the Arlingtons, and Hazel, are the only ones left who know any of the history of the block. The only ones, if I think about it now, who knew anything about Tommy.

Poor Tommy.

Our very best friends on Burlington were Rita and Mac, and they lived on the east side of Hazel. Their boys, Tommy and Darren, were so close to ours in age and looks they were almost interchangeable. They were precious to us, the whole lot of them. I meant that then, and I mean it now.

Rita and Mac were what you called a "fun couple." It was a rare thing back then, to just let your hair down. In those days people were concerned with appearances and doing what looked like the right thing. People went to work, kept their houses clean, (clean enough to annoy, Rita used to say), kids were always groomed and quiet, the lawn tidy and dandelion free.

I'm both saddened and amused when I think about how gorgeously young we were, only playing at being grown up, playing house. We were in our twenties, with little babies. Mortgages and car payments before we were thirty. Tax worries, loans, marriage problems brought on by frustration and overwork, stupidity (and a touching lack of experience with each other, in spite of the babies). We were the generation carrying the flag for our parents who had lived through the Depression. We expressed that guilt by being serious about our mortgages and lawns. We made our lives as clean and beautiful as possible, in deference to them. The Depression was the North American Holocaust and we never stopped hearing about it, trying to make up for it.

Fewer couples than you would imagine had the nerve to drink a beer on the front lawn while supervising the shingling of their roof. But that was the sort of thing Rita and Mac did. Wickedly, some would have thought.

Rita was a redhead, Susan Hayward style, in spite of her naturally straight hair, and so she spent a lot of time in curlers. In those days I was going for more of a Sandra Dee kind of thing, so my curlers came out sooner, but my hair looked odder. I always thought it looked like that high swing ride at the exhibition, especially if I was disagreeing with something and got to shaking my head. When I mentioned that to Rita, how I thought they looked like the ride at the exhibition, she made me shake my head *no* all the while humming a kind of calliope music. She was a ball of laughs, that one.

Red-haired Rita could have been bald as a cue ball for all men looked at her head. She was one of those women with enough on top to give men whiplash. She called them her "guns."

Ellen, she'd say to me, *I can get a man's wallet faster with my guns than a stick-up man can with his gun!*

When she got a little drunk, which we all did sometimes on Saturday nights in the summer playing cards, she'd tell my Dan to stick-em-up. She thought it was pretty funny. Especially after a couple-three beers.

Hey Dan! Stick 'em up! And Dan would laugh and laugh. Funny.

—*Old Vienna Lager Beer!* I can still hear the commercial playing in my head. Seems to me that commercial played every hour for years. I think of those nights when I think of that commercial. Rita and her guns. Funny stuff.

But poor Rita, Mac and Tommy. Even poor Darren, their other one. Poor all of them.

The summer I'm thinking of, they were re-shingling their roof. Rita had taken out her curlers, because the roofers were coming and they were men. She didn't mind having her hair in curlers when it was just the kids and the neighbours, but not in front of strangers or men. If she got caught out she would cover her head with her hands—*oh you caught me in my curlers!*—and run for a scarf. I've also seen her put her hair to right in seconds flat if she had to. A real gal, that Rita.

A real friend. This one time I had been trapped in the house with two sick babies for a full week. They were finally better and back in school. I had spent that day cleaning the house from top to bottom and thinking of some kind of decent meal I could serve my poor husband that night, to make up for a week of canned soup and flat soda pop. They'd had the flu and I didn't think I would ever get the smell of vomit out of the house, but I was trying.

By the time the boys got home from school, I was beat. I still had to think about supper and at that point I was thinking one more night of canned surprise was going to be it, when who shows up at my door, twenty minutes after five? Rita.

She rings the doorbell and when I answer, there she stands, in full Rita-glory: bright green shift dress clinging a little close, hair done, a scarf that matched the dress threaded through her hair like we'd seen Brigitte Bardot do in a magazine, high heels, and a clutch tucked under her arm.

Oh my god, I said, and I'm still proud of this line, *did Hugh Hefner die?*

She laughed and said we were going out for dinner.

At any other time I would have been running to the bedroom and making myself decent, but I was just exhausted and so when she said that, I was annoyed. She knew how my week had gone.

Rita, I'm just not up for dinner out.

Not you, she said. *I'm taking the boys out for dinner with us. You do whatever you like, because after dinner we're taking them to movies. There's a cowboy picture at the Park.*

I had those boys fixed up in minutes flat and they were in Mac and Rita's station wagon, pulling out of their drive before Dan was even home from work. I was as tickled with those fifteen minutes alone before Dan got home as I was with the whole rest of the evening without children. A person should never underestimate the joy of a few minutes alone without someone pawing at her skirt, and that includes her husband. It was a real treat, even if Rita felt it necessary to hang around when she dropped the boys off, nearly popping out of her dress fussing over Dan.

But that bad day that I'm thinking of, the day they were re-shingling the roof, it was just us girls and the kids. A beautiful summer day, just a week before Dan would get ten days holiday.

We were all happy that day. Rita and Mac were getting their roof fixed. Rita was going to have three men on top of her house for a week. A week of bringing out lemonade and a little harmless flirting.

(Husbands think the jokes about the milkman and the FedEx man are all funny as hell; thing is, when you're a young woman home all day with the kids and no reason to take your head out of curlers, a smiling, handsome FedEx man can make a world of difference in your day. Why do you think women had milk delivered? You think we couldn't walk down the street to the store? Our milkman's name was Stanley and I gave him a nice tip every week because he never missed a new hairdo.)

Rita was happy, and I was happy because in one week our family would be heading to the Black Hills in South Dakota, a pretty big deal for just folks. I hadn't stopped talking about it since we'd decided. The driving was the only part I wasn't looking forward to. Dan was one of those types who wrote down the mileage before he left and set a stopwatch to the whole deal just so he could brag to the bowling team when he got back, how fast he made it to the Black Hills. If you had to pee or eat, you better think of a way to do it through the window. It guaranteed at least one squabble on the way down, with a good hour of silence while one of us punched the buttons on the radio trying to find something to fill the silence (preferably a song called "I Hate You Because You're Stupid"). But I wasn't thinking about *that*.

Rita was on the front lawn with coffee for the roofers by eight A.M. I had been up an hour already. The boys were planning a scrub baseball game in the field behind the back lane, back when it was still an empty field. It's all houses now, of course. I think it was all houses not long after then.

By nine I was dressed (my curlers out) and peeking out our front window at Rita, who was staring up at the guys on the roof, one hand shielding her eyes from the sun, the other perched on her hip. Her back was to me, but I knew she was laughing, her mouth lipstick red and turned up in a sexy smirk. (*Why, you big strong boys are just going to have that roof done in no time, I can just tell!*) I watched while she picked up a tray from the lawn and went inside the house.

There were quite a few things on my list yet to do. Lists! No one makes a list like a wife. We were going to be away a week. There was the paper to cancel, the lawn to cut, the camping gear to find, still stashed from the year before, proper luggage for the hotel stay—two nights, one on the way and then on the way home.

And of course, there was the cleaning. There is always the cleaning, for a woman. It wasn't so much leaving a clean house that mattered, as it was not coming home to a dirty one. Not after a long car trip with Mr. Shaved-Two-Hours-Off-The-Trip.

I dug into the living room first. I would vacuum the rug, sofa, love seat and chair, dust, water plants, polish and oil the table in the dining room. Rita would water the plants while I was away; she and Mac would get our mail and watch the house, all of which we would turn around and do for them in one month's time, or at least we had in other years. Not that year. God no.

Probably I was thinking that I should wash the floor and not be such a lazy thing, probably beating myself up about it even as I rubbed oil soap into a table that hadn't been eaten on in six months. When I look back on my life now, I think of all those times when I was rubbing invisible dirt off something when I could have been reading a book, sewing; phoning my husband and hearing his precious voice a minute more, talking to my kids. But I rubbed that table raw. I don't even have it anymore. It's in Kerry's house now and it's cluttered all the time, like a great big desk, and whenever I see it, I both want to cheer and scream. But I think Kerry's wife has it right. She's not going to be able to discuss major days in her life by recalling what she was cleaning and a part of me is shamed that it's part of the story at all. ('Course, a sliver of me is pleased.)

Complain as I do about the cleaning, and I've always been, sad to say, a bit of a complainer about housework, there is a moment in the routine of soak, wring, wipe, rinse, repeat when the world fades away and you are alone with yourself. There's not much concentration required to polish a table or wash dishes; at some point your brain wanders off on its own. It's nice. That's when the problems are solved, when husbands are forgiven, and when, I think, a woman's life is saved.

I don't know what it's like for young women now; I don't know what different problems being a housewife and mother and career woman bring to the family, and I imagine they are substantial, but there's the point right there: *substance*. Women have an assumed substance, something automatic, now. We didn't. We had limited tools to prove our substance and without those moments of knowing who you were, you could feel yourself absolutely floating away. You had to remind yourself, *I am this house, without me they die*, or else you would just disappear into the ether one day. The women you used to see in the supermarket, their eyes staring in that Valium Vacancy? They never got the Zen-dishes thing.

But that's got nothing to do with what happened. Not really.

I just remember that I was excited about our trip, being an outdoorsy girl myself. That was something Dan and the boys admired about me, that I could paddle a canoe, light a fire, set up a tent and bait a hook.

When I finished the table, I took oil soap and rags into the kitchen and put them in the sink. I stood at the back window of the house listening for the boys until I heard the crack of the bat on the ball—a distinctly summer sound—and then I probably fixed my hair and went across the street to Rita's place, where they were fixing her stupid roof.

I'm thinking about where Hazel was during all of this. I don't mean the roof shingling or the summer we were supposed to go to the Black Hills, I mean that *time*. Because it was a time all on its own, and as far as I know there's never been a recapturing of it, but I don't know if it was a phase of life that I went through, or a phase of life the world went through. But it was a *time*.

For one thing, I don't think women stayed home with their houses and children as much after those years. The girls coming up behind me and Rita were getting jobs and apartments, not husbands and babies. Just a few years difference and everything was changing.

Dan and I got married out of high school and the first apartment either of us had ever set foot in was our first home together. We got the place on Burlington when I was pregnant with Kerry.

That was still the norm then, it was only 1965 or thereabouts; girls for the most part still waited for Prince Steady Job in their parents' home and then married him and stayed at home to raise their children, even if there was already the beginning of rumblings of other options, it hadn't changed our choices. Not then.

No one talked about it yet, not in the land of plenty where no one went hungry, when the bed you slept in was covered in clean linens and warm blankets, in a country where no one ever bombed you, invaded you, killed your neighbours. We were reminded daily about the instability of life around the world, thanks to television news, which I wouldn't let the boys watch. We were members of the luckiest society on earth and *goddamn it!* didn't they remind us. No one was talking yet about how even in the land of plenty there's a bottom rung on a ladder, and women—specifically housewives—were on it. We were duped, we women. We were told that we were the backbone of society, that without us it would all crumble, that the sacrifice of personal goals, pleasure and achievement was worth it and valued for the greater good of your family, and ultimately, society. With a smoothly running home and well-raised children, who knew what could be accomplished in the outside world? All because Mother gave up her time.

And the crowd goes wild.

What was that old joke? There are three jobs for a woman: nun, mother, witch.

That was what we were fed and we ate it. I don't even know who fed it to us; I suppose it was from watching the sacrifice of our mothers and assuming that there had to be a reason why she would do it, and a good one.

It all turned out to be unnecessary. It turned out that the fabric of society would not unravel when a woman didn't wash her floors every week, or wasn't home with cookies the minute a child ran through the front door and dropped his jacket on the mat. Men did not expire in their dirty underwear because there wasn't a roast on the table. There's been a spot of spaghetti sauce on the backsplash of Kerry's wife's stove for going on two years now. Doesn't seem to bother her at all.

Good for the girls of today. It was different for us, and not all bad, we had our ways of coping, cocktails at four notwithstanding, we had each other in a way, I think, that women don't any more. We were always there.

But where was Hazel? Hazel was Rita and Mac's neighbour, after all. I don't remember seeing her that morning, but then she could be a cipher, peering out through her curtains, only to disappear when you glanced up. I would go days without seeing her, even behind her curtains. She could have been worshipping Satan for all I knew, although that would be unlikely.

Cuth's father had died about a year before we moved into the house on Burlington and I think if we had been there for that particular human drama, that tragedy, I at least would have digested it all a little more naturally. But since I only knew that this slight, white-blonde, wraithlike woman was all alone in the world trying to raise her son I couldn't stop myself from seeing the pity in it. She was so close to us in age, I could not look at her without imagining myself in her position, a widow, not even quite in my thirties yet. Even in those early days, it bought her a lot of slack.

So I felt sorry for her. But that didn't change what she said.

I had attempted what Rita used to call a "befriendment" early in the Burlington days. When we were new to the block and I was still unpacking, I would sometimes see her in the yard. I saw all the neighbours in the yard that summer; eventually I realized it wasn't the most active gardening block ever, but that they were checking us out. We were new. I did it myself later.

Cuthbert was a year older than my oldest, Todd, then and I was getting big with Kerry. I tired easily and so instead of making sure every box was unpacked by ten, I would take it easy. The house was a mess and so Todd and I spent a lot of time in the yard.

I saw her and waved. She raised a tentative hand, flaccidly, like a sick person.

There was no Rita then—Rita was still a year away.

It was several days before Hazel came around, tugging Cuth by his arm.

She'd come to welcome me to the neighbourhood.

I laugh about that now. It was the dog welcoming the cat, except that I've always liked dogs and I think it's cats that are the sly boots. So maybe it was the cat welcoming the dog.

Hello, she said. *This is Cuthbert. He's no trouble at all.*

I told Dan that night what Hazel said and we couldn't contain ourselves. I told him how tempted I was to tell her that Todd was a modicum of trouble, but that we were working on him.

In actuality, the visit was uncomfortable and cracking little jokes was the last thing on my mind. Hazel's visit took the form of a visiting dignitary from another country, giving you their country's strange but necessary rules and tenets.

For instance, she told me that she used pesticides on her lawn so I might want to stay away. It wasn't good for the kids and couldn't be good for my "condition."

Mr. Larabee, at 370, was a policeman. Just so I knew. In case I did things that were not above board, she said.

Wanda and Matt Purdue at 349 were Jehovah's Witnesses, so if someone came to my door, I shouldn't be rude, since they might live on the block.

She suspected the Wilton teenagers were juvenile delinquents. They might even smoke marijuana. She worried because of Mr. Larabee.

And . . . she was a widow. Very matter-of-factly: *I am a widow.* Before I could even comment or offer my sympathies, she asked if my children were normal.

Beg your pardon? I said.

Your children. This one and the one on the way. Are they normal?

I wanted to say it again: *beg your pardon?* I was so taken aback by the question that I was speechless, anyone would have been. My speechlessness led to the assumption of *something* on Hazel's part and she nodded some kind of confirmation before I had a chance to even shut my gaping mouth.

Of course, I said, *they're perfectly normal—*

But I had waited a beat too long before defending them. Now I was lying, no matter what, and Hazel would take a wait-and-see attitude until they were twenty.

(Todd got his Master's Degree today, Hazel. Oh. Really? Special classes?)

His eyes are a little far apart. I was just wondering, you know, about mongoloidism. Mrs. Duncan on the 400 block has a mongoloid. She takes him to the special Olympics. He's not even that retarded.

There's nothing wrong with Todd.

It's nothing to be ashamed of, she said calmly. She opened her hands, palms up, in a fell swoop you know, like a magician or salesman. Voila.

There's nothing wrong with him.

That's good. Unconvinced.

I told her that I had much unpacking to do, but in fact I was ready to tell her to shove off. Maybe. Not likely, but in retrospect. While it would be literally months before she set foot on my lawn again, it proved nearly impossible to get her off then.

When she was finally ready to leave, she pulled Cuth out of the small, unplanted flower garden where Todd was digging with both hands and getting filthy. Cuth was clean, calm. God I felt sorry for that kid. Later you would be able to see his mind drift away and his chest heave slowly upward in a huge sigh, whenever his mother took to berating him on the lawn.

But Hazel had more to say. *Roger, my husband, worked at a bank.*

Oh, I said, lips pressed tightly together, wanting her to leave, my back aching from standing there, tenser by the moment. Then she dropped her pity bomb on me and like Japan, I was just so terribly unprepared for it.

My husband died last year, she said suddenly. She leaned in for her story, and her voice dropped. It wasn't just discretion, though. There was this feeling that she wasn't really saying it aloud yet. Like *she* herself might hear.

213

He died in our bed. I woke up and there he was, dead.

I nodded, could think of nothing else to do. What would you say? Of course Dan's face crept into the story and that was more than I could comprehend. He was, of course, my husband, lover, father to my children and I loved him—we all loved our husbands—but he was also my life support system. I knew nothing of the world. What would I have done?

And that was when this tiny, pale woman with her odd, affected hand gestures, strangely intimate questions, seemed to smack me in the head. How could I be so rude, even if I hadn't yet done anything more than think rude thoughts, I was deeply chastened.

I'm so sorry, I said. *I'm so sorry.*

She nodded and got a better grip on Cuth's arm. She had to go, she said. She had to start lunch for Cuthbert. I, she said, should probably feed my baby too. Then she looked at him, curiously.

Did you take thalidomide? I did not.

I forgot to mention that whenever Hazel sees me, when she looks over at me, there is first a blank expression and then a kind of creeping knowledge that crawls over her face. I know, I just know, she's thinking, *That's the one with the retard.*

Of course, there's nothing wrong with Todd, but for years, I couldn't stop myself from practically shouting his accomplishments in her face, rapidly and desperately, like a liar would.

He's an engineer, now. University of Toronto. Graduated with Honours.

I'm trying to tell the story about Rita and the roof. I don't like to think about that day.

The roof was a major neighbourhood project and at the end of any major neighbourhood project, such as when the Carraways put an addition on to their house taking nearly all of one summer, the neighbours were generally compensated with a party. Rita was planning a barbecue bash for the weekend coming up. It was the talk of the street. Rita was such a glamorous creature for those times, for that neighbourhood. She was so terribly pretty. She had a lovely figure and that generous set of guns. She wore sandals and pedal pushers, tied her blouse under her bosoms, told jokes that were just on this side of racy, and she was *fun.*

What Rita did, was make Burlington Street, even the whole controversial suburban neighbourhood, feel okay. Even in curlers and a house dress, Rita's laugh implied that there wasn't a damn thing going on outside the neighbourhood that was worth missing *this* for. It was all a kind of party.

So we all wanted to be at the barbecue. When I looked out at the house and saw her flirting with the roofers, and I also saw that pencil stuck in her ear, the clipboard dangling from her hand, I figured it was as good a time as any to stop cleaning and go dish about the barbecue over coffee.

Those little lifts, you know, in a regular day? The things you poke yourself with to feel alive, like it's all worth it? I have a distinct memory of that morning, thinking about that barbecue, the little thing in my day to look forward to. In fact, sometimes I was so thrilled with the quality of my life, going to the store could do the same thing. I had, *we* had, all of us, everyone on Burlington, had everything we wanted.

Hazel was always industrious, or at least as industrious as she could be given the limitations of her skills and strength. Later when Cuth was older and more capable, she made him help her with the more ambitious tasks, but delicate as she was, she did a pretty good job of things on her own. She built the gazebo in their backyard. She didn't do the really heavy lifting, she didn't put the roof on it for instance, but she was in there with the hired guy, hammering nails and holding up her end. I've always admired that gazebo, and the rare times I have seen her back there with a book in her lap, cup of tea, I thought she looked just like the rest of us, a little tired, but . . . content. From the street you couldn't see how pinched her lips were, or the lines across her forehead that were digging their way deeply into her psyche. All you could see was Hazel, the shell they gave her to work with.

The point was, she had done her share of building over the years. There had been the gazebo, and she'd had double-pane windows put in. Every year she had a crew come and clean her yard for summer, and that was two days of lawn mowers and hedge trimmers. She'd poured a new driveway, that was a guy breaking concrete for a full six hours—swear to god—and then a big, loud, stinking truck pouring cement down to two ex-cons with shovels, yelling back and forth.

Anyway: Rita never said a thing about it all. None of us did.

I was at Rita's before noon. I had taken a minute to comb my hair and put on a bright pair of shorts. I sometimes felt a little like the sandbox next to the Taj Mahal when I'd go hang out at Rita's, and I sometimes needed to put on a bit of the dog. I never went so far as making up but I would change a blouse.

Nor was I immune to the fact that I was twenty-five years old and there were three handsome young men up on the roof of my best friend's house. Maybe I put on a little lipstick, too. Who remembers so far back?

By the time I wandered over and sat in the back with Rita, the fellows on the roof were on phase two of the roof work. Whatever it was they were doing, the hammers had come out.

The sound of the banging echoed up and down the street.

Rita and I had coffee in the back and discussed the party in lazy detail. I forget now, what I was planning to bring, which is funny because such things used to occupy so much space in my mind: dessert, salad or main course, what would you bring? I had dishes that I made only for potluck parties, like Red Velvet Cake, the recipe for which I got from my mother-in-law. I had a recipe for Belgian Potato Salad that my mother gave me, that I had perfected over my years of marriage so that it was more mine than hers. I frequently had requests. But I don't remember now.

What I do remember is:

Talk was winding down. We could hear the noise of the boys coming back from their pickup game. They would want sandwiches, a gallon of milk to go with it, cake. I remember Rita had a cigarette burning in the ashtray, I brushed the smoke away from my face, and she laughed—it was interrupted by a raised voice that we could hear over the hammers. We turned our faces upwards, as though our ears were cocked, like poodles.

I remember the abrupt cease of the hammering and Hazel's distinctive voice.

Did we look at each other and laugh? We may have. However we felt about Hazel, we kept it to ourselves unless absolutely necessary.

We both stood up. The cigarette rolled out of the ashtray and onto the table—

Rita leaned over and picked it up, dashing it out in the ashtray just as—

Tommy came around the side of the house, his hand still stuck in a ball glove, fingers of his other hand wrapped around a baseball. *Mom, Mrs. Kummel—*

And she said, *I'm on it Mickey Mantle.*

I was just slightly behind Rita and Tommy.

There was Hazel, shouting up at the workers, telling them to be quiet. Telling them that it was lunch time, telling them she was a widow.

What she said once she silenced their hammers, was, *Is it necessary to make so much banging I'm trying to—*

Some of the boys were on the lawn, looking uncomfortable and interested. Donnie Bradbrook, whose parents owned a tire shop, had a grin on his face, which was red as though he'd been running. Or was embarrassed. He stared at the ground, occasionally looked over at Rita's other boy, Darren, who was beside him.

Poor Tommy.

I was looking up. On the roof, the man who had tied a handkerchief around his head, a fellow tan and dark enough to look Latin, had something in his hands. Ignoring the fuss on the lawn even as the other two were staring helplessly down at Hazel, he pulled up on something long and flat. It caught the sun and flashed terribly bright into my eyes.

I flinched and shut my eyes. When I opened them, I could see the other boys on the street. Cuth was there, one foot jauntily up on the curb, his gloved hand tucked under his arm. Just behind him was my Kerry.

I thought: *They shouldn't be on the road—*

And I was watching when Cuth's mouth dropped open and he raised his arm, pointing at the roof—

Someone shouted. I looked where Cuth was pointing and as I did, sunlight caught metal and flashed me again, blinding me; I didn't actually see although I heard, *I heard* Rita and Hazel scream and there was a terrible sound, like the whir of a jet engine, far away but I didn't see it happen—

I saw later.

Oh Tommy. Poor, poor Tommy. His head.

His head.

I didn't see Hazel when I got back from the hospital. It was dark, very late. I had my arm around Kerry's shoulders. He hadn't said a word since the accident and I only noticed then, I think, and I supposed a mother's urge is to comfort when you can't protect. There was little I could say. Everything would not be all right. It wasn't okay.

He had been standing ten feet away when his friend was *beheaded*. There were no magic words for that. A kid he'd run through the sprinkler with. A kid he'd traded Hot Wheels cars with. Slept in the backyard tent with. Stayed up late watching television with. Played ball with. I didn't know how I was going to feel in a day or two, but at that moment every nerve in my body was alive and alert.

I didn't know exactly what *he'd* seen, but I knew what *I'd* seen: when the light reflected off the piece of aluminium and flashed my eyes, I looked away. Another flash was closer to me, and then a shadow flew up and down.

Or maybe it was the sound of it, made me think I saw something. I heard it. Like a sneaker in mud. A sucking sound.

Years later, some neighbours got to talking about it. It took years before we started analyzing it, and you could tell by the tightening of voices that it was something that had stayed fresh in our minds.

John Bastion, who had not been there that day, said that it would be nearly impossible to repeat. He said that everything had to be exactly right for what happened to happen; he said the wind velocity, the angle, the timing, all of it had to have reached a kind of perfect storm.

Would have been a scrape, otherwise. Nothing to write home about, he said. Everyone stood around nodding at him, stupidly, like he was the authority on the thing that happened.

Wind velocity. Like the stuff coming out of his mouth.

On the roof of Rita's place the new shingles brightened up the house. I worried about the piece of sheet metal. I worried that they had used it on the roof. I worried that in twenty years when the roof needed doing again, some contractor was going to pull up the old shingles and find that piece of metal, a serrated edge of it still foamy with poor Tommy's blood.

I saw. The blood had foamed, like what we used to call lake spit, that bubbly white stuff that ends up on the shore.

I hoped they'd found another piece.

Rita and Mac never came back to the house. I knew they wouldn't, I guess. The family closed ranks pretty quickly and although I got lumped into the group of people *who were there that day*, and therefore possible poisonous to their minds, I continued to visit Rita in the hospital.

Only once was she straight enough to speak to me. She had been sleeping, or at least her eyes had been closed, when I came into the hospital room. Her sister Betts was there, and a nurse was fiddling with her IV. More drugs I hoped. Usually she was higher than a kite when I showed up. Who wouldn't be?

El, she said. *How was your trip?* Even though she was forming the words, her eyes were vague.

We hadn't gone on the trip. I didn't want to say that, and so like an idiot I stood there, smiling down at her. I don't know what I said, but I held her hand. It wasn't long after that that her eyes closed again. Drugs in the IV.

Rita's cousin came around to pack up the house. A bunch of us from the neighbourhood helped out. We packed their stuff into boxes. When we ran out of boxes we packed clothes into garbage bags.

The whole day there was a smell. No one mentioned it. I think everyone was thinking that given the horrible thing that had happened, that the place *should* smell bad.

It wasn't until late in that long day that I realized what it was. I opened the fridge to start emptying it, and was blasted with the most horrible, sickly sweetish bad smell I had ever encountered. Worse than the smell of the cat that had died in a pile of lumber at the back of the house one year.

There, stacked neatly on the middle shelf, were fifteen T-bone steaks. For the barbecue.

So *sad*. They'd been robbed, Rita and Mac. Especially Rita.

Stick 'em up.

I never blamed Hazel, at least not publicly. Maybe others did—neighbourhood gossip. She wasn't a good neighbour. There was something about her that *set* her outside the rest of us. There are people like that. As adults we think we can ignore differences in favour of inclusion, unlike when we're young. We think we're better once we've grown, but really, it's just more subtle. There are just people who set themselves up.

Hazel's place in the neighbourhood did not change, not on the surface. How would you tell, if it had? No one went there for coffee. No one yelled across the fence at her to come and see the new drapes. No one dropped their kids off for an hour in the afternoon to play with Cuth. No one asked her to babysit.

And they just kept at it, the not-doing.

A few days before the funeral, I was in the front yard, watering my peonies and—I think—repeatedly looking over at Rita's house and wondering how it all happened so fast.

The funeral was going to be on the Wednesday. There was no word, just gossip as to whether Rita was going to be well enough to attend. I couldn't imagine such a choice. I couldn't imagine missing my own son's funeral, but then, I couldn't imagine attending it either, and so I had no opinion on the subject. I had heard that Darren and his father were staying with family and that Darren had spent a couple of days in the hospital since the accident.

I supposed he had. Another two steps or so and it would have been his head. Or, Rita's.

Hazel saw me in the front yard. I saw her as well. I ignored her as long as I could stand it, then relented finally and met her eyes. I saw Cuth inside the house. Or rather, I saw his shadow move behind the curtains and realized he was likely getting up from in front of the television to go into the fridge and devour whatever Hazel had been planning to serve for dinner.

I looked over and let her give me one of her patented half-waves. The uncommitted alliance.

They blame me, she said.

That's not exactly the way it happened, of course. First she complimented me on my peonies, which was fair; they were beautiful that year, and they had sprung open over those few days between the accident and the funeral, as though feeding off of the anxiety and horror of the neighbourhood. They were in full bloom when Hazel stood in my front yard and uncharacteristically questioned herself. I eventually squeezed the hose in half to shut off the flow of water and stood there with her, nodding sympathetically, for the better part of an hour. Twice Dan had come to the window making vague hand gestures that could have been *Can you make me a sandwich?* or *Do you need rescuing?* equally. I didn't respond to either.

They blame me, she said. *They think it's my fault.*

Do they? I said.

It had all happened so fast that day. Even my memories of it are choppy and I was right there. I was the one who leapt forward and pulled Rita away, tucking her head as best I could into my chest. I was the one who screamed to Todd to go inside and call an ambulance. I was the one who told the rest of the kids to go across the street, to our house, to get inside and wait until someone came to get them.

Not that! I shrieked at one of the workers, when he tried to cover poor Tommy—in pieces, dear god he was in pieces—with a filthy tarp from the pickup truck in front of the house.

I had physically kept Rita from running over to Tommy's body. I had to. What would a mother do, her son lying in two pieces, there on her front lawn amidst rotting, mouldy shingles and dog shit? What would she have done? What if she had picked up his—

Rita fainted after struggling and one of the roof guys carried her inside. By then the ambulance was there and when she came to, they gave her a shot. She was hysterical. Just kept screaming. The shot shut her right up. They did that sort of thing then, without asking even. But if they had asked me—

—and it was clear who was in charge—

—I would have told them to go ahead and give it to her. Two maybe.

I called Mac at work.

It was me who packed a bag for all of them, so they didn't have to come back to the house after the ambulance took Rita away. It was me who drove Darren to the hospital.

The only thing I had no hand in, the only information I didn't create on my own, was what exactly it was that Hazel was saying to the men on the roof in the minutes before we went back there and everything happened.

It was so loud, she told me on my front lawn, hose water dripping off the shiny leaves of my peonies, like any other summer day.

I didn't mean to be a pest, she said. *I just wanted to know how long they were going to be. I'm better if I have a deadline,* she said. She smiled weakly at that, and I knew she meant it. I saw her in my head then, inside her house, checking timers, waiting for relief. It touched me. Maybe I even felt a little guilty. In the seconds that passed while she waited for me to say something, I imagined her life since her husband had died: an endless waiting for things to improve, marking time, the minimal comforts she seemed able to provide herself. The narrowness of her happiness.

No one blames you, I lied. It wasn't strictly a lie, since no one openly claimed it was Hazel's fault. But her name came up in all the conversations. Old biddy, busy-body, old witch. No one would have said *bitch,* of course, but they might have thought it.

Labels.

To Hazel's credit, she did not reply to that. *I don't know if I should go to the funeral. I don't know how it would look, either way.*

I nodded. Gave it some thought—although just for form's sake, since there was really no going around it, no matter how you think something truly is, how other people will see it, is entirely outside of most people's control. For that reason it is always important that you do what will be perceived in the long run as the *right* thing. It would only look worse if you didn't.

You have to go, I told her. *Things will be worse if you don't.*

Of course, I meant that.

We saw them again, Rita and Mac, Darren. At the funeral I spoke to a very, very stoned Rita, but it wasn't like seeing them outside the tragedy. The tragedy at that point was still going on, even if it was the last part.

Me and Dan went over to their new rented place with Mac and the cousins and helped to settle them in. It was a nice enough house, even chosen in haste.

We moved furniture and unpacked boxes that day, the reverse of what we'd done just a couple of weeks earlier. *You'll feel at home in no time*, I told Rita.

She smiled but I don't think she heard me.

Someone had picked up takeout fried chicken and we all sat around the still-unadorned kitchen table and ate primitively. There were beers and I remember thinking about how much it looked the way things used to look, and how much it was not.

Rita was a mess. She was wearing an old house dress. Her hair was like a live thing, maybe two-three days unwashed and beginning to clump. Her face was slack and doughy and I suspected she was still taking some "medication." Later I asked Mac and he said she was taking Valium for a while. Just until she felt better.

She wasn't wearing a bra. Without it, the guns hung unhappily down to her middle. It was very sad.

I think I said goodbye to her then. In my heart.

Everyone wondered if Hazel or some other helpful neighbour was going to tell prospective buyers about the accident at Rita and Mac's old place, and that may have been the case because that adorable, well-cared for little house—and let's not forget the fresh shingles—stayed empty for seven months. Just a month or so before Christmas, a young couple, no children, moved in. They looked nice. I took a cake over a week later, decorated with holly made from icing. Real holly is poisonous.

They were the Jansens. She was an educated young woman, with a Bachelor of Science and a teaching degree. He was an executive for a national car rental company. They used to live near the airport. They were looking forward to the quiet.

That made me laugh. I explained that there were at least two kids to every adult on the block and that she shouldn't expect too much peace and quiet. She reddened then and looked down shyly, whether at her expensive shoes or the cake still in her hands, or her belly. It was flat as a freeway.

Actually, she said, *we're expecting.*

Isn't that lovely! I told her.

I promised to have her over for coffee soon and she and her husband over for dinner after that. *We'll see if you like us, first*, I joked. It was strange to be standing out on Rita's stoop and to not be asked in.

She did make a gesture, of course. She said *I'd invite you in, but I'm in the middle of something.*

(Ah.)

Her name was Terry. She took her time getting around to asking about my children and I have to admit, there was a touchy moment when I was reluctant to tell her I was home all day with two kids in school. Not just in school, but actually carting themselves off to their own activities after school, also. In another year or so, Todd would be taller than me. Kerry was still working his way up.

Oh I admire you, she said. *For staying home. I just wish I could. I've been off work for two months now and I'm about going mad!*

I told her you keep busy. Once the children came along, she would have trouble finding time to (bitch) think. *Motherhood*, I said, *was all-consuming*. I even laughed a little, to soften the blow.

She did not laugh with me. Instead she nodded earnestly and said, *Do you feel like you've missed out on other opportunities? I mean, like, careers?*

I must have dropped my jaw onto Rita's stoop (not Rita's any more, I guess) because she quickly clarified what she meant. *Oh oh, please don't misunderstand, I'm only posing a question. I think it's marvellous*

(marvellous)

what you're doing, setting your own intellectual needs aside, for your family. It's the greatest sacrifice!

Oh.

In fact, she said, this time smiling slyly as though letting me in on a stock tip. Giving me the name of a horse in the third. Throwing me a bone. *I'm thinking of starting a women's consciousness raising group, right here in the neighbourhood.*

Oh.

We had one in my old neighbourhood. It was very enlightening.

I was tempted, so tempted: *we have a Tupperware group* or *we meet once a week to practise rolling over* or *we have a dusting club we like to meet for prayer meet for recipes meet to discuss keeping our mouths shut wearing saran wrap carrying a martini—*

But I said, *How interesting. Do let me know when.*

Oh, *please* do.

By June, Terry was enormous with pregnancy and looking very much a woman who might not be forming a consciousness raising group. Whatever freedoms and liberations she had gained pre-pregnancy, it was clear that they had no bearing on the fact that she was now large enough to require help up and down stairs, in and out of her husband's car, and it looked to me—when I checked—that her shoes were all slip-on. Boy or girl, that was going to be one big baby.

Her women's group in the neighbourhood never really caught fire and while the camaraderie of the Rita days had dimmed somewhat, there was still a lot of back-and-forthing among the moms and ladies of Burlington Street to raise the consciousness of whoever we needed to talk about. Course, the women's "movement" was something we had all heard about. Much was made of burning bras, something that seemed to titillate rather than enlighten, but I didn't know anyone who did it.

If we talked about Terry around the neighbourhood, and we did—as we would any newcomer, but particularly one who wanted to obliterate our way of life—it was about her surprising friendship with Hazel Kummel. I don't think anyone would have predicted that.

I understood it, though.

It was just by chance that I saw Hazel going over to Terry and Martin's house one afternoon not very long after they moved in. It was December, still before Christmas and I knew the weather would turn soon and I would be trapped inside the house, when I wasn't trapped inside the car. I decided to pull my old-lady-cart to the grocery and get some fresh air. I had an unobstructed view of Hazel, some kind of small package in hand, crossing the lane and going up the walk to the Jansens' back door. She didn't see me. It all seemed shifty and suspicious, and had I seen anyone other than Hazel skulking around the way she was, casing the joint like some nervous teenager, I might have called something out. *Hey you!* Or maybe *Excuse me!* Canadian threats.

But it was Hazel. And as she got closer to the back door I could see that the small package in her hand was wrapped in pink paper and I wondered if it wasn't a baby gift. Since that was well before Terry was showing, I realized Hazel must just know.

I guessed then that they were friends.

Really?

Looking back, it's always so very easy to see where things get started. At the time something is happening, it's less obvious that a *moment* is taking place. Case in point: when someone is murdered, no one runs up and down the street, screaming that a serial killer is on the loose. It all happens at a much slower, more stunted pace. Another body, and another body, and another body, until someone claims it was all the same knife.

It was just like that, with Hazel and that terrible song.

The folks on one side of us had a little dog by the name of Peanuts. Probably named so because he was about as smart as a bag of them. Peanuts, cute as he was, was a barker, with one of those high-pitched barks that curdle your brain. He was also reluctant to stop barking once wound up, so if you had to walk past their house, for any reason, you would set him off and then his bark would be echoing up the street for a good twenty minutes after you'd passed. Most of us learned to walk on the other side of the street. Bark, bark, bark, right next door to me. It seemed the only thing the animal could do. Cute though.

Hazel kind of hated that dog. More than once she'd knocked on their door, complaining about their dog. *Obedience school* was her stern advice. Obedience school.

Sometime after Terry's baby had been born, the disturbing little dog went missing.

It was a Monday, I think, because it seemed to me it was the night all of us usually went to the library, me and the boys.

As the boys and I were on our way out the door, the two adorable little girls from next door came up the walk with their mother, asking if we'd seen their little dog. The younger one had clearly been crying, and her sister seemed on the verge of it. They had been looking since after school. It seemed the dog might have gotten out of the house unnoticed.

The mother looked downright stricken. I remember meeting her eyes. I guessed mom might have had a distracting day, thinking groceries, lessons after school, what's for supper, anything but yappy dogs sneaking out between your legs and taking off down the street. It would have looked like a shadow. A blink of god's eye.

He'll turn up, I told her sympathetically. *I'm sure everyone will keep an eye out.*

She nodded hopefully and said it hadn't been so very long. If he had gotten out at lunch, he would be getting hungry. Someone would notice him. *He has all the proper identification*, she said. Collar, tags.

I agreed, it was just a matter of time. I volunteered the boys to go and help to look for Peanuts. And they did. We never made it to the library.

They didn't find the dog that night. They didn't find the dog until it started to smell and that took weeks because it was only spring and the thaw was slow that year. Cuth found him when he was spring cleaning the yard for his mother. I heard him telling my boys that it took him quite a while to pinpoint where the smell was coming from.

Smelled so bad it seemed like it was coming from everywhere, he told them.

I knew that. We had a cat die under a pile of lumber once. Terrible cat, a biter and a scratcher. I knew exactly how bad that smelled. Smell can stick to you for days.

Those little girls were devastated. An amateur investigation seemed to imply that the little fellow had been hit by a car in the lane maybe the day he went missing. Hit hard enough that he was thrown over the fence into Hazel's backyard. Had to be. The gate was always shut at the Kummels', and because the gate and fence ran all the way to the ground, there seemed no way for the dog to have gotten into the yard unless it was literally thrown high. Knocked airborne.

There was the slight possibility that a driver, having hit the dog, stopped the car, put it in park, got out, saw Peanuts—alive but badly injured—and chose to toss the dog over the fence, assuming maybe, that it lived there, or not caring. That seemed *much* too cruel. Even for a barky dog.

In any case, with what was likely the last of its life, the dog must have crawled under the gazebo and died. A bit of blood and a slight depression in the muddy yard seemed to indicate where he'd hit ground, and how far he'd had to crawl. Not far, really, although he had been quite a small dog.

In retrospect you could see how a person could jump to conclusions, even horrible, unprovable, conclusions.

As far as I knew, Hazel and Terry remained friends. Things went on in a usual fashion and I suppose it was all very good for Hazel, given that she seemed to have limited friendships and family was scarce. Terry and Martin were good for Hazel. And good for them, too, I suspect, since their family also seemed MIA and Hazel was handy for babysitting. For the life of me I can't think of what they named that baby.

Martin, Terry's national car rental executive husband, was in fact dropping that baby off at Hazel's on their way to something or other when the next horrible thing happened.

It didn't seem possible that *two* horrible things could happen from the same house, but then they did, just the same.

I didn't see it, myself.

It was early in the morning, and I was in the kitchen making the boys' breakfast before school, and I can even remember what it was, if only because I spilled half of it when Kerry hollered like a banshee from the front room. Peanut butter pancakes. You have to remember the little things, because they will matter.

Martin had walked over next door, and dropped off their little baby at Hazel's. He and Terry were off somewhere for the morning. He was dressed up nicely in a sports jacket and tie, casual, not his usual undertaker's outfit for the car rental place.

Donna Markem from up the street was just saying goodbye to her own husband and happened to see Martin, waving to Hazel, smiling like he didn't have a care in the world. She told me that she'd just turned to go back inside, when there was the ungodly sound of a gunning engine, wheels screeching on pavement, the grind of metal on metal, glass bursting—

And screaming.

Screaming to no end.

My Kerry just happened to open the front door at that moment, adding his own screech. I was in the kitchen and spilled the pancake batter, running to see what happened to my son.

(At the back of my mind was always that afternoon at Rita's—the whoosh, the flash of light, the horrible wet sounds that came after—I ran like a demon, truth be told.)

A car, driven by an elderly lady had gone out of control and smashed right into the side of the Jansens' sedan.

Martin Jansen was nearly cut in half. His legs were badly crushed and of course there was lots of blood. Right after dropping his baby off at Hazel Kummel's. Like any ordinary day.

He died, of course.

In retrospect, between poor Martin and that little dog—and of course poor, poor Tommy—you can see how these things might lead to speculation.

One afternoon on my way to the store, I passed a group of girls hanging around in the school yard. Singing:

Hazel Kummel's coming
She'll get you when you sleep
You'll die a thousand times
when Hazel Kummel creeps

Poor Cuth. There's always a price to pay. But he turned out well, in spite of it all.

Children are always the first ones to figure a neighbourhood out. I remember that we had been on Burlington for six years without really making many friends outside the "next doors" on the block—this is mostly due to the natural restrictions of a mother with young children. You can't very well spend all of your time running up and down the block having coffee.

Girls maybe not so much, but boys, they explore. The boys get on their bikes and ride all over hell's half acre and come home with the news; they knew, for instance, about the little dog—Peanuts—before anyone and while it was not part of the story they shared with us, their parents, I imagine that the boys found a nice long, sharp stick and poked at that little dog before they dragged it out from under the gazebo. I imagined that, *they* would hardly say so, of course. Boys get the news, girls interpret it.

Hazel Kummel's coming.

That's why I think it was a girl who worked up that rhyme. Boys lose interest. I wouldn't be surprised if it had been one of the girls who lost their dog, Peanuts. An argument could be made in their favour of course, that it wasn't really their meanness so much as their grief, and they were really just little girls.

She'll get you when you sleep/You'll die a thousand times/when Hazel Kummel creeps.

That rhyme never went away. They might still be singing it now, for all I know. I don't have small children any more, so I'm not as in touch with these things as I used to be, but I know that they say things. The kids around the neighbourhood still talk to me; I'm always friendly and my family comes around regularly—my successful boys, so handsome and smart. Very smart young men.

Successful.

So sometimes I give a passing child a cookie (this is becoming more risky, since children are no longer supposed to talk to anyone—stranger-danger—living two or three doors away from someone does not even qualify them as an acquaintance). The cookies will grease their wheels as they say, and they'll tell me things.

There's a witch lives across the street.

Oh?

She eats pets. Especially the ones you love.

Oh?

She killed a kid once. Cut off his head.

And how could she do that?

Her fingernails are like knives. At night she takes off her mask and her eyes are full of worms and her teeth are fangs she's a witch—

And when you look into her eyes you can see the abyss. Not in so many words, I guess; but that's what the kids say.

Hazel did herself no favours by sneaking around, peeking out her window instead of pulling the curtains open and giving people a wave once in a while. She kept her gate locked. She looked sideways at people when they walked by, like she was giving them some kind of evil eye.

Aging was not her friend. Too many years of hunching gave her a stooped-over look that implied a hunch, even if there wasn't one there. She kept herself indoors and was pale. She kept her hair long, even after it was thinning and had turned, not the nice silver-grey that you see now in photos for Viagra and juicers, but a muddy grey that seemed to have no colour at all.

She would yell at the kids for walking on her grass. She put a hand-lettered sign on her lawn—*Keep Off!*—like a dare.

Eventually the kids would dare each other to go touch her front door. *Hazel Kummel's coming.*

Hag. Crone. Witch. Not like she didn't have her hand in it.

I talked to her about it once. We still talked. We talk now, although it has taken on a different flavour in the last few years. I have, somehow, less contempt for her and more pity than I ever have before, but I can't bring myself to like her. Never have been able to and time has not changed that at all. Not since that time in my front yard when she asked about my boys.

Your children. This one and the one on the way. Are they normal?

But I asked once, about ten years ago, when we were both considerably more mobile than we are now, if she didn't want to go with me down to the seniors' centre where I dropped in once a week and had a visit, did some reading for folks who couldn't, dodged a lot of old and roaming hands on a lot of should-be-dead veterans (not that I worried for Hazel's sake, she didn't so much as have half a muffin for a bum, not like me, with my *voluptui*; Rita might have had her guns, but I'd always had the nicest bottom around—and if she hadn't been so busy shoving her bosom into people's faces, maybe some of them would've noticed).

Hazel said she didn't want to go. But that wasn't the first thing she said. The first thing she asked was about who was down there. Were there any old folks from the early days?

I knew who she meant and in fact, John Berth was in there, his wife having died some years earlier. Bertie and Meryl Theodore were both in there. If I remember right, then Mrs. Stanton was also still alive and in the seniors' home, although just barely.

All people from around when Tommy was killed. Just before Martin Jansen was hit by the car.

I told her they might be happy to see a familiar face. For anyone else I might have added a reminiscence about the barbecues in the summer, the Christmas lights contest on the block, the Saturday night parties in July. We'd even had a street party once. For anyone else I would have brought these things up and we might have had a nice jaw about the good old days, but I wasn't sure, even then, that Hazel would have been included.

But she brought so much of it on herself.

I can't go there, she said about the senior's home. *No one's going to like me there and then after I go home they'll all be talking.*

What would anyone have to say, Hazel? By then, I was getting old. Tired. Let's be done with it. The days are gone and past. I want to forget and let it go.

They say I'm a witch. That I killed them all. Martin. Tommy—she sucked up breath when she said his name, but god bless she said it—*poor Tommy*.

What I said was, *Suit yourself.*

I didn't do anything to those people, she said. *Not a goddamn thing.*

And she repeated it, as I crossed back to my house. *I didn't do a thing. Not a goddamn thing. You know that. You know that.*

Ad infinitum.

Now is now. Things are changing in the neighbourhood, just as they've been changing all over the world. I think about those barbecues, those parties we used to give on the Saturdays and how innocent and naive our fun was; even our occasional evil was less evil than naughty. The beer we drank, the flirting, the harmless *stick 'em up!* What was considered bad then? Adultery, probably. Drugs. Beating on your kids, your wife. Even gossip was considered a poor choice of time spent— which is why we never really talked about Hazel and Tommy, or Hazel and Martin. Hazel and that yappy little dog. People spoke facts and maybe speculated privately, or maybe after so many years had passed the outcome was no longer important. But you never really talked about things like they do now.

Last week, I had a lady from way down the street somewhere come and tell me that the police had arrested her neighbour's son. I couldn't help myself, of course—and years of self-control couldn't fight the urge—I asked why he was arrested, even though I guessed I knew.

It was drugs. He was involved in a gang.

A gang. On Burlington Street.

I imagine their Saturday night parties are much different from ours. I'm pretty sure the woman who moved into the house on the other side of Rita's old place is cheating on the nice man I think is her husband, although you can't be sure of these things any more. I see her husband leave in the morning, and this other fellow shows up a little while later. But what do I know?

I saw a kid shoplifting. Not a big kid, either, but a little one, about nine years old. He took a handful of candy bars, and saw me watching. Just walked out like Bob's your uncle.

I was in the backyard cleaning up and two young men were walking down the back lane, hurling rocks at the windows in people's garages. Then bold as you please, the skinny one took a can of spray paint out of his pocket and sprayed a name on Mr. Wyshyski's garage door. Might have said "Bunny." It was hard to read, all spikes and swirls.

We used to have tragedies on Burlington. Now there are incidents.

When you get older, it's harder to make what you would call good friends. For one thing, you've spent all those years before you got old talking and thinking about yourself and life and the world around you, so by the time you get old, you have little to debate. By the time you get old, there's so little left to say. The young kids, they don't believe it, but sure as the dead, the old ones like me, we know. I can't set the time on my DVD player, but I could explain to you what time is and where it sits in the grand scheme of things. I just don't bother.

But it makes it harder to find friends.

The friend I have made is Josie Tubman, a black woman who moved to Canada from Florida. She has a slight Jamaican accent. Josie says, *We*— and she drags out the long "e" and it's charming, *are not of dis worl any mo, eh my darlin'? Weee straddlin' the udder one!*

Josie has quite a spiritual side.

It was Josie who first mentioned that Hazel was acting oddly.

Your friend she playin wid haf a deck dese days. Someone gonna do sumting bout dat.

The madness seemed to coincide with the arrival of a new neighbour. The new guy moved into Rita's old house. It had been empty for quite a while and it was good to have someone move in. It's bad to have a house sit empty too long. Undesirable elements could move in.

That was not true in this case.

Hazel hadn't crossed that street to talk to me in quite a while, but she crossed to tell me about the new neighbour. I hadn't actually seen her do it, and I know it couldn't have been easy. I could see her in my mind's eye, taking an hour to debate it in her head. Staring out the window, peering through her curtains like some Old West coward wincing through the doors of the saloon. Working up the courage to come out in the yard. The crossing would have been the most entertaining, she would have *held her head high*, she would have *walked tall*, she would have *looked straight ahead*, except for the single furtive glance from side to side that she would not have been able to avoid.

Anyway, I was in the kitchen putting together something when she came to the door. I was surprised and I showed it, just to tweak her nose a bit.

Well, Hazel Kummel! What a surprise!

To her credit, she didn't take the bait and instead got right to the point. And what a point it was.

Something's very wrong with that new fellow, she said.

I know why she picked me of course.

This is my neighbourhood. I haven't been here the longest; that's been Hazel. But the both of us can remember when the 400-block was an empty field. Now there's not just a 400-block of Burlington, but also 500, 600 and it bottoms out at 797, where they've built a shopping centre. It hasn't done well and the parking lot is starting to look a lot like an empty field, funny that. We were here when the street behind me used to be a ball park. The boys were playing there that day when everything changed for poor Tommy. And poor Hazel, I guess. When I moved in, there was a milkman every day, and there was still an iceman if you can imagine. That was for the old folks who hadn't switched over, of course, but I can sure remember him delivering ice to the houses up the block. Department stores still delivered to the door. Seeing that truck come up the road was a big treat—someone was getting something. The kids would run out, follow the truck and then hang around on the sidewalk until the mother who got the delivery would hold up the item and show everyone.

Hazel and I knew this neighbourhood. We knew these roads. We'd seen them naked, knew what was under the concrete, under the sidewalks, under the untrimmed grasses, the fledgling gardens, the indifferent play equipment rusting into dust.

We'd watched the Masons' house go up. We all went down there every few days, the kids first bundled up in scarves and mittens, and by the time they were putting the walls up, the kids were in spring jackets. We checked the progress of that house and so we got to know the Masons before they moved in.

Odious people. Cranky. He was a drinker. Bad form.

But we knew their house. We knew a lot of the houses. We knew Rita's place, too. Sometime between Rita and Mac and the people who moved in after the Jansens, a basement was put in the house. I believe it was Terry Jansen's insurance company that had something to do with it. I just know Terry dumped the house as quickly as possible. I don't know if it was because of what happened to Martin, or if she just decided she didn't need the house anymore. Anyway, they put in a basement.

That was something.

They hacked away at the bottom of the house and then spent a few days sticking—I kid you not—jacks, like the jack you use to change a flat tire, but bigger, under the house. And then they jacked the whole thing up.

Anyway, when they were putting the basement into Rita and Mac's old place, I made a habit of walking down there in the evening, when I was out for my constitutional. Mounds of earth had been piled up toward the lane, and as the task went on, there were three piles of black dirt and I remembered wondering how mothers kept the kids out of those mountains of dirt. Dirt's a magnet to a little child. As the summer wore on, the sun would slant just so and you could see the sides of the basement taking shape, the men having dug all day.

One night when I was walking by—this was just near the end of the project as I would see later—I thought I heard a noise coming from down inside. A little noise, almost blending into the background of the night.

A little mewling sound.

I did get closer to listen, going right up into the yard and messing my shoes with clay and mud. I leaned as close to the edge as was wise and couldn't see a damn thing in the dark. The basement smelled of what it was: earth and clay. It was intoxicating.

Leaning as I did, I heard it. It was a mewling, very faint. Probably a kitten.

At the time, I smirked to myself, thinking the guys had been gone for the weekend and a mother cat had moved in and given birth in there.

In the midst of death, we are in life, a kind of reversal of the natural order.

The next day the trucks came and poured the concrete for the basement. Before I even thought about the kitten again, the basement was poured. My front door was open with just the screen in place, and I heard the truck rumble over. I heard them all applauding, and that's when I went and poked my head out the door.

The workers stood around, clapping, the terribly echoing din of the empty barrel of the cement truck pulling away, the job finished. I remember smiling, thinking *there that's done* and then the kitten ran through my mind.

I pushed it out. Reminded myself I hadn't actually seen a kitten, just thought I'd heard a kitten. I let it go for almost a month when a little boy and his sister came to the door with their wagon full of kittens just weaned and ready for new homes. Turned out they lived down the lane from the basement place.

The kittens were black and white. One of them had a little black spot right on his nose. *His name is Pepper*, the girl told me. *Like salt and pepper?* Cute as pie they all were.

I never said a thing about it to anyone. Not everything can be controlled, not everything can be managed.

That's just to say: Hazel and I, we knew the neighbourhood. That's why she came to me.

There's something wrong with the new fellow, she said.

Oh, she told me an earful.

Rita and Mac's old house—I still thought of it that way—had been empty for months. That's never good on a street like ours, where we're riding an uneasy train between neighbourhood and ghetto. If a house is empty too long the kids get to thinking it's an old toy no one wants and they start to treat it as such. Windows get broken. Beer bottles show up in the backyard. Place gets broken into and no doubt about it, before you know it, you have a crack house on your hands.

Anyway, weren't we all glad when the sold sign went up in the front. It wasn't too long a Saturday after that when a moving van showed up in front and started unloading things into the house.

No one saw much of the new owner that first day, or after that really. It was almost a non-event, just some guy moved in, end of story. He didn't play his music loud and no naked woman ran screaming out the front door, a chainsaw stuck in her backside. You never really know what to expect though.

Then came Hazel with her neighbourly ways.

He never goes to sleep, she said.

She was already upset by the time she worked up her nerve to come over to my house, to cross that great wide street. *There's something wrong with the new fellow.* She wasn't crying, or rending her flesh, but she was clearly in a state. And no slight on Josie, but she sounded sane and lucid to me. Maybe tired. And she'd always been a little crazy.

I remarked that she couldn't possibly know if he slept or not. She slept. Maybe he slept when she slept. And what was she doing peeking in at him, anyway?

She could see him through her upstairs bedroom window. The window looked down into his front room, just enough so that she could see the top of his head, and sometimes his legs. Never his feet, though.

I go to bed, he's awake, watching TV. I can see the light flicker from the set. I wake up he's still there, sitting in the same way. Watching television.

She was old, she said. It's true that the old don't sleep like the young. When we do sleep, it's fitful and filled with odd dreams. I can wake up some days and look at the clock and think, *Oh goodness I've got to get lunches ready*, and I'm halfway out of bed before I remember that my boys are grown men.

Or I can look at the clock at three A.M. and think of how time is running out. This soothes me, more than anything else. To know you're almost done, you know?

So he doesn't sleep, I offered. Gently—she did come all the way across the street, the old woman—I suggested that it really wasn't any of her business.

She shook her head. *You don't know what else*, she said. *You don't know.*

Tell me, I said. I tried to keep a noncommittal smile on my face. Tried.

It's hard to tell when an old woman is embarrassed. I don't think that we have enough blood vessels left in our rags of faces to blush, not really. And yet I think I saw her go red under her complexion, which, like mine, had darkened over the years.

Then she was stumbling, backtracking. *Never mind.*

(I insisted.

No.

Tell me.)

Will you believe me? It doesn't sound right and I know that.

I nodded, but it wasn't enough. A sort of dignity came over her, poor Hazel. In that straightening of her back I did recognize something painful, and I felt a twinge of guilt. But I was too old for guilt, for admonition.

You know me, she said. *I've been whatever I've been, but I don't make up stories. I didn't do anything and I don't tell lies about it and* you *know that.*

You know that.

There was a little too much emphasis on the *you know that*, but I acknowledged that to be true. I do know that.

The new neighbour, she said. *I think he has a tail.*

There was a guy used to walk down the block a few years back, probably as long as twenty years ago, really, who had gout. A ring around his neck that made him look uncomfortable and freakish. A lady used to have a seeing eye dog, one block over on the south side, lost her left leg up to her knee as well as her eyesight to diabetes and she used a wheelchair. Todd had an albino kid in his class for a few years around '74.

No tails though.

I brought Hazel inside and made her a cup of tea. She looked around, fascinated by it all and I realized that in fifty years, she'd probably never been closer than the front door. That seemed suddenly strange to me, and not much does any more. Not sad, but very odd, almost as if it were impossible. I tried to reverse the situation and put myself in her house. I'd never been in. I supposed I would have been as star-struck.

She looked at my pictures on the wall, some so old they were black and white. She pointed at one that had all the boys in the photo: Todd and Kerry, Tommy and Darren, Cuth, a couple of boys whose appearance was fleeting and whose names escaped with them.

I remember that, she said. The boys all had their arms around each other. Good-looking, young boys. Hazel smiled for the first time.

We sipped our tea. She grabbed looks around the house, drinking in my sofa, my coffee table, the tall spice cupboard in my kitchen.

He has a tail, you say? I wanted to hear.

Our eyes met over the table and held there, after she'd told me everything. How he caught her looking at him through his window and how he stared at her until her head hurt, how she couldn't look away—

—*tried to turn my head I really did*—

—about how the east side of her house was colder now, than the west side. *It never used to be.* One day she was in her kitchen watching him in his yard. Thought he'd been cutting the lawn. Because he was standing right there by the garden shed. Because she could smell cut grass, that heady, warm smell of fresh cut grass sort of took her away for a moment and she lost track of what she was doing until she realized she was staring right at him—

—*completely naked and his feet oh god help me*—

and he was eating grass. All around his mouth there were smears and tiny cuttings of sweet new grass. I could almost smell it, the way she described it.

What about his feet? I asked.

It took some time to unravel the order in which things had happened. Many times I thought she might cry, but to her credit, she never did. It lent to her credibility. I don't think it was easy for her.

Josie Tubman had seen Hazel in her backyard a week earlier—not long at all after our new neighbour moved in—weeping. Josie was going to ask her what the matter was; even though she wasn't exactly friendly with her, it's hard to watch a person crying like that.

Weepin lak a mudderless chile—she told me.

But what really got Josie's attention, what made Josie come and tell me the thing, was that Hazel in the midst of her weeping pulled her blouse off and wrapped it around her eyes. She said they were burning. Screamed it, actually. To no one in particular.

Josie knows it's my neighbourhood, too.

Hazel hadn't said anything about this to Cuthbert. Hadn't told her doctor. Hadn't said a word to Josie, of course. But Hazel told *me* why she wanted Josie's granddaughter off her lawn. On the surface anyway, it was nice of her, really.

But it was *just me* she told. She finally told me why she'd been yelling at that poor little girl to get her the hell off her lawn. *She might get got.*

And here we are, now.

Hazel, you have to pull yourself together.

She nods. The tea in her cup is gone, but there is still more in the pot. She's not crying or weeping in any way that Josie might call a *mudderless chile*. She's not doing anything. She's very still and sitting at my table. In her lap she has her hands clutched, like an old woman who's on the last turn of the ride and has already seen everything—in this case, a guy with a tail.

Come on Hazel, I say.

I can see her swallow and then she reaches for her tea cup, but it's empty. Very calmly—and I see her hands are shaking—she pours herself just a mouthful and then drinks it.

It's okay. Everything's okay, I tell her. I think I'm smiling. I'm thinking in my head that Cuthbert works somewhere in the north end. I would need the name of the business to get the phone number and I'm not sure where; but I know his wife is a teacher named Sarah, and she teaches near where they live. I know where they live. I can find them if I have to.

She stands reluctantly, slowly. She's probably tired. All the talking, I'm betting it's the most talking she's done in a long time, holed up in that house as long as she has been, and then this neighbour thing. She looks around my house and I know she wishes she could just stay in here forever.

At the door, I'm thinking she's sorry that she told me. Everything has a price.

I take her arm and we cross the street together. As we do, I feel our whole lives in this neighbourhood flash through my mind. As we step up onto the curb on the other side of the street, I feel so close to her. I almost love her. I give her arm a companionable squeeze. Together, we walk over to the new neighbour's house.

He sees us. He's in the backyard. He comes toward us, using a rag to wipe something off his hands. He wears a ball cap at an odd angle, jeans and a t-shirt, like one of the young men from the J. Crew catalogue. I am stricken by how handsome he is.

I smile.

Hazel stiffens beside me and I absentmindedly pat her arm. I nod. *It's okay*, I think without saying. *It's okay now.*

When he is close I look down at his feet. They are covered in sneakers, but there's something odd about them, and a suburban part of me screams that I shouldn't stare. I do, though, because I'm an old woman and I can do as I please.

His feet are round.

Hazel has gone stiff as a board beside me. *It's okay.* I say it, but it comes out in some other language, one she will not know.

I look up and he's smiling. I smile back, broadly, happily. He's just so very handsome.

Hazel, I say even though I know she's gone hollow inside. *This is my friend. His name is Legion.*

I move away from her because I want to see this final step.

He keeps smiling, a calm, warm smile that comes from his eyes and he reaches out to her, pointing his finger, like you might at a child. He taps the end of her nose very gently.

Poke.

It's not loud, but I hear her groan. I can also hear the shriek of her soul, but really, I think I could hear it before. I've been dreaming of it.

He's still smiling, even as Hazel crumbles at his feet, very dead. His teeth are white and even. Just behind him I can see his tail shudder happily. It's thick and naked like a beautiful dark penis. His eyes are blue.

He's a handsome devil.

I'm done and I know that. I go back across the street. I admit I am spent, like I used to be after hours in bed with Dan or the new neighbour, only in another form, of course, many years ago.

I'll call an ambulance and Cuth of course.

I'm a good neighbour.

I can't help it. I am stuck now, going over the past. Everything that's happened in the neighbourhood keeps running through my mind. It all comes back to that first day. Hazel never should have asked that terrible thing. The thing she said on the day we met.

Are they normal? This one and the one on the way? Are they normal?

I bet she wishes she hadn't.

I also bet Rita wishes she had kept her goddamn guns away from Dan. I bet.

Terry and her uppity ways about what women should be doing with their time.

And Hazel. Oh Hazel. She set herself up. What was I to do? Look a gift horse in the mouth? I wasn't raised that way. I also didn't sell my soul for that. Not to be pedantic, but she brought it on herself.

In fact I realize I don't feel bad about any of it. I am relieved. Maybe the little dog. *Peanuts.* And Tommy. Ah, Tommy. Of course it was supposed to be Rita. Wind velocity. Oh well. We do our best, but I think I feel bad about that, too. Maybe.

Who names a dog Peanuts? Is it supposed to be plural?

I sit in my kitchen and wait. Everything is done. I listen for sirens. I don't mind sirens.

Appendix:
The Suburbanight

a Screenplay

Introduction to The Suburbanight

I've always thought there was a great deal of potential for unwholesomeness in isolated relationships, particularly duos. I'm not alone: the *folie à deux* is a classic literary trope, not to mention a common disorder in murderous couples.

Familial relationships are so vulnerable to dysfunction, bound as they are not by lust, but by love and actual *blood*. There are also those many, many hours of the day and night when families are trapped together not only in square footage, but in a kind of *folie à deux* where the outside world is suspect, if only because that inside world is secret.

I write a little film and television in my other life, and frequently write both stories and scripts just for fun. This is one of the few that I would like to see on a screen, because it's some seriously fun shit.

The Suburbanight
by Susie Moloney

IN BLACK

THE SOUND OF A LAWN MOWER

FADE IN:

1EXT. PLEASANT AVE. A NICE SUBURBAN STREET -- DAY1

Pleasant Avenue appears empty and deserted, or still and peaceful, except for a man who mows his lawn. MR. PETERSON resolutely cuts a seemingly already trim lawn.

The lawn mower hits something and at least part of the thing goes flying out.

He stops the lawn mower, bends down to see what he's hit.

He picks it up. It's a piece of a child's toy shark. He looks next door, the only place it could have come from.

2 EXT. ARIA LEFLER'S BUNGALOW -- CONTINUOUS2

The Lefler house is much like the others, but on bong. The grass is too long, it needs a coat of paint and there is a sense of disorder to it.

Mr. Peterson walks up the walk to the front door.

He rings the bell. He puts his ear close to the door and listens to what happens inside.

3INT. ARIA LEFLER'S BUNGALOW -- CONTINUOUS3

The Lefler house is untidy, like the outside of the

244

house, but there is a good, lived-in feel to it. There are some toys scattered about, a pair of fuck-me pumps beside the basket of laundry, crayons, a child's drawings on the fridge.

A large black dog, a lab, reclines on the floor in front of the door. His head is up and facing the sound, but he doesn't move or bark. He seems a pleasant dog, not menacing.

The doorbell resonates through the house, and nothing stirs.

        4EXT. ARIA LEFLER'S BUNGALOW -- CONTINUOUS4

Mr. Peterson rings again. No one comes to the door.

Pissed off, he puts the toy piece into the breast pocket of his shirt in a way that suggests he will, indeed, return.

     5EXT. PLEASANT AVE. A NICE SUBURBAN STREET -- LATER5

The sun sets on suburbia.

The Lefler house is dark, and then the lights come on.

A SMALL ANIMAL SQUEAKS

             ARIA (O.S.)
        Stewart! Feed the pigs.

       6INT. ARIA LEFLER'S BUNGALOW -- CONTINUOUS6

Several guinea pigs shuffle over one another in a large cage in a child's bedroom.

The little boy is STEWART LEFLER, about 8. He's cute,

maybe small for his age, fair and elegant.

7INT. THE LEFLER KITCHEN -- CONTINUOUS7

Stewart opens the fridge. Inside the fridge are dark containers of unknown foods, but the fridge is mostly empty. We get only a glimpse of this, however, because Stewart grabs a Tupperware container and closes the fridge.

He carries it across the kitchen to his bedroom.

8INT. STEWART'S BEDROOM -- CONTINUOUS8

He opens the container and puts bits of vegetable into the cage for the guinea pigs. The pigs squeak and complain and eat the food.

The black dog, TANSY, is beside him and watches this process.

Stewart puts the lid on the container and watches them for a moment.

                    ARIA (O.S.)
          It's movie night.

                    STEWART
          I know. Can we watch anything?
          Anything we want?

Standing in the doorway of Stewart's bedroom is his mother, ARIA LEFLER, an attractive, youngish woman, a MILF of striking features. She looks like her son.

                    ARIA
          You mean anything you want.

                    STEWART
          I *do* mean that.

                    ARIA
What do you want to watch?

                  STEWART
Harrison Ford.

                    ARIA
Harrison Ford? You're a freak
show, kid.

Aria leaves the bedroom. Walks down the hallway to
the living room.

              ARIA (CONT'D)
(calling over her shoulder)

      You got work to do first.

              STEWART (O.S.)
I know.

                ARIA (O.S.)
Take Tansy out.

    9EXT. THE LEFLER LIVING ROOM -- MOMENTS LATER9

Aria shuffles some papers and magazines on the coffee
table in a vain attempt to clean up. She puts them
on another flat surface. She picks up a couple of
toys and tosses them into a basket already partly
full of toys. She is about to tuck into the laundry
that needs to be folded when there is a knock on the
front door.

She looks up suspiciously.

    10INT. STEWART'S BEDROOM -- CONTINUOUS10

Stewart looks up when the knock at the door sounds.

11EXT. ARIA LEFLER'S BUNGALOW -- CONTINUOUS11

Mr. Peterson stands at the door, rocking on his heels.

The door opens to reveal Aria.

For the first time we notice she is wearing mismatched pyjamas. She stares out at him. There is no love lost here.

Peterson waits for her to speak, but she does not.

             MR. PETERSON
   Hello Aria. How are you?

             ARIA
   We're good, Todd.

             MR. PETERSON
   Good, good. That boy of yours
   missing any toys?

             ARIA
   I don't know Todd.
          (sighs)
   Do you think he's missing some
   toys?

             MR. PETERSON
   I'm not sure he'd know if he was
   or not. Grass's so thick and high
   you could lose a Buick in there.

This line pleases him.

             ARIA
   Well, thanks for dropping by,
   Todd.

Aria goes to shut the door. Mr. Peterson stops her.

                    MR. PETERSON
          Wait!

He digs around in his pocket for the shark head.

                    MR. PETERSON (CONT'D)
          I'm just saying, I found this in
          the yard.

Aria takes it and examines it, knowing that it is
broken.

                    ARIA
          This is broken.

                    MR. PETERSON
          I ran over it with my mower. What
          the hell was your kid doing,
          playing in my yard? And just
          when was he playing in my yard?

                    ARIA
          I don't know, Todd. This is
          broken. You can have it.

She hands it to him.

                    MR. PETERSON
          Well what the hell am I supposed
          to do with it?

                    ARIA
          That just answers itself, Todd.
          Nice to see you again. Give my
          love to Heidi.

                    MR. PETERSON
          Heidi? It's *Nancy*.

She goes to close the door again. He again stops her.

> MR. PETERSON (CONT'D)
> Whoa, just wait a minute. That's
> not the only reason I'm stopping
> by.

Behind them in the house, the TV sound comes on.

12INT. THE LEFLER LIVING ROOM -- CONTINUOUS12

Stewart turns the TV on, but it's just an excuse to see what's going on at the door. He surreptitiously listens.

13EXT. ARIA LEFLER'S BUNGALOW -- CONTINUOUS13

Aria shifts her body so that Stewart is blocked from Peterson's view.

> ARIA
> Todd, I appreciate you dropping
> by, but I really have an awful
> lot to do--

> MR. PETERSON
> The neighbours and I have been
> talking. We pretty much agreed
> that you have to do something
> about your yard. You have to cut
> that grass. And weed that garden
> or else fill it over with grass
> seed -- if you want I can --

> ARIA
> By "neighbours" I think you
> mean you and Forrest Gump over
> there --

They both look across the street where a goofy looking
man is pretending to water his flowers in the dark,
but is listening.

                    ARIA (CONT'D)
          Got talking and decided to give
          me -- *a poor single mother* -- a
          hard time. Is that right? I work
          nights, Todd Peterson. Did you
          think of that?

                    MR. PETERSON
          No.

                    ARIA
          That's what I thought. Good
          night, Todd.
(calling across the street)
          Run, Forrest! Run!

Aria shuts the door.

          14INT. THE LEFLER LIVING ROOM -- CONTINUOUS14

                    STEWART
          Was that Mr. Peterson?

                    ARIA
          Yeah. He wanted to apologize for
          wrecking your shark.

Stewart is watching TV, sitting very close.

                    STEWART
          Huh?

                    ARIA
          Never mind. Hey, too close. And
          shut it off, you have work to do.

                    STEWART
          What about something to eat?

Aria shuts the TV off.

                    ARIA
             In a while.

                    15INT. THE LEFLER KITCHEN -- LATER15

Aria and Stewart sit at the kitchen table. All around
them are open books, papers, the stuff of school
work. The refrigerator is covered with homemade tests
declaring "Best Ever!" and "Excellent!"

The two of them are dressed now, in street clothes.

Stewart is bent over a paper, labouring. He completes
it and hands it to Aria.

                    STEWART
             Do I need to do these last ones?
             I already did them once.

                    ARIA
(looks at them)
             I guess not. Let me see how you
             did.

She takes the paper from him, begins marking it,
like a teacher.

                    STEWART
          Can I go outside?

Outside, the dog barks. It startles them and they
look towards the kitchen window -- blinds drawn --
as if unsure.

Neither of them move.

There is silence between barks, but they say nothing.

THE GUINEA PIGS SQUEAK IN THE SILENCE.

The barking stops. Aria shrugs.

>   STEWART (CONT'D)
>   I'm hungry.

>   ARIA
>   Just wait. You have another
>   chapter to read.

>   STEWART
>   I already read a half an hour.
>   You said that was all.

>   ARIA
>   Did I?

>   STEWART
>   Can I go outside then?

Aria looks at the clock over the stove. It is 11 pm.

>   ARIA
>   Okay. But we're going to start
>   the movie soon.

>   STEWART
>   What are we going to eat?

>   ARIA
>   I'll see.

Stewart goes outside.

>   16INT. ARIA LEFLER'S BUNGALOW -- MOMENTS LATER16

Aria walks down the hallway to Stewart's bedroom. The room is dark and she can hear the animals squeaking. She turns on the light.

She goes to the cage and peers inside.

She counts them.

She opens the cage door and touches the animals.

                    ARIA
          Hey. Hey.

There is no affection in it. She closes the cage door.

          17EXT. THE LEFLER BACK YARD -- MOMENTS LATER17

It is pitch black outside, except for some light from the street lamps.

Stewart and the dog, Tansy, are outside in the dark.

Stewart picks up a baseball on his way over to his back yard swing. He gets on it, and sways, tossing a ball up into the air. The dog sits beside the swing set, as if waiting.

The chains of the swing squeak. It sounds like the guinea pigs.

          18INT. PETERSON'S KITCHEN -- MOMENTS LATER18

Mr. Peterson is at his kitchen table too, and there is a contrast with the Lefler home. The Peterson house is clearly childless -- tidy, ordered. He is at the table eating a bowl of cereal, dressed for bed in robe, pyjamas and slippers.

He hears the squeak of the swing set. He stands to look out the window.

He can't really see through the window into the dark yard. But he can hear it.

He goes to the back door and peers out into the Lefler back yard.

19P.O.V. THE LEFLER BACK YARD -- CONTINUOUS19

Stewart sees Peterson at the door. He stares. He is tossing the ball up in the air and catching it.

20P.O.V. PETERSON'S BACK YARD -- CONTINUOUS20

Peterson watches the boy swing slowly and toss the ball.

From his point of view, it looks very unwholesome. Because it is.

21EXT. THE LEFLER BACK YARD -- CONTINUOUS21

Stewart stops swinging. Watches Mr. Peterson more closely. He stands and moves forward, towards the border between the two yards -- a chain link fence. He is still tossing the ball. The dog follows him, calmly.

Still holding Mr. Peterson's gaze, Stewart tosses the ball deliberately into Peterson's yard. It bounces slowly.

The dog is alert. He watches Stewart as waiting for the command.

22INT. PETERSON'S KITCHEN -- CONTINUOUS22

Peterson watches the ball bounce into the yard. He

reacts immediately. He pushes the door open, angry.

> MR. PETERSON
> Hey kid --

He is cut off in mid-sentence when he sees the dog.

Stewart stands still and expressionless at the fence as if waiting for Peterson to come out, to come close.

> MR. PETERSON (CONT'D)
> (softer, unsure)
> You better go in, kid. It's late.

Peterson closes the door, but watches. Stewart doesn't move.

> 23INT. PETERSON'S KITCHEN -- CONTINUOUS23

Peterson stands at his door, uncertain.

> ARIA (O.S.)
> Stewart, time to come in --

Peterson listens as the Lefler door opens and closes.

He looks at his clock and sees that it is 11:30. Much too late for a kid to be up.

> 24INT. THE LEFLER LIVING ROOM -- LATER24

Aria and Stewart are on the sofa in their living room. They are watching their movie, "Witness" about a weird son and his weird mother.

> STEWART
> Mom, is John Book real?

                    ARIA
          No.

                  STEWART
          I wish he was.

Outside the dog starts barking. The two of them look
at each other, then back at the TV.

The dog continues to bark. Stewart snuggles under
his mother's arm. Head to head they watch the TV.

          25EXT. PETERSON'S BUNGALOW -- MOMENTS LATER25

DOG BARKS

The lights come on in the Peterson house.

               MR. PETERSON (O.S.)
          After midnight for chrissakes --

Peterson leaves his house by the front door, in robe
and slippers, storming to Aria's house.

          26INT. ARIA LEFLER'S BUNGALOW -- CONTINUOUS 26

There is a loud banging on the door.

                  STEWART
          Should I pause it?

                    ARIA
          Better.

She rises and opens the door. Peterson is on the
stoop, bed head, mad as hell.

               MR. PETERSON
          For the love of god, it's after
          midnight, your dog is barking

like the hound from bloody hell
-- I can't take much more of
this --

                ARIA
Calm down, Todd.

            MR. PETERSON
Calm down!? You're the worst
neighbour on the street! Your
yard is a disgusting mess, toys
everywhere, grass like a goddamn
jungle, lose a goddamn Buick,
your dog barking at all hours of
the goddamn --

                ARIA
Hey! Language. I got a kid in
here --

            MR. PETERSON
And what the hell is that kid
doing up!?
(shakes his finger at her)
    You do something about that dog
right now --

                ARIA
All right. Wipe the spit off your
chin.

There is a break in the conversation and they note
the dog is no longer barking.

            ARIA (CONT'D)
There. He stopped.

Peterson appears to want to say more, but is so
angry and frustrated he simply shakes his finger at
her again. He turns and walks angrily away from the

house.

> MR. PETERSON
> (under his breath)
> ... Goddamn Buick ...

27INT. THE LEFLER LIVING ROOM -- CONTINUOUS27

Aria sits down on the couch. The movie is paused. Stewart is looking at her.

> STEWART
> I'm hungry.

> ARIA
> (nods with conviction)
> Okay.

28INT. THE LEFLER KITCHEN -- MOMENTS LATER28

Stewart is clearing books and papers from the table in preparation for dinner. He puts a table cloth down -- plastic -- and some napkins, etc.

Aria is washing her hands in the kitchen sink.

> STEWART
> Do we know any cops?

> ARIA
> No. Wash your hands, ok?

Aria dries her hands. She is looking out into the yard.

Stewart leaves the kitchen, Aria goes out into the back.

29INT. THE LEFLER BATHROOM -- MOMENTS LATER29

Stewart is washing his hands.

A LAWNMOWER STARTS

He dries his hands.

> STEWART
> (singing)
>> "Flintstones, meet the
>> Flintstones, they're a modern,
>> stone-aged famileee --

        30EXT. PETERSON'S BACK YARD -- CONTINUOUS30

THE SOUND OF A LAWN MOWER RUNNING

The back door to the Peterson's house flings open, and
Mr. Peterson stands there staring out into the dark.

He is beyond angry. He is the neighbour from hell.

He stomps again over to the Leflers', this time using
the gate to go in the back yard.

> MR. PETERSON
> This is the last straw --

He stomps up to the lawn mower only to find it lonely
and abandoned, motor running, in the middle of the
Lefler backyard.

> MR. PETERSON (CONT'D)
> What the hell?

        31INT. THE LEFLER KITCHEN -- CONTINUOUS31

Stewart and Aria watch through the kitchen window.

        32EXT. THE LEFLER BACK YARD -- CONTINUOUS32

Peterson is at the back door. He bangs. Aria calls out, sing-songy.

>   ARIA
>   Come in!

Peterson pushes his way through the door and into the kitchen.

>   MR. PETERSON
>   You better have an explanation
>   for --

Aria, Stewart and Tansy stand in the kitchen. They greet Peterson.

>   ARIA
>   Hello Todd.

Aria and Stewart smile, revealing the teeth of the vampire.

Peterson opens his mouth to scream.

It doesn't get that far. They are on him.

33EXT. PLEASANT AVE. A NICE SUBURBAN STREET - NIGHT 33

The lights go out in the Lefler bungalow.
The sun rises on suburbia.

Somewhere, a lawnmower starts up.

>   THE END

ACKNOWLEDGEMENTS

The stories in this collection were written over a number of years. I have been blessed over those years to have many friends and colleagues who have inspired, read, critiqued, grimaced at, and encouraged these stories and others. They have also provided research, desktops, tabletops, bucolic settings, food, drink, laughs, and unwavering support. In no order at all, they are: Vern Thiessen, Armin Wiebe, Josh Rioux, Dawn Cumming, John Hudson, Rick Wagner, Carmit Levite, Donna Carreiro, Sam Mollard, Andris Taskins, Billie Livingston, Mark Leslie Lefebvre, Laurence Steven, Anne Collins, Jared Moore, Stephen King, Dan Lazar, Janis Rosen, Steve George, Jeani Rector, Peter Halasz, and my Auntie Joannie. I would also like to thank Sandra Kasturi for her dedication in the editing of these stories.

PREVIOUSLY PUBLISHED

"The Audit" was originally published in the horror anthology, *A Feast of Frights*, published by The Horror Zine, April 2012, California.

"Sown," published here as "Reclamation on the Forest Floor," was originally published in the horror anthology, *Campus Chills*, edited by Mark Leslie. Stark Publishing, October 2009, Hamilton.

"I (heart) Dogs," was originally published in the Canadian literary periodical, "Prairie Fire," Volume 30, No. 1, Spring 2009, Manitoba.

ABOUT THE AUTHOR

Susie Moloney is the award-winning, bestselling author of *Bastion Falls*, *A Dry Spell*, *The Dwelling* and *The Thirteen*. Her short fiction has appeared in journals, anthologies and magazines. She lives with her husband, playwright Vern Thiessen, and a blind dog named Scrappy.

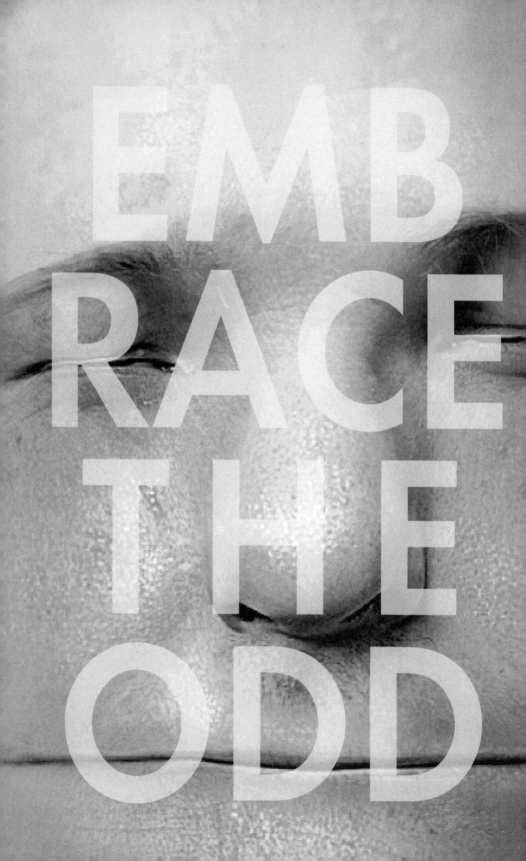

THE INNER CITY
KAREN HEULER

Anything is possible: people breed dogs with humans to create a servant class; beneath one great city lies another city, running it surreptitiously; an employee finds that her hair has been stolen by someone intent on getting her job; strange fish fall from trees and birds talk too much; a boy tries to figure out what he can get when the Rapture leaves good stuff behind. Everything is familiar; everything is different. Behind it all, is there some strange kind of design or merely just the chance to adapt? In Karen Heuler's stories, characters cope with the strange without thinking it's strange, sometimes invested in what's going on, sometimes trapped by it, but always finding their own way in.

AVAILABLE NOW
978-1-927469-33-0

GOLDENLAND PAST DARK
CHANDLER KLANG SMITH

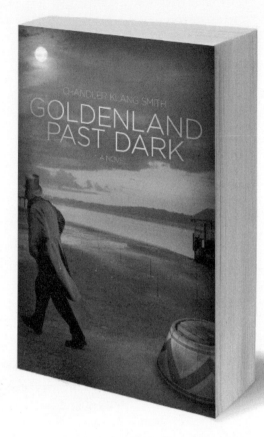

A hostile stranger is hunting Dr. Show's ramshackle travelling circus across 1960s America. His target: the ringmaster himself. The troupe's unravelling hopes fall on their latest and most promising recruit, Webern Bell, a sixteen-year-old hunchbacked midget devoted obsessively to perfecting the surreal clown performances that come to him in his dreams. But as they travel through a landscape of abandoned amusement parks and rural ghost towns, Webern's bizarre past starts to pursue him, as well.

AVAILABLE NOW
978-1-927469-35-4

THE WARRIOR WHO CARRIED LIFE
GEOFF RYMAN

Only men are allowed into the wells of vision. But Cara's mother defies this edict and is killed, but not before returning with a vision of terrible and wonderful things that are to come . . . and all because of five-year-old Cara. Years later, evil destroys the rest of Cara's family. In a rage, Cara uses magic to transform herself into a male warrior. But she finds that to defeat her enemies, she must break the cycle of violence, not continue it. As Cara's mother's vision of destiny is fulfilled, the wonderful follows the terrible, and a quest for revenge becomes a quest for eternal life.

AVAILABLE NOW
978-1-927469-38-5

ZOMBIE VERSUS FAIRY FEATURING ALBINOS
JAMES MARSHALL

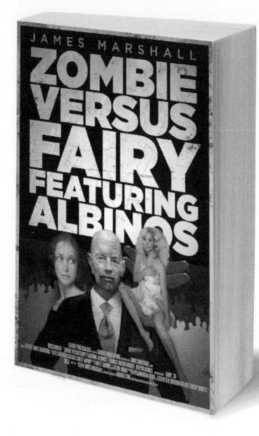

In a PERFECT world where everyone DESTROYS everything and eats HUMAN FLESH, one ZOMBIE has had enough: BUCK BURGER. When he rebels at the natural DISORDER, his marriage starts DETERIORATING and a doctor prescribes him an ANTI-DEPRESSANT. Buck meets a beautiful GREEN-HAIRED pharmacist fairy named FAIRY_26 and quickly becomes a pawn in a COLD WAR between zombies and SUPERNATURAL CREATURES. Does sixteen-year-old SPIRITUAL LEADER and pirate GUY BOY MAN make an appearance? Of course! Are there MIND-CONTROLLING ALBINOS? Obviously! Is there hot ZOMBIE-ON-FAIRY action? Maybe! WHY AREN'T YOU READING THIS YET?

AVAILABLE NOW
978-1-77148-141-0

THE MONA LISA SACRIFICE
BOOK ONE OF THE BOOK OF CROSS
PETER ROMAN

For thousands of years, Cross has wandered the earth, a mortal soul trapped in the undying body left behind by Christ. But now he must play the part of reluctant hero, as an angel comes to him for help finding the Mona Lisa—the real Mona Lisa that inspired the painting. Cross's quest takes him into a secret world within our own, populated by characters just as strange and wondrous as he is. He's haunted by memories of Penelope, the only woman he truly loved, and he wants to avenge her death at the hands of his ancient enemy, Judas. The angel promises to deliver Judas to Cross, but nothing is ever what it seems, and when a group of renegade angels looking for a new holy war show up, things truly go to hell.

AVAILABLE NOW
978-1-77148-145-8

THE 'GEISTERS
DAVID NICKLE

When Ann LeSage was a little girl, she had an invisible friend—a poltergeist, that spoke to her with flying knives and howling winds. She called it the Insect. And with a little professional help, she contained it. But the nightmare never truly ended. As Ann grew from girl into young woman, the Insect grew with her, becoming a thing of murder. Now, as she embarks on a new life married to successful young lawyer Michael Voors, Ann believes that she finally has the Insect under control. But there are others vying to take that control away from her. They may not know exactly what they're dealing with, but they know they want it. They are the 'Geisters. And in pursuing their own perverse dream, they risk spawning the most terrible nightmare of all.

AVAILABLE NOW
978-1-77148-143-4

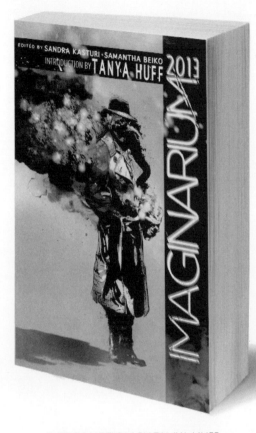

THE SUMMER IS ENDED AND WE ARE NOT YET SAVED

JOEY COMEAU

Martin is going to Bible Camp for the summer. He's going to learn archery and swimming, and he's going to make new friends. He's pretty excited, but that's probably because nobody told him that this is a horror novel.

AVAILABLE NOW
978-1-77148-147-2

TELL MY SORROWS TO THE STONES
CHRISTOPHER GOLDEN

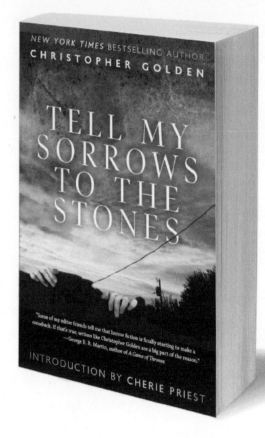

A circus clown willing to give anything to be funny. A spectral gunslinger who must teach a young boy to defend the ones he loves. A lonely widower making a farewell tour of the places that meant the world to his late wife. A faded Hollywood actress out to deprive her ex-husband of his prize possession. A grieving mother who will wait by the railroad tracks for a ghostly train that always has room for one more. A young West Virginia miner whose only hope of survival is a bedtime story. These are just some of the characters to be found in *Tell My Sorrows to the Stones*.

AVAILABLE AUGUST 2013
978-1-77148-153-3

MORE FROM CHIZINE

HORROR STORY AND OTHER HORROR STORIES ROBERT BOYCZUK [978-0-9809410-3-6]

NEXUS: ASCENSION ROBERT BOYCZUK [978-0-9813746-8-0]

THE BOOK OF THOMAS: HEAVEN ROBERT BOYCZUK [978-1-927469-27-9]

PEOPLE LIVE STILL IN CASHTOWN CORNERS TONY BURGESS [978-1-926851-05-1]

THE STEEL SERAGLIO MIKE CAREY, LINDA CAREY & LOUISE CAREY [978-1-926851-53-2]

SARAH COURT CRAIG DAVIDSON [978-1-926851-00-6]

A BOOK OF TONGUES GEMMA FILES [978-0-9812978-6-6]

A ROPE OF THORNS GEMMA FILES [978-1-926851-14-3]

A TREE OF BONES GEMMA FILES [978-1-926851-57-0]

ISLES OF THE FORSAKEN CAROLYN IVES GILMAN [978-1-926851-36-5]

ISON OF THE ISLES CAROLYN IVES GILMAN [978-1-926851-56-3]

FILARIA BRENT HAYWARD [978-0-9809410-1-2]

THE FECUND'S MELANCHOLY DAUGHTER BRENT HAYWARD [978-1-926851-13-6]

IMAGINARIUM 2012: THE BEST CANADIAN SPECULATIVE WRITING
    EDITED BY SANDRA KASTURI & HALLI VILLEGAS [978-0-926851-67-9]

CHASING THE DRAGON NICHOLAS KAUFMANN [978-0-9812978-4-2]

OBJECTS OF WORSHIP CLAUDE LALUMIÈRE [978-0-9812978-2-8]

THE DOOR TO LOST PAGES CLAUDE LALUMIÈRE [978-1-926851-12-9]

THE THIEF OF BROKEN TOYS TIM LEBBON [978-0-9812978-9-7]

KATJA FROM THE PUNK BAND SIMON LOGAN [978-0-9812978-7-3]

BULLETTIME NICK MAMATAS [978-1-926851-71-6]

SHOEBOX TRAIN WRECK JOHN MANTOOTH [978-1-926851-54-9]

HAIR SIDE, FLESH SIDE HELEN MARSHALL [978-1-927469-24-8]

NINJA VERSUS PIRATE FEATURING ZOMBIES JAMES MARSHALL [978-1-926851-58-7]

PICKING UP THE GHOST TONE MILAZZO [978-1-926851-35-8]

BEARDED WOMEN TERESA MILBRODT [978-1-926851-46-4]

NAPIER'S BONES DERRYL MURPHY [978-1-926851-09-9]

CHIZINEPUB.COM CZP

MONSTROUS AFFECTIONS DAVID NICKLE [978-0-9812978-3-5]

EUTOPIA DAVID NICKLE [978-1-926851-11-2]

RASPUTIN'S BASTARDS DAVID NICKLE [978-1-926851-59-4]

CITIES OF NIGHT PHILIP NUTMAN [978-0-9812978-8-0]

JANUS JOHN PARK [978-1-927469-10-1]

EVERY SHALLOW CUT TOM PICCIRILLI [978-1-926851-10-5]

BRIARPATCH TIM PRATT [978-1-926851-44-0]

THE CHOIR BOATS DANIEL A. RABUZZI [978-0-980941-07-4]

THE INDIGO PHEASANT DANIEL A. RABUZZI [978-1-927469-09-5]

EVERY HOUSE IS HAUNTED IAN ROGERS [978-1-927469-16-3]

ENTER, NIGHT MICHAEL ROWE [978-1-926851-45-7]

REMEMBER WHY YOU FEAR ME ROBERT SHEARMAN [978-1-927469-21-7]

CHIMERASCOPE DOUGLAS SMITH [978-0-9812978-5-9]

THE PATTERN SCARS CAITLIN SWEET [978-1-926851-43-3]

THE TEL AVIV DOSSIER LAVIE TIDHAR AND NIR YANIV [978-0-9809410-5-0]

IN THE MEAN TIME PAUL TREMBLAY [978-1-926851-06-8]

SWALLOWING A DONKEY'S EYE PAUL TREMBLAY [978-1-926851-69-3]

THE HAIR WREATH AND OTHER STORIES HALLI VILLEGAS [978-1-926851-02-0]

THE WORLD MORE FULL OF WEEPING ROBERT J. WIERSEMA [978-0-9809410-9-8]

WESTLAKE SOUL RIO YOUERS [978-1-926851-55-6]

MAJOR KARNAGE GORD ZAJAC [978-0-9813746-6-6]

"IF YOUR TASTE IN FICTION RUNS TO THE DISTURBING, DARK, AND AT LEAST PARTIALLY WEIRD, CHANCES ARE YOU'VE HEARD OF CHIZINE PUBLICATIONS—CZP—A YOUNG IMPRINT THAT IS NONETHELESS PRODUCING STARTLINGLY BEAUTIFUL BOOKS OF STARKLY, DARKLY LITERARY QUALITY."

—DAVID MIDDLETON, **JANUARY MAGAZINE**

ALSO AVAILABLE FROM CHIZINE PUBLICATIONS